G000245801

LATYMER UPPER SCHOOL

HIST

★ ★

LIBRARY

WITHDRAWN

ACC. NO. 73872	LOAN TYPE
LOCATION/CLASS. NO. 941.081 FAB	INITIAL AM
	DATE 31/1/14

WITHDRAWN

Young England

By the same author

BEACONSFIELD AND BOLINGBROKE
THE VISION AND THE NEED
PROPER STATIONS
FRENCH AND ENGLISH
BRAVE COURTIER: SIR WILLIAM TEMPLE
HIGH ROAD TO ENGLAND

Young England

Richard Faber

faber and faber

LONDON · BOSTON

First published in 1987 by
Faber and Faber Limited
3 Queen Square, London WC1N 3AU
Photoset by
Parker Typesetting Service Leicester
Printed in Great Britain by
Mackays of Chatham Kent
All rights reserved

© Richard Faber 1987

British Library Cataloguing in Publication Data

Faber, Richard
Young England.
1. Young England   *(Political movement)*
2. Conservatism—Great Britain—History
—19th century
I. Title
320.941   JN1129.C7

ISBN 0–571–14831–X

To the memory of
my Father

The Hon. George Smythe
by R. Buckner

Frederick William Faber
by Simon Rochard

Lord John Manners
by Sir Francis Grant

The papers, I see, are beginning to concern themselves with the formation of a third or middle party. Remembering with a certain tenderness what the world was pleased to call 'Young England' I look upon the 4th party with less of disfavour than some of our friends do . . .

Lord John Manners to Lord Beaconsfield,
24 November 1880

Contents

Preface

This is the story of three young men, George Smythe, Lord John Manners and Alexander Baillie Cochrane, whose brilliant promise, though briefly blossoming in the 'Young England' movement, was never quite fulfilled. It is also the story of their relations with two rather older men, Benjamin Disraeli and Frederick William Faber, who both did achieve what they set out to achieve – though they did so by leaving Young England behind them.

The three young men were the originators of the movement, which flourished during the years 1842 to 1845. Faber helped to give it its religious colouring, while Disraeli made it a political force. By the time that Young England broke up, both Disraeli and Faber were pursuing other objectives; in the end it was left to John Manners to cherish, nostalgically, the movement's ideals. Consequently, Young England's direct effect, though by no means negligible, was short-lived. But Charles Whibley, in his biography of Lord John Manners published in 1925, felt able to describe it as 'the one notable experiment in popular Toryism of which the nineteenth century was witness'. It was certainly the earliest. The ideas of Young England have always been easy to ridicule – even in this century, when they have not been forgotten, they have usually been ridiculed or patronized. But there was more to them than hostile critics allowed: stripped of their period charm, they can still be taken seriously today.

So, this is a story about people. But it is also an account of a picturesque – yet serious – episode in the history of political ideas.

As such, the story has not been told before, or at least not so fully, and that was my main reason for embarking on it. I had, besides, two personal motives. My first book, published in 1961, was an essay about Disraeli's real or imagined debt to Lord Bolingbroke. This touched on the Young England movement, as a phase in Disraeli's political thought, but left me with a wish to find out more about the other participants. In its final chapter I coined the word 'Restoratism' to describe a political tendency that Young England, Disraeli and Bolingbroke seemed to me to have in common. It is not a very lovely word (though I do not know that it is much worse than 'Conservatism') and I have never seen it used by anybody else. But I still feel that this tendency, under whatever name, deserves more attention and analysis, by writers about past or present politics, than it has been given.

My other motive sprang from family piety. Over fifty years ago my father published his *Oxford Apostles*, as 'a Character Study of the Oxford Movement'. It is in fact chiefly a study of the Movement's leading character, Newman. Frederick William Faber, who was my father's great-uncle, appears in the book, together with other lesser figures, but not in the same detail or depth. I have often suspected that Frederick Faber's influence and personality were more powerful than my father allowed himself to suggest and that they would appear so in a setting where Newman was less in the foreground. So far as I know, my father never studied the Young England movement, or his great-uncle's share in starting it. I think he would have liked to read about this political counterpart to the Oxford Movement and about the three young men who made a brief, but colourful, splash in it. If his Oxford dons were apostles, these more worldly undergraduates were their Cambridge disciples.

When he wrote *Oxford Apostles* my father was struck by the great gulf between his clerical grandfather's mind and his own, although they had shared the same sort of background and education. I too had the same sort of classical education, perhaps as a member of the last generation to do so more or less as a matter of course. As an undergraduate I worried about religion in Christ Church meadows, or imagined a renewal of Tory ideals, in quite an Early Victorian way. The particular religious problems that preoccupied my great-grandfather and great-great-uncle are nevertheless as remote to me as they were to my father. I suppose they still figure in ecumenical controversy; but it requires an effort to understand how they can ever have loomed so large. On the other hand the basic political problems that faced the ruling class of 1837–1846 seem to me wholly intelligible – and not so very different from those that still confront us.

I must add a few words in self-defence. This book is a piece of advocacy, not an attempt at wholly unbiased judgement. I have made out the best case that I could for a movement that has been too easily rejected. I hope I have not hidden its weaknesses, or ignored the criticisms that were brought against it. But I could not expect to make its ideas comprehensible without being capable of feeling some sympathy for them in the context of their time.

1

A New Reign
(1837–1841)

The dying William IV had asked his doctor to see him through Waterloo Day. The doctor obliged, or his own will-power prevailed, with a day to spare.

Disraeli had somehow contrived to see a letter from the Earl of Munster, the eldest of the King's natural children by Mrs Jordan. He passed on this account to his sister in a letter on 19 June 1837:

> The King dies like an old lion. He said yesterday to his physicians, 'Only let me live through this glorious day.' This suggested to Munster to bring the tricolor flag which had just arrived from the Duke of Wellington, and show it to the King. William IV said, 'Right, right,' and afterwards, 'Unfurl it and let me feel it,' then he pressed the eagle and said, 'Glorious day.' This may be depended on. He still lives.

The end came in the early hours of 20 June. Although William had been popular enough, as the Sailor King, and although his life had been as patriotic as his death, he had never managed greatly to awe, charm or inspire his subjects. What regret there was at his passing verged on the perfunctory. Some years later, in *Sybil*, Disraeli summed up the general feeling as one of faint praise:

> The great bell of the metropolitan cathedral announces the death of the last son of George III who probably will ever reign in England. He was a good man, with feelings

and sympathies; deficient in culture rather than ability; with a sense of duty; and with something of the conception of what should be the character of an English monarch. Peace to his manes.

It was odd to imply that the throne had become a preserve of George III's sons, when in fact George IV and William IV had between them reigned for only seventeen years. But the phrase indicates how people were ready for a change. On the whole George IV had been less respected than his brother; before them their father, once revered by the conservative masses, had been mad for several years. Thus even middle-aged men in 1837 could barely remember a time when the monarch had aroused enthusiastic devotion. The somewhat dingy lights that had settled on the throne enabled the new sun to emerge with contrasting purity.

Victoria, woken early but not too early by the Archbishop of Canterbury and the Lord Chamberlain, learned that she was now Queen and would never afterwards forget it. She held her first council in Kensington Palace ('in a palace in a garden, meet scene for youth, and innocence, and beauty') and impressed the assembled statesmen with her presence and elocution. Disraeli was not of course a witness himself; but he had accompanied his patron, Lord Lyndhurst, to the Palace gates, heard what had happened on the return journey and shared in the prevailing optimism. He recalled in *Sybil*:

A dissolution of Parliament at any time must occasion great excitement; combined with a new reign, it inflames the passions of every class of the community. Even the poor begin to hope; the old, wholesome superstition that the sovereign can exercise power still lingers; and the suffering multitude are fain to believe that its remedial character may be about to be revealed in their instance. As for the aristocracy in a new reign, they are all in a flutter. A bewildering vision of coronets, stars, and ribbons; smiles, and places at Court; haunts their noontide speculations and their midnight dreams.

Was it a dream, or a speculation, to wonder whether it would be the Queen's 'proud destiny at length to bear relief to suffering millions, and with that soft hand which might inspire troubadours and guerdon knights, break the last links in the chain of Saxon Thraldom'? What hopes did Disraeli have that he himself would eventually be guerdoned as well as inspired? At least he had every reason to think that the reign would not be a short one – and reason enough to expect it to be more stimulating than the two previous reigns. Even the Whig Sydney Smith was moved to borrow a notion from the Tory Bolingbroke when he preached in St Paul's on the first Victorian Sunday in honour of 'A Patriot Queen'.

The general euphoria was, for once, not misleading. With all her faults, and with all the increasing limitations on her power, Victoria was to prove a great queen and a source of strength to her people. Her popularity was not always at the high level of the beginning and end of her long reign. Her own wilfulness would lead her into scrapes when Albert was not there to guide her; in less than two years after her accession she was to be badly tarnished by the Bedchamber Plot and the disgraceful affair of Lady Flora Hastings. But the popular instinct had been right. Here, if anywhere, was a queen who might be expected to keep the main constitutional rules, and yet to bring back some of the magic of monarchy.

Disraeli

At the time of Victoria's accession Disraeli was still under 35, still a dandified bachelor and still out of Parliament. Desperately anxious to succeed in one career or another, he had not yet abandoned literature for politics. But, for all his sublime self-confidence, he must by now have had some inkling that the *Revolutionary Epick*, published in 1834, was not going to make him the Homer, the Dante or the Milton of the nineteenth century. Happily his political activity in 1837 would prevent the revision and completion of this majestic work, which remained a fragment, though on a monumental scale. He was to have a last fling with pure literature in his tragedy *Count Alarcos*, which unaccountably failed to secure the attention of the 'scribbling critics' in 1839: Richard Monckton Milnes told the author that it would have made Macready's fortune, but it had to wait for a performance until his first premiership when it ran for five weeks at a heavy loss.

Meanwhile Disraeli's least political novels, *Henrietta Temple* and *Venetia*, appeared in December 1836 and May 1837. The first was a love story (based on his own affair with a real Henrietta) and the second an admirable portrait of Byron, paired with a feebler likeness of Shelley. The most unpretentious of Disraeli's works – except for the first volume of *Henrietta Temple* they were written rapidly to fend off his creditors – they have charming passages and almost convince that, even without politics, he could have made a lasting reputation as a novelist. But *Venetia* was published a month before the death of William IV; her creator would soon be absorbed into the world of action, which he was never afterwards to quit.

Politically Disraeli no longer presented himself as a Tory Radical or a Radical Tory. For five years he had been trying to get into Parliament and, two years previously, he had finally committed himself to the Tory Party by joining the Carlton Club. How far this was a decision of principle must be a matter of guesswork. Certainly Disraeli had genuine Tory instincts; these strengthened their hold on him and gradually became inseparable from his political character. But he had a revolutionary as well as a conservative streak. As a young man, he could well have decided that the Whigs were more enlightened and attractive, if he had been less afraid that their exclusiveness would always keep him out of high office. According to Sir W. Fraser, Disraeli became a full Tory because his patron, Lord Lyndhurst, advised him that the party 'sadly wanted brains'. Brains, daring and ravening ambition were what Disraeli had to offer; he was right to judge that they would have more scope on the Tory side.

Lord Lyndhurst, at that time the most influential Tory after the Duke of Wellington and Sir Robert Peel, was not a hereditary peer. Son of the distinguished portrait painter, John Singleton Copley, he had been brought to England from Boston at the age of three and, by dint of ability, hard work and a fine presence, had risen to the top of the legal profession. Before and after William IV's death the Whigs were in power; but Lyndhurst had been Lord Chancellor in Tory administrations in the 1820s and in 1834–5 and was to be so again in 1841. He was a man of 62 when he first met Disraeli, who was then 30, in 1834. The two men found each other good company; the elder could sympathize with a younger, not yet so respectable, adventurer; each saw, too, how the other could be useful to him. Disraeli did some political devilling for Lyndhurst and used his pen against the Whig Government in the style of eighteenth-century intellectuals. His *Vindication of the English Constitution*, the most substantial of his early political writings, appeared at the end of 1835 as 'a Letter to a Noble and Learned Lord' who had 'honoured me by a wish that some observations which I have made in conversation on the character of our Constitution might be expressed in a more formal and more public manner'. *Venetia*, too, was dedicated to Lyndhurst, as 'a record of my respect and my affection'.

Although he had won the friendship of this leading Tory, was well known to hostesses and had enjoyed a measure of public fame since his first novel, *Vivian Grey*, it would still be several years before Disraeli was at all widely or deeply respected. An article in *Fraser's Magazine* (from a series on 'Literary Legislators' in the first half of 1847) invited its readers to look back at Disraeli's 'brilliant productions' and then to be 'struck with astonishment that he should have held, until a very recent period, so low a place in the opinion of the great mass of his countrymen . . .' It concluded that he would have been successful earlier with 'less cleverness and more craft . . . He has always been in a hurry to be a great man.' No future great man was ever in more of a hurry and yet few great men have taken so long to make their reputations. In 1837 his reputation was still to make.

But the first rungs of the ladder were about to be ascended. In the elections following the Queen's accession Disraeli came into Parliament, for the first time, as Member for Maidstone, together with another Conservative, Wyndham Lewis. Disraeli was then 33, very pleased with himself and in high spirits. This confidence was shaken, but not shattered, by a setback in the following December, when his over-elaborate maiden speech was drowned in uproar, much of it whipped up by the Irish Members. His closing words, rising above the hubbub, have become famous: 'I have begun several things many times, and I have often succeeded at the last – though many had predicted that I must fail, as they had done before me.' Then, *fortissimo*: 'I sit down now, but the time will come when you will hear me.' The time came soon. In March 1838 he made a successful speech to a full house in a debate on the Corn Laws.

It is a remarkable instance of will-power and self-discipline that Disraeli, who had seemed to lack even average judgement and self-knowledge when out of Parliament, should have learned so surely how to behave in it once he was there. In this first Victorian Parliament he managed to build up a reputation for himself as a clever, and independent, speaker, while loyally supporting his party leader, Sir Robert Peel. When the monster Chartist petition was carried to Westminster in the summer of 1839, he showed that he could still back popular aspirations. He said that, although he disapproved of the Charter, he sympathized with the Chartists: they formed a great body of his countrymen and they laboured under great grievances. He took the same line in debates in 1840, deploring what he considered the excessive punishment inflicted on some of the Chartist leaders. In July 1840 he expressed the other half of his political philosophy: 'The aristocracy are the natural leaders of the people, for the aristocracy and the labouring population form the nation.'

Two days before his first successful Parliamentary speech, in March 1838, Disraeli had heard of the death of Wyndham Lewis, his Parliamentary colleague. Then, or not long afterwards, he saw his way to the next rung of the ladder: marriage, comfort, emotional security, social respectability and control of his debts. He seems originally to have supposed that Mrs Wyndham Lewis's fortune was greater than it was; but it was quite enough to make a difference. Twelve years older than Disraeli, she was a brave and loyal, if superficially silly, woman and she certainly fulfilled her side of the marriage contract. So did Disraeli. He was implacable to those who had done him wrong; but gratitude to those who had done him right was, with his courage, perhaps his chief moral virtue. The marriage took place in August 1839 and was followed by a honeymoon at Tunbridge Wells and abroad.

Except for a few months in 1834–5, when William IV had tried to impose his will on Parliament, the Whigs had been in power since 1830. It had been, at first, a great reforming Ministry, abolishing the rotten boroughs in the Reform Bill of 1832, modernizing municipal government and introducing the New Poor Law to check the growth of pauperism. But latterly, under Lord Melbourne's cool direction, the Whigs had run out of steam; they were also running into financial difficulties. The Reform Bill had curbed the power of patronage, at least in the towns, and had extended political control to a part of the middle class. The Whig aristocrats, who still dominated their party, now found themselves in a difficult position. They had put into effect their enlightened views, with advantage to the tradesmen and dissenters with whom they were traditionally connected. But few of them wished to subvert the aristocratic system itself, or to damage

7

the prosperity and local influence of agricultural landowners such as themselves. They had got what they wanted, or most of it, and would now be relieved if the march of progress could be arrested. Disraeli saw clearly that this had lost them their political *raison d'être*. Radicals wanted further democratization and would not for long be content with the Whiggish compromise, while the conservative-minded had no confidence that the Whigs would defend the constitution in Church and State against the forces of revolution. At the same time the champions of the poor deplored distressing industrial conditions and the inhumane application of the New Poor Law; yet effective measures of relief were likely to alarm the middle-class manufacturers whose support the Whigs needed.

For a combination of these reasons the Tories, or 'Conservatives' as they were increasingly being called, were returned to power at the elections in the summer of 1841. The Whigs had been defeated on a proposal to reduce sugar duties; Peel had carried by one vote a resolution of no confidence and the Queen (now safely married to Prince Albert) had granted a dissolution. Although Victoria had clashed with Peel during the 1839 Bedchamber crisis, when her insistence on keeping her Whig ladies at Court prevented the formation of a Tory government, she soon began to regard him as politically – if not, like Melbourne, emotionally – indispensable and gave him every support. Changing constituencies, Disraeli represented Shrewsbury in the new House. He had hopes of office and even wrote to Peel to press his claim. But the answer (which perhaps reads rather more coldly than was intended) pointed out how few offices were available and how many deserving claimants.

Apparently unknown to her husband, Mrs Disraeli had also written to Peel, representing his exertions and her financial sacrifices, on the Party's behalf. 'Literature he has abandoned for politics,' she urged. 'Do not destroy all his hopes, and make him feel his life has been a mistake.'

This destruction of Disraeli's hopes, which he never wholly forgave, was in fact the foundation of his political fortunes. If he had held office he would hardly have wished, or been able, to launch the attacks against Peel, in 1845 and 1846, which were eventually to make him the leader of his party.

Smythe, Manners and Cochrane

In the course of 1841 three young men who had been friends at Eton and Cambridge came into Parliament on the Conservative side.

The Hon. George Smythe, with the canvassing help of his two friends, was returned for Canterbury at a by-election in February. He had shown his monarchism by making a speech in defence of the Queen; but this does not seem to have harmed him with his electors, although the cathedral city was Tory and the Queen still reckoned a Whig. He kept the seat, with an increased majority, at the general elections in July. At the same time Lord John Manners secured a seat at Newark, with Gladstone (not yet a Liberal) as his colleague; Gladstone described Manners to his wife as a popular and effective speaker and canvasser because of his 'general kindliness and warmth of disposition'. Alexander Baillie Cochrane, the eldest of the three, came in last. He stood for Bridport, a predominantly Liberal constituency, and was defeated – though not heavily – by two Liberals at the general elections. In September, however, the senior of those two members accepted the Chiltern Hundreds, in compromise of a petition against his return. So Cochrane, now labelled 'Liberal-Conservative', was admitted in his place.

Before the end of the year each of the three had made his Parliamentary début. Cochrane spoke briefly on 20 September, very soon after his entry, against an increased government grant to the Irish Roman Catholic seminary for priests at Maynooth. Manners, a lifelong champion of lost causes, made his maiden speech on 31 August on behalf of Don

Carlos, the Spanish Pretender detained in France. Although he was nervous at first, he managed not to break down and got a cordial reception. Smythe had the most harrowing experience. He rose on 17 May, to make a speech about sugar duties, but lost his nerve and concluded with a faltering peroration:

> Inexperienced as I am in addressing the House, I cannot give full utterance to the considerations which have brought conviction to my mind. I shall not therefore detain the House further than by declaring my intention to vote for the amendment.

Anyone who has faced a sea of amused, contemptuous or pitying faces, with a mounting feeling of despair and inadequacy, will know what Smythe felt. Although he went on to become one of the most admired Parliamentary speakers, he never forgot this moment of humiliation.

According to Sir William Gregory, Smythe 'had recently come up from Cambridge with an enormous reputation, not derived from anything he had done in the way of academic honours, but from a general belief that he was the coming young man in politics', yet 'to the horror of his Cambridge friends' his maiden speech was 'a decided failure; he broke down, and could never bear the slightest allusion to it'. In congratulating Smythe on a speech in 1845, Peel tactlessly reminded the House of this earlier failure; Gregory remarked to Smythe that the Prime Minister had given him plenty of butter; 'rancid as usual,' he replied furiously. Writing to his father from Venice early in 1846 he recalled the financial difficulties he had been in at the time, as a result of his Cambridge debts and Canterbury expenses, and the 'ruin' he had brought upon his family and himself:

> It was in this situation, weighed down by a sense of all the mischief I had done, that I tried to speak. I broke down, signally and miserably, my nerves going with a sort of

crash. What a position! I might have recovered myself, but this is not an heroic age and I took to drinking as an opiate and an anodyne ... What wonder ... that my nervous system has never recovered those years of '41 and '42.

In 1837 Parliamentary triumphs and disasters were still in the future. The characters and ideas of these three young men as they developed will I hope take shape in the following chapters. But I must try to sketch what their acquaintances knew and expected of them in the summer of the Queen's accession.

George Smythe had been born in Stockholm in April 1818. He was thus 19 in 1837 and not quite 23 when he entered Parliament – over thirteen years younger than Disraeli. He was the eldest of three sons of the sixth Viscount Strangford, an Irish peer and graduate of Trinity College, Dublin, who, after a distinguished diplomatic career at Lisbon, Rio de Janeiro, Stockholm, Constantinople and St Petersburg, was seated in the House of Lords as Baron Penshurst. (The first Viscount Strangford had married a daughter of Robert Sidney, Earl of Leicester.) Politically a strong supporter of right-wing policies, Strangford was, nevertheless, an alert and 'dynamic' diplomatist, who liked to be, and feel, in the swim. Apostrophized by Byron as

> Hibernian Strangford, with thine eyes of blue,
> And boasted locks of red or auburn hue,

he had literary tastes and had been a college friend of the poet Tom Moore. He was also a friend of Disraeli, whom he proposed for the Carlton Club and to whom he wrote a number of jaunty, man-of-the-world notes. In 1832 he expressed delight in Disraeli's *Contarini Fleming* ('Some of it is *startling*, but I like to be startled'), while he thought that the *Vindication of the English Constitution* was the best thing since

Burke. At the beginning of their acquaintance Disraeli described him as 'an aristocratic Tom Moore; his flow is incessant and brilliant'. In 1833 he wrote to his sister of Strangford greeting him like a brother, with his 'usual heartless brilliance'.

The Strangfords had fallen on evil days in the eighteenth century and Strangford was not well off. What money he had managed to save was spent on buying back a small part of his ancestors' estates in Kent; so he looked to his son to bring 'honey into the hive'. He had married for love, when he was 36 or 37, a beautiful Irish widow, daughter of Sir Thomas Burke and a few years younger than himself. She was fascinating, but delicate and excitable, alternating between gaiety and despair and neurotically sensitive to the insolence (real or imagined) of her servants. After some years of genuine, but fraught, happiness, she died of consumption at St Petersburg in 1826. After that Strangford had to look after his children – there were also two daughters – himself. According to Albany Fonblanque, who had seen family papers, and talked to his daughter-in-law, Strangford was proud of his ability at training children, but was lacking in impartiality and firmness: 'In point of fact, few men were, by temper or disposition, so little fitted for the task.'

George Smythe seems to have inherited his mother's charm, but also some of her emotional and physical weaknesses. Intellectually, he was more his father's child, though he had not been brought up in Ireland and did not share Strangford's reactionary political views. He was alternately spoilt and censured by his father – at once precociously forced and emotionally stunted. Indeed, locked in a mutual mesmerism, the father and the son had a relationship of almost incestuous intensity. Writing about George to his own mother, Strangford confessed:

His hold over my affections becomes hourly so painfully strong that I feel and fear the sinfulness of my adoration for that child, and dread the awful punishment that may one day attend it.

The motherless George responded to this emotional pressure. One or two of his boyhood letters to his father read almost like those of a petulant mistress, dreading disapproval but conscious of power to charm. Years later, in 1844, he wrote to him:

> There was never a father so appreciated by a son ... The misfortune of my life has been that I have not loved you only as a son, but with a jealous passion, which is always getting me into scrapes.

No doubt this was laid on with a trowel and for a purpose. But it is not language that most sons would use to their fathers.

At the age of 12 George was sent to Eton and stayed there five years. Although he was nearly expelled twice for insubordination, he seems to have been popular and happy there, and a favourite of his Tutor's. Afterwards he spent several months studying with the Revd Julius Hare, whom he described dutifully to his father as 'an enthusiastic scholar and evident gentleman, and, what is far more rare, a good man'. Then, in 1836, after a prolonged struggle with the impecunious Strangford, he went up to St John's College, Cambridge, (not so smart or expensive as Trinity) with financial help from his godfather, the Duke of Northumberland. At Cambridge he made some close friends – not only from among the gilded youth – read widely, spoke at the Union and wrote for periodicals; but he had not worked systematically and he got a mediocre degree.

Smythe had gone to Cambridge, 'armed with that desire for distinction which I believe that I do not share less than other men'. He at least gained a considerable political and social reputation there, even if he did less well academically than he was capable of doing. His insight into politics was already exceptional. Thus his prophecy to George Lyttelton in 1839 that the Whiggish Victoria would end 'as a Tory and something more' was as accurate as his later judgement on the aristocratic order: 'Not only on the Corn Laws, but on every other question, in every other strait, *they will give way.*' He had also demonstrated, this early, his capacity for getting into rows. In March–April 1839 he was nearly expelled from the Union for some unspecified enormity, presumably an insult, or a duel, or an attempt at a duel. At the same time the President (Beresford Hope, a fan of the Tractarians and a future Conservative Member of Parliament) had to resign, his conduct 'on Saturday evening last' being judged 'inconsistent with the established usages of the society'. Two attempts to expel Smythe were made and he was saved only by a ruling by the new President that a three-quarters majority was required. This ruling was in turn challenged three weeks later and the motion was narrowly defeated by 132 to 116. Throughout his career, Smythe's ability to charm friends was matched only by his talent for making enemies.

During his Cambridge years Smythe seems to have been very prepossessing physically. One or two accounts describe his appearance as 'dingy' or insignificant; but these seem to relate to a later period. For the elderly Disraeli, in his picture of Smythe as Waldershare in *Endymion*, he was 'not exactly handsome, but with a countenance full of expression, and the index of quick emotions, whether of joy or of anger'. The latter part of this seems to tally with Faber's more lyrical tribute:

> The light, the power, the unsettled fires that play
> Among the sleepless glancings of thine eyes,
> Thy thoughts and things of beauty, which betray
> The heart from whence they rise.

All accounts agree that, though slight, Smythe had a slim and graceful figure as well as an intelligent and expressive face. With these and with the striking blue eyes that he had inherited from his father, he quickly gained a reputation for being irresistible to women. Certainly a portrait reproduced in Whibley's *Lord John Manners and his Friends* suggests that he must have been extremely attractive as a youth, before the morning dew had evaporated. In 1835, the year he left Eton, his father wrote:

> George has grown two inches taller than I am, and looks as strong as Hercules and as handsome as Adonis. No one is more certain to achieve a brilliant future.

This youthful beauty was the outward bloom of inward enthusiasm. Later in life George Smythe liked to pose as, and to some extent was, a man without principle. He complained to his father, when he was 27:

> I am one of those miserable entities, born since 1815, who believe in all things; who can see the virtues of absolutism, democracy, autocracy, without a preference; who think the Tories quite as right as the Whigs, the Catholics as the Protestants, the Buddhists as the Christians, the Atheists as the Theists. Thus, in politics I have only had one idea – what opinion is likely to turn up trumps . . .

In the same vein, he wrote: 'Speaking morally, I do not pretend to any virtues, but I have few vices. I am too fond of wine, and I like women.' He habitually presented this rather cynical front to Disraeli, who recorded in a memorandum: 'George Smythe used to say, "I don't pretend to have any principle, but I have some heart, and I am a gentleman."' Disraeli seems to have been entirely convinced by this, though it was only one of the many things that Smythe might have said about himself. At the end of *Endymion*, when Waldershare marries Adriana Neuchatel, the verdict is that he 'did not make such a pattern husband as Endymion, but he made a much better one than the world ever supposed he would ... And Waldershare had really a good heart, though a bad temper, and he was a gentleman.' However, even the 'good heart' was denied by some. Sir William Gregory found Smythe 'selfish and heartless, but a most delightful, fascinating, companion'.

The impression left by Smythe's letters to Manners is that he was justified in claiming at least 'some' heart. As to principle, his public actions and utterances, during his brief career, were remarkably consistent, whatever doubts he may have had privately about them. Complex and emotionally unstable, he seems to have been in search of intellectual stability and to have realized the importance of adopting a reasonably identifiable public persona. Yet that persona was itself a complex one and the strain of maintaining it may have contributed to his eventual disenchantment with politics.

At any rate, at Cambridge Smythe still had principles and enthusiasms. Perhaps under the lingering influence of the Revd Julius Hare he made clerical friends there, while he inspired his friend Cochrane to write of him:

> The blue eye so sparkling at records of glory
> > Shed its beam on the altar of virtue alone;
> Sure and true is that heart which shall lead thee to story
> > For honour and principle reared thee their own.

A letter from Smythe to Manners in 1854 makes it clear that he had lost, but also had once had, religious faith. His younger sister had told him – and he seemed ruefully to accept – that he would never be religious again, because he had 'known the truth, felt it, and rejected it'. This is, again, confirmed by Waldershare's behaviour:

> At Cambridge he introduced the new Oxford heresy ...
> prayed and fasted, and swore by Land and Strafford.
> He took, however, a more eminent degree at Paris than

at his original Alma Mater, and becoming passionately addicted to French literature, his views respecting both Church and State became modified – at least in private.

The second of the three friends, Lord John Manners, was, like Smythe, handsome, graceful and romantic. But he was taller and looked more stately. He was also less brilliant and stimulating, harder working, sweeter tempered, more conscientious and much more deeply and steadily religious. As slow to make enemies as to change his gently inflexible opinions, he seems, at all periods of his life, to have provoked the same reactions of respect, affection and admiring ridicule. 'There is an impotent purity about John Manners,' wrote the exasperated Monckton Milnes, in 1848, 'that is almost pathetic.' But Milnes had also described him to Thomas Carlyle, in March 1844, as 'a very fine, promising fellow'. There was never any question of Manners's honour or intelligence, while journalists, in that still snobbish age, were glad to recognize the unmistakable stamp of 'blood' and 'family' on his bearing and features. In some ways he seemed the living embodiment of the aristocratic idealism he preached. It would be fair to say that, though he brought some ridicule on Young England through his more out-of-the-way opinions, he did far more to dispel it by his popularity and by his obvious integrity. Without them, the movement could hardly have made the headway that it did.

Lord John Manners was the second son of the fifth Duke of Rutland by a daughter of the fifth Earl of Carlisle. Born at Belvoir Castle in December 1818, eight months after Smythe, he lost his mother when he was not quite seven, but had a much less tempestuous relationship with his father than Smythe had with his. Apart from an early stammer, which he learned to control, he never seems to have caused his elders anxiety. He went to Eton in 1831. When he left it, in 1835, his Tutor wrote to the Duke:

I verily believe I speak the strict truth in saying that Lord John has carried with him the affection and respect of more individuals in various classes in this place than any boy ever did before.

At Trinity College, Cambridge, which he entered in 1836, he was popular too. He did well enough academically, if not brilliantly, spoke regularly at the Union and was an active member of the antiquarian Camden Society. His Tutor attributed to 'his example and that of others who represent him the high tone of character and conduct that distinguishes the great body of the members of the aristocracy'. The same sort of thing had been said about Sir Philip Sidney in his day. Less respectably, perhaps, Manners also became a keen disciple of 'the new Oxford heresy'.

Coming down from Cambridge in 1839, Manners travelled on the Continent with his elder brother. In Paris Lord Ranelagh suggested that they should visit Don Carlos – and so they did. Henceforth Manners, a firm believer in legitimacy, was to be as passionate a supporter of this living Pretender as he was, historically, of James II. On his return to England he filled in the time until he could enter Parliament by taking rooms in the Albany, reading for the Bar and contributing verses to the *Diadem*. At the end of 1840 he showed his loyalty to a friend, though perhaps not his judgement, by supporting the young Lord Lyttelton in his unsuccessful contest with Lord Lyndhurst for the High Stewardship of Cambridge University. It was a typically quixotic gesture, made in the face of his father's and Smythe's opposition.

Although Manners was always able to live comfortably, he was not, by ducal standards, wealthy. As a younger son he had no great landed estate. In 1880 he was glad to accept a government pension of £1,200 a year and it was at least partly on grounds of expense that he had earlier declined to serve in important posts abroad.

The third member of the trio, Alexander Baillie Cochrane

(later known as Cochrane-Baillie), was the eldest and the richest. He came from a naval family, with an Admiral of the Fleet for his father and an Admiral for his grandfather. There was a bluff breeziness about Cochrane that recalled these naval origins, although he had exchanged the quarter-deck for the library and the saloon. He was born in November 1816 and was thus about two years older than Manners. Like both Smythe and Manners he lost his mother young – when he was three – but had brothers and sisters. As the eldest son of his parents he inherited, through his mother, an estate at Lamington in Lanarkshire.

Cochrane was educated at Eton and Trinity, Cambridge, where he graduated in 1837. He served as President of the Union in the Lent term of that year; when he went down, Smythe and Manners still had two years at Cambridge before them. In the four years before he entered Parliament he must have celebrated his majority and taken charge of his estate; he also wrote and published verse and travelled abroad. The most obviously Byronic of the three friends, he started a lifelong affair with Greece, which supplied him with material for repeated Parliamentary interventions. Buckhurst in *Coningsby* (whose character was based on Cochrane's), dazzles his youthful friends with his maturity, on returning from a visit to Paris 'with his mind very much opened, and trousers made quite in a new style'. Even at Eton, at Lord Monmouth's picnic, he had precociously given his opinion 'on the most refined dishes with all the intrepidity of saucy ignorance, and occasionally shook his head over a glass of Hermitage or Côte Rôtie with a dissatisfaction which a satiated Sybarite could not have exceeded'.

Buckhurst is 'the most energetic of beings', 'fiery and generous', with an assured 'carriage' and a 'reckless genius'. Cochrane's speeches reflect this impetuosity, while his verses suggest the precocious sophistication of a boy who had had to become a person in his own right at an early age. Both display an impulsive, extrovert, open temperament. He seems to have shared in the aura of elegance that hung over his two friends (the *Morning Herald* in November 1844 taunted that nonsense 'driven from MR D'ISRAELI's novels, has taken refuge in the "graceful" MR COCHRANE's pericranium'), though his manner and his style of oratory tended to have a more straightforward appeal for the plain man. But his enthusiasms led him into greater inconsistency than either Smythe or Manners. The *Morning Herald* editorial, from which I have just quoted, was prejudiced and exaggerated, but not altogether off the mark:

> Mr Cochrane lives in a world of his own; and, as his friends the Tractarians say of their ideal Church, its development varies with climate and with race. In Greece he is more liberal than the Liberals; in France he is more legitimate than the Legitimists; in Spain he is more absolute than the Absolutists; in Ireland he is more Romanistic than the Romanists; in Scotland he is more anti-kirk than the Free Seceders; and in England he is more of a Protectionist than any farmer or squire in the land ... Extravagance, exaggeration, and vanity are the rocks on which MR COCHRANE's small abilities have foundered ...

Cochrane was certainly anti-kirk; but he was ambivalent about Romanism, while his later U-turn on Protection was spectacular. When he died, *The Times* described him as 'too fond of taking a line of his own to be a safe party man'. To this, and to his reluctance to 'consistently choose any one path', *The Times* attributed his failure to achieve fame as a brilliant speaker, or durable literary work, or high office. Yet, according to this obituary, he left Cambridge 'with a reputation for ability and accomplishments' and with 'all the world before him'.

This is to anticipate. What needs to be noted now is that, if only because of his age, Cochrane was not as close to his two friends as they were to each other. This would have disqualified him from taking the leading part, even if he had been as original in his ideas as the other two and had not been inhibited by the hero worship he felt for Smythe. In practical matters he was no doubt often to the fore; he was no less in the limelight than the others, but he did not dominate the imagination and ideas of his contemporaries in the way that Smythe could, when he made the effort. Although Cochrane was closely involved in the formation of the Young England group, he must have had some sense of not being in the inner ring. It would be difficult otherwise to explain a passage at the beginning of *In the Days of the Dandies*, which he contributed to *Blackwood's Magazine* in January 1890. Asked whether he had been in Parliament with the Young England party, the anonymous author replies:

> Yes; but I was an outsider. I joined them much later. Young England, so called, was a body of young men who had grown up together from Eton days.

Perhaps this is not meant to be Cochrane himself, but an imaginary supporter of the movement. After all, Cochrane had been at Eton with the other two, if rather before them. But it seems more natural to suppose that the passage reflects something of what Cochrane felt about his own connection with the movement.

If Cochrane was not the leader of Young England, who was? Was it Smythe or Manners? It has usually been assumed that, so far as Young England was not Disraeli's creation, it was, basically, Smythe's. This is partly because Smythe was the closest of the three to Disraeli (and was chosen to take the lead in *Coningsby*); partly because he was the most fascinating socially; and partly because, at his best, he was the most brilliant speaker. Moreover Manners himself, from the earliest days, had elected to give him the lead.

Years later, after Smythe's death, Manners wrote about him to Lyttelton:

> Memory ... settles upon those joyous days at Cambridge, when he was the sun and centre of my happiness, and when we never tired of arguing for him a dazzling career of glory.

Yet Smythe himself treated Manners as at least an equal in the enterprise. In 1839 he cautioned his friend: 'I must most sincerely deprecate all such hallucinations as those under which you labour, when you talk of my being your leader.' *Fraser's Magazine* for May 1847 described Smythe as having 'adopted and re-echoed some of their [Young England's] favourite views, without allowing himself to be carried away by their enmities'. This was after the Young England group had broken up; but it would still be odd language to use if Smythe had been generally and indisputably recognized as its leading spirit. In fact there is a good case for regarding Manners both as the chief begetter of Young England's most typical ideas and as their steadiest and (after Disraeli) most effective exponent to the public.

Smythe's and Manner's careers at the Cambridge Union followed a pattern later to be repeated in Parliament. Both of them, together with Cochrane, spoke in the negative on 'Is Mr O'Connell a benefactor to his country?' in December 1836. This seems to have been the only time when all three took part in the same Union debate; the next term Cochrane became President and then faded from the scene. Smythe did not speak again until October 1837, after which he made eight set speeches in the period up to December 1838. One of these speeches, against the 1688 Revolution, was delivered (Manners wrote to his father) with 'wonderful eloquence'. Sir William Gregory, an Oxford contemporary, recalled him as 'quite the first speaker at the Cambridge Union, though he never spoke without great preparation, and indeed, elaboration'. Meanwhile Manners played the tortoise to Smythe's hare. Without opening any debates, he spoke on twenty occasions between November 1836 and March 1839. He wrote to Lyttelton:

> I am quite sure Smythe and I look upon the Union in a very different point of view. I love and reverence it, and would no more think of treating it slightly than my best friend; he, unless I mistake greatly, despises it, and it is but natural he should do so.

All of this might apply to their later Parliamentary experience. Smythe never made a speech without tension and effort; according to his sister-in-law, Lady Strangford, he was 'never a very ready speaker; he had to be wound up under the pressure of a high nervous excitement'.

The Union in this period of Whig government seems to have been predominantly Tory in tone. Current problems were often approached through debates on dead statesmen – Canning versus Castlereagh, for instance, or Fox against Pitt. Both at Oxford and at Cambridge the Stuart Age, and particularly the Civil War, was a fertile mine of debating topics. Either Smythe or Manners, or both, spoke for Pitt, against Fox, against the Puritans, against the 1688 Rebellion and against the abdication of James II. They both attacked Melbourne's foreign policy, the idea of universal education and the establishment of an Ecclesiastical Commission. Manners supported the King of Hanover, and the Established Church in Ireland; he deplored the French occupation of Algiers, the Ministry's conduct to Lord Durham, the introduction of the Ballot, Whig internal policy and the admission of dissenters to Oxford and Cambridge degrees. He was neutral on Astrology and Press Control, but definite that Alfred Tennyson's poems did *not* 'shew a fine poet' (this was established by the President's casting vote). The two friends spoke with the majority except on one or two topics, notably universal education and the 1688 Revolution. When they both took part in debates they did so on the same side, with the single exception of 7 November 1837. Then Smythe argued that the New Poor Law had been 'beneficial to the pauper population of this country' and Manners argued that it had not been. In this instance, at least, it was Smythe, and not Manners, who eventually came round to the other's point of view.

Faber

Victoria was crowned Queen on 28 June 1838. The day was spent by a young Oxford don in 'a willow-shaded spot', within the reach of 'dreamy sounds of never-ending bells from Oxford's holy towers'; there he was able to meditate tranquilly on the past and the future. It was his own birthday and he put his feelings into a poem called 'Birth-day thoughts'. Religiously dated, in the pedantic Tractarian way, the poem celebrated the Feast of St Irenaeus, the Vigil of St Peter and the Coronation of Queen Victoria, as well as his own anniversary. After a nod towards each of the saints the poet devoted two stanzas to the Queen:

> It was the day whereon a Sovereign knelt
> > Before the Altar high,
> And through the realm was heard one loyal cry,
> > One beating heart was felt.

> And thoughtful men were startled at the sound,
> > And good men fell to prayer,
> For with the glory and the pageant rare
> > Shadows were gathering round.

Then he turned to a more immediately absorbing theme – himself, his homelessness, his fatherlessness, his restlessness, but also his cheerfulness. Here too he expected shadows to gather:

Sunny and wild all earthly things do seem,
　　Like an enchanter's show,
And yet it frets me all the while to know
　　That this is but a dream.

I cannot burst the fetters of the spell:--
　　The silvery light of mirth
Streams from within me over all the earth,
　　As from an endless well.

So bright of late the unsetting sun hath played,
　　Its evening must be near,
When Hope shall win fresh loveliness from fear,
　　And Memory from shade.

The poet knew himself well and his intuition was right. After a final blaze that summer his sun was to go behind a cloud. When it rose again, it would shine with a less worldly, and (at least as the world sees) a less mirthful, light.

Frederick William Faber was born in 1814, nine years after Disraeli and four years before Smythe. He was to become a close friend of Smythe and Manners and to encourage them in their ideas. He may well have met Cochrane on one of his visits to London; but there seems to be no record of this, though Cochrane quotes from Faber's poetry in *In the Days of the Dandies*. Nor is there any evidence that Disraeli ever met Faber, though he had heard a good deal about him from Manners, got Manners to lend him one of his books and used him as a model for a character in *Sybil*.

Faber was born into a clerical environment. His ancestors had originally been sheep-farming Yorkshire yeomen. But Frederick William's grandfather was Vicar of Calverley in Yorkshire; his father was Secretary to the last Bishop Palatine of Durham; his uncle was Master of Sherburn Hospital and a noted evangelical controversialist. His paternal grandmother came from a French family of Huguenot gentry who had taken refuge in England after the Revocation of the Edict of Nantes; this gave a number of people, including Manners himself, the mistaken impression that the Fabers were predominantly of French Huguenot stock. Like all three Young Englanders he lost his mother during his boyhood – though not until he was 15. He had a sister and three elder brothers, but he was his mother's Benjamin and later confessed to having been too much indulged as a child. While treasuring the memory of his 'sainted Mother', he was also much attached to his father (who died, without leaving any fortune, in 1833) and to his elder brothers, who looked after him until he was able to make his own way.

Faber's early schooldays were spent at Kirkby Stephen, in Westmorland. He wrote in 1857, in a preface to his long poem *Sir Lancelot*, of his 'perfect acquaintance with all the nooks and angles of the Westmoreland mountains' and of the long, rapturous, solitary holidays he spent as a boy among their 'ruined halls and castles and moated houses':

> From earliest times it was to me the land of knightly days, and the spell has never yet been broken. When it became the dwelling-place of manhood and the scene of earnest labour the light upon it only grew more golden; and now, a year-long prisoner in the great capital, that region seems to me a home whence I have been exiled, but which, only to think of, is tranquillity and joy.

When he was 11 Faber went for two years to Shrewsbury and then on to Harrow, where he stood out both for brilliance and for piety. But the piety was shadowed by doubts and by wild moods of rebellion, so that, later in life, he believed that he had been very wicked as a schoolboy. Henry Wilberforce recalled him declaring that 'in that thunderstorm he stood on a tomb in Harrow Churchyard, and lifted up his hand to heaven, defying God, if a God there was, to strike him dead!' He also reproached himself, when an Oxford undergraduate, for having surrendered himself at Harrow 'so wholly and unreservedly to the more easy charms of modern literature, that I fear it is too late now to make myself a proficient in the studies of antiquity'.

These self-reproaches seem to us a trifle priggish. But it was an age when it was thought proper for boys who expected to become clergymen to take a solemn view of their failings and duties. It is clear that, in spite of this, Faber was a lively and enchanting companion. A contemporary at Harrow exclaimed: 'I cannot tell why it is, but that Faber fascinates everybody.' Piously, if again somewhat priggishly, Faber decided that he ought 'to lay this talent at the feet of my Redeemer'. His brother, writing an account of his early life after his death, quoted from *Cymbeline*:

> Such a holy witch,
> That he enchants societies unto him:
> Half all men's hearts are his.

Faber's power to fascinate was reinforced by the beauty of his appearance when he was a young man. This was admitted by all, though some found it more admirable than others. A hostile obituary remembered him at Oxford as 'handsome with a feminine sort of handsomeness'; a friendly obituary, referring to the same period, wrote of 'a grace of person and mind rarely to be met with'. At a slightly later period (1841) there is the convincing testimony of the Eighth Duke of Argyll, who met Faber briefly in Edinburgh.

> He struck me at once as an interesting and attractive man – very good-looking, with eyes of a fine blue, set in deeply hollowed sockets, an aquiline nose, and a general expression wild – imaginative – unsettled.

These were the sort of looks to appeal to a generation nursed on Shelley and Byron. It was a time, too, when clergymen exuded more glamour than has sometimes been the case. Faber might have inspired W. S. Gilbert's song:

Time was when love and I were well acquainted;
Time was, when we were ever hand in hand;
A saintly youth, by worldly thought untainted –
None better loved than I in all the land!

Time was when maidens of the highest station,
Forsaking even military men,
Would gaze upon me, rapt in adoration –
Ah me! I was a pale young curate then.

Faber did not actually become a (part-time) curate until 1837; but it was understood, throughout his time at Oxford, that the Church was to be his destiny. It was of course only as a clergyman that he could become a College Fellow, like his elder brother Frank, ten years his senior, who was a Fellow of Magdalen. Frederick William went up to Balliol in 1833. He lived a full life as an undergraduate, busying himself with the *Oxford University Magazine* and with the Union, where he was elected Secretary for the summer term of 1834. During the few months in which he was a regular speaker at the Union he moved 'That the reign of Charles 2nd was a less disastrous period of English History than the Commonwealth' (carried without a division) and 'That Wordsworth is in every respect a superior poet to Lord Byron' (lost by 14 votes to 34). He also opposed, with the majority, a motion of Whiggish tendency that 'no Ministry can hope to carry on the Government of the country, which is not formed as well upon a principle of extensive practical Reform, as of preserving the established rights of Property'.

In 1836 Faber, who had moved to University College, disappointed himself and his friends by getting only a Second Class in Greats. If he had read too much modern literature at Harrow, he had (from an academic standpoint) worried too much about religion at Oxford. However, he compensated by carrying off the Newdigate Prize, with a poem on 'The Knights of St John', and the Johnson Divinity Scholarship. In January 1837 he was, in spite of his Second Class, elected to a Fellowship at University College. Mark Pattison, who did not like Faber, had also entered for this Fellowship; in his *Memoirs* he described Faber's success as natural enough: he was a 'flashy talker' and 'a great favourite in his college'. This is itself evidence of Faber's general popularity. But he had detractors as well as admirers; there were those who called him a tuft-hunter, or reproached him with soft living, or were resentful at the way in which his charm could be turned on and off. He became known as 'Water-Lily Faber' after a poem he wrote in his first year at Oxford; this cannot have been a recommendation to the sporting, or hard-reading sets. Malicious gossip, partly deserved, contributed to Faber's eventual feeling that he must leave Oxford, though it was a place he had greatly loved. But he had other, more personal, reasons for not being very happy in 1839 and 1840.

However exciting, or depressing, Oxford might be, Faber found a second home, at Ambleside in the Lake District, that never disappointed him. He renewed his boyhood love of mountain scenery, celebrated it in his most authentic poetry, and worked off some of his formidable energy in immense walks and discussions. During the university vacations he virtually took over the running of the parish from Mr Dawes, who was elderly and infirm and had been the incumbent for a quarter of a century. The church in those days was St Anne's Chapel, enlarged in 1812 but never large enough for its congregation, set on a hilltop with commanding and intoxicating views. The famous Rushbearing Festival was still celebrated at Ambleside – and still is, in the larger church which was built in the valley a few years after Faber left. A note in the new church records that Faber was the first to use wax candles in the services. He was also long remembered for his sermons and for his pastoral work in the parish.

Faber was ordained deacon at Ripon in August 1837. It was in that long vacation that he first went to Ambleside, with a small reading party of undergraduates. The district had of course been made famous by the Lake Poets; the Wordsworths were living at Rydal Mount, within easy walking distance. That summer William Wordsworth himself was away but, towards the end of August, the newly fledged deacon paid the first of many calls on Rydal Mount. Mary Wordsworth wrote about his 'simple but beautiful language' to her husband:

> When he called upon me, I took him for a Modest Boy. He has 3 or 4 Pupils and takes the Sunday duty ... The chapel at A. is filled to overflowing ... All the *non* gentry who have seats are as much edified as the grandees. Mr. F. is the reigning subject – Q. Victoria has sunk into nothing among the conversationalists.

Three weeks later she reported that, having heard so much of this nice young man, she had not been able to resist hearing one of his sermons. She had been much impressed, particularly by his 'modest but animated fervent manner'. 'Our John was quite fascinated ...' she wrote, and it seemed that the preacher maintained this high standard every week.

Faber, who was ordained priest at Oxford in May 1839, was to keep his connection with Ambleside until the end of 1842. Since 1838 he had known William Wordsworth as well as Mary. In June 1839 Wordsworth went south to Oxford, to be honoured by the University, rather belatedly, with a DCL. Both the Faber brothers gave breakfasts for him. Frank reported that his had gone off 'with wonderful éclat ... Professor Keble was exactly opposite and was very pleasant and full of animation. Newman was quite at a distance ...' Frederick's breakfast, attended by the future Bishop of Salisbury and the Prussian Ambassador, was even more brilliant. The elderly poet gave great satisfaction by 'most

magnificently' reciting 'Yarrow Unvisited'; according to
Frank: 'It was a morning of great enjoyment, such as could
hardly be expected to occur again.' Indeed the whole week
was treasured in Frank's memory. He wrote to his fiancée:

> Well! I have dined with the Poet, breakfasted with the
> Poet – walked arm in arm up High St. with the poet!!!!
> Perhaps you think I ought to exclaim with Sir John
> Falstaff 'now let me die, for I have lived long enough' –
> but I am not quite so romantic. Fancy walking up the
> very place wh. he has immortalized in his sonnets.

The same letter gave a glimpse of his younger brother:

> Fred joined us at dinner and then accompanied us for a
> walk to some beautiful gardens. I regret to say that C.
> fell in love with him – e.g. 'Frederic is very handsome.'
> 'Yes.' 'Don't you think him very sweet looking?' 'I don't
> know what you mean by sweet looking.' 'Why he has
> such a sweet mouth.' 'I don't know what a sweet mouth
> means.' 'Why . . . a mouth one would like to give a kiss
> to'!! Whereupon Tom and I expressed similar senti-
> ments as to the mouth of Signora Albertazzi, one of the
> singers. XXXX

The long vacation of 1840 was enlivened by the visit of
Queen Adelaide, the Queen Dowager, to Ambleside. She
arrived in some state, visited the church and took refresh-
ments at Rydal Mount before leaving. The loyal Faber must
have been in his element. He was about to publish, rather
successfully, his first volume of verse, *The Cherwell Water-Lily*.
He had also provided for his immediate future by leaving
Oxford and becoming Tutor in the Harrison family, who
lived at Ambleside and were connected with the
Wordsworths. In February of the following year, while
Smythe was taking his seat in the House of Commons, Faber

embarked on a tour of the Continent, with his pupil, Matthew Harrison. They spent some time in Italy and Greece, visited Constantinople and returned through central Europe, reaching England in September. They had meant to go to the Holy Land, but were prevented by reports of plague; Faber wrote to a friend that he might have taken the risk himself, if he had not been responsible for his pupil. Faber was a determined traveller, often more or less unwell but soon recovering, gallantly enduring dirt, fleas and discomfort, enraptured by scenery and recording it in beautifully written letters, sympathetic to foreigners yet stoutly English – particularly in his frequent consumption of strong, scalding tea. On his return he went to Ambleside and spent most of 1842 there.

One of Faber's most obvious weaknesses, at least in these earlier years, was his tendency to exaggerate. A close friend, Roundell Palmer, described him, after his death, as

a man of genius, though not of that kind in which strength predominates. His nature was tender and emotional; he thought and felt in superlatives; and though his thoughts and feelings were real and true, they were surrounded by a *nimbus* of artificial light.

Wordsworth admired Faber as a man, and almost revered him as a clergyman, but wrote to Isabella Fenwick in 1844 that he was 'in the habit of using strong expressions, so that what he says must be taken with some qualification. This practice in so very pious, good and able a man is deeply to be regretted ...' Frank Faber thought that the 'use of exaggerated forms of expression' by his brother was due to there having been nobody 'to assert equality with him' in the nursery. It was an undoubted fault but a superficial one, he wrote, and less apparent as he got older.

No doubt Faber expressed his views strongly on political, as on other, matters. It is clear that, from his Union days onwards, he was never a revolutionary democrat. Although he felt strongly the obligation on the wealthy to help the poor, he would have been horrified at any idea of subverting the aristocratic order or the authority of the Crown. He was, of course, a devoted monarchist; he wrote to Smythe in May 1839 that he would 'preserve my loyalty to the last, and evince it by giving the Queen precedence in the journey . . .' But he does not seem to have been a violent political partisan. He confessed to John Manners: 'I always go wrong upon politics, I will give then up now. You shall be my Pope in politics.' According to Crabb Robinson he declared, during a four-hour walk to Easedale Tarn on 30 December 1842, 'his indifference to Whigs, Tories, and Radicals, having no predilections'. What, nevertheless, gave his opinions a Tory edge was his concern for the Church and his disgust with reforms likely to weaken the hold of the Church over the nation. Thus he deplored the threat of a Royal Commission on the universities and wrote in 1837 that he was 'quite sick of all Reformers'. But increasingly he saw salvation in the separation of Church and State; as early as 1835 he held that in 1827 (?1828, when the Test Act was repealed), the legislature had 'ceased to be a Christian body and by consequence the State to be a Christian state'.

Faber had been brought up as a boy in a twilight of ecclesiastical splendour at Bishop Auckland, where the Bishop of Durham was still Count Palatine and a temporal prince, holding his own courts, appointing local magnates and moving between Durham and Auckland in a coach with six horses and armed outriders. In 1836, when the privileges of the Palatinate were transferred to the Crown, Faber wrote a poem on the funeral of the last Palatine and lamented, 'There is a glory less upon the earth':

> This thought a light o'er my old age will shine,
> A grandeur, now no more on earth, touched me
> With its last outskirts, for on bended knee
> I oft was blessed by that Last Palatine.

That must have been a real laying on of hands. From his boyhood on, Faber was obsessed by the need to restore the Church – menaced by Revolution, Reform and Materialism – to a central place in the scheme of things. He was not only moved by the past, but excited by what he foresaw of the future. Thus he opened *The Cherwell Water-Lily* with a quotation from de Maistre: *Nous touchons à la plus grande des époques réligieuses.* He expanded on this in a versified Preface:

> An Age comes on, which came three times of old,
> When the enfeebled nations shall stand still
> To be by Christian science shaped at will;
> And Taste and Art, rejecting heathen mould,
> Shall draw their types from Europe's middle night,
> Well-pleased if such good darkness be their light.

Like Hurrell Froude, as described by Newman, he was 'smitten with the love of the Theocratic Church'.

It was this same sense of a Church in danger, but shaking its sinews, that impelled the whole of the Oxford Movement. As Newman wrote in his *Apologia*:

> While I was engaged in writing my work upon the Arians, great events were happening at home and abroad ... Shortly before (1830), there had been a Revolution in France ... I held that it was unchristian for nations to cast off their governors, and, much more, sovereigns who had the divine right of inheritance. Again, the great Reform Agitation was going on around me as I wrote. The Whigs had come into power; Lord Grey had told the Bishops to set their house in order, and some of the Prelates had been insulted and threatened in the streets of London. The vital question was, how were we to keep the Church from being liberalized?

For Newman the Church must not be liberalized, because it was God's means of enabling men to see and share in His truth without being solely at the mercy of their individual consciences. There would always be forces seeking to undermine the Church; but the aim must be to keep it as nearly as possible in the pristine state in which it had come from the Maker. The Bible was not enough: 'A book, after all, cannot make a stand against the wild living intellect of man, and in this day is beginning to testify . . . to the power of that universal solvent, which is so successfully acting upon religious establishments.' What was needed was to restore, in a second Reformation, 'that primitive Christianity which was delivered for all time by the early teachers of the Church, and which was registered and attested in the Anglican formularies and by the Anglican divines'.

It is impossible to read Faber's correspondence without being struck by the extent to which, even in his most worldly moments, religion coloured his deeper thoughts. Fond of reading, and himself a writer, he loved the classics. Yet at Oxford he regretted having to spend so much time studying them, when he wanted to learn and think about religion. As with many other religious men, his belief passed through various stages, but he always knew that what really mattered to him was his relationship with God and Christ. For most of his time as an undergraduate he was inclined to evangelical views; Frank Faber attributed this to the influence of 'a clergyman who lived near his friends in the country, the late Rev. W. W. Ewbank'. But gradually, at Oxford, he decided that the evangelical school was not intellectually satisfying. He told Newman on his deathbed that 'the turning point of his life' had been one of Newman's sermons at St Mary's, soon after he had come up to Oxford, which had given him the first notion he had of supernatural grace. But this only started the process. It was apparently a sermon by Edward Pusey, in 1836, that finally made Faber a 'Puseyite' or 'Tractarian'.

Of course, in the long run, there was nothing final about this either. Faber had convinced himself, or been convinced, that the Church was the main vehicle of God's truth. With his usual vehemence he told Crabb Robinson, during their trudge to Easedale Tarn, that 'without the Church, the Scriptures could not suffice to convince him'. But then the question arose: Which Church? Tastes and traditions might differ from nation to nation. But God's truth must be universal and could not be self-contradictory. The Anglican Church claimed a genuine Apostolical succession. Was this justifiable? Even if it was, how could Anglicanism be made, or revealed as, fully Catholic? Could a common basis for belief and worship be found in the origins of both the Anglican and the Roman Catholic Churches? If the gulf between them was too wide to bridge, which Church had the better claim to represent the early traditions? The Anglicans were a relatively small splinter group from a worldwide organization. What if the Roman Church still were, with all its imperfections, Peter's Church? What if Henry VIII, rather than the Pope, had been moved by the spirit of Antichrist? What if the Reformation had been, at best, a hideous mistake, at worst, the diabolical fruit of sinful self-will?

This struggle for the soul of the Oxford Movement occupied, roughly, the decade from 1835 to 1845. It was an exciting, though a deeply disturbing time for the clergymen who were caught up in it. With his charm and intellect, and with the hypnotic force of his personality, Newman was of course the leading figure; but he was sometimes led as well as leading. In December 1849 he explained to Frank Faber that, up until Michaelmas term 1839, he 'honestly wished to benefit the Anglican Church at the expense of the Church of Rome'. Between then and 1843 he wished to benefit it 'without prejudice to the Church of Rome'. In Michaelmas term 1843 he 'began to despair of the Anglican Church and gave up all clerical duty', but he did not wish positively to injure it. A year later he 'distinctly contemplated leaving it' and so told his friends.

Frederick Faber, with others, followed in Newman's wake; but their pressure sometimes forced Newman's pace. Minds with a love of certainty and the absolute – minds given to employing 'strong expressions' – found this state of ecclesiastical limbo uncomfortable and were unlikely to endure it, willingly, for long. In the earlier stages, however, there was more hope than fear. Faber wrote busily for the new movement and went on missionary forays to Cambridge. Newman summed up one such visit, in a letter of December 1838:

> Faber has returned from Cambridge with doleful accounts, as he gives them, though I have not confidence in his representation. However, I doubt not he has done good by going. He says that two parties are formed, Hookites, which *in fact* includes us, and a sort of Latitudinarians, who *consider* they maintain Oxford views.

Although the two men were to be closely associated, and although Newman was to write admiringly about Faber's 'remarkable gifts' after his death, he never really got over his personal distrust of his disciple. Faber remained touchingly, if sometimes tiresomely, loyal to Newman; he thought that the misunderstandings between them had been put right 'and righter than right' on his deathbed. But Newman's written comment on this final interview was that Faber had done almost all the talking and that his own view of him 'poor fellow, is not much changed . . .'

The Long Vacation of 1838

Manners was happy at Cambridge, but happiest during the long vacation of 1838 which he spent in the Lake District. We have his own words for it:

The most salient feature of the happy two years I spent at Cambridge was the long vacation of 1838 which, in company with Newport, now Lord Bradford, I spent at his father's charming cottage, St Catherine's, above Windermere, reading with John Morse Heath. It was there I first fell in with Frederick Faber, and heard him preach in Ambleside Church. The magic of his voice and the charm of his society and conversation were irresistible. I at least found them so, and his influence over me was great until he entered the Church of Rome.

Over thirty years later St Catherine's still had charm for Manners. He wrote to Disraeli in September 1873, on revisiting:

this romantic spot . . . It has been to me like going back to boyhood. In this cottage (as it then was) Bradford and I spent the summer of '38 and from it explored nearly every nook and corner of what poor Faber called these 'unworldly lakes'. Now another storey has been added to the house, and the views from the new Drawing room are quite exquisite.

Unworldly lakes! The words were taken from a poem by Faber bidding farewell to his friend Thomas Whytehead, a contemporary of Smythe's at St John's, who was about to go out to New Zealand as a missionary, and to die there in 1843. During that long vacation of 1838 Whytehead, too, was in the Lake District, at Keswick together with Smythe and Goulburn. Faber's poem recalled their rambles together:

> Unworldly lakes! – Did we not dream away
>   Part of our manhood by their inland coves,
> Living, like summer insects, all the day

> In summer winds or shade of drowsy groves?
> And with our endless songs and joyous airs
> Made wings unto ourselves as bright as theirs?

In his obituary on Faber Manners portrayed the 'poet-priest ... habited in a blouse with a broad-brimmed straw hat flapping behind his back', striding over the fells with a group of high-spirited boys at his heels. 'To the young and enthusiastic it was fairyland,' he wrote, 'each mountain clothed with glory, each lake a well of inspiration.'

But the highest summits seem to have been glimpsed during Faber's sermons in St Anne's Chapel. His style of preaching was 'poetical and vivid'; one sermon in particular, preached on Rushbearing Sunday about 'The Dignity of Little Children', was delivered with 'electrical' effect. After the service the congregation of local people and reading parties would gather in the windy churchyard, with its glorious views, to meet and congratulate the preacher. Faber, flushed with a feeling of success in God's service, and presenting a fine figure in his fluttering robes, would find the right words to say to each of them. He was conscious of unusual power that summer. In 'An Epistle to a Young M.P.' (Manners) at the end of 1841, or the beginning of 1842, he wrote:

> In that old rambling year of Thirty Eight
> Thou knewest me encircled with a state,
> And retinue of vision, feeling, thought,
> Joy, fear, and hot conception, all inwrought.
> That pageant is worn out ...

It was in St Anne's churchyard that Manners met Faber for the first time. He recorded in his Journal for 22 July:

> To Ambleside to hear Smythe's idol, Faber, preach; did not quite like his style of reading prayers; too inanimate; the high church idea of not presuming to invest things

sacred with any human ornaments. Sermon on reading Old Testament as well as New, and all parts alike – eloquent, earnest and gorgeous beyond what I had anticipated; expressions and similes drawn from nature, glowing and glorious; he insisted that every word of the Bible was inspired by God . . . altogether I was charmed, and highly gratified at being introduced to him by Smythe.

The words 'highly gratified' were no mere polite formula. In November 1846, when Young England was no more, Smythe wrote to Manners, invoking their past friendship and hoping it would survive any loss of esteem:

Love me in the Past and in memory: with thoughts of Keate's Lane, and your first introduction to Faber after church, and Cambridge rides, and Commons speeches, and Carlton suppers . . .

The use of the vogue word 'idol' in Manners's Journal shows that Smythe's own acquaintance with Faber must have been of earlier date. Perhaps they had met during one of Faber's Cambridge visits.

It is clear from Faber's poems that, during the next few weeks, he saw a lot of Smythe, hiking with him to Furness Abbey and spending 'three happy days' in the 'awful hills', talking of 'great and solemn things'. There were, of course, other lions in the neighbourhood. Whytehead was able to compare Southey's restlessness with Wordsworth's calm. Wordsworth entertained the young university men to tea, where they met Dr Thomas Arnold, whom Manners found 'ugly' but 'clever-looking' (he was prepared to revise his unfavourable opinion of him, since everybody who knew him seemed to like him). But all these excitements had finally to end. When Smythe had left the Lake District, Faber wrote, on 12 September:

Brother, brother! thou art gone, and I will not mourn
  thy going.
Though thou hast been unto me like a river in its
  flowing;
For many a fresh and manly thought, and many a
  glorious dream,
Like fruits and flowers of foreign lands, have flourished
  by the stream.

Perhaps it was during these manly conversations that Faber
first advised Smythe against becoming a Roman Catholic; in
1857 he reproached himself (in a letter to the Duke of Norfolk) with having '*hindered* his [Smythe's] being a Catholic in
1839'. That Smythe was indeed at one stage tempted by
Catholicism is confirmed in a letter from him to Manners:

> If I could summon the pluck . . . I would go over heart
> and soul to Rome . . . Otherwise I see no bulwark, which
> can stand the assaults of the Printing Press and other
> damnable engines in sapping and modernising all good
> old prejudices.

Smythe was, too, impressed by Newman's personality: he
described him as 'more simple than any man I ever met
except the Duke of Wellington'. However, lacking the pluck
or the conviction, he remained an Anglican until he lost his
faith.

It was not only Smythe whom Faber set out to fascinate
during these seminal holidays. His friendship with Manners
blossomed rapidly, too. By January 1839 he could write about
him to his Cambridge correspondent Beresford Hope in the
following terms:

> I think one of your clique is safer, sounder and wiser
> than all the rest put together; and love him because the
> inward counterpart of earnestness goes along with the

outward progress of his opinions. It shows a solid soul, and a loyal one in the sight of God, and precious to the Church . . .

This was one of the sound judgements that Faber, even in his wilder moments, was capable of making about other people. Towards the end of 1838, after a visit to Cambridge, he dedicated a sonnet to Manners's patriotism. It confirms that they discussed political, as well as religious, topics:

Thou walkest with a glory round thy brow
Like Saints in pictures – radiant in the blaze
And splendour of thy boyhood, mingling now
With the bold bearing of a man, that plays
In eyes which do with such sweet skill express
Thy soul's hereditary gentleness.
Thou art my friend's best friend; and higher praise
My heart hath none to give, nor thine to take;
So I have loved thee for my brother's sake.
But when thou talk'st of England's better days,
And from its secret place thy soul comes forth,
And sits upon thy lips as on a throne,
Then would I fain do homage to thy worth,
And worship thee for England's sake, and for thine own.

For his part Manners was impressed by the serious talks he had with both Smythe and Faber. On 4 August he recorded in his Journal a conversation with Smythe:

We have now virtually pledged ourselves to attempt to restore what? I hardly know – but still it is a glorious attempt, and he is really well qualified to take the lead in it, but what rebuffs, sneers and opposition must we expect: however, I think a change is working for the better, and all, or nearly all, the enthusiasm of the young spirits of Britain is with us.

This seems to have been the moment when Young England's first flame was lit. It was lit by Smythe and Manners – perhaps originally by Smythe – but with a spark from Faber's fire.

On 28 August Manners made another entry in his Journal:

> I had a deal of talk with Faber, his idea is that Church and State must first of all be separated; then for a crash to end in the supremacy of the Church. Eager as I am, I hardly know how to agree to this, and ventured a suggestion as to the necessity of postponing by all means in our power this internal crash, till the external one, which is evidently nigh at hand, has taken place. He admitted there was some reason in that, but thought the internal struggle would soon be over, though fierce and keen, and that it would leave England in a purified and consequently robust state. I wish I could be as sanguine.

This is the language of revolution, however theocratic; it seems unlikely that Faber used it for long. However, nothing that he said seems to have shaken Manners's allegiance – not even his abuse of James II. 'I only wish I could remember more Faberisms,' Manners concluded. 'Of a surety something must come of all I have heard this day.' A year later and, from the Park of Pau, he could still look up to Faber as an apostle:

> This time last year! and we were roving then
> On Loughrigg's brow, or up St. John's wild glen;
> Friends of an hour, and thou gav'st utterance
> To words which cold and worldly-hearted men
> Might deem too full of wrath; and yet perchance
> The hour may come, and come unlooked for when
> Things shall prove true that scared thy prophet's ken.

The effects of all this talking soon began to strike other people. The Revd J. W. Blakesley, of Trinity, Cambridge, wrote to Lyttelton on 10 December 1838 about the curious influence that the Oxford School was beginning to exert in Cambridge:

> It is quite obvious, however, in all cases that are most conspicuous (viz. Smythe, John Manners, and Hope, the two former of whom were bitten by one Faber at the Lakes during the rainy weather last summer) that the religious views have grown out of the political, and that if we strip off the hide of Newman we shall find Filmer underneath.

But Newman himself, in the passage already quoted from his *Apologia*, wrote of 'the divine right of inheritance'; Tractarian beliefs harmonized quite comfortably with an exalted view of monarchy. It is likely enough that the Young Englanders began to form their political opinions at Eton, before they had acquired advanced religious views. In the end, however, it became very difficult to separate the religious and political strands of the Young England movement. As we shall see, the Church was intended to play a vital role in realizing the ideals of the movement. When the Church failed to respond, the whole fire went out.

2

Poetry and Passion

_____

Young England was a party of youth. It reacted against the
political assumptions of the older generation, particularly
reliance on the profit motive and on rational calculation,
rather than sentiment and faith, as the mainspring of government. These assumptions owed much to the teachings of
Jeremy Bentham and the political economists, who were not
among Young England's heroes. More positively, the party
had the romantic idealism often associated with youth: the
belief that, if proper attitudes could only be inculcated, both
in rulers and ruled, the world could be made a better and
happier place. Still more to the point, it was in fact made up
of young, or youngish, men. Its main supporters, inside or
outside the House of Commons, were in their twenties or
thirties. Even Disraeli was under forty when the movement
was launched.

This is not to say that the Young Englanders pictured
themselves, in any sense, as protesting against their elders. In
the early days Disraeli even saw the elder John Walter – a
man of 66 – as a possible leader. Cochrane thought this an
excellent idea (so long as the leadership was *nominal*), in order
to ensure the support of *The Times*. But Manners wrote
strongly against 'so stupid a choice', presumably because the
elder Walter, unlike his son, was known to distrust the
Oxford Movement. There is nothing to suggest that Walter
was considered too old for the job. According to Cochrane (*In
the Days of the Dandies*), elder statesmen, like Lyndhurst and
Brougham, were kind to the young men, giving them good
advice, which was modestly digested.

Nor was the name 'Young England' chosen by the Young Englanders themselves. In a speech at Bingley, in October 1844, Disraeli made it clear that this title was a taunt 'given to us in derision', but that the Young Englanders had accepted it and believed it had brought 'hopeful tidings' throughout the realm. Yet it had taken them some time to see the title's advantages. According to an article in the *Morning Post* on 18 July 1843 the name had been given to the movement 'on a recent occasion' by the Radical, Joseph Hume, and had since been very generally adopted. For their part the *Morning Post* (supporters of Young England) protested against it; what *they* wanted was 'a recurrence to the principles and feelings of "OLD ENGLAND" '. In this the newspaper was certainly reflecting what Manners, for instance, felt.

Nevertheless, the rapid way in which this title spread suggests that what struck outsiders most about the movement was the obvious fact of its members' youth. Before Young England existed, Disraeli had virtually coined the name in a casual phrase to his wife, when (in February 1842) he told her how well a speech of his on the consular service had been received: 'All Young England, the new Members, etc., were deeply interested.' This youthful image was of course at once a help and a hindrance. Whether attracted or irritated by it, older men were likely to react more kindly, but also with more ridicule, than might otherwise have been the case. The benevolence allowed the movement to take root; but the ridicule hampered its subsequent growth.

That the protagonists were very conscious themselves of their youth was only to be expected. At the end of *The Cherwell Water-Lily* Faber spelt out the readership he had had chiefly in mind:

> YOUNG Reader! – for most surely to the old
> These loose, uneven thinkings can but seem
> Unlifelike and unreal as a dream . . .

Smythe quoted these lines in his *Historic Fancies* and in the shape of Waldershare) was himself described by Disraeli as 'one of those vivid and brilliant organizations which exercise a peculiarly attractive influence on youth'. Manners wrote about 'the enthusiasm of the young spirits of Britain', while the best pages in Cochrane's novels are those recapturing a youthful feeling of enjoyment. Writing to his brother Frank (17 November 1840) Faber excused his youthful indiscretions in *The Cherwell Water-Lily*:

> You see all your objections (to all wh I partially suc-
> cumb) are such as belong not to *me* personally, but to
> *youth* universally – such as must inevitably adhere to all
> young publications, and the question is whether it has
> been well to publish so young. Had I kept my MSS I shd
> have felt enthralled. As it is I feel disenthralled, and at
> liberty to go my own gait and do better – so I don't
> repent. I am in a desperate hurry.

Another man in a hurry! Between Disraeli and Faber the three younger men had little chance of maturing slowly. But, if they had waited for maturity, they would never have made the particular contribution which was in them, as young men, to make.

Poetry

Byron, Shelley and Keats had all died young, while Wordsworth and Coleridge both owed their reputations as poets to their youth. In the wake of the Romantic movement young men with any literary pretensions tended to regard poetry as a sacred mission – or, if not quite that, at least as an emotional phase that they ought to experience, and then put behind them. In that post-Georgian period not even the mild-est social stigma seems to have attached to versifying; on the whole it was rather a source of prestige. Young men, even 'of the highest station', could dabble in it without any sense of losing caste or neglecting sterner duties; they paid their early sacrifices to the Muses with an enthusiasm unequalled since Tudor or early Stuart times.

All my five heroes wrote and published verse at one time or another, between them covering a wide range of the best English styles. A fierce critic might dismiss Faber's poetry as Wordsworth and water (or Wordsworth and milk), Manners's as Pope and water, Cochrane's as Byron and selzer water, Smythe's as mulled Macaulay and Disraeli's as Shakespeare and/or Milton neat. That would be fiercer than they deserve. All five wrote verse that was at least surprisingly competent. Even Disraeli's lines – though almost wholly devoid of original poetic genius – can express interesting ideas with force and point. The three younger men tended to write more unevenly, with less force, but with more appeal. Faber, though guilty of much that was mawkish, pietistic and derivative, had still more appeal, with moments of genuine poetical inspiration. His poetry is sincere, even when derivative; it is pleasantly rhythmical and agreeable to the ear. What gives it its quality, however, is the way in which his better lines do rise gently above the commonplace with some quiet felicity of language or imagination. It was this, as much as his religious modishness, that appealed to the Young Englanders – good enough critics if only moderate poets – and to Wordsworth, whose ability to recognize poetry had survived his own much greater inspiration.

Some of the quotations from Faber's poetry in this book will show him in a sentimental and rather ridiculous light. At his best he had a sensitivity to moods, a moving simplicity of language and an eye for nature that induced Wordsworth to say of him, when he opted to become a full-time parish priest: 'I do not say you are wrong; but England loses a poet.' Here is one sonnet, from *The Cherwell Water-Lily*, that seems to deserve to last:

Keswick, August 3, 1838

Some fall in love with voices, some with eyes;
Some men are linked together by a tear;
Others by smiles; many who cannot tell
What time the Angel passed who left the spell.
It comes to us among the winds that rise
Scattering their gifts on all things far and near.
The fields of unripe corn, the mountain lake,
And the great-hearted sea – all things do take
Their glory and their witchery from winds;
All save the few black pools the woodman finds
Far in the depths of some unsunny place,
Which stand, albeit the happy winds are out
In all the tossing branches round about,
As silent and as fearful as a dead man's face.

Faber published two volumes of more or less lyrical verse –
The Cherwell Water-Lily and Other Poems, which came out in
September 1840, and *The Styrian Lake and Other Poems,* dedicated to John Keble, which came out towards the end of 1842.
On the whole the earlier collection is the more secular and the
more interesting poetically. At the end of 1844 he produced a
long poem, *Sir Lancelot – A Legend of the Middle Ages,* set in the
Westmorland mountains in the reign of Henry III. Its object
was dear to Faber's heart – he wished to show how appreciation
of natural beauty could be combined with Christian sentiments. He had worked hard at this poem; but, by the time it
was out, he was no longer ambitious to make poetry, whether
Christian or otherwise, his life's work. His last volume of
poetry – *The Rosary and Other Poems* – appeared in 1845, was
dedicated to Beresford Hope and in aid of the restoration of
Elton Parish Church. At the end, as a kind of farewell to the
Muse, he reproduced the epitaph written by Chiabrera for his
own tomb, which he had seen at Savona in the spring of 1843
and which struck him as a divine warning to himself to seek
consolation in religion rather than in poetry:

Amico, io vivendo cercava conforto
Nel Monte Parnasso;
Tu, meglio consigliato, cercalo
Nel CALVARIO!

In so far as Faber was a poet, he was so instinctively. Newman, with perhaps a touch of disdain, called him a poet, even when he had more or less abandoned poetry. Faber himself admitted that he relied on 'mysterious perceptions and half-truths' which he could hardly express in logical form; he thought that '. . . imagination, when it comes near any truth, has a mysterious and instinctive yearning towards it . . .'. His uncle accused him of being influenced 'rather by warmth of imagination; than by severity of close investigation'. This was, surely, the true poetic mentality. But it was also one type of religious mentality and Faber always had a difficulty in reconciling his practice of poetry with his practice of religion. In his early days he thought he could marry the two; he claimed to a friend (in October 1840) that he had 'almost invariably subdued my poetry under a stern theological carefulness'. Perhaps that was the trouble; perhaps that was what prevented him from writing poetry that would really last. As it was, the priest inevitably came to predominate over the poet. By the time he took to writing hymns he had deliberately turned his back on poetry, like Plato abandoning Art for Philosophy, and cared nothing for the poetic distinction of what he wrote, so long as it helped to save souls. His simplicity of language was then almost his only poetic gift to survive. Manners, in his obituary of his friend, claimed that

> The service demanded by the Church of his choice dimmed the fine gold of his genius, and trailed through his later devotional writings that thread of coarse exaggeration and materialistic devotion to the blessed Virgin and the saints which shocked many of the older school of Anglo-Roman Catholics . . .

Wordsworth reported Faber, in July 1842, as 'writing poetry at an immense rate, meaning to have a volume (*The Styrian Lake*) out before his departure in January for the Continent'. That was the other part of the trouble: Faber's flow was too rapid and facile. By October 1844 the Laureate had decided that, though his young friend had an even better eye for nature than himself, he was not going to be a poet after all. He wrote to Isabella Fenwick:

I have told him what I thought of his Poem [*Sir Lancelot*] as far as I have read it. It is a mine of description, and valuable thought and feeling; but too minute and diffusive and disproportioned; and in the workmanship very defective. The Poem was begun too soon and carried on too rapidly before he had attained sufficient experience in the art of writing, and this he candidly and readily admits. Some of his Friends wish and urge him to continue writing verse. I had a long conversation with him upon the subject yesterday, in which he gave me such an account of himself that I could not concur with those advisers in their opinion. A man like him cannot serve two Masters. He has vowed himself as a Minister of the Gospel to the service of God. He is of that temperament that if he writes verse the Spirit must *possess* him, and the practice master him, to the great injury of his work as a Priest.

Mark Pattison was almost certainly the author of an unsympathetic obituary on Faber published in the *Saturday Review* for 10 October 1863. He castigated *The Cherwell Water-Lily* as

a now forgotten volume, but full of the Faberian characteristics from end to end. It was very ecclesiastical, very imaginative, very unreal, very full of dedications to Lord John Manners, George Smythe, Roundell Palmer, and notabilities in general, not invariably grammatical, and not unfrequently very silly.

As an example of silliness, he quoted a verse from 'Three Happy Days', in which Faber had described – without mentioning any names – a moment of relaxation with a friend after earnest discussions on Church and State (the friend was clearly Smythe):

> We pulled each other's hair about,
>   Peeped in each other's eyes,
> And spoke the first light silly words
>   That to our lips did rise.

Mark Pattison was not the only reader to be taken aback by the picture conjured up by these lines. Frank Faber seems to have remonstrated with his brother about them. Frederick defended himself and claimed that 'Three Happy Days' figured on two lists from admirers as a favourite piece. But, as usual, he attended to criticism, while appearing to resist it. Although a kind of holy silliness remained one of his ruling characteristics, he was careful to maintain a more sober tone in *The Styrian Lake*.

However much Faber would have denied it, 'Three Happy Days' seems to have escaped through the net of the 'stern theological carefulness' that was supposed to mount vigil over his work. But even Homer nods. Faber's considered attitude to other English poets was as stern and theological as might be wished. Milton, although a great writer, was an 'execrable rebel and heretic' – heretic because he depreciated the Godhead of Christ and, in his own pride, sympathized with Satan's. Wordsworth overvalued Milton, had an 'unfortunate theory of poetry' and adopted a regrettably Pantheistic attitude in *Tintern Abbey*, but was otherwise to be loved and admired. So was Coleridge. But Byron – much read by Faber at Harrow – was 'godless and obscene', having abandoned his duties at home for a 'filthy and lascivious exile'. As for Shelley, he was 'a low unprincipled scoundrel, not a romantic dreamer; but I owe so much to him of joy and pleasure that his death has given a melancholy interest in my eyes to this Gulf of Spezia . . .'. Yet, 'I have never repented the hour when at Univ I threw into the fire my beautiful 4 vol edition of Shelley.' Finally there was Keats, whom Faber admired more than some contemporary critics; he thought the 'Ode to a Grecian Urn' 'a very classical poem . . . whose real merits false principles of taste and a singularly feeble dominion over his mother-tongue have perhaps too much over-shadowed'.

If some of these judgements seem a trifle vehement, it has to be remembered that, for Faber, the Devil really was walking about, seeking whom he might devour. Life was a perpetual struggle against the Devil's wiles – or a gradual submission to them. A childlike silliness was, in one sense, a defence against them, since it at least kept out the Satanic vice of Pride. In Faber's English New Testament, given him by his mother, the fly-leaf contains two Latin objurations: *Fide: tantum fide* and *Obsta diabolo*. Below them three strange, elongated crosses are stabbed – as if in an agonized attempt to ward off the Devil's onslaughts.

To move from Faber's poetry to Disraeli's is like travelling from a landscape of showers and pale sunshine to the dazzling aridity of the desert. Arid because, clever though he was, Disraeli was never really a poet. Both he and Faber were distracted from poetry – one by religion and the other by politics; but Faber's emotions at least needed to be expressed in verse, whereas Disraeli's – if he wanted to express them at all – could just as well, if not better, have been entrusted to prose. In fact *The Revolutionary Epick* is really a dissertation on political theory, which might be interesting, and even brilliant, if expounded in Disraeli's usual pregnant and sardonic sentences. As it is, it would be tempting to regard it as an elaborate hoax, but for conclusive evidence that it was his one serious attempt to create a poetic masterpiece. It none the less deserves to be looked at politically, rather than poetically.

The Revolutionary Epick, designed to do for the current Revolutionary epoch what Homer had done for the Heroic age and Virgil for the Augustan era, portrays the titanic struggle of Magros, the Spirit of Feudalism, with Lyridon, the Spirit of Federalism. Magros gets the first innings. He claims that aristocracy's seeds are sown deep in the human heart and that its real basis is the power of Genius. The Feudal/ Aristocratic system nurtures Civilization. What constitutes a PEOPLE?

> The lore
> Long centuries yield; refined arts; and faith,
> Honour, and justice; love of fatherland
> By olden thought endeared . . .

EQUALITY? 'The cry of feeble spirits . . . Is Nature equal?' Philosophers are 'a prating crew'; Imagination, not human Reason, drives Mankind. All this sounds like a very dry version of the basic philosophy behind Young England or behind Disraeli's own mature views. However, we move from argument to action. Faith and Fealty flee the earth at the advent of Change (the French Revolution). Magros goes to earth to strike Change down, but finds (to his horror) that, behind Change, looms another Spirit of his own weight – Lyridon.

It is now Lyridon's turn to tell us that it is his office 'To teach to monarchs and to multitudes their duties and their rights . . .' He dwells on the evils of Tyranny and Superstition and thinks much better of Equality than Magros does:

> . . . EQUALITY!
> Thou art indeed a God. Thy sacred fire
> Burns now in later temples, not to fall
> Like thine old shrines . . .

Then he turns to Liberty. Athens and Rome used to be free. Liberty left the earth in the reign of Nero, but returned with the invention of printing. In England John Hampden and Sir John Eliot were its high priests; in America Labour is honoured and the drones are banished; in France Reason has been given a dwelling.

Demogorgon, invited to choose between these arguments, gives his statesmanlike decree: 'In man alone the fate of man is placed.' Let them look to a great man (Napoleon) now rising on the earth. So we adjourn to the Conquest of Italy. Lyridon is the quicker off the mark, visits Napoleon in his camp and inspires him. Magros works on the King of Sardinia, but too late. There is a clash; Italy is freed; and the fragment ends.

The curious thing about this lengthy fragment is that, so far as it goes, Lyridon gets the better of Magros, though Magros is on the whole given the more sophisticated arguments to deploy. Presumably, if it had been completed, the poem would have developed some sort of synthesis, perhaps symbolized in Napoleon's later compromise with feudalism. Nevertheless Disraeli was not only ready to publish this incomplete work in 1834, but also to have it republished thirty years later. It is as if, however deeply committed in practice to Magros-type attitudes, Disraeli retained some sympathy for the ideals of the French Revolution and, at least as a poet, was not afraid to reveal this in public. For that matter, intensely ambitious and realistic though he was, the younger Disraeli was seldom afraid to reveal his deepest thoughts in public. *Tancred* might almost have been written expressly to prevent himself ever becoming a Conservative Prime Minister.

Perhaps this ambivalence over the French Revolution was characteristic of most early-Victorian intellectuals. In France itself writers like Chateaubriand and Balzac were clearly schizophrenic about the recent history of their country. So it is not surprising to find a similar schizophrenia in the

Gallomane Smythe. In his *Historic Fancies* (1844) he produced some brilliant and sympathetic prose portraits of French Revolutionary leaders, alongside rousing verse in honour of the old *noblesse*:

> Then grant, God, grant, that day may come, and long
>   shall it endure,
> For the poor will find true friends in those who have
>   themselves been poor;
> And the Noble, and the People, and the Church alike
>   shall know
> A Christian King of France, in King Henry of
>   Bordeaux.

Historic Fancies was dedicated

> To the Lord John Manners, M.P., whose gentle blood
> Is only an illustration of his gentler conduct
> And whose whole life
> May well remind us that the only child
> Of Philip Sidney became a Manners,
> Because he is himself as true and blameless,
> The Philip Sidney of our generation.

There are Stuart pieces (Mary Stuart, Charles Stuart, 'the Catholic Cavalier'), French pieces ('the Loyalist of the Vendée', 'the Jacobin of Paris', the death of the Duke of Orleans), a sonnet to Faber, another to Manners, and a poem on Ambleside Church. One piece, apparently advocating a renewal of the royal Touching for the Evil, earned a certain amount of derision; but Smythe himself described the practice as a 'graceful superstition' and praised it only as an instance of 'direct communication' between highest and lowest. A comment on James II is typical of Young England: 'Oh when will the rulers of the earth understand that their natural allies are the Many, their natural enemies the privileged and few!' There is a scene of Bolingbroke in his old age

('His memory is mostly associated with his light, and graceful, and gifted youth, the very idea and type of universal fascination'). That, too, is typical enough of Young England. Less typical, though characteristic of Smythe personally, is the rollicking invocation of 'The Merchants of Old England', with which the collection ends.

Some of this is the sort of stuff that a clever schoolboy might write; the verse is oddly prophetic of Kipling. But the studies of French Revolutionary leaders are mature as well as brilliant and suggest that Smythe's considerable literary talents really lay in the field of higher journalism. Certainly he went on to write much effective journalism, but never published any more verse. Yet what he did publish was successful enough at the time. *The Times's* review of *Historic Fancies* (on 4 July 1844) found 'fire and force' in his poetry, particularly in 'The Merchants of Old England', which was the finest thing in the volume and 'really a great national strain'.

Smythe's sonnet to Faber, as passionate though less single-hearted than those he received from him, indicates that his esteem for Faber survived the comparative cooling of their relationship after 1839:

Dear Master – I do love thee with a love
Which has with fond endeavour built a throne
In my heart's holiest place. Come sit thereon
And rule with thy sweet power, and reign above
All my thoughts, feelings, they to thee will prove
Loyal and loving vassals, for they burn
With a most passionate fire and ever yearn
And cleave to thee as ne'er before they clove
Dearest, to others. Oh for some strong spell
To give me back my childish heart, to shrine
Treasures I love too dearly and too well
To mar by contact with this life of mine.
Yet am I full of fears. Alas – beware
For knowing me, is ever knowing care!

The word 'albeit' makes at least three appearances in *Historic Fancies*, although Faber had written to Manners a few years earlier:

> I am so glad you put *albeit* into your sonnet. It occurs in every poem G.S.S. ever wrote; nearly every one F.W.F. ever wrote; and it is not infrequent in your own productions. It is a very unprotestant word. Put it in right and left. Esoterically we will be the *albeit* school; Catholics *albeit* we are Anglicans; free from Rome *albeit* near to antiquity; Jacobites *albeit* sub-Guelphians; mysterious to others *albeit* with no secrets to each other; faithful *albeit* all about us are unfaithful; boys in heart *albeit* men in years; lakers *albeit* not of the lake school.

Cochrane, who had not shared in that magical Lakeland vacation, was hardly a member of the '*albeit* school'. His poetry is less political and more heterosexual than that of his *albeit*-minded friends. It is mostly straightforward Byronic stuff (*Childe Harold*, rather than *Don Juan*), very flowing and efficient, seldom obviously immature, but without much distinctive power. The first slim volume appeared as early as 1838, in a private edition of only twenty copies; like the second volume it was dedicated to Cochrane's father. The subject matter ranged from a historical *fragment* and a poem on Scott's death to orthodox love poetry and panegyrics on Liberty. Two years later a collection called *The Morea*, after its principal poem, added the Greek dimension. It also included the lines in honour of Smythe already quoted, as well as a poem to Laura insisting that friendship between man and man cannot compete with 'the sympathy of a woman's heart'. At the end there are some prose 'Remarks upon the Present State of Greece', the burden of which is as Byronic as the poetry. Cochrane had expected to find 'a regenerated country', but it was 'in the last stage of misery'; Great Britain had guaranteed the Greeks a constitution, which they had still not got; 'Russia still breathes ruin over Greece ... surely it is in our interest to weaken Russian influence.' There is little in either of these collections that seems typically 'Young England', except some admiration of Strafford (very much *à la mode*) and some execration of Thomas Cromwell.

Manners's main poetic effort was *England's Trust and Other Poems,* published in 1841. The dedication ran:

> To the Hon. George Percy Sydney Smythe
> This volume
> Parvum non parvae pignus amicitiae
> is
> most affectionately and admiringly dedicated.

There was a long political poem in heroic couplets ('England's Trust'), a poem on King Charles the Martyr, a comparison of the Civil War period with 'these our days of restlessness and strife', tributes to Smythe and Faber and 'Memorials of Other Lands' dedicated to the author's elder brother. The poem to Faber ('friend most dear') is steeped in religious emotion:

> Surely, if ever two fond hearts were twinned
> In a most holy, mystic knot, so now
> Are ours: not common are the ties that bind
> My soul to thine; a dear apostle thou,
> I, a young Neophyte, that yearns to find
> The sacred truth, and stamp upon his brow
> The Cross, dread sign of his baptismal vow!

The references to Smythe are rather more secular, though no less emotional. In one poem ('Leaving Cambridge') Manners looks back on the 'brightest spots' as 'the hours that I did love to spend with thee, or listening to thy frequent praise'. In another ('The Meeting') he 'fondly prophesies the time when thy most glorious name shall blaze with clear undying light in nobler days . . .' There is, too, a suitable aura of stained glass and devotion about a passage regretting that Smythe was not with him during his travels abroad:

> But most at Rome, while hanging o'er the tomb
> Of those, the last of Stuart's line,
> Shrouded from gazers by the evening's gloom,
> My sighs did yearn to melt with thine.

But the poem of chief interest is 'England's Trust' which, until Disraeli wrote *Coningsby* and *Sybil*, was the most complete manifesto of Young England's basic philosophy. That is to say, it expressed Manners's philosophy, rather than Smythe's less monolithic opinions; but, since Manners quietly dominated the Young England movement – and, in a sense, incarnated it – it was as good a statement of the assumptions of the movement as was available at that time. It was also the most obviously Augustan of Manners's poems. By a curious paradox of taste, although in architecture he was a committed supporter of the Gothic style (regarded by Puseyites as being both more religious and more truly national than the Classical style), Manners seems to have admired the Classical Pope more than the later, Romantic, poets. In this, perhaps, he followed Byron, or perhaps some Eton master; or perhaps he simply liked Pope's style, because it was gentlemanly and hard-wearing.

Because this poem gives the fullest and most unreserved account of what the young Manners believed, it is necessary to quote rather fully from it. A text from Isaiah at the beginning strikes the keynote: 'In returning to rest shall ye be saved; in quietness, and in confidence, shall be your strength.' At least in Manners's conception, Young England does not have a *dynamic* vision: it does not want to advance to revolution, or to multiply change and activity. It wants to restore a more static, and more contented, condition of society. That condition is vaguely situated in the Middle Ages. St Alban's Cathedral makes the poet think

> of a nobler age
> When men of stalwart hearts and steadfast faith
> Shrunk from dishonour, rather than from death,
> When to great minds obedience did not seem
> A slave's condition, or a bigot's dream . . .
> When kings were taught to feel the dreadful weight
> Of power derived from One than kings more great,
> And learned with reverence to wield the rod
> They deemed entrusted to their hand by God.

In those happy days the nobles reverenced God's ministers, the monks practised charity and all classes felt a common kinship:

> Each knew his place – king, peasant, peer or priest,
> The greatest owned connexion with the least;
> From rank to rank the generous feeling ran,
> And linked society as man to man.

Contrast this (the poem urges) with modern capitalism. Wealth is expended on ease and comfort, while 'the modern slave', motivated by a false love of independence, treads 'his lonely path of care and toil'. Contrast the happy Tuscan peasantry with the English industrial work force.

Of course (Manners continues) we cannot go back to the pre-industrial age. But it does not follow that we should sacrifice our remaining traditions at the altar of Equality, or fancy that constitutional checks and balances will suffice to restrain 'the pent-up violence of man':

> Must we then hearken to the furious cry
> Of those who clamour for 'equality'?
> Have not the people learnt how vain the trust

On props like that which crumble into dust?
Are the gradations that have marked our race,
Since God first stamped His likeness on its face,
Gradations hallowed by a thousand ties
Of faith and love, and holiest sympathies,
Seen in the Patriarch's rule, the Judge's sway
When God himself was Israel's present stay,
Now in the old world's dotage to be cast
As weak pretences to the howling blast?
No! by the names inscribed in History's page,
Names that are England's noblest heritage,
Names that shall live for yet unnumbered years
Shrined in our hearts with Crécy and Poitiers,
Let wealth and commerce, laws and learning die
But leave us still our old Nobility!

This last couplet, quoted and misquoted *ad nauseam*, looks itself like living 'for yet unnumbered years', though not to Manners's or Young England's advantage. It was used against him by electoral opponents during his life and is still held up in lecture rooms as an example of aristocratic fatuity. Though urged to do so, Manners would never withdraw or explain away these lines. It is clear from the context that he is not just thinking of 'Nobility of Character', though that has been suggested. Smythe was nearer the mark when he advised him in 1849:

Say a word, if you can, at the declaration of the poll, about the couplet, that it was writ at 20 and that your idea of 'Nobility' applies, as I know it does, more to the 'statesmen' in Cumberland, or the yeoman of the South, with Squire everywhere, and the artisan ... than to modern Peers, and the Brummagem coronets of successful chicane, or sinister intrigue.

This was no doubt true. But it was not the whole of the

matter. Manners must have been proud of his own family's historical record (although his ancestor had been on the Parliamentary side in the Civil War!). In any case, what he was arguing for in these lines was not so much a particular class, or classes, as the hierarchical principle as such.

For the author of *England's Trust*, however, the ultimate salvation did not lie in the aristocracy, but in the 'healing power' of the Church. Meanwhile each 'earnest-minded man' must 'make some duty his peculiar care' and 'leave the rest to Faith'. There were still uncorrupted people:

> Simple are they. They never learned to scan
> With haughty pride the wrongs or rights of man,
> Nor deemed it wisdom to despise and hate
> Whate'er is noble, reverend, or great.
> O'er them no lurid light has knowledge shed,
> And Faith stands them in Education's stead.
> . . .
> Oh! may the holy angels guard and bless
> Their modest homes from modern restlessness.

'Modern restlessness': if any two words could sum up what Young England most disliked in contemporary civilization, these were they. Disraeli might bring himself to put up a theoretical case for Equality; not Manners. Of the three ideals of the French Revolution Manners could approve wholeheartedly only of Fraternity. Even Liberty should be tempered by Obedience. As to Revolution itself, Manners agreed with Newman: it was a type of Man's rebellion 'against his Maker . . . The Church must denounce rebellion as of all possible evils the greatest.'

Passion

In her short memoir of her brother-in-law, published as an introduction to his novel *Angela Pisani*, Lady Strangford wrote of Smythe, Faber and Whytehead: 'For many years these three were constantly interchanging poems, of which only a very few have been published.'

The Cherwell Water-Lily contains twelve poems addressed to Smythe, three of them actually entitled 'To G.S.S.' and two using one of his names, Sydney. They were written mostly between July and September 1838. One of the poems 'To G.S.S.' ends with the verse:

> Ah, dearest! – wouldest thou know how much
> My aching heart in thee doth live?
> One look of thy blue eye – one touch
> Of thy dear hand last night could give
> Fresh hopes to shine amid my fears,
> And thoughts that shed themselves in tears.

If this is not love poetry, it would be difficult to know what is. Hopes and fears, joy and heartache, delight and doubt, alternate in these poems, together with an increasing sense of uneasiness that the loved one is imperfect, that the lover's feeling for him is a sort of madness – and yet that this love is an inescapable fate.

Manners was not exaggerating when he wrote, in his obituary of Faber:

> It was friendship, and not love, as conventionally understood, that tuned his lyre and inspired his lays with expressions as passionate as were ever devoted by troubadour to his ladye-love.

It would be wrong to infer from this typically archaic comparison that, when he wrote passionately to his friends, Faber was merely practising a rather strained literary convention. It has sometimes been argued that that is enough to explain Shakespeare's Sonnets to his young patron. Faber used strong expressions habitually, in almost every context; but he did so because he felt strongly and found it difficult to play the hypocrite. At first he seems to have thought that there was no harm in having strong feelings about other men. When he began to suspect that his soul might be in danger from his love for Smythe, he painfully disciplined himself until he was no longer passion's slave. He was able to sublimate most of his other friendships, so that they helped, not hindered, his spiritual life. In his passion for Smythe, however, there was something he could not control and which he had to brace himself to jettison.

Up to a point, of course, the ideal of 'passionate friendship' was acceptable socially at this time. After all, Tennyson became a Victorian Poet Laureate, although he had written *In Memoriam* as a passionate tribute to a male friend. There were famous Classical (and even biblical) examples of male friendships, which were reverently cited at public schools. Faber's poems to young men other than Smythe, including Manners, were passionate enough; so, for that matter, were the poems exchanged between Smythe and Manners and the poems each of them addressed to Faber. Roundell Palmer, in his *Memorials Family and Personal*, wrote of Faber as an undergraduate: 'In person he was extremely prepossessing ... almost feminine grace ... our affection for each other became not only strong but passionate.' All of this was, presumably, just on the right side of the line between propriety and impropriety. But some of Faber's poems to Smythe seem to have crossed that line. He was reproached with this and – whatever he might say at the time – he took the reproaches to heart.

This is what he did say, in a letter dated 17 November 1840 to his brother Frank:

Strong expressions towards male friends are matters of taste. I feel what they express to *men*: I never did to a born woman. Brodie (a school friend) thinks a revival of chivalry in male friendships a characteristic of the rising

65

generation, and a hopeful one. So he probably would not object to it. What I say of friendship in 'First Love' and to which Roundell (Palmer) objects so much *aesthetically* will probably keep me from it in future.

'First Love' was a poem about Faber's wish for a home and his feeling for a young girl. According to his brother, Frank:

> Those verses refer to something real, which came to nothing; and though I have seen him in after years smile at the recollection, yet I can bear witness that his interest was strong enough in the matter at the time the lines were written.

Real or unreal, the feeling did not last long. Yet Faber contrasts it, in 'First Love', with 'false friendship's wildfire sweet':

> It is not passion's lurid light,
>   Nor friendship's meteor way,
> False gleams that through pale summer nights
>   From far-off tempests play.
> But one rich golden orb that shines
>   Steady and large all day.

It is clear that, for Faber, friendship had become something false and fascinating – not at all the humdrum, virtuous relationship that the word usually conveys.

There might possibly be room for doubt about the reality of Faber's feeling for Smythe if it were not for what he himself confessed to Manners on at least two occasions. In a letter from Oxford, in January 1839, he described his friendship with Smythe as 'unsound – he fell in love with my intellect – not with my heart ... he has raised passions and violences that marked my schoolboy days when I was an infidel ...'. Again, in May, a week before his ordination, he wrote that he was 'quite unfit ... I am all of earth ... My head

66

and heart are full of love . . .'. Since knowing Smythe, he said, he had 'never known quietness'; he might have to leave Oxford, and spend one or two years abroad, for his peace and even for his 'hopes of heaven'. Besides, he reproached himself that his 'idols are in such a different rank of life with such different objects and interests'. What had he and Manners in common? Perhaps 'religious principle'. But what had he and Smythe in common?

Faber had paid two visits to Cambridge since the summer of 1838. He had other purposes; but the wish to see his 'idolatry' must have been foremost in his mind. During his first visit, however, he was hardly able to see Smythe and, when he did, he had

> not one kind word from him. He did not look like himself to me, except just 5 minutes before he went away; and then I could have cried in the streets. I have written twice to him this Vacation – my last childishly affectionate. But no answer. Not a word.

On the second visit he seems to have been luckier, but distressed to find few signs – except in Manners himself – of 'grave inward life':

> I have lectured Smythe so much lately that to have done so this last time would only have endangered my influence over him without any prospect of good . . .

Smythe was one of the communicants when Faber celebrated the Eucharist for the first time. In November 1839 Faber still expected him to contribute to a church in which he was interested. After that they seem to have drifted apart, though Faber never lost his affection for Smythe – he blamed himself for the excess of his passion and was determined that it should not turn to bitterness. Smythe, for his part, was proud of Faber's friendship; he described him to his father, in 1846, as 'a man who gives up all he has in the world for conscience'. This was in a letter in which he claimed that Manners, Lyttelton, Faber and Whytehead, the 'most virtuous and amiable of my contemporaries . . . love or loved me'.

Evidently Faber had, for at least several months in the years 1838 and 1839, a homosexual infatuation for Smythe. At other times in his life, both before and after, he seems to have had sublimated homosexual feelings for a number of other young men. It does not of course follow that either as a boy or a man he ever had any kind of sexual relations with them, any more than with women. He would have regarded any breach of his celibacy as a dreadful sin. His main emotional needs were satisfied by religion. Physically, he may have been late in developing, while from quite an early age he began to be weakened by a dropsy due to kidney disease. Even when strongly tempted he could summon up his will-power, which, for all his restless delicacy of feeling, was at bottom exceptionally strong.

Faber himself seems to have thought that God's grace had kept him clear of 'impurity', both at school and at college. When writing to Manners about his 'wildness' at Harrow, he hastened to add that 'sins of impurity' were 'utterly and absolutely unknown to me'. Frank Faber (himself a married clergyman) emphasized in the *Early Life* he wrote of his brother:

> I believe that he passed, by the blessing of God, through the ordeal of an university life without any cause for that regret which early years so often bequeath to others. It is my firm persuasion, and I have good reason for saying so, that the purity of his life was without soil or blemish. *Soli Deo gloria.*

John Bowden, Frederick's biographer, shared this persuasion: 'He resisted from first to last the temptations to which many succumb, and by the grace of God was able to preserve unstained the purity of his life.' According to Roundell Palmer, who knew him well at Oxford, his life and conversation were 'pure and without reproach'.

If there seems to be a little too much protestation in these testimonies, it could be because Faber's willowy elegance at Oxford had exposed him to some suspicion. Mark Pattison (if he was indeed the author) indulged in some unpleasant innuendo in his obituary of Faber in the *Saturday Review*, though he explained his ungraciousness as a reaction to the semi-canonization that had been going on:

> In all the non-masculine virtues he (Faber) was admirably calculated to shine ... he was entirely the man for pretty little chorister-boys, feminine or semi-feminine confessions, and the imaginative or imaginary Paradise with which he eventually surrounded himself. He was very amiable; he was decidedly ornamental; he had a world of good qualities about him, if he would only have let them alone.

This obituary was avowedly coloured by anti-Catholic prejudice. It provoked an indignant response, in the *Dublin Review*, from somebody who had known Faber both at school and at college:

> It is hardly credible that among us there should be found a man – and he must be also an Oxford man, we fear, and perhaps once a friend – who could describe such a man and such a life as one 'who would have made his fortune as a pocket-handkerchief preacher in a fashionable chapel', and whose proper sphere was among choristers and effeminate minds.

Faber's avoidance of sins of 'impurity' was not due to any permanent lack of temptation. In 1844 he wrote to a friend that God had for some time delivered him wholly 'from even a half-formed thought of impurity', but he did not know how long this would last. He described his temptations, before then, as 'miserable and hellish'. Again, in November 1845, he told Newman that, for two days, he had had 'most violent assaults of impurity'. These assaults were the Devil's work; they were recognized as such, but none the less disturbing for that.

To understand Faber's relations with Smythe and Manners it is important to bear in mind that, at that time, homosexuality was scarcely discussed by respectable men – and never in front of respectable women. Men who had been to boarding schools inevitably knew something about it; but, boarding schools apart, it was concealed by a conspiracy of silence. When homosexual vice was discovered and punished, it was subject to terrible penalties; the sentence of capital punishment for sodomy was not lifted until the 1860s. But the sheer unthinkableness of the physical offence (outside those circles where it was secretly practised) made it possible for men openly to advertise romantic friendships without fear of having them dubbed homosexual. They could demonstrate affection to other men in public without arousing suspicions of being 'queer' or 'gay'. If they had felt inhibited by such fears and suspicions, Faber, Smythe and Manners could never have exchanged ardent poems, and had them published, in the carefree way that they did. Faber's cheerful admission to his elder brother that he had had strong feelings for men, but not for women, shows how little shame he felt about this – or felt that his clerical brother would feel. In this he was only partly right. When his letter was made public in *The Early Life of F. W. Faber* a crucial sentence, and still more crucial 'n', were omitted. The original passage is still perfectly legible in the MS letter:

Strong expressions towards male friends are matters of taste. I feel what they express to *men*: I never did to a born woman.

In *The Early Life* it appears as:

> Strong expressions towards male friends are matters of
> taste. I feel what they express to *me*.

Of the three Young Englanders Cochrane – in spite of his
hero worship of Smythe – was probably the most conventionally heterosexual. This appears from his poetry and
novels. It is also suggested by his relatively early marriage at
the end of 1844, when he was 28, to a niece of John Manners.
There were a son and three daughters of this marriage.

Both Cochrane and Manners seem to have lived their
private lives free from scandal, although they were both
active and prominent in society throughout their lives. Manners was of course like Faber in that he devoted himself
consciously to religion. His character, with its sweet temper,
its loyalty, its refinement and its gentle obstinacy, was notably
lacking in male *machismo; Fraser's Magazine* in 1847 described
his look when speaking: 'His face becomes radiant with intelligence, and the play of his mouth is almost feminine.' It
seems quite possible that he retained his 'virginity' until he
married, in 1851, at the age of 32. He then wrote, apprehen-
sively, to Disraeli:

> A piece of news which I fear may perhaps be not
> altogether agreeable to you – I marry Miss Marley. But
> do not think my poor services, such as they are, will
> consequently be lost to you in St Stephen's.

Of course he got back a letter of warm congratulations. After
three supremely happy years Manners had to write again to
Disraeli, when his wife died of scarlet fever. 'She was to me
during that little period of happiness,' he burst out, 'an Angel
of light, purity, and innocent mirth – and she has, my soul
tells me, gone back to the Heaven she came from.' There was
one son by this marriage. In 1862 he married again; from

this, earthier, union there were five sons and three daughters.

Smythe remains more of an enigma. He had, and probably deserved, a reputation as a womanizer, who collected women with ease and discarded them without compunction. According to Sir William Gregory his fascination over women was 'quite remarkable', but it was a bad day for every one of those who fell under his spell, for he was 'as remorseless as he was capricious'. Yet he never seems to have been deeply under a spell himself, unless in 1842–3 when he claimed to his father to be gravely in love with 'a young girl of inexpensive habits'. This affair was finally broken off 'upon a question of settlements' early in 1844.

Unlike his friends Smythe did not manage to avoid scandal, though he was never actually ostracized, or at least not for long. In the summer of 1846 he pursued Lady Dorothy Walpole, whom he had probably first met at breakfast with the Disraelis, while she was staying with her parents near Andover. He was discovered with her in a summerhouse and the worst suspicions were aroused when she subsequently fell ill. Her mother, when she heard the rumours, indignantly maintained that Smythe had had a *female* with him in his Andover hotel, and that it had been a case of mistaken identity. In December 1847 Lady Dorothy was safely married to a cousin. But, a year earlier, Lord George Bentinck had reported to Disraeli that it was much discussed whether Smythe would be received in society after getting an Earl's daughter pregnant – if pregnant she turned out to be.

Smythe's charm seems to have depended on a nice blend of masculine and feminine characteristics. The *Fraser's Magazine* reporter (who seems to have had an eye for such things) emphasized his slim, graceful and juvenile appearance. He also contrasted Smythe's physical and mental attributes 'in the latter, a vigour the most masculine: in the former, what might almost be called effeminacy'. Like Disraeli, Smythe enjoyed the company of young men and old women. According to Gregory his first affair was with 'a most charming old lady of a

72

great French house, who was old enough to be his grand-mother'; he wrote to Manners at the end of 1850: 'I adore all old women as you know.' As to young men, there is no evidence of practising homosexuality, though there might be a hint in what he wrote to his father before Confirmation at the age of 17 (he was then under the care of the Revd Julius Hare):

> I believe that I am, and I trust shall continue, in a healthier and purer state of mind than when exposed to the profligacy which, with most boys, goes hand in hand with the upper parts of a public school.

He also referred, in a letter to Disraeli early in 1846, to having been pursued to Paris by one woman and to having got entangled with another – and then to having had 'other affairs of debauch' at Venice. But there is nothing to indicate what sort of debauches these were.

It is of little importance whether or not Smythe, like Byron, was active homosexually, at one time or another, as well as heterosexually. What does matter, for the purpose of this story, is that, having been left motherless, he seems to have felt a recurring need for the guidance, and perhaps the admiration, of some older man whom he could respect; he felt this need, yet he chafed against it. Various men – his father, the Revd Julius Hare, Faber, Disraeli – filled the exacting role he required of them with varying success. Smythe never wholly accepted their direction, but never wholly rejected it; he was certainly resentful when he found his own role as an influential disciple usurped. After a visit to the Disraelis at Hughenden in 1853, he wrote to Manners:

> Puzzled I was (I have been staying with him) to see how really and apart from all paradox Diz. is governed by H. Lennox. I see now how vain an ass I was in my Young England days, when I attributed to my intellect the

favour, which I see he must have accorded to his personal friendship only, for myself.

If Faber was right, what Smythe wanted from his older friends was intellect rather than heart; but of course it was difficult to procure the one without the other.

For much of his short life Smythe was oppressed by the awareness that, if he was to master his debts, let alone bring some 'honey into the hive', he must marry money. In the event he did marry, but not until his father was dead and he himself on his deathbed at the age of 39. Six years after his death Disraeli recorded in a memorandum:

> George Smythe was very rich when he had made up his mind to marry an heiress, and gave his instructions to all the ladies who were, and who had been, in love with him, to work for his benefit. 'Family', he used to say, 'I don't care the least for; would rather like to marry into a rich, vulgar, family. Madness no objection. As for scrofula, why shd I care for it more than a King? All this ought to be a great pull in my favour.' Strange to say, he succeeded and married an heiress – but literally on his deathbed.

Disraeli himself made a successful marriage and had had at least one or two fully-fledged affairs with women beforehand. But he always had a weakness for youth and a taste for elegance. (The aristocratic backgrounds of the three Young Englanders – for Faber both an attraction and an embarrass-ment – were, for Disraeli, an essential part of their charm.) He could write convincingly in *Contarini Fleming* about his hero's boyhood infatuation with another boy. In *Coningsby* he described schoolboy friendship as

> a passion. It entrances the being; it tears the soul. All loves of afterlife can never bring its rapture or its wretchedness ... 'Tis some indefinite recollection of

these mystic passages of their young emotion that makes grey-haired men mourn over the memory of their schoolboy days. It is a spell that can soften the acerbity of political warfare . . .

More discreetly he commented on an adult male friendship in *Tancred*:

Of all the differences between the ancients and ourselves none are more striking than our respective ideas of friendship . . . As we must not compare Tancred and Fakredeen to Damon and Pythias and as we cannot easily find in Pall Mall or Park Lane a parallel more modish, we must be content to say that youth, sympathy and occasion, combined to create between them that intimacy which each was prompt to recognize as one of the principal sources of his happiness.

It was this sort of intimacy that bound the three Young Englanders together; Faber and Disraeli were each included, for a time, in its spell. All three young men had lost their mothers in childhood and must have felt, more acutely than most, the need for affectionate sympathy. The intimacy between them survived political triumph and political failure alike. It helps to explain how the Young England movement came into being and how it broke up – though without recriminations – when its founders were divided by diverging lives.

Prose

The three Young Englanders did not only lisp in numbers. They were also quite prolific in prose. Smythe contributed to periodicals, besides writing the greater part of a novel, which was published after his death. Manners also wrote for periodicals and published a few tracts. Cochrane published quite a number of works – historical studies and two full-length novels among them.

The Times, in its review of *Historic Fancies*, described Smythe's prose as 'sparkling, and always exact'; it had 'much grace', though it sometimes lacked breadth and was 'a little wire-drawn'. This was fair criticism. Its judgement on the book as a whole was also fair, though perhaps a trifle complimentary: it exhibited 'great talent, and indicates a greater promise'; it was 'full of freshness and vigorous fancy; there is no commonplace in it'; it produced 'results which may be in some instances crude, but which are always genuine'. All this is certainly true of Smythe's private letters. It was not quite so true of *Historic Fancies*, which on the whole strikes a modern reader as a rather callow medley of insights and fancies. But the book came out at a time when Young England had made a bit of a stir; it was certainly original; and it had at least a veneer of brilliance which people remembered after much else that Smythe had done was forgotten. Manners wrote to Disraeli about its reception, with avuncular pride, on 5 August 1844:

> I hope and believe 'Historic Fancies' is fairly settled as a success; tho' to be sure after Coningsby a second Edition mayn't seem much.

Smythe spent a part of his life writing, more or less regularly, for the *Morning Chronicle*; he was described by his sister-in-law in 1875 as having been the 'first member of the aristocracy who became a steady contributor to the press'. Some of his journalistic output had more than ephemeral interest. Thus in 1845 he wrote two articles on Grey and Canning for the *Oxford and Cambridge Review*, which were both of the same high standard as his studies of the French Revolution in *Historic Fancies*. The former contains a passage on the Tory and Whig Parties, written with an interesting detachment from party prejudice:

Each represents a necessity for England. The creed of this is love of antiquity and abhorrence of disorder, the creed of that, desire for improvement and detestation of oppression. To different temperaments each has its particular charms.

Disraeli might have written something like this, though only (I think) in a less political context; it is difficult to imagine Manners writing anything so uncommitted anywhere.

Another example of Smythe's journalism at its most effective can be found in a study of Disraeli, reproduced in *Chiefs of Parties* by D. O. Maddyn (1859). This ascribed Disraeli's current influence not so much to his *public* as to his *private* life: 'a noble disposition which attaches men'. It also acknowledged his power of 'charming the imagination of the "new generation"'.

> The career of the late Chancellor of the Exchequer is not closed: we believe its brightest position is in the future. We have watched its wonderful vicissitudes with a deep interest since our college days, when we read for the first time *Contarini Fleming* with a glowing heart and a kindling cheek ... when the world has believed him beaten, he has always been on the eve of his greatest victories.

Not unnaturally, Disraeli was delighted with this. He recommended it to a correspondent in 1860 as 'a sketch of my character and career, especially with reference to my political position, which is written with great power – and worth looking at'. It was the work, he said, of 'a personal friend ... who had a very fine taste and quick perception'.

In January 1846, Smythe wrote a letter to Disraeli, in which he mentioned an affair at Paris with a woman 'who gave me mortification and heart-burning enough – all which I wrote in a book which will never see the light'. This was presumably his novel *Angela Pisani*, which he seems to have written at Venice at the end of 1845. He told his father: 'I have written 500 pages of a novel which I have begun with high dreams of elevating fiction, and of achieving a work of art which should endure . . . Strange to say the style became, willy nilly, picturesque . . .'. The novel was never completed, but was published by the last Lady Strangford, his sister-in-law, in 1875, when Disraeli was Prime Minister for the second time. Impressed by the 'exceeding cleverness and beauty of the greater part' she sent the Prime Minister the proofs (they are still among the Hughenden papers), assuring him: 'Every line of it will bring George Smythe with vivid recollections to your mind; and in many places you will recognize the apt and loving pupil of so great a master.' The book was published in time to give a melancholy pleasure to Smythe's old Tutor at Eton. The Revd Mr Cookesley, now a country clergyman of 73, commented: 'It is wonderfully like Smythe, full of coruscations of genius – of refined, deep and subtle thought. It is a mere outline, but it gives us a noble idea of what Smythe had in him – of what he might have done.'

Angela Pisani is set largely in France in the early nineteenth century, though it has a prelude in the time of Louis XV and Madame de Pompadour. The main interest of the book lies in the contrast between two young men – Lionel Averanche, who is idealistic and soft-hearted, and Charles Denain, a graceful, heartless materialist. The author seems mainly to identify with the former, who on the whole fails in life; but at the same time he evidently admires the style and success of the latter. In a sense, then, the book plays out the conflict between Smythe's two selves (or two of a number of selves) and is essentially introspective. It has some romantic devices typical of the age; various historical glimpses of an idealized Napoleon, Louis XVIII at Hartwell, Byron and Warren Hastings (!); a good deal of psychological finesse; an excellent picture of schoolboy life; and a tone, at once smart and thoughtful, worldly and unworldly, that does indeed conjure up the strange man who wrote it. It also contains some interesting, and characteristic, allusions: a defence of free trade; praise of the commercial instinct; criticism of the wealthy English aristocracy for preferring their horses to their poor; a picture of France under the First Empire as being 'essentially aristocratical' and the 'golden age of society'; a good word for Canning; and a reference to the 'eclecticism of our times', which had affected Averanche so that 'he could feel as strongly on one side as the other, while his judgement declared by turns for different opinions.'

That last passage is an unmistakable reflection of Smythe's own predicament. Two other passages are also worth quoting for their bearing on his life. In the first, a character maintains that the English system is not really worked by the aristocracy, which ostensibly governs, but by

> journalists who originate and clerks who administer. Journalists who, in the first instance, give you the idea which finds its way into the Legislature, but whose names you never hear and scarcely whisper; clerks who govern the vastest empire on earth, but whose individuality is unknown out of a street.

The second seems to reflect the loving/hating feud between Smythe and his father:

> Who does not . . . know that there are no resentments so violent as those which result from inverted affection, from the horrible feeling that you admire and adore where you are rejected, despised, insulted, trampled on?

Perhaps this helps to explain what Lady Strangford had in mind when she wrote that, though Smythe had 'a bright, deferential, sweetness of manner', he was also ready to ridicule his dearest friend: there was 'an underlying current of bitterness within'.

So far as I know, Manners never tried his hand at a novel.

79

His most celebrated prose publication was a pamphlet that came out early in 1843: *A Plea for National Holy-Days*. If *England's Trust* was the first manifesto of the Young England movement, *A Plea for National Holy-Days* was its first appeal for specific reform. Manners argued that the English people were becoming more discontented and morose:

> Will the old parish church send out of its time-honoured portals and old men and women, the lads and lasses, to the merry green, where youth shall disport itself, and old age, well pleased, look on? Alas! no. Utilitarian selfishness has well nigh banished all such unproductive amusements from the land . . .

Still under Faber's spell the author cited the Lake District as a part of England 'where old customs and the old character still linger'; he offered the Ambleside Rushbearing Ceremony as an example. As in *England's Trust* he stressed the vital importance of the Church in the work of restoration/ improvement: 'It is the Church now that will restore to us . . . the frankness and good humour, the strength and glory of the old English character.'

The vision of 'the old parish church' and 'the merry green' had a tint of Technicolor, which tended to put off the cool-minded. It was one of Young England's difficulties that the symbols that attracted some Early Victorians automatically repelled others. But, underneath the symbols, Manners had hit on an obvious – and to us even a glaring – truth: that the workers of that time, and particularly industrial workers, had totally inadequate time for relaxation. Force of habit, or absorption in *laissez-faire* theories of economics, blinded contemporaries to a need that was increasingly recognized in the course of the following century. Young England may have called holidays 'holy-days'; but in substance it was struggling for a change of attitude that has since come about.

In a fine speech at Bingley in October 1844 Disraeli noted the progress already made towards such a change:

> I remember when my noble friend near me first pub-
> lished a slight pamphlet – slight in form but not in spirit
> – which was to advocate the proper and just recreations
> of the people. (Hear, hear.) I, who knew him well, know
> the strong convictions which impelled him to take that
> step. I remember – and it is barely twenty-four months
> ago – the frigid reception with which even many who
> were intimate with him greeted it, the ready ridicule
> which was lavishly bestowed by opponents.

Yet, Disraeli added, a week ago he and his friends had been at Manchester, where £21,000 had been subscribed 'to form parks for the people'.

Smythe, at least, was enthusiastic from the beginning. With his usual ability to flatter and caress (Disraeli's terms) he wrote to Manners:

> You have gone and done it! I have only just been able
> to-day to get your pamphlet, as I have only come back
> from the Deepdene three hours ago. It is not only far
> the best thing you ever wrote, but it is the best modern
> pamphlet I have ever read.

In the long run it must have done Young England good to be associated with a plea for more popular recreation. Another, earlier, pamphlet by Manners can hardly have been so helpful to the movement. This was *What are the English Roman Catholics to do? (The question considered in a letter to Lord Edward Howard by Anglo-Catholicus)*, published in June 1841. It appealed to those Roman Catholics 'who desire to stand upon the old ways ... keep up the old English aristocracy ... preserve what little remains of old-fashioned charity and social intercourse between the higher and lower classes', to rally to 'the side of order and religion' and to withdraw from 'the fellowship of the Atheist, the Democrat, the Dissenter and the Leveller'. That might not have grated too much on the ordinary Tory. But he would have judged some of the language rather injudicious and he might have been puzzled to learn that the reign of James II heralded a brighter era of loyalty and integrity. He would have found it difficult, too, to swallow his distrust of Popery to the extent recommended by 'Anglo-Catholicus':

> Let them (the Roman Catholics) know, if they do not know it already, that there are many amongst us who have never harboured an ill thought, nor cherished an unkind feeling towards them – who have been willing and glad to recognize in them the descendants of the loyal adherents of the STUARTS – and who would mourn over and deprecate, with truthful regret, the necessity of classing them among the Jacobins and Democrats of the day.

In 1841, of course, most British politicians regarded 'Democrats' with the same sort of suspicion that most modern American businessmen regard 'Communists'. Our constitution was considered free, and allowed to contain an element of democracy; but it did not profess to be democratic as such.

Public fear of Lord John's Popish leanings was increased when he mooted in Parliament the revival of monastic institutions to help fill the religious void in the manufacturing towns. He wrote an article on this theme in the *Morning Post*; it was subsequently printed in pamphlet form under the title *The Monastic and Manufacturing Systems*. A less controversial work – *Notes on an Irish Tour* – was published in 1849, with the object of mitigating 'the angry feeling with which some of my countrymen are now disposed to regard everything Irish'. It is not too kind to the political economists as a class;

but its language is more prudent, and its tone more mature, than in Manners's earlier publications.

Cochrane had more time and energy for writing than either of the other two. *A Young Artist's Life* (1864) is 'a brief sketch of the life of a young man very singularly gifted, which, unhappily, set quick as a winter's sun'. That sounds a rather Smythe-like hero: *Historic Pictures* (1865) certainly contains a Smythe-like mixture of French and Stuart themes. But these are only two among a number of varied works. The chief evidence of Smythe's influence is Cochrane's dedication to him of the novel *Ernest Vane* (1849) 'in the presumptuous hope that their two names may be associated in literature, as they have been in long and uninterrupted friendship'.

Ernest Vane even contains an admiring portrait of Smythe, who has nothing to do with the plot but appears in the person of 'George Percy' (Percy was another of Smythe's names) at a dinner of smart young men:

> ... the beloved of all, with his ready wit, his retentive memory, and his abundant reading. Brilliant, above all, where none were wanting in brilliancy, possessing that most enviable of all qualities, a perfect readiness, a power of calling up any faculty of the mind whenever it was required. Quick in his temper, but so easily convinced of error, that every slight cause of difference only ended in endearing him still more deeply to the circle of his friends. He was one of those favoured beings whose society, after having been long enjoyed, becomes indispensable; whose appearance is the signal for a burst of enthusiasm, and whose absence is a prolonged regret.

This passage reminds us how the Young Englanders, particularly Smythe, shone in society, at a time when it was homogeneous and (at its best) both aristocratic and intelligent. That was of course one way, though never the most important way, of acquiring political influence.

Ernest Vane was described in *The Times* obituary of Cochrane as 'gloomy, persistently gloomy'. I should rate it as intermittently gloomy; but it is certainly not an exhilarating read. It has some touches of Young England about it. The House of Rochdale 'had not imbibed those lessons of wretched philosophy which would degrade the sovereign into a chief magistrate, and would strip him of all that mysterious divinity which dignifies the act of submission . . .'. The 'master manufacturers' are castigated for treating their workers as machines. The Whigs are described as at once 'haughty and condescending – universal and exclusive'. Charles I is 'the greatest sovereign, the most admirable gentleman that England ever saw . . .' The French aristocracy are 'swept away with all their light-heartedness, their wild gaiety, their joyous vivacity, into the dark vale of revolution'. Ernest is impressed by the devoutness and charity of a Trappist monastery, which he visits; he tells the Prior: 'I have always thought it was religion alone which prevented the people rising from the depths of their misery to overturn all our institutions, all classes, all degrees . . .'; he does not reproach the upper classes with being careless of their fellow creatures, but thinks there has been too rapid an accumulation of wealth and luxury in England.

Lucille Belmont (second edition in 1849) also ends gloomily. Unlike *Angela Pisani* it has a straightforward moral: the author 'wished to show that the best impulses, the fairest and noblest purposes, are worthless, unless they are associated with high principles . . .'. The novel contains eulogies of both Canning and Castlereagh. It is also complimentary to Peel, whose 'calm and temperate reason' is contrasted with Canning's 'gorgeous and dazzling eloquence'. There is a mild flirtation with Roman Catholicism: in Venice the hero is soothed by 'the heavenly smile of the Virgin' and makes his confession to a priest, who assures him that 'the mother church . . . is universal in her love'. There is an echo of *England's Trust* in the exclamation: 'Will its [society's] members never learn, that the people, the masses, are, after all, governed by ideas, by sensations, more than by reason?'.

Like Cochrane's poetry, these two novels show some ability and are by no means lifeless. The style is imitative, rather than original, and the maturity of the execution contrasts with a certain psychological *naïveté*. But there is in both of them a genuine sense of the elasticity of youth.

The writings of the three Young Englanders, whether in prose or verse, have long been virtually forgotten. Disraeli's prose works, however, have remained famous; two or three of his novels are still quite widely read. The chief works in which he was, or had recently been, engaged at the time of Victoria's accession have already been mentioned. In the following decade he was to write his celebrated trilogy of political novels – *Coningsby*, *Sybil* and *Tancred*. These have a direct bearing on the Young England movement and will be discussed in a later chapter.

Faber, while still an Anglican, wrote a number of religious tracts and saints' lives, as well as poetry. After his conversion to Roman Catholicism he produced several devotional books, which were treasured by the devout in their day. Before then, almost immediately after his conversion, he published a rather aggressive booklet (attack being his form of defence) entitled *Grounds for Remaining in the Anglican Communion. A Letter to a High-Church Friend* (1846). This is worth noting here, because of what it has to say about Young England.

The burden of the booklet is that its author 'left the Establishment because I felt morally certain that I could not be saved, if I remained in it ...'. He urges his 'High-Church Friend' not to let political considerations deflect him from facing this supreme truth. A suspicion has crossed his (Faber's) mind:

Is not your reluctance to become a Catholic connected with some idea you have of political changes, effected by the youth of the rising generation, which will restore the feelings of personal loyalty to the sovereign for which England was once so famous, revive the fallen aristocracy, and bring back so much at least of Jacobitism as was generous, lofty-minded and self-devoting? Do you not feel that a Church must, after the failure of previous experiments, be the chief engine of this ... have you not a fear lest by becoming a Catholic you, so far forth, give up these beautiful day-dreams of your enthusiastic politics?

Faber does not reprove these day-dreams. He says that he is far from wishing to ridicule 'these airy citadels – these schemes for young England to carry old England, like pious Aeneas, safely out of the conflagration of the nineteenth century'. He is still in favour of enthusiasm; though what is to be restored must be a matter for subjective choice and 'to my taste, the England of Augustin and Cuthbert, of Wilfrid and Boniface, and the canonized builders of the Norman abbeys, is a more delectable object than the England of Laud and Andrewes, of Herbert and Sancroft'. However, that is not the point – neither that, nor the conviction that the Protestant Establishment 'dwarfs all greatness amongst us' and that to better the poor materially, and to rescue the nation from money-grubbing and disbelief, must be a delusion without the Holy Roman Church. The essential point is the salvation of the individual soul; how can 'poetry and romance and Jacobite hopes' be more to a man than that? In their desire to restore *practically* 'a dream of chivalry', some good men are aiming 'at an uncertain good in an uncertain way'. Money-making is actually more innocent than worldly chivalry, because it is less likely 'to take people in, and frustrate higher vocations'. The conclusion of the whole matter: seek *first* the Kingdom of God and then 'whatever comes of poor England be conformed to his blessed will'.

It was a moot question whether this booklet was more likely

to attract or to repel converts. Newman, who always thought that Faber wrote too much, was not at all pleased; Faber was contrite, but never quite understood what Newman's objections were. The writing of the *Letter* had been a psychological necessity for him. Its vehemence of language can be explained – as far as the paragraphs on Young England go – by the obvious inference that Faber was wrestling with his former self. It was not his 'High-Church friend' but himself who had had these delusions of chivalry, these enthusiastic political day-dreams. They were the sort of things he had discussed with Smythe and Manners during that glorious Lakeland summer of 1838. Personal loyalty to the Sovereign. Revival of the Aristocracy. A leading role for the Church. Bettering the poor materially and the rich spiritually. That was, in summary, the whole Young England creed. As to Chivalry, a letter from Faber to Hope on 23 January 1839 had suggested that the most chivalrous countries in the Middle Ages were the least Roman – France, first, and then England: 'We had a glorious immunity from the grinding littleness of Rome, compared with most other nations.' In 1839 this had been a source of pride.

A minor theme in the lines just quoted is intriguing. This is the preference for medieval, over Stuart, nostalgia. Faber had had a feeling for the Middle Ages since he was a boy. He probably communicated some of this feeling to the Young Englanders (except for Cochrane, who told the House of Commons in March 1843 that he suspected people were led astray by romantic notions of the state of medieval society – 'the serf and villein system was most deplorable'). However, Faber had also shared Young England's Stuartomania. Manners, in his obituary of his friend, wrote that Newman's influence over him was 'aided by the young inquirer's study of George Herbert, Andrewes, and other writers of the Stuart epoch . . .'. In November 1839, when Faber needed money to spend on a Church at Sandford, he told Beresford Hope that he had 'sold all my pictures but Laud – even Chas I and

Strafford are gone . . .'. Here again, the Faber of 1846 was sacrificing a former self.

One other prose work by Faber is relevant to a study of Young England, since it was borrowed by Disraeli when he was working on *Sybil*. This was *Sights and Thoughts in Foreign Churches and among Foreign Peoples,* published, with a dedication to Wordsworth, at Eastertide 1842. Almost the first letter from Manners to Disraeli, in the Hughenden papers, is one from Kendal dated 5 August 1844. It includes the following paragraph:

> The day before I left London Smythe told me you wished to have Faber's Foreign Churches and Peoples; but in the bustle of departure I forgot to send it to you; if you will send for it, my housekeeper will let you have it.

Disraeli was not a great reader of contemporary literature. But *Sybil* was intended to glorify the Church, while one character in it, the young clergyman Aubrey St Lys, was to be based on what Disraeli had heard about Faber from Manners. We shall see later that the book may have given Disraeli one or two ideas.

Sights and Thoughts is an interesting, though somewhat uneasy, mixture of travel-writing, historical references, political/social comments and theological arguments. It was written at Ambleside during the winter of 1841, when Faber had returned with his pupil from their Continental tour. There are some exquisite descriptions of scenery; but otherwise the religious atmosphere of the book is a little overpowering and there are not many signs of the author's usual lightness of touch. One of the interesting features of the book is the way in which Faber satisfies his classical as well as his religious leanings by attributing real, if embryonic, religious value to Greek paganism. This enables him to have a dream of pagan beauty, near the Greek oracle of Trophonius, with a clear conscience:

Infinitely as most northerns, we children of mists, clouds, woods and weeping rain, may prefer the beauty of mystery and indefiniteness, that is, romantic beauty, still we may feel a keen pleasure in definite beauty, so mightily triumphant as it is in the Parthenon and Olympeion and the gorgeous Propylaea, if gorgeousness can be predicted of a splendour pure even to severity.

He recalls how, as a schoolboy, he had actually experienced a vision of the Homeric Gods. Indeed, almost anything connected with any sort of religion, even the Muslim religion, tends to inspire his instinctive reverence.

Another attempt to get the best of both worlds is his sympathy with the Italian Carbonari, in spite of a feeling near to 'reverence and affection' for 'the paternal government of Austria':

I have little sympathy with democratical feelings; and of course secret societies ... must lead men into sins ... [but] ... all things being candidly considered I should not hesitate to assert that the reviled Carbonari of Italy are more respectable than almost any other democratical party with which history makes us acquainted.

There are some echoes of Young England. Faber idealizes 'Charles the Martyr' and cherishes the memory of Marie Antoinette, though without sharing Manners's devotion to Don Carlos: 'It is really difficult to interest one's self in the royal families of Spain and France. There is so little about them to which any rightly directed sympathies can cling.' He believes that 'an hereditary aristocracy purifies and invigorates the life of a whole nation, unless it be itself utterly licentious and corrupt ... We know, from our own English experience, how much prouder, meaner, and more insolent towards inferiors an aristocracy of wealth is, than an aristocracy of blood ...' He deplores the way in which the utilitarian 'system-mongers' have assailed the relics of antiquity. As to Chivalry, there is a foreshadowing of *Grounds for Remaining in the Anglican Communion:* it 'meant well, but the truth is, the Church is sufficient for all these things'.

The book contains an odd invention in the person of a mysterious representative of the medieval Catholic Church, who appears from time to time and has dialogues with the author. He is stern, penetrating and apparently omniscient; he displays a 'dignified tranquillity' and has 'scarcely any upper lip'. Manners disliked this invention; looking back, he thought that 'the goodly volume in which Faber summed up the results of his tour in 1842 is rendered obscure and unreal by the introduction of a fictitious character styled the Stranger, whose arguments and criticisms are, to our mind, sadly out of place ...'. On the other hand Faber's Catholic biographer, Bowden, thought that the Stranger's appearance 'adds very much to the attractiveness of the book', while Frank Faber commented:

> I remember a friend congratulating him on the happiness of the thought, and telling him that no such originality had been given to a book of travel since Lawrence Sterne published his 'Sentimental Journey'!

In one of their dialogues the author tells the Stranger that he means to travel to the Lord's Tomb, if possible. He 'would fain see Jerusalem before I visit Rome'. The Stranger warns him about the plague, but devoutly crosses himself on describing Jerusalem as 'even a more awful place than Rome ... Europe, if ever outward unity be vouchsafed her again, will turn her eyes thither once more. There will be another crusade, though after a different sort from what has been heretofore.' In the event Faber never got to Jerusalem, whether on this or on two other occasions when he might have done so. In 1851, after he had been advised by his doctor to take a six-month break, he set out for the Holy Land with a companion. But he fell ill again and got no further than Italy. When he recovered, he returned to England, after an absence of only two and a half months. It was as if, deep down, he felt that he had wanted the inspiration of Jerusalem as an Anglican, but that Rome was now as far as he need travel.

The Stranger has some other advice on a subject close to Faber's heart. He gives him 'nineteen reasons why I think it would be expedient, for a clergyman to live a single life'. The main reasons are that continence is a spiritual gift to be 'coveted earnestly'; that celibacy enables priests to concentrate on their work and at the same time to make a suitable sacrifice/atonement; that it is a cure for some defects of character (such as an 'unhealthy appetite for sympathy'); and that it would open 'a stronger feeling of communion with the rest of Western Christendom'. One of the reasons evidently had a particular application to Faber's own case:

> If a person in this age of such general impurity, has been at school and college, by God's *seemingly* accidental mercy, kept clear of overt sins, specially condemned in Holy Scripture, does not celibacy seem hinted to him in such a Providence?

Young Elton

Faber spent most of the year 1842 at Ambleside. His *Sights and Thoughts* came out over Easter and his *Styrian Lake* poems in the autumn. Writing apart, he was trying to get to know himself better, to purge himself of his youthful effervescence and to dedicate himself more absolutely to religion. One of his *Styrian Lake* poems was 'An Epistle to a Young M.P.' (John Manners), who must have urged him to leave his Lakeside seclusion. He replied that he had become a different, steadier, person:

> love is unto me a different birth
> From what it was in our old boyish mirth,
> And hath a deeper root in this kind earth.

He added that the glory of 'our own summer year of Thirty
Eight' was a thing of the past and that Manners ought not to
stay entranced by it. For himself it was 'a faded year':

> Faded in all save truest love for thee,
> And that high-souled young priest beyond the sea,
> And that dear bard, whose life is like a river,
> Singing and sighing on its road for ever.

(Manners, Whytehead and Wordsworth – he did not mention
Smythe.) His own boyhood was over; but

> I shall heave anchor when the ship is due,
> And come within thy sight to seek a part
> In the world's fretful glory, where thou art –
> A man in place with boyhood at thy heart.

What sort of share in the 'world's fretful glory' was it that
Faber envisaged? When he did eventually come to work in
London, it was as a Roman Catholic priest, entirely devoted to
the business of his Church.

It was in the year 1842 that the Young England movement
began to take shape as a Parliamentary force. Faber was
evidently consulted by Manners about this, but seems to have
sounded a note of caution. According to the late Father
Addington, who had had access to correspondence at Belvoir
Castle:

> Faber actually tried to prevent Manners forming his
> 'party within a party' in 1842, partly because he thought
> he was too young to be successful, but mainly because he
> considered that direct political action would harm the

Church of England rather than help her ... that more social justice could be achieved by religious and moral revival than directly through politics.

Presumably, when he saw that Manners and his friends were in earnest, Faber abandoned his opposition. But he remained detached. He knew nothing of the Parliamentary situation; he was immersed in his own religious plans and worries; perhaps he was already moving towards the attitude to Young England revealed in *Grounds for Remaining in the Anglican Communion.*

Towards the end of the year Faber was offered, and decided that he ought to accept, a prosperous college living at Elton in Huntingdonshire (now Cambridgeshire). He seems to have stipulated that this should not interfere with plans that he had already made to take his pupil for a second visit to the Continent in 1843. He thought that ignorance explained some of the English prejudice against the Roman Catholic Church; though still an Anglican, he wanted to find out more about how Roman Catholicism actually worked.

At the end of 1842 the diarist Henry Crabb Robinson, friend of Wordsworth, Lamb and Coleridge, saw quite a bit of Faber at Ambleside and was torn between personal liking and religious disapproval. He wrote at Christmas time that Faber was 'a flaming zealot for the new doctrines':

Last year we had with us an admirable and most excellent man – Dr Arnold ... we have this year a sad fanatic of an opposite character ... This Faber is an agreeable man. All the young ladies are in love with him. And he has high spirits, conversational talent and great facility in writing both polemics and poetry.

On Christmas evening Faber preached a sermon displaying 'a sentimentality approaching to eloquence which pleased the ladies' but which Crabb Robinson himself 'could not relish'.

On 30 December these two very different men went for a long walk. Faber defended himself against the charge (provoked by one of the Stranger's remarks in *Sights and Thoughts*) that he favoured religious persecution. On the contrary, he would like Church and State to separate; he thought the Church could manage without endowments and even gain by it. He felt certain that he personally would 'never go over to Rome, though he rather regrets not having been born in that communion'; he was not hostile to *born* Dissenters and thought there should be a separate university for them.

> Nothing could be more agreeable than his manner, and he impressed me strongly with his amiability, his candour and his ability. But I could agree with very little indeed.

There was another walk on 1 January, when they talked about poetry and Goethe, perhaps with more agreement; then again, with Wordsworth on 5 January. Crabb Robinson observed that Wordsworth's 'tone was that of deference towards his younger and more consistent friend'. On Saturday, 7 January, two days before his departure, Faber dined for the last time with the Wordsworths, playing whist in the evening as usual; he preached a farewell sermon the following day. Next week Crabb Robinson reported to a correspondent that the 'ultra-Catholic' Faber had left the neighbourhood:

> he carries away the affections of all the people, having been very zealous and charitable to the poor – he is in fact a very amiable and interesting young man ... He may become a nuisance to the world.

Despite his distrust of Faber's doctrines Crabb Robinson invited him to a male dinner party in Russell Square in March 1843. The company was a mixed religious bag, but they all succumbed to the young clergyman's charm. By December 1845, however, Faber's conversion to Roman Catholicism had eclipsed the charm and sharpened the disapproval. Crabb Robinson took the elderly Wordsworth sternly to task:

> On my reminding him he had not executed his purpose of introducing in the new edition a note expressing his regret that he had ever uttered a word favourable to Puseyism, he said that his only reason was that he was at last quite tired – a very insufficient reason. And I fear he will never do it. Nevertheless, he expressed himself strongly against Faber . . .

These strong expressions were perhaps partly for Crabb Robinson's benefit. In December 1846 Wordsworth could write quite amiably that he heard that Faber was well 'though he had a frightful accident, having fallen down the mouth of a coal pit . . .'. Whatever words had been said on behalf of the Oxford Movement were never recanted. Four years later the Poet Laureate was dead.

On 2 April 1843, Faber read himself in at Elton Church. The next day he left with his pupil for France and then for Italy. (Originally he had meant to go to Spain and Sicily.) He wrote to Frank Faber from Rouen:

> I read in at Elton on Sunday and preached in a very crowded church: I left it, tower, rectory and all, looking most beautiful . . . the reception given me by the poorest in whose cottages I went being full of warm affection and . . . reverence. I was really on the point of crying.

He did not return until October, thus missing the first exploits of Young England in the House of Commons. It was in that autumn that Newman began 'to despair of the Anglican Church'.

Faber spent most of the next two years at Elton, except for

visits to Ambleside, in the autumn of 1844, and to Oxford. In the summer of 1844 Frank Faber was thought to be dying; Frederick joined him in Oxford and helped to nurse him through. In August of the following year, in one of his last acts as an Anglican priest, he officiated at his brother's wedding. Meanwhile his attachment to Anglicanism had been shaken by his trip to Rome (Manners wished that he had never made it) and by the impression made on him at his Papal audience. He went through a period of great mental strain, which Manners thought 'laid the foundations of future disease'. In spite of this he worked hard in his parish and achieved remarkable results there. According to Manners, even the railway navvies at Elton 'then a sort of proscribed class in England . . . accepted his ministrations with gratitude'. Manners stayed at Elton in the Passion Week of 1844 – an eagerly awaited visit, though Faber feared it was too great a pleasure for the season.

Other visitors included the Beresford Hopes, the Wordsworths and Roundell Palmer. Wordsworth wrote that they had found Faber 'doing a great deal of good, among a flock which had been long neglected'. Roundell Palmer recalled him living 'in his household and among his parishioners in a very primitive fashion, taking no account, in his behaviour towards them, of the difference between poor and rich, but winning the hearts of all . . . That he was in all respects prudent I cannot affirm; but he carried into his work a spirit of love and ardent zeal . . .'. He planted trees, put in new stained-glass windows and an oak pulpit, proposed to convert the parsonage stables to alms houses, visited the poor and sick and collected a small band of devoted adherents who eventually followed him to Rome. One of these, Tom Godwin, remembered

Faber preaching under the acacia, a venerable remnant of a tree still standing on the lawn, and the garden was thronged by a crowd of old and young, rich and poor, who all afterwards joined in the Te Deum, the Old Hundredth, and other Psalms, with an energy which caused them to be heard far and wide.

The *Saturday Review* obituary was of course as cutting about this phase of Faber's life as about others. It seemed to grudge his obtaining, unusually young, a college living 'of fair value':

Unluckily 'young England' was in the ascendant with him for the moment. Instead of rehabilitating the 'nest' he gratified his tastes by constructing a very grand chancel, and turning his gardens into an aesthetic promenade for the unappreciative parishioners.

Orthodox people, according to this obituary, were scandalized by Sunday cricket matches organized by the Rector in the Rectory grounds.

Games on Sunday afternoons, after church, were certainly part of what Young England, particularly Manners, advocated. On 15 August 1843 Manners asked the Attorney-General about the fining of some young men for playing cricket on a Berkshire common after divine service. If the fining was legal, 'was it legal for the rich to have their horses and carriages and other enjoyments at the same time?' Frank Faber wrote to his fiancée in November 1843:

I quite agree with Fred's cricket. A 'quiet walk' is well enough for the old – but a merry innocent game is better for the [word indecipherable] of the young. Fred will combine the proper pursuits of the day with recreation – only let him avoid two things – ordinary labor, or puritanical gloom. Those long-faced groaning scoundrels in Charles's time began with little, but they ended in slaughtering both King and Primate – and the horrid reaction of Charles II's court of immorality was a natural legacy bequeathed us by the Roundheads.

Perhaps the best judgement on Faber's time at Elton was made by the future Dean Stanley, who had been a friend of his at Oxford, though not a very close one. Stanley had heard strange acounts from Faber's successor and from one of the Elton churchwardens. He wrote to his sister on 7 December 1845:

> It seems that Faber had devoted himself wholly to the parish, and with the great energy of his character and fascination of his manners had produced an effect on the people which I should think was really very extraordinary, whilst the faults which his friends knew did not strike them. He had lived on terms of great familiarity with them, having the young men, etc., constantly to dine with him, and read with him in his own drawing room, and having pulled down all the divisions in the Rectory grounds so as to turn it into a kind of park, and throw it open for the whole parish to walk in, so that on Sunday evenings there used to be promenades of one hundred or three hundred people, the poorer classes, and he walking about from group to group, and talking to them. And thus, while the old people liked him for his kindness there had grown up a 'young Elton' which quite adored him . . .

But, by the time that Stanley wrote this letter, Faber's attempt to develop a 'young Elton' in the likeness of Young England had come to an end. It was not because his energy failed or because his vision was inherently impracticable; it was not because his parishioners were unappreciative. This unique social–religious experiment was short-lived, because Newman was received into the Roman Catholic Church in October 1845. Faber, not without anguish, followed him a few weeks later. As if in renunciation of his time as an Anglican poet, and of the idols he had then set up for himself, he sent to Beresford Hope a portrait of Manners he had had commissioned in 1839 and at which he had been used to gaze until, in his own words, he had begun to worship it.

The *Oxford and Cambridge Review*, one of the chief organs of the Young England movement, carried an article on 'The Recent Secessions' in 1845. Although deeply regretting Faber's conversion, it praised him at once for 'the beauty of his fervid and elegant poetry', and for his 'deep and humble piety':

> All sincere friends of our Church must regret the loss of such a man as Mr Faber: very few are there who can supply his place.

3

Party Within a Party
(1842–1846)

'Why are the Tories like walnuts? Because they are troublesome to Peel.' This witticism enclosed in a nutshell the Parliamentary stituation in the five years 1842–1846.

The Whig Government was defeated in July 1841 on a proposal to reduce duties on imported sugar; the Opposition was able to carry an amendment against this, on the ground that it would encourage the production of slave-grown sugar. Ministers did not resign; but they were in financial difficulties and Peel carried, by the narrowest margin, a vote of want of confidence. There was a dissolution, leaving the Whigs in a minority. When Parliament met in August, Ministers were defeated and resigned. Peel formed a Conservative government that held office for five years.

Peel had been Prime Minister only once before, for a few months from the end of 1834. But he had had considerable experience of government, particularly as Home Secretary in the 1820s. He had led the Opposition in the House of Commons for over a decade and his authority and prestige as a Parliamentarian were immense. In his Tamworth Manifesto of 1834 he had recognized that, after the 1832 Reform Act, the Tory Pary could not afford simply to stand for reaction; he had done more than any other man to make it possible for the Party to return to power. Both in intellect and in practical ability he was head and shoulders above the average Tory Member. With all this to recommend him, why was he turned out, through a revolt of many of his supporters, in June 1846?

The basic cause of Peel's loss of power in 1846 was that he

could not persuade enough of his Party that free trade in corn was desirable and inevitable. He might not have felt the need – or seen the opportunity – to convince them of this, if it had not been for the Irish potato famine. The Tories might for their part have accepted his continued leadership, though grudgingly, if Disraeli had not seized the chance to launch a series of lethal attacks. It was possible for Disraeli to make these attacks, and to be applauded for them, because the average Tory Member had come to the conclusion that Peel expected his support without being prepared to take serious account of his views. Once in government Peel saw himself as serving the Queen and her people, not his backbenchers; his aim was to create a measure of national consensus and to preserve aristocratic government, by giving it a reasonably popular and 'caring' image. In defining this image to himself, he was influenced by the views of the wealthy middle class to which he himself belonged.

Peel, though educated at Harrow and Christ Church, was the son of a cotton manufacturer. The Tories began to suspect that his real sympathies did not lie with the landed class, with which most Conservative MPs were connected, but with the industrialists and businessmen who were jostling with them for political control. They had also not forgotten how Peel had betrayed the orthodox wing of the Party by dropping his resistance to Catholic Emancipation in 1828–9. Disraeli wrote that Peel, although 'a very good-looking man' had 'the fatal defect . . . of a long upper lip'. Disraeli's heroes, like the Stranger in *Sights and Thoughts*, showed their breeding by keeping their upper lips to a minimum.

As we now know, the 1832 Reform Bill, which had suppressed the Rotten Boroughs and extended political power to a part of the middle class, was nothing like a definitive solution of the constitutional question. As soon as it was accepted that the voting pattern should be rationalized, and not left to the vagaries of tradition, there was no sufficient reason why the suffrage should not in time become universal. No arrangements restricting it to a particular class or classes could be confidently accepted as final, whether by oligarchs or by democrats. However, in the 1840s, the question of extending the suffrage was dormant as a topic of Parliamentary debate. Governments were less inhibited by the need to attract mass support at elections than by the fear of violent revolution. The year 1830 had been one of revolution in Europe; 1848 was to be another. Peel was no demagogue; he wrote in 1833 of 'the real tyranny which mobs and newspapers, if aided by a popularity-hunting Government . . . will infallibly establish'. But he became increasingly preoccupied with the need for the governing class to avoid revolution by showing a care for popular interests; the lower class would then feel justified in continuing to trust its rulers. At the same time he thought that it was only by increasing economic prosperity that the lot of the poor could substantially be bettered. He was not prepared to impose restrictions on manufacturers that might put economic expansion at risk. For one thing he feared that, if a land-owning legislature were to seek to impose such restrictions, the conflict between the landed and entrepreneurial classes would intensify.

Outside Parliament the Chartists continued to press for universal suffrage as the first of the five points in their programme of constitutional reform. Disraeli said publicly in 1840 that, though he disapproved of the Charter, he sympathized with the Chartist grievances. He took the same view, retrospectively, when he wrote *Sybil* at the end of 1844: the hero, Egremont, advocated 'obtaining the results of the Charter without the intervention of its machinery'. Before writing *Sybil* Disraeli had had access to Chartist correspondence. He told his readers that, when the Chartists presented their National Petition to Parliament in 1839, they did not believe that their objects would be obtained in the short term, but hoped that at least there would be a 'solemn and prolonged debate'. When this was denied them, they despaired and 'reckless counsels' began to prevail. Thenceforward most respectable politicians, including Disraeli and his friends, tended to view Chartism as a threat to public order; there was even less disposition at Westminster than there had been to regard it as a serious political movement.

Although constitutional reform was in abeyance, there was no lack of other controversial topics to keep Parliament busy. Apart from Irish affairs the political scene from 1841 to 1846 was dominated by three problems: the nation's finances; the 'condition of the people'; the corn laws *versus* free trade. With the first Peel was particularly successful; the financial muddle was sorted out; trade and prosperity began to improve; an income tax made possible a reduction in indirect taxation. As to the second, in his last book, *Endymion*, Disraeli described the condition of the country early in 1842 as 'not satisfactory', with a depression in manufacturing business that increased throughout that year. In his view it was the railway boom that pulled the country out of its depression. 'What with these railroads,' says the Duke of Bellamont in *Tancred* (speaking in 1845) 'even the condition of the poor, which I admit was lately far from satisfactory, is infinitely improved. Every man has work who needs it, and wages are even high.' Whatever the cause, the 'condition of the people' did begin to look up a bit with the improved economic climate. But then there was the potato blight in England and, more importantly, in Ireland. Peel came to the conclusion that the government could best help by making bread cheaper. He was very far from being callous towards the misery of the poor, either in Britain or in Ireland. He told a French statesman that the state of the working classes in England was 'a disgrace as well as a danger to our civilization'. When he resigned, he ventured to hope that he might

> leave a name sometimes remembered with expressions of good will in the abodes of those whose lot it is to labour, and to earn their daily bread by the sweat of their brow, when they shall recruit their exhausted

strength with abundant and untaxed food, the sweeter because it is no longer leavened by a sense of injustice.

It is tempting to represent the opposition to Peel, from within his own party, as merely ungrateful, obscurantist and self-interested. But of course there was another side to the question. Able though he was, Peel had no very clear ideas of his own about the direction in which society should move. His grasp of facts was more impressive than his imagination. Perhaps, too, there was a touch of vanity, as well as a deal of conscientiousness, in his eagerness to settle crucial conflicts. Nothing forced him, except his own changed beliefs, to bring in a measure not merely suspending, but ultimately repealing, the corn laws. By any standards this was a remarkable volte-face on a major point of party policy. Nor was the case for free trade in corn as unanswerable as its champions thought it to be. The landowners could argue that they had traditionally borne the responsibility and expense of rural government; they believed, wrongly, that cheap bread would simply enable manufacturers to lower wages; they feared, rightly, that, without protection or subsidy, British agriculture would sooner or later wither. Some of them, like Manners, thought that the whole question had been inflated; the repeal of the corn laws was neither the disaster nor the necessity that had been claimed; if so, why should a Prime Minister determine on wrecking his own party in pursuance of it?

It was against this background that the Young England movement had its season of notoriety. A powerful leader irking some of his supporters. An attempt to cure social distress by giving the market free play. A question whether or not to put party policy before national consensus. Like all conservatives, Peel wanted to preserve existing institutions and make them work. But he was a crypto-Liberal, by the ideological standards of his own time, in that he looked to the free market to lower the cost of living and thus relieve social distress. (By contrast, the Tory Party had been traditionally

104

associated with a system under which the State protected the landlords, while the landlords paid for poor relief through the rates.) More generally, Peel was a consensus rather than a party politician. He was prepared to ignore the feelings of his more extreme supporters; he reached out beyond them to achieve as wide a measure of national support as possible; this effort strengthened and shaped his own convictions.

Spring

By the end of 1841 the three Young Englanders were all safely seated in Parliament and had made their first speeches. Disraeli already knew Smythe, but had not much taken to him. He met Manners for the first time at a dinner party in February 1841. On that occasion Manners did not take much to Disraeli: 'D'Israeli talked well, but a little too well,' was his comment. Cochrane does not seem to have had much to do with Disraeli before the autumn of 1842.

Smythe and Manners had kept up their friendship and had not forgotten their Ambleside ambitions. When the House rose they paid a visit together to the manufacturing districts of Lancashire. There they came across some manufacturers who treated their men well, such as the Grants, the originals of the Cheeryble Brothers in *Nicholas Nickleby*. But they also found low wages and much misery, together with radical employers who put the blame for everything on the land-owners. Disraeli was to make an effective episode in *Coningsby* of this enterprising attempt to bridge the gap between land and industry, between the aristocracy of birth and that of wealth. As often, the reactions of the two friends, though broadly similar, were not identical. Smythe saw the great cotton-spinners, romantically, as 'legitimate heirs of the Eliza-bethan adventurers'; Manners thought his companion had 'run aristocracy-of-wealth mad'. Some of Smythe's feeling of industrial romance was to penetrate the *Coningsby* account. Manners's sense of romance was stirred by other scenes and periods; he was clear that 'nothing but monastic institutions can christianize Manchester'.

After the visit Manners wrote to his elder brother, Granby:

> It's all very well for the Manchester Radicals to rail against an aristocracy, but between you and me there was never so complete a feudal system as that of the mills; soul and body are, or might be, at the absolute disposal of one man, and that to my notion is not at all a bad state of society; the worst of this manufacturing feudalism is its uncertainty, and the moment a cotton lord is down, there's an end to his dependents' very subsistence: in legislating, this great difference between an agricultural and a trading aristocracy ought not to be lost sight of.

This was intuitive reaction, rather than considered thought, but Manners did not mean it as a paradox. Young England believed that society should rest on a 'feudal' system of reciprocal obligations. Under such a system people would be treated as people, and not as machines, and those in power would have to take responsibility for the welfare of the masses. Of course the rulers, like the medieval kings in *England's Trust*, must be taught 'to feel the dreadful weight of power derived from One than Kings more great'. For Young England almost the worst state of society was the one prevailing at that time, when (apart from the workhouse, some 'feudal' factories and some charitable efforts) the welfare of large sections of the population was left entirely to market forces.

In February 1842 Smythe set out in Parliament to efface the impression left by the failure of his maiden speech. He supported what was still Peel's policy of 'gradual, safe and moderate reformation' of the corn laws and, fresh from his industrial tour, displayed his Liberal streak:

These were not the times to reject God's gifts. Let them appreciate the great boon and blessing of machinery without which Manchester would have been as Wood-stock, Liverpool a fishing village on the Mersey . . .

He had no doubt that free trade in corn would benefit both the revenue and the consumer; but protection should be abated gradually, out of respect for the agricultural interest. He complimented the Minister for 'having sought, in the words of a Stuart King, rather to rule for the common weal than the common will'. This was greeted with some applause, though according to *The Times* reporter, 'owing to the great impetuosity of his manner and the occasional indistinctness of his utterance, a considerable portion of his speech was wholly unintelligible in the gallery'. Disraeli's comment to his wife was crustily Tory:

> George Smythe made a most elaborate speech; very Radical indeed, and unprincipled as his little agreeable self, but too elaborate – his manner affected and his tone artificial, and pronunciation too; but still ability though puerile.

It was not long before Disraeli began to find Smythe more agreeable; after making his speech about the Consular Service at the beginning of March, he reported the 'enthusi-asm of young Smythe' as 'extraordinary'. They were soon dining quite regularly in each other's company. Smythe, whose manners could be very finished when he chose, seems to have treated Mrs Disraeli as her husband treated Queen Victoria, though impertinence would sometimes break through. Sir William Gregory gives a glimpse of Mrs Disraeli saying to a party of young men: 'Would you like to go and see the room where Dizzy was brought to bed of *Coningsby*?' Smythe took the lead, amidst roars of laughter, went into the wrong room, fell into Disraeli's bath and came down drenched. Mrs Disraeli asked him placidly whether he had seen the place of birth: 'I know nothing of his place of birth, but I know I have been in the room where he was recently baptized.'

Cochrane spoke briefly about copyright in the House of Commons on 8 Februry 1842; a month later he made a longer speech in favour of the rights of Scottish proprietors over Church patronage. On 24 June he touched a subject nearer to Young England's, or at least to Manners's heart, when he stressed the unpopularity of the New Poor Law (1834). This had been designed to discourage pauperism by centralizing relief in workhouses; outdoor relief remained in fact much more extensive than indoor; but the new law's opponents argued that it had been put into practice without compassion. Both Cochrane and Manners, with the general support of Young England, were to launch a more powerful attack on the New Poor Law two years later.

Manners began speaking regularly in Parliament, as he had done at Cambridge, though in 1842 he confined himself to making some characteristic, and not too lengthy, interventions. In February he urged relief for distress at Bolton, having seen the extent of it himself; he also spoke on the corn laws – perhaps they could be improved, but he could not agree that they were the sole, or main, cause of popular distress. In April he taunted 'gentlemen opposite' with approving of revolutions; he himself 'conscientiously believed all revolutions to be wrong'. In May he supported the Income-Tax Bill, because he looked upon it as a bold, and believed it would be a successful, attempt to diminish the influence of wealth; to this, and not to the influence of aristocracy, 'a great part of the present evils were to be attributed'.

Equally characteristic were Manners's private reflections on the Fancy Dress Ball that the Queen and Prince Albert gave in May in aid of the distressed silk-weavers of Spitalfields. The Royal Pair appeared as Edward III and Queen Philippa;

Manners was Sir Kenneth from Scott's *Talisman*. Though with some misgivings, he determined to look on the bright side:

> Now am I altogether wrong in thinking that good may come from all that enormous waste? Many hundreds of the higher orders have been led to look into the domestic histories of their forefathers, to adopt their picturesque dresses, to learn something of their manners.

This Ball is a striking reminder that medieval nostalgia was by no means confined to Young England. It was in the air of the age. Three years earlier Lord Eglinton, a young Scottish nobleman, had expended large sums in reproducing a medieval tournament on his estate, in the hope of retraining the *jeunesse dorée* in the valorous exercises of their ancestors. The tournament attracted immense interest, though the jousting proved tame and the rain relentless. On a humbler scale Miss Thorne, in *Barchester Towers*, was still trying, though failing, to revive the quintain in the late 1850s. If any one man was responsible for all this medievalizing, it was Sir Walter Scott.

Meanwhile Manners was painfully conscious of the 'tremendous volcano' on which the rich and the powerful were dawdling. He wrote to his Cambridge friend, Lyttelton: 'The mists are rapidly rolling away, and the alternative will soon present itself – a democracy or a feudalism.' Naturally he preferred the latter. As he wrote to Granby in September, the aim must be to show the people 'that we are their real friends', by giving them public baths, public games, public walks and holidays; there was a great need for more *personal* intercourse between rulers and ruled:

> That's my vision; it may be a wrong one; but if, as I believe, the Whig one of giving the people political power and prating to them of the rights of man, the glories of science, and the merits of political economy is

wrong, I can see no other way save the old and worn-out one of *'laissez-faire, laissez-aller'*. . .

Young England was not formed, as a party within a party, until the end of 1842. It was not really until the summer of 1843 that it made much public impact. As early as March 1842, however, Disraeli began seeing the possibilities of such a party for his own position. He wrote to his wife on 11 March:

> I already find myself without effort the leader of a party, chiefly of the youth and new members. Lord John Manners came to me about a motion which he wanted me to bring forward . . . Henry Baillie the same about Afghanistan. I find my position changed.

But these approaches were, at that stage, only an indication of what might happen. Cochrane was insistent, in his old age, that although Disraeli attracted the group with his genius, and so came to lead it, he had nothing to do with its original formation. A satirical song of the time, quoted by Cochrane, represents Young England as being born in the City of Oxford. It was indeed a political offshoot of the Oxford Movement. But its actual begetters were Smythe and Manners, who had pledged themselves at Ambleside to a campaign of restoration and who were now to renew these pledges to each other at Geneva.

Some time in the summer of 1842, presumably in the earlier part of June, Smythe and Manners met in Geneva and, in the intervals of reading Gibbon, decided to launch their movement. Manners, regarding Smythe as his leader, agreed that he should enter into negotiations with third parties; but this does not necessarily prove that Smythe took the leading part at Geneva. Manners had got more self-confidence since the summer of 1838; at the end of June he wrote in his Journal: 'If we keep together, we might be formidable;

110

considerable attention is even now paid to our movement.' By July a first approach had evidently been made to Disraeli. Manners recorded:

> D'Israeli wishes us to form a party with certain general principles, not to interfere with acceptance of office. He says even six men acting so together would have great weight. I think a great deal about our present and possible future state; perhaps there never was a House of Commons in which there was so much young talent frittered away.

These political visions did not prevent Manners from continuing to believe, like Faber, that salvation must primarily come from the Church. Not that Faber and Manners were eccentric in this view. The young Gladstone was no less theocratic; he told Manners in early July that 'he had no faith at all in political remedies; that it all depended on the Church, and on this hope he seemed sanguine . . .'.

The Disraelis spent the winter of 1842–3 in Paris. By early October they were installed in the rue de Rivoli and they did not return to London until the end of January. The wealthy Henry Hope of Deepdene, who was four years younger than Disraeli and was to be one of Young England's backers, arrived in Paris about the same time. On 13 October Smythe and Cochrane, who were also in Paris, dined with the Disraelis, who had already made 'a charming pilgrimage to the Luxembourg' with Smythe. The results of these, or perhaps other, meetings appear in two letters written by Smythe after returning to London.

The first of these letters, dated 19 October, was written to Manners. It gave an impression of difficult, but triumphant, negotiations:

> We have settled, subject to your approval, to sit together, and to vote together, the majority deciding.

Beyond this we have settled nothing, because I have no authority from you, in relation to individual details or to political principles. As to the bond of self-denial and refusal of office, Cochrane and Disraeli were violent for it, but I saw objections, which I will give you *viva voce*, and it remains on this footing, that any such overture shall be communicated to the party acting together, although it shall be in the option of the individual offered to refuse or to accept.

Smythe's objections to self-denial of office were presumably connected with his father's wish for him to 'bring honey into the hive'. Disraeli seems to have changed his own view about this since July; perhaps he had had some fresh reason to think that Peel would never give him the chance to refuse; he was also in a sanguine mood about his Parliamentary influence. Smythe went on to magnify this in his letter to Manners; the two Hodgsons, Quintin Dick, Walter and Henry Hope were probable supporters, he wrote; Henry Baillie (Smythe's brother-in-law) would also be invited to 'sit with us': 'We four vote, and these men are to be played upon, and won, and wooed, for the sense in which we esoterics may have decided.' Cochrane, he said, was rather suspicious of Disraeli and wanted an exclusive trio of the three Eton/Cambridge friends; but, 'that will always be, and being together from personal attachment'. The trouble was that Cochrane, though 'a noble creature' and growing on Symthe's liking, did not know Disraeli well 'and sometimes dreads his jokes, and is jealous of his throwing us over'. But it was better to be in a position to be thrown over than to be nothing at all. If the three friends were ever to be 'of power, or fame, or even office', they needed all the support they could get.

In the second letter, written the following day, Smythe told Disraeli that he had fulfilled his instructions and written to John Manners and H. Baillie, though more guardedly to the latter ('the Celt'). Cochrane was being difficult and jealous; Disraeli must work on him.

Next month, on 14 November, Smythe was able to report to Disraeli that a conquest had been made of Cochrane, 'who writes full of your praises'. H. Baillie, he said, was afraid, 'the paucity of our numbers' would provoke ridicule; but he would come along 'if there was any prospect of serious damage to Peel'. Smythe himself suggested that they ought to think about a witty anonymous pamphlet 'to give nerve to disaffection':

> Seriously – something ought to be done – *something that should not commit us* – before Parliament meets to vex and bully Peel and to give a notion of disaffection. Otherwise – if the sky be entirely serene – the grumblers will believe that the rest of the party are in a state of halcyon satisfaction – and will not have the courage to move.

That 'noble creature' Cochrane was perhaps unaware of the extent of these anti-Peel intrigues. To his later recollection:

> The Young Englanders were not supposed to adopt a factious line: they simply expressed in bright and vigorous language fresh political views, which they hoped to see adopted by the Government, so they sat on the bench exactly behind the Ministerial or Leader of the Opposition.

Cochrane continued to resist too much expansion of the group and to regard Disraeli's 'vast combinations' as grandiose and unrealistic; Disraeli's conquest of him was clearly not yet complete. On 3 December he reported drily to Manners from Paris:

> Disraeli's salons rival Law's under the Regent . . . while the great man is closeted with Louis Philippe at St

Cloud, and already pictures himself the founder of some new dynasty with his Manfred love-locks stamped on the current coin of the realm.

Meanwhile the 'great man', who had indeed been hob-nobbing with Louis Philippe, was immensely enjoying the heady sensation of international power without responsibility. He had in mind the formation of a sizeable party of Conservative MPs who, while sympathizing in general with Peel's domestic policy, could 'dictate the character of his foreign' policy, to the benefit of Anglo-French relations. He went so far as to give the French King a memorandum in November in which he had this to say about the proposed new party's leadership:

> A gentleman has already been solicited to place himself at the head of a Parliamentary party which there is every reason to believe would adopt the views on the Foreign Policy of England referred to, a party of the youth of England, influenced by the noblest views and partaking in nothing of the character of a Parliamentary intrigue; and if he has not at once accepted an offer which it is known he esteems the greatest honor that he ever received, it is only because next to the responsibility of forming a Government, is in his opinion that of leading a party.

Nothing seems to have come of this extraordinary *démarche*. It is not at all clear what Louis-Philippe's reaction was meant to be – whether benevolent interest or a cheque drawn on his secret funds. Disraeli's hero, Bolingbroke, was thought to have sought help from French secret funds when in opposition a century earlier. If Disraeli had any such idea, he must have felt very certain of keeping the transaction confidential, however enlightened the objective of closer Anglo-French understanding might be.

There is nothing to show that the three Young Englanders were involved in this unorthodox diplomacy. During the next two years Young England was active both inside and outside Parliament. This must have involved some expense, though hardly on a massive scale. So far as funds were needed, they could readily have been supplied by Henry Hope or other rich friends; there is certainly no trace of any kind of foreign subsidy. Nor was the party ever organized on the scale envisaged in the salons of the rue de Rivoli.

In fact the party never acted as a disciplined Parliamentary group. On quite a few occasions even the four 'esoterics' took up different positions. The others, who were to be 'played upon, and won and wooed', can hardly have amounted to more than ten and certainly had no Young England Whip at their tails. The group could count on two or three wealthy supporters outside Parliament. Inside Parliament it had, apart from the 'esoterics', at least two active and more or less committed supporters, as well as two or three less committed friends, who were nevertheless much in the Young Englanders' company. There were a few others, who were sometimes sympathetic to Young England, but seem to have had less share in the direction of the group. Throughout this book I have concentrated on the four leading spirits, who launched the movement and gave it its character. But some of the others were prominent in it at the time and deserve to be listed, however briefly.

The election for Nottingham of the elder John Walter (proprietor of *The Times*) was declared void in 1842; his son did not secure his father's seat until 1847. The father had been opposed to the New Poor Law like the Young Englanders, but – not at all like them – distrusted the Oxford Movement. The son was a good deal more sympathetic to 'the Oxford heresy'. Altogether *The Times* gave Young England and Disraeli considerable support, including (according to Cochrane) 'a small room, where we had all the advantage of early information and competent advisers'. But neither

Walter was in Parliament during Young England's heyday. Henry Hope, too, was no longer in Parliament to support the movement in its prime, though he encouraged Disraeli to write *Coningsby* and frequently entertained the Young Englanders at his country house, Deepdene. The Walters also entertained them at Bearwood.

Inside Parliament the three main champions of Young England, apart from its founders, were Peter Borthwick, W. Busfeild Ferrand and Augustus Stafford O'Brien (later known simply as Augustus Stafford). Two distinguished Conservative MPs, Richard Monckton Milnes and A. J. Beresford Hope, younger brother of Henry Hope, were sometimes reckoned as fellow-travellers. Henry Baillie, Quintin Dick, R. Hodgson and T. Bateson (a young Irish landlord) may have been counted as occasional, and lesser, supporters.

Peter Borthwick (1804–1852) had been educated at Edinburgh and Cambridge. J. G. Lockhart, consulted by John Wilson Croker about the new movement in the summer of 1843, said that Borthwick had been 'a notorious man in the Scotch newspapers of 1822' and that he had also been 'a tragic actor at the minor theatres for some years'. In spite of this shady past, he was returned to Parliament in 1835 and sat there, as member for Evesham, until 1847. In 1850, two years before his death, he became Editor of the upper-class Tory *Morning Post*. (The *Morning Post*, which had strong paternalist views, was sympathetic to Young England from the start.) He seems to have been a prompt and effective speaker; at one time he had intended to take Anglican orders.

W. Busfeild Ferrand (1809–1889) was squire of Bingley in Yorkshire. According to Cochrane he had a 'Dantonesque appearance and stentorian voice'. He was vehement on the malpractices of manufacturers, a strong supporter of the Ten Hours Bill, a strong believer in the virtue of allotments and a strong opponent of the New Poor Law. During the 1841–6 Parliament he was involved in an endless row with Sir James Graham, the Home Secretary.

Augustus Stafford O'Brien, a Cambridge friend of Manners, was at once an Irish landlord and a Northamptonshire squire. He was a member of the Anti-League of Protectionists, an epigrammatic speaker and a fine performer at country-house charades. He became Secretary of the Admiralty in 1852.

Beresford Hope (1820–1887) was originally Faber's disciple. In January 1839 Faber wrote to him: 'I never saw a man adopt views with such *mere* enthusiasm as you do; I say *mere* enthusiasm, and I use enthusiasm in a bad sense of course ... If you think [this] very severe you have only to imagine yourself still in the Shell at Harrow, and I a monitor in the scholastic sense of the word ...'. Hope, who was a strong churchman, took this spiritual chastisement meekly; he remained Faber's friend, though he stoutly resisted later appeals to join him in the Roman communion. He was also a Cambridge friend of Manners and Smythe and a fellow member of the Camden Society; he entered Parliament in June 1841 and published some poems in 1843. In 1842 he married Lady Mildred Cecil, the daughter of the Marquess of Salisbury. Although an eager Oxford Movement convert he kept some distance from Young England, because he distrusted Disraeli. In 1867 he called him 'the Asian mystery'; Disraeli retorted with 'Batavian graces' (the Hopes were of Dutch extraction). Nevertheless, Cochrane's satirical song included 'Hope with his opera-hat' as one of Young England's offspring, while both Gregory and Cochrane reckoned him a member of the group.

Richard Monckton Milnes was an associate, but hardly a full, member; according to Cochrane's song he was 'not yet tinctured with Puseyite leavening'. Born in 1809, he was educated privately and then at Trinity, Cambridge. In 1837 he became Conservative MP for Pontefract. He published volumes of poetry in 1838 and 1840, gave famous breakfast parties, joined the Liberals, was created Baron Houghton in 1863 and died in 1889. He and Smythe irritated each other;

they would have come to a duel once, if Smythe had not apologized. On the other hand Milnes admired Disraeli and, as we shall see, was upset when Disraeli failed to turn him into a character in *Coningsby*.

It was accepted from the start by the four 'esoterics' that the movement was to have a High Anglican bias. Cochrane wrote to Manners that Disraeli had agreed 'that the High Church doctrines must be our standard of Christianity – this must please you'. Smythe made one of his acute comparisons: 'Dizzy's attachment to moderate Oxfordism is something like Bonaparte's to moderate Mohammedanism.' But it was as much as the cause required. Of course the four must also have exchanged views on other topics such as the monarchy and popular welfare, though Manners and Smythe at least already knew each other's mind on them. But there seems to have been no attempt to put on paper any set of common principles.

This left each of the four free to put forward his own views publicly as he chose. Others might or might not assume him to be speaking for the movement as a whole; there was no means of confirming or refuting this. The group would naturally avoid criticizing each other; they would concert together on specific questions, where they were agreed. But their individual priorities were not necessarily the same. For Cochrane in later life the first principle of Young England was the desire to 'lighten their [the people's] servitude' and to add to their enjoyments – in fact to restore 'Merrie England'. The others would have agreed with this objective, but might not have given it such priority or expressed it quite in that way.

So long as the Disraelis were wintering in Paris even informal exchanges of views cannot have been easy. However, they returned in time for the 1843 sittings of Parliament, to find 'Peel feeble and frigid, I think, and general grumbling'. When there was time for Disraeli to be fully briefed on the historical views of the younger men, including their enthusiasm for the Stuarts, he knew better than to pooh-pooh them. To some extent these views fitted in with his own; in any case temporary use could be made of them and they could always be dropped later if they became too embarrassing.

Many readers of Disraeli will feel for Manners in what he wrote in his Journal some months later: 'Could I only satisfy myself that D'Israeli believed all that he said, I should be more happy: his historical views are quite mine, but does he believe them?' The answer surely is that Disraeli was always less interested in the truth of ideas, than in the use that could be made of them. What he really wanted was power. But he had a genius for *manipulating* ideas – and this could be a substitute when power was not to be had. In one sense he believed in virtually nothing, except himself and one or two central ideas (the Jewish race and the 'territorial constitution'), which had become essential to his personal or political existence. In another sense, he was ready to believe in virtually anything that struck his fancy.

Meanwhile Manners had brought out his Holy-Days pamphlet and, early in 1843, had paid a visit to another potential Young England sympathizer. This was Ambrose Lisle March Phillipps (De Lisle) (1809–1878), a former undergraduate at Trinity, Cambridge, whose father had estates in Leicestershire and who had been converted to Roman Catholicism at the age of 15. In 1835 he had given 230 acres of land in Charnwood Forest for the re-establishment of the Cistercian order, exactly three centuries after its suppression. He also maintained for several years an ecumenical correspondence with the leaders of the High Church party at Oxford. Manners found him 'something between Faber and Gladstone'. No doubt Phillipps helped to sustain Manners's belief in the value of monastic institutions.

In Parliament Manners was still assiduous, speaking on behalf of Don Carlos, against the Afghan War and against the appointment of a Bishop of Jerusalem. On 14 March he argued that allotments, by affording 'the labouring poor the opportunity of healthful out-of-door amusements' would 'greatly improve their physical and moral condition'. On 18 May he spoke in favour of 'principles which, while they would render the Church triumphant, and the monarchy powerful, would also restore contentment to a struggling, overworked and deluded people'. He maintained that:

> As power was taken away from the mitre and the crown and transferred either to the people in that House or out of it, their physical and moral happiness had been lessened ... He would extend the feeling of responsibility between the rich and the poor, and shorten the interval which in his opinion was growing too wide between those for whom wealth was made and those who made it.

Cochrane, too, spoke quite regularly. He opposed money for Maynooth as a Protestant, though he respected the Roman Catholic faith of his ancestors and preferred 'the arrogance of the Church of Rome to the hypocrisy of the Church of Scotland'; in fact he was against 'ecclesiastical domination' of any kind. On 14 March he said that England owed much to 'manufacturing prosperity', but not necessarily to individual manufacturers; he would be happy 'if the present surplus could be got rid of; but the overthrow of the agricultural interest was too great a price to pay for such a boon'. On 10 May he deplored the distress of manufacturing workmen; he 'would far prefer to see our country humble in its relations with other nations ... if the distress of the people were lessened, and their sufferings more mitigated'. But he doubted whether corn law repeal would help, since it would 'lesson the price of labour, and reduce wages'. He took a surprisingly last-ditch stand on behalf of his fellow landowners:

> The only way to arrest the march of revolution in this country was to decide at once against all concession . . . if the agricultural party were only true to themselves, no influence . . . would be able to destroy them . . .

Manners had sounded an authentically Young England strain on 18 May; but otherwise these proceedings did not give much evidence of a new, organized, Parliamentary group. Indeed on 14 March 1843 there had been some evidence to the contrary. Smythe supported a motion to set up a Select Committee to inquire into the burdens and privileges of the landed interest; Manners and Cochrane, with Peel, voted against.

However, a speech by Disraeli to his constituents at Shrewsbury, on 13 May, suggests that, at least to some extent, he and the Young Englanders were by now thinking on the same lines. He put 'the preponderance of the landed interest' above all else, though he interpreted this as including much more than 'squires of high degree'. He dwelt on the 'estate of the poor' and on the 'great estate of the Church'. He regretted that there were not more relics of the feudal system remaining. What was its fundamental principle? That the tenure of all property should be the performance of its duties – 'the noblest principle that was ever conceived by sage or ever practised by patriot'.

Even before this speech, on 18 April, Manners had been able to record in his Journal that the movement had survived its teething troubles:

> Our *partie carée* is still in existence after many dangers. Disraeli is a very easy man to get on with, and incomparably clever; we had many coquettings with newspapers, and it seemed once as if 'The Times' was to be our organ; if young Walter was to have come in for Nottingham, he was to have joined us.

In another three or four months Young England was to get all the publicity it could wish.

Summer

In the two years of its Parliamentary blossoming, no topic absorbed more of Young England's time and effort than the state of Ireland. Perhaps there was no other topic on which its efforts were quite so fruitless, or which split the movement more. But, equally, there was no other topic that procured it so much public attention.

In the spring of 1843 Smythe and Manners, sensing the potential importance of the Irish question for their group, prepared themselves by paying a joint visit to Ireland. Both of them could claim some hereditary interest in its problems. Smythe's parents were Anglo-Irish; his father had been educated at Trinity, Dublin. Manners's grandfather, the Fourth Duke of Rutland, had been, before his early death of a fever, Lord Lieutenant of Ireland under the younger Pitt.

The two friends turned this visit to account when they were back in London. On 19 June, Manners made a speech in the House of Commons condemning Irish destitution. Smythe's opportunity came the following month, when Smith O'Brien brought forward a motion inviting the House to consider Irish discontent 'with a view to the redress of grievances and to the establishment of a system of just and impartial government'. On 11 July Smythe made his first effective speech at Westminster, on behalf of a conciliatory Irish policy; he urged the Government to approach Ireland in the spirit of Chesterfield and Pitt. But the 'esoterics' had failed to win over their rank and file, who preferred a tougher policy. Smythe, Manners, Cochrane and Ferrand voted with the minority for Smith O'Brien's motion; the opposing majority included Borthwick, Stafford O'Brien, Milnes, Beresford Hope and Bateson.

Sir William Gregory, though critical enough of some

aspects of Smythe's character, recorded later that he felt 'the most unbounded admiration for the courage as well as the political foresight, with which George Smythe, a young man like myself, treated Irish questions, social and religious, although he represented the extreme Tory, and indeed, retrograde element of a cathedral city'. The Liberal *Morning Chronicle*, in an editorial on 18 July, was surprised and pleased to see 'some members of the Tory party' more or less advocating the governing of Ireland 'on a sound liberal system', though it did not care much for their cult of Puseyism or their regrets for the 'Toryism of Strafford'. The views and language of these young men were confused and extravagant, but they seemed to 'have a very sincere sympathy with the great mass of the people'. In any case any stick to beat the Government with was a good one: 'Sneers at "Young England" are just now more palatable with your good Tories than even abuse of O'CONNELL.'

Smythe himself realized that he had put himself at risk with his constituents. On 18 July he wrote an open letter to the Electors of Canterbury explaining his vote on Smith O'Brien's motion. This is worth quoting rather fully, as a summary of his political views at this time (or such of them as he wished publicly to profess):

> Upon the hustings I told you that if you did me the honour to elect me you would elect 'an old Tory' – one who believed that the principles advocated by the 'old Tory' party, now more than a century ago, through contumely and proscription, through great numerical disadvantages, in opposition and decline, were still, with the exception of mere ephemeral and party detail, the soundest principles of government.

He said that he had held then, and still held, that:

> ... monarchy is a principle rather than an instrument ...

. . . the Church ought to be placed in a less dependent and circumscribed position . . .

. . . in trade and commerce the old Whig policy of restriction ought to be replaced by a larger and freer system . . .

. . . in foreign policy the French alliance is the best guarantee for the peace of Europe and the prosperity of England . . .

. . . Ireland ought to be governed in sympathy with Irish feelings.

He concluded:

I am not going to alter my opinion about men or measures. I am not going, because on this occasion I think for myself, to abandon the lead of the conservative statesmen in the Commons . . . if I have voted against Sir Robert Peel's Irish policy, he at least will know that, as I have never sought a favour at his hands, so I am not influenced by any motive of pique or disappointment.

The Governmental *Morning Herald*, in publishing Smythe's letter on 20 July, expressed scathingly the plain Conservative point of view:

In style this letter is ridiculously affected, in matter it is extremely unsatisfactory. Mr Smythe was returned for Canterbury to support the leaders of the conservative party as the proximate Ministers, and not to form within that party a rebelliously opiniative *clique* . . . *Old Toryism* . . . is but a new name for modern 'liberalism' . . . Mr Smythe is one of those smart, fine, generalising gentlemen who discover 'principles' in door-posts and are perpetually talking about what they don't understand. Lord John Manners . . . sighs for a Strafford . . . These two gentlemen are the prime movers of *Young England*;

and that tomfoolery is the political offshoot of Tractarianism. Mental dandyism is its chiefest characteristic.

This was strong stuff; but the use of such heavy artillery showed that the party organizers were worried. It also showed that Young England was getting itself talked about. A letter from Macaulay to Napier, on 22 July, described the Tories as 'broken up into three or more factions, which hate each other more than they hate the Whigs – the faction which stands by Peel, the faction which is represented by Vyvyan and the *Morning Post*, and the faction of Smythe and Cochrane'. 'Faction' was an ugly word in good Tory vocabulary; but at least it was something to be recognized as a distinct group.

In spite of Smythe's eclecticism, the record of his short Parliamentary career is remarkably consistent – certainly more consistent than Cochrane's. He was consistently a supporter of the monarchy, an adherent of the Stuarts and an admirer of Bolingbroke, Pitt and Canning. At the same time he was consistently an advocate of free trade (which he associated with Bolingbroke and Pitt) and of enterprising manufacture. He consistently spoke in favour of some reform of the corn laws; voted with the Government and the industrialists on factory hours; and refused to put agricultural interests automatically first. He consistently favoured Anglo-French understanding (in *Historic Fancies* he said that he wished to promote 'a gentler feeling' between the two countries). He consistently urged conciliation in Ireland and consistently spoke in favour of grants to Maynooth.

This record, whether right or wrong, is hardly 'unprincipled', however lacking in principles Smythe was, or pretended to be, in himself. Most of the positions that he adopted in Parliament can be traced to the explanation he gave to his constituents on 18 July 1843. If he adopted them simply because he thought they would turn out trumps, he must at least have been taking a disinterestedly long-term view. Of course his attitude struck his contemporaries as a strangely paradoxical blend of 'old Tory' and 'Liberal' views. According to *Fraser's Magazine*, in May 1847, he 'adopted and re-echoed' some of Young England's opinions, but was not to be confounded, in his political liberalism, with Manners and Disraeli. His sister-in-law, in her memoir in *Angela Pisani*, also stressed his Liberal differences from the other Young England leaders.

These differences became clearer in the future, although they were implicit from the start. It is noteworthy that, in his letter to the Electors of Canterbury, Smythe did not mention the 'condition of the people'. However, in a letter from Deepdene in September 1843 he took pains to assure Manners that his heart was in the right place:

> I cannot help feeling (to another it might seem presumption to say so) that there is a position given us, by which we may be of good to the poor masses in this country. This is a grave and great responsibility which I the more sensibly feel perhaps, that I have not those other supports which spiritualize your resolution, and sustain your purpose.

This is to anticipate a little. In July–August 1843 the Young England leaders, having just acquired a name and a public identity, were at their most united. On 1 August Manners, supported by Borthwick, moved: 'That it is inexpedient, in the present condition of the country, to continue the existing restrictions on the exercise of private charity and munificence'. Millions in England and Ireland were 'suffering from the extreme of want, ignorance and misery,' he argued. If the State would not help, at least let it facilitate private munificence; as it was, the Mortmain Act of George II, which imposed restrictions on the devising of property to charitable uses, stood in the way. The re-establishment of religious houses would also help to bring the most benighted areas 'within the pale of Christian civilization'.

> In an age confessedly devoted to money-making ... I ask you to have the courage to believe in the nobler impulses of our nature; to appeal to the glorious spirit which built our cathedrals, our colleges, our convents ...

Manners did not divide the House on his motion, which was opposed (not too roughly) by the Home Secretary. In May 1844 he moved a committee of inquiry into Mortmain; in 1846 and 1847 he continued to press that the law on pious and charitable bequests should be changed; but he had to wait until 1888 for the George II Act to be rescinded.

The following day Cochrane added his voice against the Government's Irish policy, claiming from Peel 'a nobler and more becoming tone of feeling towards those who found themselves compelled to differ ...'. On 7 August he joined Manners in deploring the French treatment of Don Carlos. On 9 August Disraeli and Smythe both spoke on the Irish Arms Bill. Disraeli called the measure 'contemptible' in relation to the current state of Ireland. Smythe accused Peel of using an 'intolerant expression' against his followers and criticized his 'do-nothing' Irish policy. He would be less anxious if Peel were more so; the Arms Bill was 'a measure efficient only to irritate'.

Press comment was, again, extensive and mixed. The *Morning Post* defended Young England, having itself become thoroughly disenchanted with Peel: 'Sir Robert Peel *was* a Conservative leader, but he is not so now.' Besides, Tories should guide and protect 'those below'; Peel, on the other hand, supported 'a sordid, mechanical, unfeeling policy, which is subversive of the glory of the nation, and inimical to the happiness of the people'. The *Post* argued that it was a mistake to attribute a Puseyite attitude to this new

'Conservative section' (Young England). Every sound Tory must be 'a lover of discipline and deference'; these principles might be generally held by 'Puseyites', but they were not 'Puseyism' in themselves.

The Times, though sceptical about the 'Cavalier' bias of Young England's Irish policy, was polite to its leaders personally ('men of by no means inconsiderable talents, information, and eloquence') and strongly vindicated their right to think for themselves.

The *Morning Chronicle* prophesied that the new Conservative section 'which has just begun to attract notice . . . though at present small in number, will become daily of more importance . . . these gentlemen . . . are evidently not expediency men, and there is an instinctive antipathy between them and Sir ROBERT PEEL . . .'. It did not of course follow that they were faultless: 'They are strongly embued with the Puseyite theology, and their views of the remedies which our social evils require, involve a sufficiently large measure of absurdity.'

The *Morning Herald* was strongly opposed to the revival of monastic institutions (so was the *Morning Chronicle*) but admitted that Manners had otherwise put forward a good case for revising the law of Mortmain. On 4 August, however, it launched another blistering attack on the movement:

> . . . the clique of aspiring young politicians known as *Young England*; the chief qualifications for enrolment in whose ranks are a very hearty contempt for Old England, a perfect horror of Bonnie Scotland, a yearning for the descent of miraculous power on the Church, and a miracle-working Minister on the State, and a liberal-loving patronage of Romanism.

This was directed mainly at Cochrane. Nearer the bone was an extract from the *Globe*, which appeared in the *Herald* the following day:

It appears to us that Lord John Manners, and all that school of politicians, are pre-occupied to a puerile degree by the rage of attributing every *new* unfavourable symptom in our condition to neglect of same *old* practice.

Meanwhile, respectable Conservatives were waxing indignant about Young England's subversive behaviour. Charles Greville noted in his diary, on 11 August, that, during the Irish Arms Bill debate, 'D'Israeli and Smythe, who are the principal characters (together with John Manners) of the little squad called 'Young England' were abusive and impertinent.' Croker, the former Secretary to the Admiralty who had invented the term 'Conservative' in 1830, asked J. G. Lockhart, Editor of the *Quarterly Review*, for information about the new group. Lockhart replied that Smythe, whom Croker had omitted, was 'the cleverest of the set, I believe':

> Milnes, Disraeli, Cochrane, are poets. Cochrane not the worst of the three. He is a Cochrane ... but not a bad fellow. A little *notice* would have made him and Smythe all right. Disraeli and Borthwick are very necessitous, and wanted places of course.
>
> I fancy Young England has in some degree at least associated itself with *Urquhart* [David Urquhart, Turcophil diplomatist and critic of the Afghan War].

Croker proceeded to pen a footnote to one of his political articles, dealing politely with the members of the group, as individuals, but accusing them of 'endeavouring to create distrust of the only statesman in whom the great Conservative body has any confidence, or can have any hope'. Mr Smith O'Brien's motion was 'the most offensive to *Old England* which has been made for many years'. The Young Englanders should not be 'deceived as to the quality of the notice which their singularity has obtained; it has in it more of

129

wonder than respect . . .'. Croker also seems to have written to Graham, the Home Secretary, who replied at the end of August:

> With respect to Young England, the puppets are moved by Disraeli, who is the ablest man among them . . . I think with you that they will return to the crib after prancing, capering, and snorting . . . Disraeli alone is mischievous.

Peel reported to the Queen that, in the July Irish debate, four members of the party had voted against the Government; he also told her that, in the Irish Arms Bill debate, Disraeli and Smythe had made speeches apparently indicating that they would in future oppose the Government. In September the Conservative Whip, Freemantle, warned Peel that, if Borthwick failed to get a diplomatic appointment, he might join 'the party of malcontents, G. Smythe, D'Israeli and Co.'. At the start of the 1844 session Freemantle asked Peel whether he should send the usual letter requesting attendance to Manners, Smythe, and Cochrane. Peel told him not to write to Disraeli or Smythe, though he readily accepted Disraeli's assurance that he had misinterpreted his attitude.

Smythe's relations with his father cannot have been helped when the Queen's reactionary uncle, the King of Hanover, wrote to Lord Strangford (in October): 'According to my opinion, these self-pretended Tories, such as G.S., Lord J. Manners, and others, are all distracted, having no one fixed principle upon which to go, whether religious or political.' This was, no doubt, the reaction of most of the older Conservatives. It was true enough of Smythe who, though consistent, was consistent to conflicting principles. It was very untrue of Manners.

However, there were compensations, as 1843 drew to a close. Young England had made a decided impact on the country. In September the Disraelis and Smythe all spent some time at Deepdene. One night Disraeli sat next to the widowed Mrs Evelyn of Wotton: 'Her son, the present squire, there also; a young Oxonian and full of Young England ... The journals daily descant on the "new party" that has arisen to give a new colour to modern politics, etc.'

Young England was still absorbed in the Irish question when the 1844 Parliamentary session opened. On 14 February Cochrane blamed 'the constant changes and breaking up of property' in Ireland for much of the trouble there. He hoped the Government would 'take into consideration the sympathies and affections of that most noble and gallant-hearted nation'. Two days later Disraeli spoke at length about Ireland; he wanted to see it governed in accordance with true Tory principles; in the best Young England style he evoked the 'benignant policy' of Charles I. On 19 February Smythe spoke briefly, trusting the Government would come forward 'with some well-timed measure', such as the settling of relations between landlord and tenant.

In the course of his speech Disraeli expressed the hope that, in fifty years' time, the Irish people might be found 'a contented and thriving peasantry':

> He looked to no foreign, no illegitimate influences for bringing about that result – not to the passions of the Irish people, not to the machinations of their demagogues, but to a power far more influential, far more benignant – a power more recently risen in the world, not yet sufficiently recognized – [Mr Ward: 'What Young England?'] – No, not Young England, but a power which Young England respects – that irresistible law of our modern civilization which has decreed that the system which cannot bear discussion is doomed.

Ward's interjection was not the only evidence in early 1844 that the Young England group was by then firmly labelled as such in Parliament. On 27 February both Smythe and

Cochrane rallied to the support of Manners, when he raised yet again the plight of Don Carlos. One member (Trelawney) said that 'the party of Young England had shown a great deal of misplaced sympathy for Don Carlos'. Borthwick was stung into a schoolboyish retort: 'A certain school, designated "Young England" had obtained some notoriety, but there was another school of youths – the young Boeotians – who were very talkative in that House.'

Smythe's Don Carlos speech seems to have drawn cheers even from the ranks of Boeotia. He had by now got the ear of the House and, according to *The Times* report, he was greeted with 'loud and general cheering' (Manners and Cochrane only rated 'Hear, hear', while Palmerston got 'Cheers'). Loyally and diplomatically, he referred to Louis Philippe's 'example of domestic happiness and unassuming worth . . . to which there could only be a parallel in the English contemporary court'. If Queen Victoria read this tribute, she was not mollified by it.

On 22 March the new group showed less unity when Manners made a long speech advocating the ten-hour limit for work in factories by boys under 18. He earnestly appealed to the House not to dash 'the cup of hope' untasted to the ground. In the vote Smythe sided with the Government, who favoured a twelve-hour limit, while Manners, Disraeli, Cochrane, Borthwick and Ferrand were all in the ten-hour minority. Cochrane made two subsequent interventions on behalf of ten hours. Disraeli tried to speak before the division, but could not get a hearing; he did not actually speak in favour of any factory act till 1850.

Smythe's apostasy did not go unnoticed. Later in the year the *Morning Herald* argued that Young England had done nothing *practically* to help their fellow men: 'All that we can at present call to mind, is a rather awkward vote of one of their number – Mr. SMYTHE, *against* the ten-hour clause . . .'. It was hardly for the Governmental *Herald* to cast this particular stone. The Government feared that the imposition of a ten-hour limit would disgruntle the manufacturers and reduce their competitive ability in world markets. The Queen herself believed that a ten-hour limit would injure the country's trade and split the Peel Government. Smythe presumably voted with the Government either because he felt obliged to please his father by supporting Peel or, more probably, because he agreed with the Prime Minister that the Conservatives ought not to antagonize the manufacturers.

The leading spirit in the move to shorten factory hours was of course Lord Ashley, the future Earl of Shaftesbury. Before him the Tory social reformers Richard Oastler and Michael Sadler had also laboured in this vineyard. Ashley was suspicious of Young England and the Tractarians, because his own religious views, though as strong as theirs, were deeply evangelical. He was also a difficult man personally; when Manners and Smythe made their tour of the manufacturing districts, he had been convinced that their object was to undermine his personal influence. He came to regard Manners (as everybody did) as 'a really well-intentioned fellow'; but he nevertheless suspected that *The Times*'s support of him was designed 'to raise up a Tractarian champion for the poor in opposition to myself'. Perhaps this suspicion was not entirely neurotic. After becoming a Roman Catholic Faber promoted schools for the Catholic poor, with the express object of counteracting 'the pernicious effect' of Ashley's Ragged Schools.

Young England's support for shorter factory hours, though incomplete and not immediately successful, was not without effect. The elderly Cochrane held that it had been 'greatly by the energetic action of Young England that the Factory Acts were passed'. *The Times* obituary of Manners, while admitting the short-term failure of his efforts on allotments and Mortmain, attributed the first Factory Act of 1847 largely to the 'exertions of Lord Ashley, Mr. Fielden and Lord John Manners'.

An opportunity soon occurred for Smythe and Manners to

present a united front again. On 24 April 1844 there was a full-scale debate in the House of Commons, when the Home Secretary rose on a question of privilege about a speech by Ferrand, published in *The Times*, containing charges against him (Graham) and Hogg. The speech had been delivered at a meeting in Leeds on 8 April, also addressed by the 'factory king' Oastler, in the cause of the Ten Hour Bill. Ferrand had accused Graham and Hogg of unseating Walter at Nottingham, his friends there having spent between £30 and £40 in treating. Walter had been penalized, Ferrand suggested, as an 'advocate of the poor': 'No man has resisted the New Poor Law more rigorously or at a greater sacrifice of time and money than Mr. Walter.'

Disraeli had himself served on the Nottingham Election Committee, which split down the middle – three Tories for Walter, three Whigs against – leaving its Chairman to decide the matter. Although not approving of Ferrand's attack on Graham and Hogg, he thought that Ferrand should not be hounded for it. Smythe and Manners also spoke in support of Ferrand, the former once again eliciting 'loud and long repeated cheers'.

In June the Government risked coming to grief, as their predecessors had done, on a question of sugar. A majority carried against the Government a proposal to reduce the duties on all *free-grown* sugar, with the object of helping the British colonial growers. The four Young England 'esoterics', except for Cochrane, voted with this majority. Peel stuck to his own proposals and was thought to have been unconciliatory at a party meeting. Disraeli, expecting Peel to fall and the Whigs to come in, made a stronger attack on the Prime Minister than he had yet done: 'I think the Rt. Hon. Gentleman should deign to consult a little more the feelings of his supporters.' He was much applauded and his friends rallied round him, including Cochrane who, in spite of his previous vote, spoke up for 'the independence of the House of Commons'. Nevertheless, the House rescinded its earlier decision, as the Government wished, though only by a narrow majority of twenty. Queen Victoria wrote to her uncle, the King of the Belgians: 'We were really in the greatest possible danger of having a resignation of the Government without knowing to whom to turn, and this from the recklessness of a handful of foolish half "Puseyite", half "Young England" people.'

Coningsby had come out in May and was having a great success. *Historic Fancies* would be out in July. Now that Irish affairs had receded into the background, the increasingly confident Young England leaders were able to concentrate on the plight of the poor. Disraeli began to plan *Sybil*. Cochrane considered a motion against the New Poor Law. On 19 June Manners had a chance to champion the Church and the poor simultaneously by deploring an attack on a Bishop:

> He should have regretted to have such an attack made upon any Prelate, but he regretted more the attack upon the right rev. Prelate in question, because he knew that there was than that right rev. Prelate no more warm or consistent advocate of the best interests of the poor.

He himself advocated these interests in a number of Parliamentary interventions in July.

On 4 July Cochrane brought forward his motion: 'That the new Poor Law, though improved by the proposed amendments, is still opposed to the ancient constitution of this realm, and inadequate to the necessities of the people.' He condemned Malthusian doctrines as 'tending to harden the human heart'; he argued that the law 'tended to diminish and repress those kindly feelings which ought to exist in every relation of life'; he claimed that the manufacturers did not bear their share in maintaining the poverty they created. Borthwick, Ferrand and Manners spoke in support. When it came to a vote they were joined by Disraeli, Smythe and Milnes – all seven being in a small minority voting for adjournment of the debate. Smythe had defended the New

Poor Law at the Cambridge Union; either he had changed his mind since then, or he was determined to avoid another appearance of group disunity.

Young England was united in opposition to the New Poor Law, both because its members wished to maintain the 'parochial constitution' of the country and because they deplored the severity of the new provisions for relief. At least in theory the object of the law was to restrict relief to those who were really destitute by applying the 'workhouse test' — under which claimants for relief had to enter workhouses where the standard of maintenance was deliberately austere. This involved, among other hardships, the separation of husband and wife. Although Borthwick described the Act as 'unsound in principle and oppressive in operation', Young England failed in its attempt to get it rescinded. But the Government did bring in some amendments to mitigate the Act's severity and declared that the 'workhouse test' was in fact only very partially applied. Cochrane claimed that the Home Secretary now 'took a very different view of the question from that which he had formerly avowed and acted upon'.

The Times had been tenacious in urging the evils of the new system. It commented bitterly on 5 July that there was 'certainly a most dire aversion felt in the House of Commons to having the state of the poor brought before them. It is a sore subject indeed. They had rather talk about any other.' However, by the following day, the editorialist had recovered his serenity. After all, the debate had gone off 'very satisfactorily'; Ministers had conceded an important point in abandoning the 'workhouse test' as the principle of the Poor Law. In any case, the attitude of *The Times* towards Peel had been becoming increasingly critical during this session. So it was glad to be able to congratulate Manners for taking the Prime Minister to task, 'very sharply and successfully', over the grudging way in which the Government had brought in amendments to meet the Law's opponents.

Two days earlier *The Times* had reviewed Smythe's *Historic Fancies*:

> This volume is calculated to attract a considerable share of public attention; not merely because it exhibits great talent, and indicates a greater promise, but because it represents in its various pages of mingled prose and verse a picture of that youthful and stirring mind which has recently so much engaged the observation and in a great degree the sympathy of the public.

Of course, as always, it depended on which public you happened to meet. The observation of the politically conscious public had certainly been engaged, together with the sympathy of many. But the aura of Popery created by some of the things that Manners and Cochrane had written and said had deterred many others. At the end of August Disraeli visited his Shrewsbury constituency. He wrote to his wife that the reputable tradespeople 'quite approve as to the attack on the Government, but a little alarmed in some quarters, I find, about Popery, monasteries, and John Manners. This I shall quietly soften down . . .'.

Hitherto the Young Englanders had concentrated on the House of Commons. Now that they had got some reputation they were in demand as speakers elsewhere in the country. For a short season in the autumn of 1844 they accepted invitations to speak outside Westminster and their own constituencies; it was only because of their own misgivings that this did not snowball into a longer campaign.

Manners was invited to became a patron of the Birmingham Athenic Institution, which (according to a booklet of Young England addresses published in January 1845) had been established 'a few years ago for intellectual culture and for the enjoyment of the old English manly sports by respectable young men in that town'. On 26 August 1844 he presided over their first annual dinner, having written to Disraeli beforehand: 'As I know nothing whatever about its chances of success, I shall go like a knight-errant alone: they seem fine straightforward fellows.' He must have found the atmosphere as congenial as he had hoped; he told these latterday Athenians that it was 'a high treat to ... hear their sentiments, which might be described as truly English, and so excellent in every respect'. He went on to make three points. First, the 'hardworking men of Birmingham' must protest against 'the modern political dogma which would seem to assume that no recreation was necessary for the working population ...'. Second, he stressed the aim of 'uniting together again the different classes of society'. In the old days, there had been much more peace, happiness and security than under the present class system (*loud applause*): 'In the palmiest days of feudalism the barons of England were accustomed to sit at the same table and partake of the same fare with those beneath them.' Third, there was the Institution's plan of mental improvement. He did not share the view that education was not suited to the working classes and he hoped the Institution would let him present them with a set of 'the Englishman's Library'. His conclusion was optimistic: 'A great improvement is taking place in the tone and feeling of society. In many parts of England great efforts were being made to restore amongst the people, the ancient games and field sports ...'.

Nowadays, it would be impossible to make such a speech without appearing absurdly condescending. At that time most of Manners's hearers must have felt genuine gratitude to him, a Duke's son, for sharing their table, their fare and their hopes. In that structured society – only recently emerging into industrialism from the semi-feudalism of the rural areas – appeals to class unity and common inheritance could strike a deep emotional chord. Besides, Manners was himself so likeable, so patently honest and so full of obvious goodwill, that only the 'ill-conditioned' could resent it if he made one or two of his points a little clumsily. There were unlikely to be many such malcontents in this gathering of fine, straightforward fellows.

A more spectacular event was a 'Grand Soirée' organized by the Manchester Athenaeum in the Great Free-Trade Hall on 3 October, with an audience of over three thousand and Disraeli in the chair. This was a strictly middle-class affair: tickets were 5 shillings (member and lady) and Evening Dress was worn. The Bands of the 5th Dragoon Guards and of the 67th Regiment of Infantry had been engaged, together with Horabin's Double Quadrille Band. Carriages were 'to set down with the horses' heads towards Deansgate, and to take up in the opposite direction'. 'Doors open at 6 – chair taken at 7 – dessert at 9.'

It was not at all a party-political occasion. Disraeli made an uplifting speech on the theme 'Knowledge is power'. He spoke of the need to 'emancipate this country from the degrading thraldom of faction ...'. He appealed to the Youth, as 'the trustees of Posterity' and told them 'to aspire'.

Manners, mildly aspiring, welcomed the Athenaeum's attempt 'to soften the harsh tendencies of toil and wealth by the gentle means of literature and art'. He said that past history should not be regarded as 'a mere record of the kings who reigned and the battles they fought'. He rejoiced that Christian Art was having a happy revival.

Smythe, hectically aspiring, enthused over the old, natural, alliance between literature and commerce. The literature arising from 'such a meeting as the present' would not be a literature of patronage, but 'free, independent, universal, and above all tolerant', like Manchester's commerce. He referred to Canning as 'our last great man' and praised the spirit of British Commerce for having nothing small or sectarian about it. He ended with a proclamation of the banns of marriage between spirit and matter, between an industry 'which has conquered the world' and 'an intellect which is young, which is of the people, and which, by God's help, shall continue pure'.

This was Smythe the Liberal speaking. It was exactly what Manchester wanted to hear. Manners wrote to Cochrane:

Smythe's eloquence was really surpassing, and electrified the audience. They rose like one man, or one woman, when he had finished, and gave him a burst of cheers; it was a spontaneous tribute to unwonted eloquence.

Even the King of Hanover liked the reports he read of the speech – he must have found cultural democracy a less alarming prospect than political. The success of this evening was really the climax of Smythe's career. He wrote later to his father: 'In '44 ... I wrote and spoke with some success; I made a great hit at Manchester and I lived a happy season with you because you understood my objects ...'. Similarly he expressed his gratitude to Disraeli, early in 1846:

I never shall forget how you found me low, abased in my own esteem and that of others, morbidly doubting my own powers and how you made a man of me ... and set me on my legs at Manchester, and have ever been to me the kindest and gentlest of counsellors.

Newspapers had their predictable reactions. The *Morning Chronicle* found the speeches uniformly good, 'but that of Mr Smythe as one of the most influential and clever of the party called "Young England" deserves special attention'. The *Chronicle* was particularly pleased with him for vindicating the importance of journalists. Its overall verdict on the movement was:

With all this conceit, *Coningsby*ism, and silly stuff about the 'pure Caucasian breed', we think that Young England has done and is doing no little service, and may yet accomplish, under better guidance and better direction, vastly more.

The *Morning Herald* urged the movement to reduce its 'opinions' to a comprehensible system, but grudgingly admitted that games and sports could be a valuable political medicine. However, 'because highly-coloured tradition tells us of a happy peasantry under the regime of priestcraft', that was no reason for saddling us again with the 'corporations of bachelors' (monasteries). The *Herald* reassured itself and its readers that 'the mouthing of "Young England", even at a gala *soirée* at Manchester, is as harmless as the pipes of the Strephons, with whom one of its young members would cover the grass-grown ruins of that important town'.

Harmless, but seductive – at least to a certain type of religious person with a social conscience. An anonymous Tract in the British Library, written at the end of 1844 and entitled *Regeneration Social, Moral and Spiritual,* had to borrow Carlyle's style to express its enthusiasm:

> Numberless 'Athenaeums', 'Athenic Institutes' and the like – with their books and tracts – are loudly cried for these days, to stem the torrent of licentiousness which foams over the framework of society. Honor to ye 'Young England' – Honor to Manchester! that with brave effort and noble aim – ye stand out there to fight for Education and to give the people 'Bread of Life' instead of this horrible Bread of Death.

From Manchester Disraeli and Manners went on to Bingley, where they stayed with the Ferrands. Mrs Ferrand had appropriated some acres for field-garden allotments and had also promoted the establishment of a cricket club. So there was, naturally, a dinner, presided over by her husband. Manners, replying to a toast of the agricultural interest, said that large farms ought not to swallow up all the smaller ones; the peasant with some land of his own was 'likely to be a better man, a better citizen, and a better member of society, than he who merely works for another'. Allotments could help towards this; they would also provide agricultural training, increase sobriety and promote food production:

> That estrangement ... which unfortunately has undoubtedly taken place between the various classes of society, where your good example is followed will give place to cordial sympathy, to the performance of duties and responsibilities on the part of the rich, and to contentment and loyalty on the part of their less fortunate fellow-countrymen.

Disraeli's speech was not so much a political address as a sermon, preached on the text that 'society, like man, has a heart';

> We are on the eve of a great change, which will bring back some of those old feelings, some of those ancient hereditary sentiments of loyalty and good faith and mutual trust, that once made England great, and which, in my opinion, alone can keep England great.

The essence of Young England is in these two revivalist speeches. They could be, and were, criticized for their practical vagueness; but they struck a precise emotional chord.

After these meetings Manners paid a pilgrimage to the Lake District, where he visited Wordsworth: 'I had the great satisfaction of receiving his thanks for my public conduct, the reward I most covet.' But, in spite of this laurel wreath, a note of doubt is detectable in Manners's letters to Disraeli at this time. On 24 October he takes it that 'some of the gentry are not best pleased with our movement'. On 4 November he remarks: 'There are at least half a dozen "Young England" newspapers and magazines bursting the shell; poor proprietors.' On 17 November he feels he should concert with Disraeli and Smythe over an invitation to a Young England dinner at Wakefield. His father does not like him taking part in political meetings out of his 'own district and sphere'. Besides, it looks like 'popularity-hunting', and setting up as 'a distinct political party, which he is against.

So the year seems to end with Smythe in an expansive, and Manners in a rather recessive, mood, with paternal pressure relaxing on the one and increasing on the other. The Wakefield invitation was presumably declined, as was an invitation to address the Manchester Operatives' Conservative Association the following March. Manners told them he was otherwise engaged, adding that 'Conservatism' was not enough; there was a need for 'more distinctive principles and more decided acts'. He ended with 'a hearty wish that old Tory principles and sympathies may once more strike a deep root into English soil'.

Meanwhile Cochrane had also been making news. This was at Bridport, his constituency, on 13 November. He defended his 'sense of honourable opposition' and represented himself as an unflinching advocate of Protection: 'I consider the repeal of the Corn Laws will be the forerunner of a revolution.' He painted a dramatic picture of poverty, misery and neglect in the industrial centres. The reforms to insist on were 'ventilation, drainage, supplies of pure water and improved buildings', rather than 'scientific literature for the poor, or warm baths and washing establishments'. The allotment system, national education and the abolition of the New Poor Law were excellent objectives in their way; but the central need was to put some check on machinery and to assess it more highly to the poor rates: 'The surest pledge of the stability of our commerce – of our greatness – is to protect the poor man, who is the humble instrument of our greatness.' Several toasts followed 'and the harmony of the evening was kept up by some excellent songs by Captain Steele until about 10 o'clock'.

The *Morning Herald* could hardly contain itself. Apparently drawing on Lockhart's letter to Croker, it exclaimed:

> One would really suppose from such flights of absurdity that Mr. COCHRANE, like his friend Mr. PETER BORTH-WICK, was stage-struck and accustomed to enact tragedy heroes at some of the minor play-houses. Rant of this sort is, happily for commonsense, confined to *Young England*; and even amongst those 'exquisites', Mr. COCH-RANE is its DEMOSTHENES – its first fiddle.

Cochrane wrote to the *Herald* on 19 November complaining that it had used 'partial and garbled' extracts from his speech. The *Herald* commented that there were no London reporters present and that the matter was now too stale for it to publish a full version.

Cochrane seems to have deployed at Bridport the *sanitas sanitatum* theme, which Disraeli was to develop, as a major concern of Conservative policy, several years later. With typical gusto, Cochrane had preferred it to other measures of social reform, including some dear to Manners's heart. Manners, who perhaps had had access only to 'partial and garbled' extracts, found what Cochrane was reported to have said unhelpful, but took it with his usual good nature. He wrote to Disraeli: 'I see Cochrane has been throwing cold water on our fires; the dog – '. Yet this was perhaps – so soon after Young England's finest hour – another small nail in its coffin.

These private symptoms of doubt and disagreement did not prevent the shell-bursting, on 4 January 1845, of a weekly newspaper, called *Young England, the Social Condition of the Empire*. (There are fourteen numbers of this, up until early April 1845, in the British Library collection.) It aimed to provide a wide, and professional, coverage of news, as well as comment on Young England's various themes. Its tone was radical and practical; it suggested a whole range of topics for reform – the condition of the manufacturing population, sanitary regulations, the exchange rate, Ireland, colonial emigration, crime prevention, taxation (more direct and less indirect), Church government, the pew system, facilities for manly sports, Mortmain, the window tax, the game laws, baths for the labouring classes, etc. While respectfully following the lead of the movement's leaders in Parliament and, like them, calling for the 'sympathetic union of all classes', the weekly was a good deal less restoratist in tone. It was dedicated to a new future and spurned the 'extinct system of tyranny and intolerance usually denominated Toryism'.

It would not be surprising if the Young Englanders in Parliament began to wonder whether they had started a process that was going to be increasingly difficult to control.

Autumn

Just as Young England was never formally set up, so it was never formally disbanded. It could almost be represented as having a shadowy existence, until Peel's fall, in June 1846. At that time Disraeli and Manners, together with a majority of those who had been Young England associates, were still opposing Peel from within the Conservative Party. On the day of his triumph Disraeli wrote to his wife from the Carlton Club: 'The Ministry have resigned. All *Coningsby* and "Young England" the general exclamation here.'

But of course it was not Young England that in the end defeated Peel. It was the majority of Protectionist Conservatives, who either voted against Peel or abstained – ostensibly on the Irish Coercion Bill, but actually as a protest against the policy of repealing the Corn Laws. This latter was a question that split the Young Englanders, as well as the larger party to which they belonged. Years later Cochrane held that the Corn Laws had caused 'the first difference of opinion in the Young England party'. This is not strictly true; there had been other, less important, differences since the outset. But Young

England had been able to survive those differences. The Corn Laws crisis, which cast its shadows well ahead, was another matter. It mattered enough to divide the whole Conservative Party. Young England could have continued to play an effective role within that party only by taking a firm stand on one side of the dispute or the other. Since two of the four 'esoterics' in the end supported Peel's Corn Laws policy, and two opposed it, this was clearly impossible.

When the members of the Carlton Club gave '*Coningsby* and "Young England" ' the credit for Peel's defeat, they must have been primarily congratulating Young England's leader on having done more than anybody else to bring the Prime Minister down. They cannot have meant that Young England as a whole was still a force to be reckoned with and that it was this force that had dislodged Peel. But they could also have had in mind that Disraeli's earlier attacks on the Government had been mounted under Young England cover and that, without this process of sabotage over three years, it was improbable that sufficient numbers of Conservative Members would have withheld their support from Peel when the decisive moment arrived. In this sense not only Disraeli, but Young England as a whole, can take the praise – or the blame – for Peel's resignation. 'The "boys" beat him at last,' says Coningsby in *Tancred*, referring at once to Sir Robert Walpole and Sir Robert Peel.

Young England had in fact ceased to operate effectively some time before the 1846 Parliamentary session. It had started 1845 rather hesitantly, as if a little afraid of the genies it had conjured up. Very little happened during that session to boost the solidarity or the reputation of the group as a whole. There were differences of view within the group, one of them on an Irish/religious topic that was important to them. In the individual contributions of its three younger members there was an evident lack of fresh ideas. Nevertheless, nothing happened in 1845 to make the collapse of the group inevitable; there is some evidence that, at the end of the year, Disraeli was still hoping to do something with it during the 1846 session. If so, he was prevented by events beyond his control. For all practical purposes Young England was moribund throughout 1845 and a spent force by the end of January 1846.

Almost the only instance of concerted action by the group, during the 1845 session, was on 20–21 February, when the Post Office was charged with having opened letters under a Home Office warrant. (The original letters were Mazzini's; but a Radical MP claimed that his letters had had the same treatment.) Disraeli, Manners, Ferrand and Milnes all spoke in favour of setting up a Select Committee of Inquiry. A week later, in a follow-up to this exchange, Disraeli made his famous speech about Peel having walked away with the Whigs' clothes while they were bathing. It culminated in a masterly personal attack on Peel, who had been incautious enough (given his own supposed past treatment of Canning) to quote against Disraeli some lines of Canning on the perils of having a candid friend. 'The theme, the poet, the speaker,' exclaimed Disraeli to loud and prolonged applause, 'what a felicitous combination!' George Smythe was as excited as anybody; he wrote to Mrs Disraeli: 'It would have made you cry with delight to have heard the thunders of cheering.'

Even on this affair, however, Young England was not united, since Cochrane, Borthwick and H. Baillie all voted for the Government. Cochrane made a brief speech to explain why; otherwise he seems to have been rather uncharacteristically subdued throughout this session – apart from occasional remarks about Greece. He always had, personally, a considerable admiration for Peel and he may have been made uncomfortable by Disraeli's continued attacks on the Prime Minister. In the middle of March, Disraeli launched another bolt at Peel in support of a county Member's proposal to afford relief to the agricultural interest. In a superbly comic passage he accused Peel of abandoning his first love, 'the great agricultural interest'; he also took the opportunity of 'expressing thus publicly my belief that a Conservative Government is an organized hypocrisy'. This time Smythe parted company with Disraeli, though without any personal rupture. He spoke briefly to the effect that he would differ from Disraeli in his vote, but that he would stand by him (Disraeli) against any attempts to tar him with inconsistency. Smythe's own stand was of course consistent with his steady refusal to put the agricultural interest automatically first. Borthwick, Milnes and H. Baillie voted with Smythe and Peel; Manners, Ferrand and Stafford O'Brien with Disraeli.

Meanwhile Manners continued to speak regularly and predictably throughout the session. On 6 February he discussed agricultural protection, though not as a violent partisan: 'We are all too much disposed in this House to look upon ourselves as agricultural or manufacturing Members, and too little disposed to take into consideration the more important question of rich and poor in this country . . .'. On 4 March and 9 April he brought up allotments again; on 6 March he spoke about art museums and on 5 June he resuscitated Don Carlos. At the end of May he opposed the Government's policy on academical institutions in Ireland: 'I think the Government would make a very bad exchange of a faithful and believing people for those who possessed a mere mass of secular learning.' *The Times*, in commenting on the second reading of this Irish Colleges Bill, referred to Manners's 'characteristic straightforwardness'.

For Young England the most divisive question of the session was the Government's proposal to convert an annual grant of £9000 to Maynooth, the Irish seminary for Roman Catholic priests, into a permanent endowment of £30,000 a year. In the vote on this proposal on 18 April Smythe, Manners and Milnes supported the Government, while Disraeli, Ferrand, Stafford O'Brien, Bateson and Q. Dick opposed them; Disraeli spoke on the one side; Smythe and Manners on the other. Manners recalled that in 1843 he had been one of the few Tory Members who had thought there was scope for some remedial action. Smythe made a particularly fine speech; he had shared Manners's opinion in 1843: 'Unfortunately my watch was upon this, as upon other occasions, five minutes too fast.' In spite of his own feeling for France he warned the House that, if the *entente cordiale* were ever to fail, the nation would not be secure without an *entente* with the Irish people. He displeased his father by supporting Peel over Maynooth, as he had displeased him by opposing the Government on other matters. Peel himself was delighted; he congratulated Smythe and forecast great things for his future. Nobody could have foretold that it was almost the last time Smythe would address the House, except on foreign affairs.

Disraeli later said that it was his own opposition to the Maynooth Bill that had broken up Young England. This may have seemed true in retrospect; it may even have been part of his feeling at the time. But, if Young England had still had real life in it, it could have lived down this difference on a question of religious conscience, as it had lived down earlier differences. In one sense the movement was already finished, in that it had either to advance or to recede and – at least for the time being – seemed incapable of advancing. In another sense it was still in being, if dormant, and would remain so as long as its four leaders kept together, and sometimes acted together, in Parliament. It was not Disraeli who prevented their doing so; he would surely have preferred to keep them with him, if he could. When this proved impossible, it was natural enough that he should choose to remember, and wish others to suppose, that it was he himself who had broken up the movement. Some years later, he recorded in a memorandum:

> ... between 1844 and 1847 when *Tancred* was published (*Sybil* in 1845, and *Tancred* was intended for 1846 – but the publication postponed in consequence of the great Corn Law Repeal) much had happened in my position: the Young England myth had evaporated, and I had

149

become, if not the recognized leader, at least the most influential organ, of a powerful parliamentary party . . .

Young England, having expired, had to be regarded as a myth – and one that he himself had dispelled. But it would not have become a 'myth' if it had continued to serve Disraeli's purpose. And, even if that were all that it was, the man who dispelled it was Smythe.

Sybil came out in May 1845. It might have been expected to re-animate the movement. But, though it was full of Young England's ideas, it did not specifically ascribe them to Young England characters. The hero was some years older than Coningsby and there was no mention in the book of Young England as such; it was not until *Tancred* that the *Coningsby* characters reappeared. In *Coningsby* Disraeli had figured – slightly off-stage – as Sidonia, only a mentor (though a very influential one) of the young men who took the limelight. In *Sybil*, although he has no particular role to play in the cast, he seems to come forward and occupy the centre of the stage himself.

Newman was received into the Roman Catholic Church in early October 1845; Faber followed him a few weeks later. Manners must have foreseen, and feared, these conversions several months beforehand, perhaps even as early as 1843. An anonymous pamphlet published in 1872 (*Lord John Manners, A Political and Literary Sketch, comprising some account of the Young England Party and the Passing of the Factory Acts. By a Non-Elector*) ascribed the breakup of the Young England party to the effect of the conversions on the Tractarian movement. According to *The Times* obituary of Manners, 'the High Church party were cast into temporary gloom by the secession of Dr. Newman and his friends to Rome': they could no longer look to an ecclesiastical revival for the regeneration of the country. This gloom would be easy to imagine, even if the mutual dependence of Young England and Tractarianism had not been underlined in Faber's *Grounds for Remaining in the Anglican Communion.* For Manners personally the conversions were a bitter cup to drink; they must certainly have deepened the depression that he would in any case have felt about the Corn Law controversy. Believing that both sides attached an exaggerated importance to repeal, he even had thoughts of retiring from the House of Commons in the winter of 1845. Stafford O'Brien, a convinced Protectionist, had to urge him (in a letter of 21 December) to stay firm by the cause: 'Do not be the Peel of Young England.' In the end it may have been his disapproval of Peel's conduct, as much as anything, that kept Manners by Disraeli's side. As he wrote to Lyttelton, in January 1846:

I think Sir Robert Peel is corrupting the intellect and ambition of the country, and unless checked in time will at his death or decay hand over the management of Church and State to political eunuchs.

Manners was not the only member of Young England to feel Newman's and Faber's secessions as a severe blow. Disraeli himself wrote, in his General Preface to the collected edition of his novels (1870):

The writer and those who acted with him looked, then, upon the Anglican Church as the main machinery by which these results might be realized. There were few great things left in England, and the Church was one. Nor do I now doubt that if, a quarter of a century ago, there had arisen a Churchman equal to the occasion, the position of ecclesiastical affairs in this country would have been very different from that which they now occupy. But these great matters fell into the hands of monks and schoolmen; and little more than a year after the publication of CONINGSBY, the secession of DR. NEWMAN dealt a blow to the Church of England under which it still reels. That extraordinary event has been

151

'apologized' for, but has never been explained. It was a mistake and a misfortune. The tradition of the Anglican Church was powerful. Resting on the Church of Jerusalem, modified by the divine school of Galilee, it would have found that rock of truth which Providence, by the instrumentality of the Semitic race, had promised to St Peter. Instead of that, the seceders sought refuge in medieval superstitions, which are generally only the embodiments of pagan ceremonies and creeds.

Much earlier, in his 1849 Preface to the fifth edition of *Coningsby*, Disraeli had used similar terms to emphasize the Church's importance in Young England's programme:

> In considering the Tory scheme, the author recognized in the CHURCH the most powerful agent in the previous development of England, and the most efficient means of that renovation of the national spirit at which he aimed.

Even Smythe, although no longer a convinced Christian, must have felt that the secessions had made Young England's position less tenable. In the latter part of 1845 he was plunged in love affairs, and/or dissipations, at Paris and Venice. He had also embarked on the writing of *Angela Pisani*. For months he had no contact with Disraeli, who wrote to Manners from Paris on 17 December:

> As I see you are at Melton, furiously hunting, this will reach you. Where is G.S.? I have not heard from him for months, and expected to find him here in vain. Has he gone on to Stamboul? If not, and in England, I wish you would send him a line and beg him to write to me, or come over.

It sounds very much as if, late in December, Disraeli still regarded Smythe as a Parliamentary ally, with whom he wanted to confer before the 1846 session. He did not, however, hear from Smythe until the middle of January, when he got a letter from him breaking the news that he had had an offer from Aberdeen (the Foreign Secretary) and that, succumbing to parental pressure, he meant to accept it. Smythe evidently realized, and nervously regretted, the pain that his becoming a Peelite would give to Disraeli – though he wrote to his father that the 'same boat' could no longer hold them both. The offer was to become a Junior Minister (Under Secretary of State) in the Foreign Office.

Smythe needed to please his father; he also needed a salary. He realized that he was committing himself to supporting a policy of Corn Law Repeal; but, though he saw disadvantages in this, he was not in principle opposed to it. Perhaps he really had had enough, for the time being, of Disraeli's guidance. He probably felt that it would harm his career if he were to turn down his first offer of a Ministerial post. In any case it must have seemed to him that, given the secessions to Rome and the approaching Corn Law crisis, there was little prospect that Young England could be effectively revived. So it is not surprising that he accepted Aberdeen's offer. Yet it turned out to be his biggest mistake. He was not a great success as a Junior Minister; Gregory said that 'he paid no attention to his work, and was thought very little of at the Foreign Office'. In any case in a few months' time he and the other Peelites had to go into opposition. If he had stayed with Disraeli he would still have been in opposition, but more enjoyably and brilliantly and (as it turned out) with rather better prospects for the future. He probably realized all this soon enough; he had certainly realized it by 1852, when the Conservatives were briefly in power again.

That Disraeli deeply resented Smythe's decision seems clear from what Smythe wrote to him in July 1852:

Well might I have faith in your star.
For since it has ceased to shine on my fate, since I

severed our destiny, I have eaten my heart away in utter indigence of action – the result of a humiliation – which you did all things – and you alone successfully – to make me feel.

But I was more loyal to you, in the M. Chronicle and otherwise, than you think.

Parliament met on 22 January 1846. Soon afterwards Cochrane revealed that he, too, had become a Peelite. On 9 February he said that no sacred principle was involved in the Corn Laws, denied that Parliament ought to appeal to the People on the question and defended Peel's change of stance as a result of changed circumstances. Making one of Smythe's favourite points he said that great Ministers (Pitt, Huskisson, Canning) had favoured Free Trade. He ended with an ingenious, if not wholly convincing, attempt to square what he was now saying with what he had said before:

I vote for this measure, because I prefer legislation to agitation; moreover, because I am a sincere advocate for protection . . . not to one . . . but . . . to all classes.

It is difficult to be certain what made Cochrane change his mind about the Corn Laws. Smythe's example must have had some effect on him; the dedication to *Ernest Vane* suggests that Cochrane was still idolizing him in 1849. But he was also inclined to idolize Peel. He wrote in *In the Days of the Dandies:*

Those of our party who cared for men rather than measures resolved to consult the great man himself . . . if we were nervous, Sir Robert Peel was much more so . . . Still, when once he began to explain the position, no words could be heartier, no expression of feeling nobler.

During the next couple of months Cochrane confined himself to questions about Scottish entailed property and Greece.

Soon he was no longer in a position to ask any questions at all. In his Dorset constituency, Bridport, the Liberals were normally in a majority. Henry Baillie, Smythe's brother-in-law, had stood, but failed, as a Conservative in 1837. Cochrane did better than him in 1841, but would not have got into Parliament if the senior of the two Liberal Members had not accepted the Chiltern Hundreds. In May 1842 there was a debate in the House on the Bridport elections; Peel himself intervened with a long speech; Smythe, Manners, Ferrand and Stafford O'Brien supported Cochrane in opposing the setting up of a Committee of Inquiry. In spite of these agitations, Cochrane managed to keep his seat until March 1846, when he in his turn felt obliged to accept the Chiltern Hundreds. He was re-elected, by one vote; but there was a petition against this and he was declared unduly elected on 27 April. Accused of bribing voters (a frequent enough occurrence in the years following the 1832 Reform Bill), he complained in the House on 25 April of having 'been left most unusually in the dark about the complaints'.

Cochrane stayed out of Parliament from the end of April 1846 until the General Elections of July–August 1847, when he came top of the poll – nine votes ahead of the more successful of the two Liberal candidates. Thus, by May 1846, of the four founders of Young England, one had become a Junior Minister, one had lost his seat and the third (Disraeli) was completely absorbed in his struggle with Peel. Manners alone was left flying, a little limply, the flag of Young England ideals.

Young England wanted both to maintain the landed hierarchy and to bring relief to the industrial masses; its ideals were almost equally compatible with the maintenance of the Corn Laws and with their total or partial repeal. So at least thought Manners, though he was more of a Protectionist than not. But the group had a bias towards tradition and most of its MPs were more definitely on the side of Protection. During the 1846 session there were three important votes on Peel's measures. On 27 February Smythe, Milnes and H. Baillie voted for Peel's commercial policy, while Disraeli, Manners, Borthwick, Ferrand, Stafford O'Brien, Beresford Hope, Q. Dick, T. Bateson and R. Hodgson voted against it. The line-up was the same on 15 May, for the Third Reading of the Corn Importation Bill, except that Baillie was absent and Hodgson and Bateson were paired. On 25 June, when the Corn and Customs Bills finally passed the House of Lords, the Corn Laws were, effectively, repealed. That same evening a large number of revengeful Protectionists with-held their support from Peel on a division in the Commons about the second reading of his Irish Coercion Bill. On this occasion Beresford Hope and Bateson joined Smythe and Baillie in supporting Peel; presumably, although Protection-ists, they felt unable to oppose his Irish policy. Milnes, on the other hand, joined Disraeli, Manners and the rest of their friends (Ferrand and Hodgson were absent). On 29 June Peel announced his resignation; Russell and Pal-merston formed a Government; the Whigs, surviving the General Elections of 1847, held office until 1852.

Soon after Peel's fall Manners, aware that his Newark con-stituents were disturbed by his Maynooth vote, his Anglo-Catholicism and his only moderately Protectionist views, decided that he would not apply for their votes at the next elections. In 1847 he tried for Liverpool; but he was charged with Puseyism and came bottom of the poll. He did not return to the House until 1850 when, with Disraeli's heavy backing, he got a seat for Colchester.

Since Manners was not in the House of Commons at the time that Lord George Bentinck resigned from leadership of the Protectionists there, he had no chance of succeeding him – as he otherwise might well have done. He never showed any regret for this and Disraeli had no more loyal friend. But at one time Disraeli seems to have thought that he might one day find himself Manners's lieutenant, rather than the other way round. At any rate he took time off from finishing

Tancred, in September 1846, to send Manners an oracular message:

> The past is a dream and the future a mystery. I cannot read it, but feel persuaded that, if we only stand together, I shall yet see you Prime Minister.

It was left to the mysterious future to reveal, in its own good time, that, though the pair had stood together, this was to bring Disraeli, not Manners, to the top.

Smythe felt yet more dejected towards the end of 1846, than Manners had done towards the end of 1845. Although he does not seem to have taken much pleasure in routine work at the Foreign Office, he can hardly have relished losing office only a few months after his appointment. In the autumn of 1846, in the midst of the scandal caused by his assumed affair with Lady Dorothy Walpole, he was at a particularly low ebb. Still a young man of 28, he wrote to Manners as if his life and career were over:

> I have only one regret, that I did not die younger. I shall never know half so much, feel half so well, as I was at twenty . . . I am full of vanity, and hope my promise will not be judged by those damnable travesties of my elaborate speeches in Hansard. *The fire is out* – and I never can say what I have done in the pluck of my young earnestness again; and this little, which was good, for it was subjectively (*qua* myself) all true, is most exquisitely ridiculous as it remains . . .

For the next few years, perhaps for the rest of his life, Smythe was to alternate between gaiety and heavy depression. What he said or wrote in his depressed moods was sincere, but it was not the whole of the picture. He overrated his powers – and then, by reaction , he underrated them. The accounts of his speeches in Hansard do not read today like 'damnable travesties', though there is more obvious brilliance in his *obiter dicta*. Yet there is no doubt that they made a more vivid impact then than now. According to *Fraser's Magazine* they inspired delight: 'so pregnant with thought and illustration, so powerful and polished in their language ... passages in them which have not been surpassed by even the most gifted of our parliamentary orators'. The *Magazine* hinted that Smythe's 'capabilities for business' might not be very great; it reported that some people confidently predicted his failure 'when he comes to hard blows'. But it nevertheless concluded, as late as May 1847:

> Unless some strange fatality should intervene to blight his powers, we should be inclined to predict with confidence that he will one day attain a very high eminence ...

Unlike Manners, Smythe found himself back in Parliament, still as Member for Canterbury, after the 1847 elections. At those elections he presented himself once again to his constituents as a true, or 'old', Tory. He argued that support for Corn Law reform was fully consistent with true Toryism, which was not a whining 'for a yesterday' but 'the true party of progress and the people'. Was it not

> a succession of heroic spirits, 'beautiful and swift', ever in the van, and foremost of their age? – Hobbes and Bolingbroke, Hume and Adam Smith, Wyndham and Cobham, Pitt and Grenville, Canning and Huskisson? Are not the principles of Toryism those popular rights which men like Shippen and Hynde Cotton flung in the face of an alien monarch and his mushroom aristocracy – that long line of democratic measures which begin with the Habeas Corpus Act and end with Corn Law repeal? – Are not the traditions of the Tory party the noblest pedigree in the world? Are not its illustrations

that glorious martyrology that opens with the name of Falkland and closes with the name of Canning?

Smythe had already identified himself with Free Trade, Anglo-French understanding and Irish conciliation, in the letter he wrote to his constituents in 1843. He now went on to add secular education for the masses, extension of the franchise and abolition of religious disabilities to his list of true Tory causes.

It is difficult to imagine how the burghers of Canterbury reacted to this stirring vision. Perhaps they were dazzled with eloquence, or perhaps they took it with a pinch of salt. The King of Hanover, with his feet firmly planted on the ground, found it a 'damnably radical' speech. It was a more daring attempt than Cochrane's to reconcile a Peelite present with a Tory past. It was also, in its baroque way, more personally consistent. Smythe had always been determined to combine progress with tradition.

Once returned to Parliament Smythe made little attempt to further any cause, whether progressive or reactionary. Between 1847 and 1850 he spoke, briefly, only on foreign affairs – Cracow, Montevideo, Greece and the *entente cordiale*. He made one big speech, on the Ecclesiastical Titles Assumption Bill, on 24 March 1851. He regarded this, quite rightly, as 'a sham bill ... against a sham aggression'; the Pope had accorded 'certain territorial titles, but no territorial faculties'; in fact Rome's current power was due to her withdrawing herself, bit by bit, 'from State connection and Erastian domination'. His peroration revived the marriage metaphor which had been so successful at Manchester six years before:

She [Rome] has read here in England the first banns of those free nuptials between liberty and faith – between modern liberty and ancient faith, which, in my conscience, I believe in no remote age will yet regenerate the West.

Smythe was in a minority of Peelites, Irish and Radicals in voting against the Bill. Except for Beresford Hope, his former friends voted with the majority. But at least this, his last speech in Parliament, may have given some pleasure to a former friend outside Parliament. If it was read by Faber, now head of the London Oratory, it may have given him some slight hope that an erring sheep might yet be received into the true fold.

Why did Smythe allow his Parliamentary reputation to dwindle in this way? Partly because of laziness and depression. He had always found it an effort and a nervous strain to make a major speech; the more he lost his faith, the more he became attached to his own comfort. But his refusal to play an active role in the Parliament of 1847–52 had deeper roots than that. He must have had increasing doubts about his own suitability for either a Parliamentary of a Ministerial career. Even without these doubts, he must have realized that the division of the Conservative Party did not bode well for his future success. He was critical of his own chief, Peel, and disenthralled with the whole Parliamentary conflict. So he considered whether there was anything else he could do, to earn some money, to make some reputation and to have some influence on the course of events.

He chose journalism – an unusual enough career, for an aristocrat, to appeal to his sense of romance. He persuaded himself that journalists were the creators of ideas and the unacknowledged legislators of the future. The journalistic profession had been coming into prominence, both in France and in England over the last two decades. In Balzac's *La peau de chagrin* (1831) a journalist, Emile, says to the hero that power has been transferred from the Tuileries to the press:

> Le journalisme, vois-tu, c'est la religion des sociétés modernes, et il y a progrès . . . les pontifes ne sont pas tenus de croire, ni le peuple non plus . . .

If he read this passage, which is likely enough, it would have appealed to Smythe's romantic cynicism. In a less cynical mood he might have agreed with Charles Reding, in Newman's novel *Loss and Gain* (1848):

> My father never could endure newspapers – I mean, the system of newspapers; he said it was a new power in the state. I am sure I am not defending, what he was thinking of, the many bad things, the wretched principles, the arrogance, and tyranny of newspaper-writers – but the press comes in, to fill a constitutional gap, since the great body of the people are very imperfectly represented in Parliament.

He himself made a character in *Angela Pisani* remark that, in the English system, it was not really the aristocracy that governed, but the 'journalists who originate and the clerks who administer'. He had said at Manchester in 1844 that he would rather be 'one of the journalists who led than of the statesmen who followed in the path of reforms'.

Deciding to join the originating élite, Smythe began writing regularly for the *Morning Chronicle* not long after the 1847 elections. The *Chronicle* had always been kind to him, even when it had been a Liberal newspaper and he had been a 'Liberal-Conservative'. In any case it was acquired by Lincoln and Herbert 'as an organ of Peelite opinion' in 1848.

Smythe gained something of an international reputation for his articles on foreign affairs; Metternich arranged for a number of his *Chronicle* contributions in 1848 to be translated and published in the German newspapers. Yet before long he seems to have tired of journalism, too. Between 1850 and 1852 he hankered after a revival of Young England. To this end he made tentative moves to renew his political ties with Disraeli, now leader of the Conservatives in the House of Commons, and with Manners. But it was too late. Disraeli no longer needed Young England, while Manners, newly married to Miss Marley, was steeped in domestic bliss.

4

A Faith at Last

When *Coningsby* was published, in May 1844, the reaction of
Young England's inner circle was ecstatic. For a young man to
have his character portrayed – and still more his views
expounded and improved – by a sympathetic and very clever
writer, is a rare, and must be an exhilarating, experience.
Disraeli reported Hope as 'enchanted ... Cochrane raving:
Manners full of wild rapture'. Smythe wrote, while still under
the book's spell, in a riot of enthusiasm:

> Dear Diz,
>
> I have just finished it. What can I say, or write, or
> think? I am so dazzled, bewildered, tipsy with admir-
> ation the most passionate and wild!
>
> I never read anything, thought of anything, felt any-
> thing, believed in anything, before.
>
> Thank God I have a faith at last! 'The blessing of all
> the prophets be with you' is the prayer of a disciple more
> enthusiastically devoted than any they ever counted.
>
> Yours ever most affectionately,
G. S. Smythe

It is as a faith, rather than as an intellectual blueprint or a
series of practical measures, that Young England ought to be
judged. During its three years in Parliament, as a 'party
within a party', it was active and enterprising and attracted
much attention. It showed the public that politics could be
viewed and practised in a new kind of way; that the traditional labels of Whig/Tory, or the more modern labels of

Liberal/Conservative, did not cover the whole gamut of political conduct – at least not in the sense in which these labels were currently understood. It helped to create a new sense of *noblesse oblige*, which was to make itself felt, in social as well as in political dealings, for years, and even decades, to come. It would be quite impossible to quantify this influence at any stage. But (to take one small example) every time a Victorian squire gave a party for his tenants or servants he was, directly or indirectly, influenced either by the Young England movement itself or by the currents of opinion which set it afloat.

In terms of positive, identifiable, achievement, the record of the movement seems at first unimpressive. Inside Parliament Young England's activities had little immediate effect, except that of contributing to Peel's fall from, and Disraeli's rise to, power. A detailed study of the years 1842–5 shows that there were very few occcasions on which even the four 'esoterics' were able to present a combined front on matters of substantial importance. Irish policy (other than Maynooth) and the New Poor Law were the only major topics on which the four were completely united. In neither case did Young England manage to do more than exercise a marginal influence on Governmental attitudes.

What the group achieved, or tried to achieve, in Parliament is a measure of its sincerity, but not of its success. To judge this one must take into account the wider impact made outside Parliament as as a result of newspaper reports of its members' views. Yet even this impact would have been limited and ephemeral if it had not been for the brilliant way in which Disraeli marshalled and presented Young England's ideas in his celebrated trilogy (*Coningsby*, *Sybil* and *Tancred*). The success and wide sale of the trilogy, particularly of the two earlier volumes, ensured the propagation of these ideas in those social circles where fashionable books were part of the furniture of life. The effect was no doubt more immediate than lasting; bewildered readers must often have been inclined to mistake froth for liquor and then to pour away the liquor with the froth. But the ideas were so seductively presented, that they cannot have failed to make some impression, especially on the tender young.

In his General Preface to the Novels (1870) Disraeli pays tribute to George Smythe ('a man of brilliant gifts; of dazzling wit, infinite culture, and fascinating manners. His influence over youth was remarkable, and he could promulgate a new faith with graceful enthusiasm') and to Henry Hope ('learned and accomplished ... a penetrating judgement and an inflexible will'). But he contrives to give the impression that Young England's ideas were basically his own:

> I had been some time in Parliament and had friends who had entered public life with myself, and who listened always with interest and sometimes with sympathy to views which I had never ceased to enforce. Living much together, without combination we acted together.

In actual fact, a comparison of what Disraeli said and wrote after he came to know the three Young Englanders, with what he had said and written before, strongly suggests that, although he did indeed already hold some ideas which confirmed theirs, or made them more articulate, there were other ideas which he absorbed from his friends. His chief contribution seems to have been that of an editor, or impresario, rather than a creator. *Fraser's Magazine* put it very accurately, in February 1847:

> He [Disraeli] certainly imparted vigour and coherency to the significant, but uncombined speculations and desires of that band of original thinkers who were so much ridiculed as the Young England party ...

How far were the three Young Englanders themselves 'original thinkers'? Their 'speculations and desires' were not of course wholly peculiar to themselves. They developed them because they were young, earnest and imaginative and were not content with the commonplaces of the time. This personal bias made them ready recipients of new (or old) ideas already stirring in some more or less original minds in reaction to events in the world at large. New ideas seem to spread most easily in two different circumstances – either in the face of outworn systems, no longer capable of satisfying modern needs; or when some process of thought or behaviour has been carried to an intolerable extreme and a reaction becomes inevitable. The French Revolution occurred in the first of these circumstances; the movement of reaction that followed it was a type of the second.

Young England could be viewed as a provincial offshoot of the early nineteenth-century movement that strengthened ecclesiastical and social hierarchies throughout Europe against revolutionary excess. The Young Englanders reacted against the abuse, or the illusion, of equality and democracy, by opting for an interdependent feudal society run on supposedly traditional lines. In doing so they were not simply opposing revolution; they were also opposing the rational, enlightened, doctrines of writers like Voltaire, who had created the mental climate in which revolution became possible. They were Romantic, rather than Classical, in that they put Imagination before Reason; but theirs was a type of Romanticism that subjected the individual to historical and religious restraints. They were of course also reacting against the ugly side of industrialism, and the misery that unchecked capitalism seemed to cause. But their solution lay in a restoration of stability, order and contentment – not in an advance to some new, liberated world.

The ideas that the Young Englanders absorbed were part of a tide that was bound to flow after the bloodshed and tyranny/anarchy of the French Revolution had shocked moderate-minded people everywhere. It was the 1789 Revolution, or the prospect of future revolutions, that gave these ideas their emotional urgency. But the Young England doctrine was anti-rational as well as anti-revolutionary. It was an affirmation that human reason was not enough to ensure happiness and virtue; that the world needed the discipline of graded society; that even non-revolutionary, rational theories – like utilitarianism – were callous and inadequate guides for the government of men.

People who thought on these lines were likely to look to the past for reassurance and guidance. The young, idealistic Tory of the 1830s and 1840s could find encouragement in Canning's liberal Toryism in the 1820s, or in the reforming years of the younger Pitt before the nation became immersed in the struggle with France. The earlier part of the eighteenth century was (for this young Tory) a dreary waste of corrupt Whig rule. But he could go back to the colourful Stuarts and particularly to Bolingbroke, their last talented servant; the Stuarts, at their best, had had a paternal concern for their people and for the welfare of the Church. The Tudors were more suspect, because they had brought about the dissolution of the monasteries and the break with Rome. For real inspiration it was necessary to go back before these sad events: to the Middle Ages, mysterious, unfamiliar, but thought to have been merry and known to have been devout.

The past had to be approached through teachers or through books. By their own admission, or by obvious inference, the Young Englanders were influenced by a number of past and recent writers. But they were also influenced by teachers at Eton, as well as by Faber and other Oxford Apostles whom they met as undergraduates. In *Coningsby* Disraeli characterized Peel's *Tamworth Manifesto* (1834) as 'an attempt to construct a party without principles'. At Eton, he said, there was a general feeling in 1835 in favour of Conservative principles, but doubt as to what these should be was already reaching the school from the universities. These inquiries

> were whispered in conversation by a few. A tutor would speak of them in an esoteric vein to a favourite pupil, in

whose abilities he had confidence, and whose future position in life would afford him the opportunity of influencing opinion.

Ought we to recognize in the Revd W. G. Cookesley (1802–1880), Smythe's Tutor, himself educated at Eton and King's (we last met him enjoying *Angela Pisani* in his old age), one of the godfathers of the Young England movement?

Its Prophets

All three Young Englanders, of course, had been brought up on the Greek and Latin classics. Mr Cookesley was a distinguished classical scholar, who published selections from Greek and Latin poets, as well as maps of ancient Athens and Rome. Readings and teachings from Plato and Aristotle, or lessons drawn from the history of the Greek city states, would have given all three their first ideas of political theory, of the relative advantages of monarchy, oligarchy and democracy. The manner, if not the matter, of what Smythe wrote to Manners in April 1842 is entirely classical:

> I believe the government of the One is for the good of the many, the government of the Few for the good of themselves, the government of the Many for the good of the One. From Monarchy results the Commonwealth. From oligarchy – oligarchy, from democracy – a tyranny.

Non-British writers of the early nineteenth-century ecclesiastical reaction must have had their influence on Faber and, through him, on Manners. Faber prefaced his first volume of poems with a quotation from Joseph de Maistre. Manzoni's *I Promessi Sposi* (1825–7) was a favourite novel, with its picture of the Church providing guidance and compassion at a time of social unrest. In *Endymion* Waldershare became 'passionately addicted to French literature'. Presumably this was also true of Smythe, on whom Waldershare was closely modelled. But French literature was not responsible for Smythe's Young England views; these were derived from native sources.

The novels of Walter Scott had brought the Middle Ages before the imagination of the general reader. It is almost impossible to exaggerate the effect of these works, which conferred a sort of rough nobility on every period they evoked. We have seen how Manners went to the Queen's Fancy Dress Ball as a character from *The Talisman*. Newman, in his *Apologia*, writing about the reaction against 'the dry and superficial character of the religious teaching and the literature of the last generation', did not disdain to notice Scott's impact: he 'turned men's minds in the direction of the Middle Ages'.

The imagination once roused, there was a need for more or less accurate information. According to his biographer, Manners, at the age of 16, was looking into Henry Hallam's *View of the State of Europe during the Middle Ages*. This celebrated history, which first came out in 1818, had a sixth edition in 1834. Hallam was a Whig and disapproved of monasteries, denying that they did for the poor what was later done by the Poor Laws; Southey attacked his anti-Tory and anti-Church tone in the *Quarterly Review* for January 1828, describing his *Constitutional History* as the production of a decided partisan. But even Hallam admitted that the monks were 'protectors of the oppressed' and made some effort to relieve indigence. He believed that 'the labouring classes, especially those engaged in agriculture, were better provided with the means of subsistence in the reign of Edward III, or of Henry VI, than they are at present'. He also saw in chivalry a 'great source of human improvement' and appeared almost to regret the decay in the spirit of gentlemanliness since the late seventeenth century. All this was grist to Young England's mill.

Manners, a member of the Camden Society since his Cambridge days, must have met antiquarians at its meetings. A distinguished antiquarian, Sir Francis Palgrave, Deputy Keeper of the Public Records, was described by the *Morning Herald* in November 1844 as Young England's tutor in matter of Mortmain. His book *The Merchant and the Friar* (1837) was praised in Faber's *Sights and Thoughts* as Sir Francis Palgrave's 'delightful volume on the Middle Ages'. Like Hallam, Palgrave did not simply preach what Young England wanted to hear: he thought that restoration was impossible ('the King never gets his own again') and that visions of perfection were always delusions, even when supplied by the past. However, he admired much in the Middle Ages that Faber must also have admired: the unity of Christendom; the value of the apprenticeship system, which 'rendered the Master and the Servant members of one household and family'; the religious basis of the Guilds; and the penitentiary system of punishment for the clergy. Looking towards his own times Palgrave regarded the continued existence of the clergy as 'a tribute which the powers of this world are compelled, however unwillingly, to render to an authority beyond the world's control', while the Anglican Church was 'the democratic leaven of our balanced monarchy. The dignified Ecclesiastics of the Church of England were, during the Middle Ages, always the best, and not unfrequently the only advocates of the poorest, and, therefore, the most defenceless classes.'

Another well-known antiquarian, Sir Samuel Rush Meyrick, may have been in Thomas Love Peacock's mind when he wrote *Crotchet Castle* (1831). Meyrick, who was knighted by George IV for arranging the arms and armour at Windsor Castle, himself accumulated a magnificent collection. He was born in 1783 and died in 1848. Among other scholarly works, he published in 1824 three quarto volumes of a *Critical Enquiry* into armour from the Norman Conquest to the reign of Charles II.

In *Crotchet Castle*, one of the more sympathetic characters is 'a good-looking young gentleman' called Mr Chainmail 'with very antiquated tastes'. Lady Clarinda describes him as

> fond of old poetry, and . . . something of a poet himself. He is deep in monkish literature and holds that the best state of society was that of the twelfth century, when nothing was going forward but fighting, feasting, and praying, which he says are the three great purposes for which man was made.

Mr Chainmail, unlike the 'march of mind' Mr MacQuedy, finds that Scott has misrepresented the twelfth century by making it worse than it actually was. The people then had their beef and ale:

> They were not, and could not be, subjected to that powerful pressure of all the other classes of society, combined by gunpowder, steam and *fiscality*, which has brought them to that dismal degradation in which we see them now.

He prefers 'the religious spirit' to 'the commercial spirit' and sees no modern compensation 'for the religious charity of the twelfth century':

> Now we all wear one conventional dress, one conventional face; we have no bond of union, but pecuniary interest; we talk anything that comes uppermost, for talking's sake, and without expecting to be believed; we have no nature, no simplicity, no picturesqueness; everything about us is as artificial and as complicated as our steam-machinery . . .

Mr Chainmail has his hall hung with armour and dines with all his household at two old oak tables. He believes that 'poverty in despair' creates insurrection and that the 'way to

170

keep the people down is kind and liberal usage'; he wants to restore the twelfth century's 'community of kind feelings between master and man'.

Faber, though rather more forward-looking, would have had great sympathy with Mr Chainmail. Peacock portrays the young antiquary as excessive and slightly ridiculous – like all his characters – yet gives the impression that he also feels respect and affection for him. Nearly a decade before the Young Englanders began to make their views known, Mr Chainmail embodies much of what they held dear. He is, as it were, the medieval half of the Young England ideal – without the other half of Stuart sophistication.

Another contemporary author who found inspiration in the Middle Ages and communicated it to a whole generation, was Kenelm Henry Digby (1800–1880), a graduate of Trinity, Cambridge, and an early convert to Roman Catholicism. He wrote much, but his first book was his most famous: *The Broadstone of Honour, or Rules for the Gentlemen of England*. The first edition came out in 1822; an enlarged four-volume edition (respectively entitled *Godefridus*, *Tancredus*, *Morus* and *Orlandus*) appeared in 1826–7; other editions in 1828–9, 1845–8 and 1876–7. It now seems a turgid and unreal work; but, at the time, it struck a vein of high-minded nostalgia that had a widespread appeal. It was 'a history of heroic times, arranged chiefly with a view to convey lessons of surviving and perpetual interest to the generous part of mankind'. It preached reverence for antiquity and a revival of chivalry. Chivalry was not the property of any one class, though the happiness of society required 'the preservation of degree'. Religion was the source of chivalry; both religion and chivalry urged kindness to the poor. There was no need for the young in heart, who 'still lives in the sweet land of poetry, in the grand days of knighthood', to feel that chivalry had had its day: 'The earth is again walked by heroes ... the age of indifference is gone!'

This can give only a slight flavour of what is, after all, a remarkable book, which did much to shape the poetic ideal of the Victorian gentleman. It certainly had a deep effect on the Young Englanders. Ambrose Lisle Phillips, who became Manners's friend, had been on intimate terms with Digby at Cambridge. Disraeli, like Digby, was inspired by Tancred's career; he could well have had Digby's concluding rhapsody in mind when he wrote in *Sybil*: 'We live in an age when to be young and to be indifferent can no longer be synonymous.' Faber, as a young man, had felt the full force of Digby's eloquence, though he later came to believe that the pursuit of chivalry could distract from religious truth. He wrote in *Sights and Thoughts* that Chivalry 'meant well, but the truth is, the Church is sufficient for all these things'. In an obvious allusion to Digby's work, he added: 'The broad stone of honor sank into the earth when it ceased to rest itself against the corner-stone of the Church.'

The Young Englanders belonged to a generation that rediscovered the virtues of the early Stuarts, particularly Charles I. Clarendon's *History of the Rebellion* was one guide to this period. Disraeli's father, Isaac D'Israeli, was another. The elder D'Israeli published in 1816 *An Inquiry into the Literary and Political Character of James I*, which defended the King against Puritan/Whig misrepresentations. He went on to publish in 1830–2, *Commentaries on the Life and Reign of Charles the First*. He did not idealize Charles and claimed to write 'as a philosopher, not as a partisan'; but he nevertheless gave an overall impression of qualified approval; he was certainly critical of Puritan excesses, like the suppression of country 'Wakes and Ales'. The younger D'Israeli, in editing this work at the end of 1850, stressed the relevance of the period to 'the events, the thoughts, the passions and the perplexities of the present agitated epoch . . . when we read of the conversions to the Roman faith then rife, especially among the elevated orders of the community, we seem to be listening to the startling narrative of the hour'. Faber quotes an earlier edition of these *Commentaries* in his *Sights and Thoughts*. It seems likely that this was what he was reading when he wrote to Manners in 1839, a week before taking orders, that he was 'reading D'Israeli when I ought to be reading Bishops and Doctors . . .'. He said: 'I am quite unfit . . . I am all of earth . . . My head and heart are full of love.' Perhaps it was to satisfy Smythe's Stuartomania that he was studying D'Israeli.

Even when his father and grandfather had been rehabilitated, Charles II continued to have a bad name with the Early Victorians, because of the immorality of his Court. But Smythe and Manners at least had a phase of revering James II. As a corollary, they tended to execrate William III. William was a Whig hero; Hallam regarded reverence for his memory as an essential test of Whiggism. Some Tories, like Disraeli, respected him as a great man who 'would not be a Doge'. But, for Manners, he was 'cold Dutch William'. In Newman's *Loss and Gain* Mr Reding says of his religious-minded son Charles:

'I never knew a boy who so placed his likings and dislikings on fancies. He began to eat olives directly he read the Oedipus of Sophocles; and, I verily believe, will soon give up oranges from his dislike to King William.'

'Every one does so,' said Charles: 'Who would not be in the fashion?'

The 'Jacobitism' that tinged the Young Englanders' earliest aspirations was in fact less based on love of the Stuarts themselves than of the idea of Legitimacy (the most absolute antidote to Revolution) and of the virtue required to keep faith with it. This was what Faber meant when he wrote of Young England wishing to 'bring back so much at least of Jacobitism as was generous, lofty-minded and self-devoting'. It was not so much a question of restoring an old royal line as of restoring an attitude of uncalculating devotion.

It is odd that the profligate Bolingbroke should have escaped the censure passed on Charles II; but then his old age, if cantankerous, was decorous enough. It is odder that both Disraeli and Smythe should have taken him, separately, as a prophet, when there is little trace of romantic monarchism in his writings, or of feudal concern for the poor; when he admired Elizabeth, not the early Stuarts; when he took little trouble to hide his own free-thinking Deism. Still, there were points in his favour: he served the Stuarts (including, briefly, the Pretender); he championed the Church party under Queen Anne; much later, he wrote *The Patriot King*. He was, in any case, the most articulate Tory leader of the eighteenth century, and the man who prepared for the Party's return to power by ridding it of outmoded doctrine. Deserved or not, there was a considerable cult of him in the 1820s and 1830s – as early as 1826 there had been a respectful reference to him in Disraeli's first novel, *Vivian Grey*. When Faber was Secretary of the Oxford Union, in 1834, he recorded the thanks of the Society to Mr Yonge of St Mary Hall for a present of Burke's copy of Bolingbroke's works. Disraeli made much of Bolingbroke in his *Vindication of the English Constitution* (1835), though misleadingly. Smythe made much of him, less misleadingly, in his *Historic Fancies*. The central ideas of *The Patriot King* – that *tone* in a monarchy is of great importance, that a monarch ought to be popular and that creation of the right atmosphere can make a good deal in politics possible – were genuinely part of Disraeli's and Smythe's creeds.

Disraeli also had a case for claiming that Bolingbroke had sanctioned a policy of freer trade and of understanding with France. In *Sybil* he summarized 'the Bolingbroke system' as:

> a real royalty in lieu of a chief magistracy; a permanent alliance with France, instead of the Whig scheme of viewing in that power the natural enemy of England and, above all, a plan of commercial freedom . . .

These were three of the five points that Smythe had put to his constituents in 1843, having already made them in his 1841 campaign. None of these points figures in the eulogy in Disraeli's *Vindication* (1835), which is concerned simply with Bolingbroke's party record. Originally a Gallophobe, Disraeli had become Francophile by the winter of 1842; he began representing free trade as a traditionally Tory policy in Parliamentary speeches in May–July 1842. By this time he was beginning to see a lot of Smythe and it is difficult not to conclude that he picked up from him these fresh slants on Bolingbroke's career. He had certainly borrowed a deeper admiration for Charles I by the time he wrote his trilogy; in the *Vindication* he had included Henry VIII, Coke, Pym, the Protector and William III (all anathema to Young England) among the twenty 'wise ancestors, in a political sense, since the Reformation'. In 1856 Disraeli wrote to a new young protégé, Lord Henry Lennox, that he had inherited his views on Anglo-French alliance from Lord Bolingbroke; it is at least a question whether this inheritance did not reach him through Smythe.

It was perhaps a reading of Burke's *Revolution in France*, at the age of 16, that first gave Manners his horror of rebellion. If the Young Englanders went on to read Carlyle's *French Revolution* (1837) they would have found more understanding of the causes of the Revolution, but little reason to feel less horror at the result. Carlyle was not anti-revolutionary, in the way that Newman and Manners were; but he treated revolution as a savage interlude, before the inevitable imposition of fresh order. As usual, Smythe's views were more complex than Manners's. According to one of Disraeli's memoranda, Smythe thought Burke wrong on the French Revolution as on the other two great occasions of his life – India and America. It is easy to see that Smythe would have sympathized with Warren Hastings (who is respectfully introduced into *Angela Pisani*). He could well have wished to maintain a link with the American colonies. But he cannot seriously have thought approval of the French Revolution compatible with his other principles; after all, he looked forward, in one of his poems, to the restoration of Legitimacy in France. Presumably he blamed Burke, not for deprecating the Revolution, but for creating excessive emotional prejudice against it, for surrounding it with enemies and so making it worse. This would accord with a passage in *Sybil*, where Disraeli suggests that Burke had internal motives for his diatribe:

> Burke poured forth the vials of his hoarded vengeance into the agitated heart of Christendom; he stimulated the panic of a world by the wild pictures of his inspired imagination; he dashed to the ground the rival [Fox] who had robbed him of his hard-earned greatness; rent in twain the proud oligarchy that had dared to use and to insult him . . .

The young Wordsworth had greeted the French Revolution with fervour; but, by the time that the Young Englanders were boys, he, Coleridge and Southey were all supporters of Church and State. Here, in the Lake School, were three poets who could be admired with no political, and few religious, scruples. Faber and his friend Roundell Palmer had revelled in the poetry of Wordsworth and Coleridge at Oxford. The young Disraeli, with his usual lack of poetic discrimination, told Lady Charlotte Bertie in an opera box in 1833 that 'he thought Southey the greatest man of the age; he was really a great man . . .' (Lady Charlotte confided to her Journal that it was 'beautiful to hear him talk of Southey'). Newman recognized high principles in Southey and Wordsworth; he thought that Coleridge, in particular, 'installed a higher philosophy into inquiring minds than they had hitherto been accustomed to accept'.

Coleridge's *On the Constitution of the Church and State* was first published in 1830. Politically he must have appealed to Young England by his historical and traditional caste of thought, by his doctrine that property holding conferred obligations as well as rights, and by his disbelief in automatic progress. This last attitude was bound to encourage nostalgia and 'restoratism', though Coleridge himself wished to strike a balance between progressive and conservative forces. He wrote in *The Statesman's Manual* (1816):

> The notion of our measureless superiority in good sense to our ancestors, so general at the commencement of the French Revolution, and for some years before it, is out of fashion . . . among men of influence and property, we now have more reason to apprehend the stupor of despondence, than the extravagancies of hope . . .

Coleridge was susceptible to the mystique of Land: 'Agriculture requires principles essentially different from those of trade . . . a gentleman ought not to regard his estate as a merchant his cargo, or a shopkeeper his stock . . .' He also highly valued the role of the 'Clerisy, or national Church', which he held to have originally 'comprehended the learned of all denominations'.

In some other respects Coleridge's views were out of sympathy with those of the Oxford Movement, which was only beginning to emerge at his death. He was strongly anti-Papal; strongly anti-Stuart (the Commonwealth was 'that narrow interspace of blue sky between the black clouds of the first and second Charles's reigns'); and strongly anti-celibate (the celibacy of the clergy was 'the most efficient of all the means adopted by the Roman pontiffs' to extend their sway). He thought that Henry VIII did right to take the land from the monasteries (to rescue 'the Nationalty' from foreign domination). But the King should not have put it in private hands. It should have been devoted to maintaining schools and universities; keeping 'a pastor and a schoolmaster in every parish'; church and school building; and maintaining 'the infirm poor whether from age or sickness'. Here at any rate was a programme with which Young England could wholeheartedly concur, provided the Church had its full share in it.

Perhaps there is an echo of these ideas in *Coningsby* and *Sybil*.

Southey, who was at one stage much admired by Smythe and Manners, as well as by Disraeli, shared Colderidge's doubts about 'the improvement of the world'. In his *Colloquies* (1829) he made Sir Thomas More query whether 'even in this country there may be more knowledge than there was in former times, and less wisdom . . . more wealth and less happiness . . . more display and less virtue'. And again:

> The root of all your evils is in the sinfulness of the nation. The principle of duty is weakened among you; that of moral obligation is loosened; that of religious obedience is destroyed. Look at the worldliness of all classes . . .

Southey disapproved of Cobbett as an agitator. Yet, although I have found no reference to him in the writings or speeches of Young England, Cobbett seems an even more obvious inspirer of *Coningsby* and *Sybil* than either Southey or Coleridge. His *History of the Protestant Reformation in England and Ireland* (1829) set out to show 'how that event has impoverished the main body of the people'. He argued that it had given them pauperism instead of easy, monastic, landlordism and 'Old English hospitality'. He anticipated the Young Englanders in his dislike of political economy and in his Tory feeling for the past. On one of his rural rides he told his son that Winchester Cathedral 'was made when there were no poor wretches in England, called *paupers*; when there were no *poor-rates*; when every labouring man was clothed in good woollen cloth; and when all had plenty of meat and bread and beer'. This might almost have been Manners speaking, though Manners would not of course have endorsed Cobbett's violent denunciation of the civil and religious authorities of his own day.

Dickens, although reacting to social distress with the same kind of indignation as Cobbett, did not share his love of 'the good old days'. Nevertheless, Faber relished Dickens's novels all his life; their dramatic sentiment and emphatic colouring suited his flamboyant taste. *Oliver Twist* and *Nicholas Nickleby* were both published before 1840 and are likely to have confirmed the Young Englanders in their view of social evils. Oliver Twist is himself a victim of the New Poor Law. Nicholas Nickleby admires the generosity of the Cheeryble brothers, self-made manufacturers: 'Good Lord! and there are scores of people of their own station, knowing all this and twenty times more, who wouldn't ask these men to dinner because they eat with their knives and never went to school!' These were the Grant brothers of Manchester, with whom Dickens had dined and whom Smythe and Manners met on their industrial tour.

But the contemporary writer most concerned with the sort of problems that worried Young England was Carlyle. Of course he had no sympathy with the Tractarians; his style of thought, life and language was completely different from that of Disraeli and his friends. But he shared with them an aristocratic bias – at any rate he wanted a 'real' aristocracy. He despised the 'Aristocracy of the Money-bag'; and he felt deeply that the hungry masses were looking up and not being fed. He was a friend, and regular correspondent, of Richard Monckton Milnes, a member of the Young England social set. There is a quotation from Carlyle in Cochrane's *Lucille Belmont*, while Manners, in his *Notes on an Irish Tour*, refers to Carlyle's 'category of "shams" '. So it appears that the Young Englanders were among his readers. Carlyle himself had mixed feelings about the movement and regarded Disraeli as 'a superlative Hebrew conjurer'. When he was offered a GCB and pension at the end of 1874 (he declined, but was glad to have had the offer) he felt that Disraeli had heaped coals of fire on his head.

Carlyle's *Chartism* was published in 1839. He noted a decay of loyalty and religious faith in the lower classes all over Europe, but 'more painfully and notably in England than elsewhere'. The significance of the French Revolution had been that 'it was a revolt of the oppressed lower classes against the oppressing or neglecting upper classes'. In England the upper class, imbued with *laissez-faire* doctrine, was neglecting, rather than oppressing. This would no longer do: 'The working classes cannot any longer go on without government, without being actually guided and governed.' Democracy could provide no permanent answer. Even at Rome and Athens 'we shall find that it was not by loud voting and debating of many, but by wise insight and ordering of a few that the work was done'. What was needed was to find a *real* aristocracy, that would *really* work. Cash payment had made the old feudal system obsolete; a new nexus was required to bind society together.

In *Past and Present* (1843) Carlyle even indulged in some medieval nostalgia. Drawing on papers published by the Camden Society, he contrasted the current state of things with the condition and rule of a twelfth-century monastery, rather to the advantage of the latter. He admired the *reality* of faith in the twelfth century, the feudal bond between classes, the capacity for hero worship and the *real* governing powers of both aristocracy and priesthood. He had some harsh things to say about current 'Dilettantism', which had produced Puseyite religion and 'a Governing Class who do not govern'. The Corn Laws should be repealed; but land was, nevertheless, the right basis of an Aristocracy. As to Factory Legislation, it was not for him to judge; but it could not be left to the 'lawless anarchy of supply-and-demand'. Above all was the need for a new social structure in which Independence, having properly got rid of his 'sham-superiors', would find his true ones:

> Isolation is the sum-total of wretchedness to man. To be cut off, to be left solitary; to have a world alien, not your world; all a hostile camp for you; not a home at all, of hearts and faces who are yours, whose you are! It

is the frightfullest enchantment; too truly a work of the Evil One.

Democracy was advancing 'irresistible, with ever-increasing speed'; he feared it would 'go its full course'. But the 'Toiling Millions' would find out its inadequacy before long. If not, England would 'cease to exist among nations' and, by worshipping 'ever-new forms of Quackhood, go down to the Father of Quacks'.

These were the two of Carlyle's books most likely to have influenced the Young England movement. Apart from the attack on Puseyism, there is virtually nothing in the two preceding paragraphs that Manners would not have eagerly endorsed. Carlyle placed more value on Independence. He thought that Independence should 'seek out his real superiors', whereas Manners might have advised him to make the best of his present ones. This – though it is certainly a difference – is perhaps in practice a 'sham' difference, rather than a 'real' one.

This brief summary of the movement's 'Prophets' suggests that, though Young England may have been politically eccentric, it was supported by many tendencies in the thought of the time. There were several mentors ready to advise the Young Englanders that previous ages, particularly the medieval and early Stuart eras, had had some advantages over the present. There were others who could warn them – if any warning was needed – of the evils of Revolution. Romantic notions of chivalry were fashionable as a reaction to the drab precepts of political economy; they had been eloquently proclaimed in a recent book addressed to, and with a wide appeal for, the English gentry. The Young Englanders were far from being alone in their distress at the conditions in which many of the poor lived and worked. In their attachment to Church and State they were at one with the chief poets of the previous generation – at least those who had not died young. The leading sage of the time preached ceaselessly that there was need for a governing class that would care for the masses and really govern.

All these influences would have been at work, even if the Oxford Movement had never been launched. But it was the Oxford Movement that covered these undercoats with its distinctive gloss.

Disraeli's Trilogy

By the end of 1841 the three Young Englanders had already assembled the main parts of their creed. Smythe had addressed his Canterbury constituents; Manners had had *England's Trust* published; they had both taken at Ambleside a pledge to embark on a campaign of restoration. It is more doubtful whether Cochrane's views were concerted with those of his friends at this early stage. But, where there is later evidence that he shared their outlook, there is at least a strong possibility that he thought the same way in 1841.

It was not until the spring of 1842 that Smythe and Disraeli began seeing much of each other. Manners had not met Disraeli at all until a dinner party in the spring of 1841; he did not make any political overtures to Disraeli before the session of 1842. Cochrane still regarded Disraeli as a stranger in the autumn of 1842. It follows that, in their essentials, the ideals of Young England were established before Disraeli had had the opportunity to influence them. Of course he had come to some of the same conclusions independently; so had other contemporaries, who confronted similar problems with similar casts of mind. He strengthened the movement, both practically and intellectually; but he was in no way its originator.

Before we look at Disraeli's trilogy it may be helpful to summarize the main principles of the Young Englanders, at the time when they began to launch their movement.

All three agreed that government could not depend simply on Reason, but needed to harness Imagination and Faith.

They disliked Utilitarianism and the dictates of the political economists. They believed that the links between the classes should be closer and kinder, and that society should rest, as the feudal system had rested, on reciprocal obligations. They wanted to use Restoration to avoid Revolution. (Cochrane was probably a less eager restorer than the other two.)

Smythe was convinced, and the other two agreed, that the Crown must be restored to a central place, both in the process of government and in the imaginations of the people. The sovereign would not be bound by the interests of a small class, but would take care of the Many as well as of the Few. (Neither Disraeli nor his friends ever explained how this change was to come about. If they meant it really to be a change – and not just a transformation effect – they must surely have meant that the sovereign, like Bolingbroke's patriot king, would once again choose his own ministers. This in turn would imply that the Crown, relying on its wider popularity, would have to develop a body of support in Parliament. It is ironical that, if the Queen had really been able to choose her own Ministers, Peel would never have fallen.)

All three accepted the need for an aristocracy to serve the crown and lead the people; they were not believers in Equality as such. But the aristocrats must learn to show a proper concern for the welfare of the masses. (Smythe was more inclined than the other two to hanker after a 'real' aristocracy. Similarly he was less attached than them to the landed interest and readier to enthuse about merchant adventurers and manufacturers. This soon appeared in his Liberal attitude towards Protection. Cochrane was a convinced Protectionist until he changed his mind in 1846; Manners took a balanced view.)

Manners strongly advocated, Smythe accepted and Cochrane conceded that the Church – clothed in Tractarian robes – should play a major role in regenerating the nation. (By 1841 Smythe had probably lost most of his own faith, but he may have compared his position in a Church party with that of the free-thinking Bolingbroke over a century before. Cochrane was against 'priestly domination', but had a soft, if rather secret, spot for the old religion.)

They all attached great importance to improving 'the condition of the people'. For Cochrane, reminiscing, this was the main aim of Young England; he described the party's 'great object' as being 'to relieve the working classes from the tyranny of the manufacturers and employers'. (It was certainly a primary object of Manners's, though perhaps a secondary object of Smythe's.) All three wanted to humanize the Poor Laws. Both Cochrane and Manners were prepared to envisage governmental interference in factories; Smythe was more reluctant to disturb market forces. Manners thought the government should facilitate private and ecclesiastical charity to the poor; he also wanted more missionary work done among industrial workers, with the aid of monastic institutions.

These were the main articles of faith, together with the aim (which may not have been explicit in 1841) of conciliation in Ireland. In addition Smythe was already maintaining that Anglo-French alliance and freer trade with the Continent were in the true Tory tradition. Manners must also have been evolving his proposals for social reform – allotments and smaller agricultural holdings; holidays; public amenities; Sunday sports.

It was probably at a rather later stage that Cochrane developed the *sanitas sanitatum* programme, which he expounded at Bridport in November 1844. It may also have taken time for the group to accept the need for greatly increased popular education. At Cambridge both Smythe and Manners had resisted proposals for universal education. But by 1844 the latter was telling the 'hardworking men of Birmingham' that he did not share the view that education was unsuited to the working classes. Manners indeed preferred education with a religious bias; but Smythe was ready to advocate secular education for the masses, as a Tory cause, at

Canterbury in 1847. In *Coningsby* the hero liked to think of an 'educated people', who would be able to control events through the medium of a 'free and intellectual press'.

Faber would have shared all these ideals, though he relied more exclusively on the Church for their realization. It is impossible to judge to what extent he influenced, or originated, the entire Young England body of belief. On the whole it seems likely that, in political matters, he encouraged rather than created – though he may well have helped Smythe and Manners to think through their arguments and present them in a more plausible way. In religious matters, on the other hand, Smythe and Manners would have taken their tone from him. In the practical promotion of the ideas, of course, Faber, unlike Disraeli, had no part to play.

In the General Preface to his Novels, written in 1870, Disraeli noted that the 'general spirit' of his trilogy ran counter to the 'utilitarian' views that had long prevailed in England. The three volumes

> recognized imagination in the government of nations as a quality not less important than reason . . . In asserting the doctrine of race, they were entirely opposed to the equality of man, and similar abstract dogmas . . . Resting on popular sympathies and popular privileges, they hold that no society could be durable unless it was built upon the principles of loyalty and religious reverence.

He also listed the tasks of 'a reconstructed Tory Party', as he saw them at the time of the trilogy:

> to 'change back the oligarchy into a generous aristocracy round a real throne';
>   to 'infuse life and vigour into the Church, as the trainer of the nation';
>   to 'establish a commercial code' on the principles of Bolingbroke and Pitt;

to govern Ireland 'according to the policy of Charles I and not of Oliver Cromwell';

to 'emancipate the political constituency of 1832 from its sectarian bondage and contracted sympathies';

to 'elevate the physical as well as the moral condition of the people, by establishing that labour required regulation as much as property';

'and all this,' he emphasized, 'rather by the use of ancient forms and the restoration of the past than by political revolutions founded on abstract ideas . . .'.

Now, except for the mention of 'race' (which was Disraeli's special interest) and the masterly sentence about the political constituency of 1832 (written after the Second Reform Bill), these objectives are virtually identical with those that the Young Englanders seem to have evolved before they had any connection with Disraeli.

Of course there was a great deal else in the trilogy that was entirely due to Disraeli's own cleverness. The whole work, with its marrying of politics and literature, was, and still is, unique. Disraeli's systematic rewriting of history was a remarkable – and not wholly misleading – *tour de force*. None of his three young friends could have produced work of such brilliance. But it is a mistake to suppose that they got their *ideas* from Disraeli; on the whole the evidence is rather the other way round. When Smythe thanked God, and Disraeli, that he had a faith at last, he meant that he was at last satisfied that his opinions could be made to stand up. Disraeli was not a great creator of ideas, any more than of characters. As Lord Blake has pointed out in his biography, 'The truth is that Disraeli lacked imagination.' He was, however, extremely adept at taking other people's ideas and then deploying them for his own purposes. Similarly he was adept at taking characters for his novels from living men and women.

No doubt the process was often unconscious; no doubt Disraeli came genuinely to believe that he had himself originated ideas that in fact he had absorbed from others. For that matter, such rapid and successful absorption is almost as impressive as creation, particularly when allied with such a formidable ability to make use of the result. But this tendency in Disraeli may help to explain the extraordinary fits of plagiarism in which he now and then – it seems unintentionally – indulged. The classic example is his use of a passage by Thiers in a panegyric he had to deliver on the Duke of Wellington in 1852. He explained this, with obvious sincerity, to Richard Monckton Milnes:

> The passage in question seized upon me, as passages in Mr Burke, for example, which I have not read for a long time. It was engraven on my memory . . . Association of ideas brought it back when musing for a moment, amid the hurry and strife of affairs, over a late solemn occasion, and I summoned it from the caverns of my mind. Unfortunately the spirit was too faithful.

Disraeli's respect for national institutions – including the Throne and the Church – of course ante-dates his acquaintance with Smythe and Manners. His wish to improve the condition of the poor goes back at least to his first electoral contest in 1832. But the peculiar, historically slanted veneration that Young England felt for the Throne and the Church begins to colour Disraeli's references to them after his involvement in the movement. In his *Vindication of the English Constitution* (1835) Disraeli was already a strong opponent of Utilitarianism and of abstract principles in general; he was already a strong champion of national character, precedent and antiquity. But he made none of the special appeals on behalf of Crown, Church or People that he was to make in the trilogy. The *Vindication*'s emphasis was essentially – and almost exclusively – aristocratic. It valued the two Houses of Parliament. It derived from the equality of our civil rights 'the sympathy which has ever existed between the great body of the English nation and their aristocracy'. It paid a magnificent tribute to the 'gentlemen of England', whose party the author had recently joined:

> a class of individuals noble without privilege, noble from the generosity of their nature, the inspiration of their lineage, and the refinement of their education; a class of individuals who, instead of meanly submitting to fiscal immunities, support upon their broad and cultivated lands all the burthens of the State; men who have conquered by land and sea, who have distinguished themselves in every honourable profession, and acquired fame in every department of learning and in every province of science and art; who support the poor instead of plundering them, and respect the court which they do not fear; friends alike to liberty and order; who execute justice and maintain truth – the gentlemen of England; a class of whom it is difficult to decide whether their moral excellence or their political utility be most eminent, conspicuous and inspiring.

With such a lesser aristocracy, what need of a 'real' one? Smythe, too, was an admirer of the squirearchy. But it was not central to Young England's preoccupations (although its chief source of support) and, in the trilogy, there is no special attempt to woo this particular class.

Coningsby

The first volume of the trilogy, *Coningsby*, came out in May 1844. It was dedicated to Henry Hope, who had urged 'the expediency of my treating in a literary form those views and subjects which were the matter of our frequent conversation' at Deepdene; it was subtitled *The New Generation*. This was, then, Young England's book from the start. It was about the young men who launched the movement. It was described, in at least one contemporary advertisement, as Young England's 'manifesto'.

The underlying purpose of the book was unashamedly partisan. The author aimed to reveal 'the true character of political parties'; to show up the Whigs as the 'Venetian' party who, since the seventeenth century, had emulated the Venetian Constitution (an oligarchy headed by a Doge); and 'to vindicate the just claims of the Tory party to be the popular, political confederation of the country'. The attempt to make the conserving Tories look popular, and the reforming Whigs exclusive, was not so paradoxical as might at first appear; but it involved some characteristically Disraelian interpretation of political developments since the beginning of the century.

It is clear that to rehabilitate his party in popular esteem, thus enabling it to compete in a century that looked like being a century of progress, was what mattered most to Disraeli. This aspect of the book was his own idea and achievement. But, even here, Smythe had something to offer. Standing for Canterbury, in 1841, he had told his constituents that he stood as an 'old Tory'; he could not have done this without implying that the 'new' Conservatives had departed from an older, more popular, tradition. His view of old Toryism must have reinforced, if it did not prompt, Disraeli's.

Indeed, if *Coningsby* is Young England's book, it is, more especially, Smythe's book. It is he (Coningsby) who preaches the pure Young England doctrine to his bemused/disgusted grandfather:

> Let me see authority once more honoured; a solemn reverence again the habit of our lives; let me see property acknowledging, as in the old days of faith, that labour is his twin brother, and that the essence of all tenure is the performance of duty . . .

It is he who develops the monarchical theme that dominates so much of the discourse. The author lends his own authority to it: 'It is not impossible that the political movements of our time, which seem on the surface to have a tendency to democracy, may have in reality a monarchical bias.' The wealthy and knowledgeable Jew, Sidonia, is able to put this more daringly: 'The tendency of advanced civilization is in truth to pure Monarchy' and the House of Commons 'will in all probability fall more rapidly than it rose'.

But it is left to Coningsby to expand on this monarchical future. He says he has no faith 'in the remedial qualities of a government carried on by a neglected democracy, who, for three centuries have received no education'. If Class Legislation is to be avoided, then 'the only power that has no class sympathy is the Sovereign'. Like all holders of power the Sovereign needs some check; but this must be supplied by public opinion; after all, the representation of the Press 'is far more complete than the representation of Parliament'. He (Coningsby) does not want to do away with Parliamentary government, since he looks upon 'political change as the greatest of evils'. But he would 'accustom the public mind to the contemplation of an existing though torpid power in the constitution, capable of removing our social grievances':

> Let us propose to our consideration the idea of a free monarchy, established on fundamental laws, itself the apex of a vast pile of municipal and local government, ruling an educated people, represented by a free and intellectual press.

As to the Church, Coningsby regards it as 'the estate of the people' and thinks, like Faber, that it should be released from its union with the State so that it can freely carry out its function of regenerating the national character.

There is much of the real Smythe in Coningsby's championship of the Sovereign and the Press – perhaps even in Sidonia's depreciation of the House of Commons. In spite of some truthful touches, however, very little of Smythe's personality comes across in Coningsby's blameless character. It has often been remarked that Disraeli's heroes have little life of their own; they behave beautifully, but colourlessly. We are continually hearing in *Coningsby* about its hero's great abilities, without being given much evidence of them. We can believe that he had a 'quick and brilliant apprehension' and 'a memory of rare retentiveness'. But this is because we know that these were qualities in the real Smythe, as were Coningsby's ascendancy over his friends and his good, slightly formal, manners. Almost the only new discovery that we make is a 'vein of simplicity' in Coningsby resulting from 'the earnestness of his nature' (the over-earnestness could explain why Smythe took such frequent refuge in cynicism):

> There never was a boy so totally devoid of affectation, which was remarkable, for he had a brilliant imagination, a quality that, from its fantasies, and the vague and indefinite desires it engenders, generally makes those whose characters are not formed affected.

Coningsby's physical appearance becomes conventionally handsome, and attractive to women, as the book progresses. But, at the beginning, he recalls the real Smythe in his 'limber and graceful' figure, his interesting though not extremely regular features, and 'the deep blue eyes' which haunted Faber's sleep. He also has the short upper lip, without which none of Disraeli's heroes can afford to be.

The golden light bathing Coningsby's years at Eton is probably in accord with Smythe's memories – certainly Manners and Cochrane were both passionate Old Etonians. But Smythe's career at Cambridge was rather more turbulent than Coningsby's. Coningsby found his time there something of an anti-climax after Eton, though he concluded at the end that 'he had passed three serene and happy years in the society of fond and faithful friends, and in ennobling pursuits'. There is, of course, no hint of debts, nor of Union rows.

The character of Lord Henry Sydney (based on Manners) adds some simpler and quieter thematic material, mainly for the woodwind section of the orchestra. We hear of his sweet disposition, of his enthusiasm, of his intelligence and of his happy home life. At Cambridge he 'was full of church architecture, national sports, restoration of the order of the Peasantry, and was to maintain a constant correspondence on these and similar subjects with Eustace Lyle' (Ambrose Lisle Phillipps). He 'devoted his time and thought, labour and life to one vast and noble purpose, the elevation of the condition of the great body of the people', both physically and spiritually. He 'represented to the Duke [his father] that the order of the Peasantry was as ancient, legal, and recognized an order as the order of the nobility'; he stressed the importance of the 'parochial constitution' of the country. He visits his friend, Eustace Lyle, at St Genevieve, looks at its pictures of the Civil War, and laments his ill-luck in not living at that time. His brother-in-law, who scoffs that Henry thinks 'the people are to be fed by dancing round a maypole', asserts that life is much easier now than it was then; Coningsby denies this: 'Manners are easy and life is hard'; Lord Henry wishes the reverse: 'The means and modes of subsistence less difficult; the conduct of life more ceremonious.'

Another theme associated with Lord Henry and with Lyle is Paternalism. Lyle holds an alms-giving ceremony at St Genevieve, in supposedly medieval fashion, explaining that he wishes 'the people constantly and visibly to comprehend that Property is their protector and friend'. At Beaumanoir, the seat of Lord Henry's father, the ladies are 'deeply sensible of the responsibility of their position' and the consequences are noticeable in the superior tone of the peasantry. The Duke is well aware that 'the ancient feudal feeling that lingers in these sequestered haunts is an instrument which, when skilfully wielded, may be productive of vast social benefit'.

Cochrane, transformed into Sir Charles Buckhurst, has fewer ideas, but seems to be the man of action of the trio. He hits on the secret of Young England's brief success:

> I dare say the only way to make a party in the House of Commons is just the one that succeeds anywhere else. Men must associate together. When you are living in the same set, dining together every day, and quizzing the Dons, it is astonishing how well men agree.

Lyttelton, Smythe's and Manners's Eton and Cambridge friend, appears as 'the calm and sagacious Vere', the son of a Whig Minister; the younger Walter is Millbank, who goes to Oxford, instead of Cambridge, and whose sister Coningsby marries. Croker's attacks on Young England are revenged by his caricature as Rigby, the parasitic man of business of Coningsby's grandfather, Lord Monmouth. The book ends with a series of questions about the future of the group. In particular:

> Will they maintain in august assemblies and high places the great truths which, in study and solitude, they have embraced? Or will their courage exhaust itself in the struggle, their enthusiasm evaporate before hollow-hearted ridicule, their generous impulses yield with a vulgar catastrophe to the tawdry temptations of a low ambition?

The future answered both questions with a qualified 'Yes'.

Sybil

Sybil, or The Two Nations came out a year later than *Coningsby*; it was dedicated to Mrs Disraeli. This is Disraeli's own book, as *Coningsby* was Young England's. More serious historical and social research went into the making of it than into his other novels. Young England, and its originators, do not appear, even in disguise. The hero, Charles Egremont, though an Etonian, goes to Oxford, not Cambridge; he is older than Smythe and Manners, since he seems to be 25½ when the book opens in 1837 (it ends in 1842). Disraeli wrote *Sybil* in the last months of 1844, when Young England was making its greatest public impact. But perhaps he already had a feeling that it would be a mistake to nail his own colours too irretrievably to its mast; or perhaps he simply wanted more freedom to put his views across in his own way. At any rate there are fewer constitutional fireworks in *Sybil* than in *Coningsby*. It concludes with a summary of some political convictions that Disraeli claims to have held and promulgated himself for 'nearly fourteen years' – ever since the start of his political career in 1832.

The book is nevertheless full of Young England's views. The Monarchy is again exalted, though less prominently than in *Coningsby* and perhaps in more Disraelian language. The two main subjects of the book – the condition of the poor and the 'great estate of the Church' – are conceived very much as Manners conceived them. Indeed, where this is not Disraeli's book, it is Manners's rather than Smythe's. Perhaps there is an echo of Smythe (who was to write to Manners in 1849 about 'Brummagem coronets') in a new concern about the genuineness of the aristocracy. This appears in a reference to the 'pseudo-aristocracy of this country'. It also appears in the family trees of the characters. Both the Marneys and the Mowbrays are relatively *parvenu*, while the Duke of Fitz-Aquitaine is descended from a royal bastard and the Marquis of Deloraine, who marries Egremont's widowed mother, is the grandson of an attorney. Fortunately, good marriages have refined his blood. Similarly Lady de Mowbray, daughter of an old ducal house, can call on reserves of real blood when the mob advances to her castle.

If the aristocracy is frayed round the edges, it is still sound at the core. We are given a genuine young noble to admire in

Lord Valentine, who goes to the Queen's Ball as Richard Coeur de Lion, clad in an old family suit of armour. Egremont tells Sybil that 'the People never can be strong', but says he sees a dawn:

> [the] new generation of the aristocracy of England are not tyrants ... Their intelligence, better than that their hearts, are open to the responsibility of their position ... They are the natural leaders of the people, Sybil; believe me they are the only ones.

This is surely Disraeli speaking himself. At the same time he has allowed himself to hint that some men in low places, like Walter Gerard, may be more genuinely aristocratic than some in high. At Wodgate the ruling clique of barbarous, uneducated, ironmasters is 'a real aristocracy; it is privileged, but it does something for its privileges'.

The re-writing of history in *Sybil* is more extensive than in *Coningsby* and goes further back. In the eighteenth century we rediscover Lord Shelburne, as the statesman who passed on the Tory 'apostolic succession' from Bolingbroke to Pitt. In the seventeenth century we learn that 'bribery was unknown in the time of the Stuarts'; that Charles I was 'a virtuous and able monarch', who tried to tax the rich directly (Ship Money) rather than the poor indirectly; that he laid down his life for 'the cause of the Church and the cause of the Poor'. In the Middle Ages we are taught to see the Church dispensing charity and the monks as easy landlords; there were yeomen, then, not simply two classes of masters and slaves; there was real community instead of modern aggregation. In a glowing notice of *Sybil*, soon after its publication, the *Oxford and Cambridge Review* found these 'views of English history as novel as they are correct'. How far they were in fact correct does not matter to an understanding of Young England; but it is fair to recognize that there was a case of this kind to be made.

There are a remarkable number of good Roman Catholics in *Sybil*: the Gerards, the paternalist Traffords, even the genealogist, Hatton. But the religious honours of *Sybil* go to Mr St Lys, the Anglican Vicar of Mowbray. St Lys is not an exact portrait of Faber, whom Disraeli may never have met. He is about 34 (a bit older than Faber at the supposed time of action) and he is 'a younger son of the most ancient Norman family in England', which is certainly more than Faber was. But otherwise, with his beauty ('the Norman tempered by the Saxon; the fire of conquest, softened by integrity'), his 'serene, though inflexible habit of mind', his charitable work in his parish and his ability to bridge class differences, he is a type of Faber, as seen through Manners's eyes. Like Faber, St Lys has been a College tutor; like him, too, he tells Egremont that 'nothing would ever induce him to marry'. The disagreeable Lord Marney does not care for St Lys 'preaching in cottages, filling the people with discontent, lecturing me about low wages, soliciting plots of ground for new churches, and inveigling Arabella into subscriptions to painted windows'. But then Marney is a great supporter of the New Poor Law, 'fierce against allotments' and strongly anti-ecclesiastic; he ascribes all the misery to over-population and believes in emigration as the only solution.

Lord Marney may see St Lys as a trouble-maker. But, in times of trouble, the clergyman is the best friend the land-owners have. At the end of the book he preaches to the Trades of Mowbray, assembled in his church, on 'Fear God and Honour the King'. He tells his parishioners that it will support them 'at the judgement' if they help him to clear a way for Lady de Mowbray and her party to escape from the mob. Before the crisis the radical journalist Morley says that the People are not ready to rise: 'Besides there is a priest here, one St Lys, who exercises a most pernicious influence over the people. It will require immense efforts and great distress to root him out.'

St Lys blames the Church to Egremont for all that has

occurred: 'The church deserted the people; and from that moment the church has been in danger, and the people degraded.' Forms and ceremonies 'represent the divinest instincts of our nature'; they go back to Judaism and 'Christianity is completed Judaism or it is nothing'. This is Disraeli rather than Faber speaking. But Faber, in his Anglican period, would no doubt have concurred with Disraeli in placing Jerusalem higher than Rome. Otherwise Disraeli does not seem to have made much use, in writing *Sybil*, of the copy of *Sights and Thoughts* he borrowed from Manners. Its influence may be more detectable in some of his later books.

The conclusion of *Sybil* is worth quoting at length as an avowed statement of Disraeli's own views after two years of working with Young England:

> It is the past alone that can explain the present, and it is youth that alone can mould the remedial future. The written history of our country for the last ten reigns has been a mere phantasma ... Oligarchy has been called Liberty, an exclusive Priesthood has been christened a National Church; Sovereignty has been the title of something that has no dominion, while absolute power has been wielded by those who profess themselves the servants of the People. In the selfish strife of factions, two great existences have been blotted out of the history of England – the Monarch and the Multitude; as the power of the Crown has diminished, the privileges of the People have disappeared; till at length the sceptre has become a pageant, and its subject has degenerated into a serf.

Tancred

Tancred, or the New Crusade followed in March 1847, after Peel's fall and well after Young England had ceased to operate effectively as 'a party within a party'. Publication had been intended originally for 1846, but was held up by Disraeli's absorption in the political crisis. The book is set in 1845. When Disraeli began writing it – presumably in the autumn of that year – he could still treat Young England as a cohesive, if no longer a highly creative, force. 'Young England' is in fact mentioned by name (for the first time in the trilogy) and the *Coningsby* characters – Coningsby, Lord Henry Sydney and Sidonia – reappear in the earlier part of the book. It looks as if Disraeli touched up this section, without altering it substantially, nearer to publication date. Coningsby himself is represented as a political and social success; he and his wife – who has become worldly and fashionable – give dinners of forty covers at their country house. Egremont, the hero of *Sybil*, now Lord Marney, has found in Coningsby's 'vivid and impassioned intelligence . . . the directing sympathy which he required'; the party hack, Tadpole, regrets that he should have thrown away his chance of being Lord Privy Seal 'for the nonsense of Young England'. But the general effect of Coningsby's reappearance is somehow that of a tune repeated in a minor key. There is even a hint of criticism in the remark that prosperity had developed in Coningsby 'a native vein of sauciness which it required all the solemnity of the senate to repress'. This must surely have been put in after Smythe had become a Peelite.

Buckhurst does not reappear at all, since Cochrane was not only a Peelite but unseated when *Tancred* came out. Lord Henry, on the other hand – modelled on the one member of the trio who was still working with Disraeli – is as nice as ever and has become a politician to reckon with. His object remains 'to elevate the condition of the people'. He 'took an habitual part in debate and was a frequent and effective public writer'.

The boy . . . intent upon the revival of the pastimes of the people had expanded into the statesman who . . . had shown that a jaded population is not a source of national prosperity. What had been a picturesque emotion had now become a statistical argument.

He seems destined for an important future:

Richly informed, still studious, fond of labour and indefatigable, of a gentle disposition though of an ardent mind, calm yet energetic, very open to conviction, but possessing an inflexibility amounting even to obstinacy when his course was once taken, a ready and improving speaker, an apt and attractive writer, affable and sincere, and with the undesigning faculty of making friends, Lord Henry seemed to possess all the qualities of a popular leader, if we add to them the golden ones – high lineage, an engaging appearance, youth, and a temperament in which the reason had not been developed to the prejudice of the heart.

As a portrait of Manners this could hardly be bettered. Disraeli may not have been able to create characters; but he could certainly assess them.

A fresh member of the Young England set, Richard Monckton Milnes, makes a slightly ridiculous début as Vavasour, the great giver of breakfast parties. He bickers with Coningsby, as the two originals did in real life. Disraeli later noted, in his private memoranda, that 'Milnes was 25 years speaking in Parliament and he is the only man of whom it can be said, that beginning badly, every time he spoke worse'. He added that Smythe used to compare Milnes with Boswell and to call him Sancho Panza; once, in Easter 1846, Milnes, 'who had not a rural taste or accomplishment' came to the House 'in a squire's cut away green coat'; casting a contemptuous eye Smythe exclaimed: 'See Dicky – Protection looking up.' Another memorandum explains that Milnes was himself responsible for Vavasour's entry on stage:

When I published Coningsby he [Milnes] complained to me, that I had not introduced his character among the Young England group, to which he was attached in feeling, and with whom he wished to act – and had sometimes. He spoke to me on this matter with great earnestness – tears in his eyes – I had never appreciated him, and all that sort of thing. As his father was a friend of mine, and I always wished to be on good terms with Milnes (tho' George Smythe hated him with a sort of diablerie and treated him with a fantastic insolence wh. requires a great pen to picture) I at length promised, that if the opportunity offered, I would remember his wish. Accordingly, when I wrote 'Tancred' in wh. the Young England group reappeared, I sketched the character of Vavasour and made it as attractive as I cd. consistently with that verisimilitude necessary. I don't know whether he was over-satisfied – but betwn. 1844 and 1847 when Tancred was published (Sybil in 1845, and Tancred was intended for 1846 – but the publication postponed in consequence of the great Corn Law Repeal) much had happened in my position: the Young England myth had evaporated, and I had become, if not the recognized leader, at least the most influential organ, of a powerful parliamentary party. Milnes was full of envy.

There is not much about the British political situation in *Tancred*. We are given the impression that Disraeli still relies on a mixture of aristocracy and monarchy to put it right. But the young hero decides that what is really needed is faith and that, without it, the people are 'kept in some rude provisional discipline' only 'by the remains of that old system which they are daily destroying'. So he goes to the Holy Land to try to find faith and, through faith, duty.

Europe in general, and England in particular, are put firmly in their place. Progress mistakes 'comfort for civilization'. The Church of England has got into difficulties 'mainly from its deficiency of oriental knowledge' and consequent 'misconception of the priestly character'. Anglican bishops were 'tattoed savages' a few centuries back; Rome at least 'was founded by a Hebrew and the magnetic influence lingers'. As to Parliament, it has been superseded by public opinion and no longer 'does the real work'. Tancred is glad to be travelling to a land never 'blessed by that fatal drollery called a representative government, though Omniscience once deigned to trace out the polity which should rule it'.

When he gets to the Near East Tancred has some initial difficulty in getting in touch with Omniscience. But his thirst is eventually assuaged by the Angel of Sinai who reveals the following secret to him:

> The equality of man can only be accomplished by the sovereignty of God. The longing for fraternity can never be satisfied but under the sway of a common father ... Cease, then, to seek in a vain philosophy the solution of the social problem that perplexes you. Announce the sublime, and solacing doctrine of theocratic equality.

If this means anything, it seems to mean that political problems can be solved only with the aid of religion. Tancred strikes up a close friendship with Fakredeen, who has Smythe-like qualities – charm, delicate sympathy, financial embarrassment, love of intrigue, genuine but unstable emotions. Between them they puzzle over the enforcement of 'theocratic equality'. Tancred tells his friend that 'equality, properly developed, is in fact the patriarchal principle' of the desert. They brood over 'a new social system, which was to substitute the principle of association for that of dependence as the foundation of the Commonwealth, under the sanction and superintendence of the God of Sinai and Calvary'. But we are not vouchsafed any details. Tancred merely announces to the Queen of the Ansarey their joint ambition 'to conquer that world, with angels at our head, in order that we may establish the happiness of man by a divine dominion, and, crushing the political atheism that is now desolating existence, utterly extinguish the grovelling tyranny of self-government'.

'Theocratic equality' – the Fatherhood of God and the Brotherhood of Man – is of course at the core of both Christianity and Islam. The Angel of Sinai had been brought up in the best Semitic tradition and His message was as orthodox as one would expect. Its value as a guide to politics seems limited to persuading people that the religious is more important than the political plane and that they are equal on the first, if not on the second. Perhaps, as a reaction against Young England, Disraeli really did have a momentary vision of British society moving from dependence towards association; perhaps, in a sense, that is what it has since done; perhaps he helped the process by the Second Reform Bill. But, if he really did envisage this in *Tancred*, he also envisaged the Multitude under strict theocratic control, presumably exercised by Crown and Mitre; he did not think of them as self-governing. In actual fact his whole career remained true to the principles of aristocracy and dependence, which he had shared with Young England and which were central to its doctrine. He modified them to suit the wider franchise; but he never abandoned them. Equally he never in practice tried to circumscribe Parliament's power, either in the interest of the Monarch or in that of the Multitude.

Disraeli and Faber had very little in common, except that they could both write, had both visited Constantinople and were both friends of Smythe and Manners. Whatever interest Faber had for Disraeli must have faded after he became a Roman Catholic. There is nothing to show whether, for his part, Faber ever read *Coningsby* or *Sybil*. Since he was still at Elton when they came out, and still a close friend of Manners, it seems quite likely that he did. If so, he must have found their tone worldly, but perhaps he would not wholly have disapproved of them. Different as the two men were in their ambitions and temperaments they did share a certain flamboyance of taste which led to a faint resemblance of literary style in some of their passages. It seems to appear, for instance, in the rather theatrical, highly coloured way they both have of describing Mediterranean scenery – though this may simply reflect one of the fashions of the age.

One of the oddest scenes in *Tancred* is that in which Tancred and Fakredeen are shown by Queen Astarte 'what the eye of no stranger has looked upon' – a 'variety of sculptured figures', the relics of Antioch, representing the Gods of the Greeks, who are also Gods of the Ansarey. The insertion of these symbols of classical myth into the extremely monotheistic, and Semitic, framework of the rest of the story seems almost deliberately designed to bewilder and disorientate the reader. The scene is, however, curiously reminiscent of a similarly bizarre passage in *Sights and Thoughts*. This is where the clerical author, in a dream near the Greek Oracle of Trophonius, is conducted to the home of the worshippers of the beautiful and admires the Schools of Sculpture:

Have I forgotten [writes Faber] the steep, breezy slope, that choice elm-girdled field, where one bright school-day, the Monday dedicated to Homer, that same coronel of deities looked down upon me out of the blue sky, imprinting their beautiful features and symbolical attire deeply and with separate distinctness upon my memory, while my worn and blotted Iliad lay beside me, and I was not sleeping? Could I not then judge the works of Phidias, when I had seen in pure vision that beaming assembly?

If Faber, a priest, could admire the Greek Gods, while

devoting his life to a jealous Semitic God, why should not Disraeli, a politician, attempt the same feat? For Faber, Christianity was a crowning revelation; but other religions had been groping, in their different ways, towards God. For Disraeli, it was 'all a matter of Race'. Providence had entrusted divine truths to the Semitic Race; but other races had contributed their lesser patterns to the vast design.

It does not seem to me too far-fetched to detect another trace of Faberian influence in *Tancred*'s subtitle. One half-concealed thread running through Faber's book is his thwarted ambition to travel to Jerusalem: 'I would fain see Jerusalem,' he tells the Stranger, 'before I visit Rome.' Tancred realizes this ambition, thus performing (as the subtitle proclaims) a 'New Crusade'. In *Sights and Thoughts* the Stranger reveals to Faber: 'There will be another crusade, though after a different sort from what has been heretofore.' It is doubtful whether he was thinking of Tancred; it is not impossible that Tancred was thinking of him.

It is tempting to pursue parallels further. What Faber had to say in *Sights and Thoughts* about secret societies and the Italian Carbonari ('the convulsive struggles of the heirs, to whom great Rome has bequeathed her tremendous legacy of stirring associations, must be objects of interest and sympathy') has conceivably an echo in Disraeli's *Lord George Bentinck* (1852) and in *Lothair* (1870). I have even wondered whether Disraeli might not have got his first idea for Sidonia from Faber's Stranger; they share an almost supernatural authority, as well as an inhuman omniscience. In that case, when he borrowed *Sights and Thoughts* from Manners in the late summer of 1844, it was not to read it for the first but for the second time.

Its Critics

Young England has had its share of abuse. The jeers of the *Morning Herald*, during its lifetime, have continued to sound in the ears of later critics. Morley wrote of its 'childish bathos';

Fonblanque, the biographer of the Lords Strangford, dismissed it, more kindly, as 'a pretty and a harmless dream'. *Fraser's Magazine* rightly remarked, in an article on Manners in March 1847, that: ' "Young Englandism" was a sentiment, not a political system. It aimed at moral regeneration ...'. Hence the vital importance of the Church to the movement. Those who expected a complete political system, of a predominantly secular kind, were bound to react with disappointment or contempt.

Others attacked 'Young England' because they found it – particularly its picturesque trimmings – ridiculous. The idea of reviving medieval attitudes was as ludicrous to some as it was appealing to others. In 1849, when Manners unsuccessfully contested the City of London, his 'old nobility' couplet was held against him; his opponents described him as a member of the 'white waistcoat' party – a benevolent association of young gentlemen formed to effect the restoration of medieval institutions. Manners's belief in the social value of monasteries and Smythe's regret that the Touching for the Evil no longer brought the Sovereign into intimate contact with his subjects were particular targets for ridicule, together with the notion that the Young Englanders' remedy for social distress was to erect maypoles in every village.

Cochrane's obituary in *The Times* for 17 February 1890 shows how easy it was for a supercilious writer to wrap the whole movement in a fog of derisive innuendo:

> It is hard nowadays to do the 'Young England' party full justice, or even to treat its members half as seriously as they viewed themselves. They had so many obvious foibles that their good points have been almost forgotten ... They had a hazy notion that a little modernized feudalism, with monasteries and illuminated manuscripts, would be an excellent antidote to the prevalent poison of the Manchester School. One at least of them was not sure whether something might not be said for

reviving the ceremony of touching for the King's evil. Hodge was to be handled in a parental spirit; the Church was to be made popular and picturesque; the Bishops were to be tribunes of the people; and it was the common badge of all the School to denounce the cruelty of the New Poor Law . . .

This is at once a very accurate and quite misleading account of the aims of the movement. Nothing in it is untrue; but it gives the impression that the Young Englanders cared only for trifles; thus it avoids the need to take seriously their deeper preoccupations. Disraeli, at the end of *Coningsby* and elsewhere, recognized ridicule as one of the chief dangers that the movement had to face. Some of the things that seemed ridiculous then (more holidays, more sports, more public amenities, more allotments) do not seem in the least ridiculous now. But the ridicule tends to remain, while the achievement is forgotten.

Although ridicule of this kind has been Young England's main stumbling block, it has of course always been possible to find fault with the movement on more serious grounds. For one thing, to the extent that it was based on restoration, critics could plausibly claim that the past was not better, but worse, than the present. (Even Cochrane had his doubts about the Middle Ages.) For another, plain men were right in detecting a lack of coherent principle. Manners himself did his best to create a basis of such principle, with rare consistency and doggedness. But his conception of an essentially paternalist society was not always shared by his comrades. Cochrane was a maverick, who was, as his obituary remarked, 'too fond of taking a line of his own to be a safe party man'. Smythe tried to weld increasingly liberal ideas on to an orginal bed of Jacobite prejudice. He did this by describing his own brand of Liberalism as 'old Toryism', in the hope of making it more acceptable to the electors of Canterbury. Disraeli sometimes practised the same method, though with rather more plausibility and discretion. The general result was that even sympathizers were left bewildered. Where did 'Liberalism', 'Conservatism', 'Old Toryism', 'new Toryism' and 'Radicalism' each begin and end?

Even if Manners's views are taken as representing the true spirit of Young England, they are of course open to serious objections, as are all political philosophies. One of the best criticisms is in a review of *Tancred* by Richard Monckton Milnes, which we will come to shortly.

Meanwhile Disraeli's support was not an unalloyed blessing for the movement's public image. At this stage of his career, before his attacks on Peel had shown how formidable he could be, he was not taken wholly seriously by serious people, whether as a politician or as a writer. The commercial success of *Coningsby* and *Sybil* (by the standards of those days) and their vogue in smart society provoked other authors to find them flashy and cheap. Even Wordsworth, though he congratulated Manners on his public conduct at the end of 1844, was ready to have a professional fling at Disraeli. He wrote to Edward Moxon on 21 July 1844, two months after the publication of *Coningsby*:

> How can any one when such trashy books as Disraeli's are run after expect any portion of public attention, unless he confines himself to personalities or topics of the day?

Some months later he was still irritated enough to refer to 'Beardless Boys' in a peevish sonnet:

> YOUNG ENGLAND – what is then become of Old,
> Of dear Old England? Think they she is dead,
> Dead to the very name?

(This burst of patriarchal indignation may have been provoked by the new weekly, *Young England*, which was much more dismissive of 'Old England' than Manners and his friends.)

So far as I know, Dickens did not attack Disraeli personally. But, in *Bleak House* (1852) he criticized the movement in terms reminiscent of the editorial in the *Morning Herald* on 20 July 1843. The *Herald* had then described the 'tomfoolery' of Young England as 'the political offshoot of Tractarianism. Mental dandyism is its chiefest characteristic.' Dickens in *Bleak House* discovered a sort of Dandyism that 'has got below the surface' in the 'brilliant and distinguished circle' at the Dedlocks' country seat:

> There *are*, at Chesney Wold this January week, some ladies and gentlemen of the newest fashion, who have set up a Dandyism – in Religion, for instance. Who, in mere lackadaisical want of an emotion, have agreed upon a little dandy talk about the Vulgar wanting faith in things in general; meaning, in the things that have been tried and found wanting, as though a low fellow should unaccountably lose faith in a bad shilling, after finding it out! Who would make the Vulgar very picturesque and faithful, by putting back the hands upon the Clock of Time, and cancelling a few hundred years of history.

This was to measure Medievalism by Radical standards and to find it irrelevant to the real problems of the time. Thackeray concentrated on the movement's surface oddities. He satirized Young England – or rather a certain type of young Tractarian – in *The Book of Snobs* (reprinted from pieces in *Punch* 1846–7). A banker in Carmarthenshire, Sir Thomas Muggins, has a son who blossoms out as Sir Alured Mogyns Smyth de Mogyns, with a lengthy genealogy, a crest of a 'tom-tit rampant regardant' and a motto of 'Ung Roy ung Mogyns'. His eldest son, born in 1819, has taken his father's seat in Parliament and has of course joined Young England. He is the only man in the country who believes in the De Mogynses, and sighs for the days when a De Mogyn led the van of battle. He has written a little volume of spoony puny poems. He wears a lock of the hair of Laud, the Confessor and Martyr, and fainted when he kissed the Pope's toe at Rome. He sleeps in white kid-gloves, and commits dangerous excesses upon green tea.

But Thackeray had begun his attack on the movement by mocking Disraeli personally. He reviewed *Coningsby* in the *Pictorial Times* for 25 May 1844, describing it as 'seemingly very deep, but in reality very easy of comprehension' and as having everything needed to make a book popular, since it made the reader laugh 'not only with the author, but at him'. He also contributed '*Codlingsby* by B. de Shrewsbury' to *Punch* in 1847 (this concentrated, not very liberally, on the Jewish angle). In *The Book of Snobs* there is a passage which Disraeli would have found particularly irritating:

> I don't know anything more delicious than the pictures of genteel life in 'Ten Thousand a year', except perhaps the 'Young Duke', and 'Coningsby'. There's a modest grace about *them*, and an air of easy high fashion, which only belongs to blood, my dear Sir – to true blood.

The Young Englanders had their revenge. One of Disraeli's memoranda records Smythe as exclaiming that, since novelists are always said to draw their own characters, 'he wished to God Thackeray wd draw his own – that wd be a character! The Cynic Parasite!' In *Endymion*, the novelist St Barbe is amusing, but absurdly envious. (His great rival appears under the neatly derogatory name of Gushy.) St Barbe writes *Topsy Turvy*, which has an immense success and 'if the knowledge of society in its pages was not so distinguished as that of human nature generally, this was a deficiency obvious only to a comparatively limited circle of its readers'. Endymion finally gets the better of St Barbe – though does not win his gratitude – by securing him a pension.

Another contemporary novelist who thought little of Disraeli as a writer was Anthony Trollope. He admitted in his *Autobiography* that Disraeli had had the genius to strike the young with astonishment and to arouse 'in their imagination ideas of a world more glorious, more rich, more witty, more enterprising than their own'. But it was no more than the 'glory of pasteboard', the 'wealth of tinsel', the 'wit of hairdressers' and the 'enterprise of mountebanks'. Trollope wrote this while Disraeli was Prime Minister and he reserved his most scathing judgement for *Lothair*. But, even as a young man (and he was only a year older than Cochrane), his sturdy sense of independence must have steered him away, temperamentally, from Young England. He described himself, in his *Autobiography*, as 'an advanced, but still a conservative liberal'; the Young Englanders could well have described themselves as 'retarded, but still liberal, conservatives'.

In *Barchester Towers* (1857) Miss Thorne of Ullathorne is a 'dear good old creature' who still cherishes, in an extreme right-wing form, some of the principles that Young England was propagating over a decade before. She looks back 'to the divine right of kings as the ruling axiom of a golden age' and keeps 'low down in the bottom of her heart of hearts, a dear unmentioned wish for the restoration of some exiled Stuart'. Both she and her brother are unflinching conservatives, totally opposed to free trade; indeed, Miss Thorne is herself not yet reconciled to the Reform Bill:

> She ... constantly thought of good things gone by, though she had but the faintest idea of what those good things had been. She imagined that a purity had existed which was now gone; that a piety had adorned our

pastors and a simple docility our people, for which it may be feared history gave her but little true warrant.

Charles Kingsley, in *Yeast* (1848) gives a fuller, and more balanced, account of Young England's strengths and weaknesses. Colonel Bracebridge comes to see the hero, Lancelot Smith, after staying with 'young Lord Vieuxbois, among high art and painted glass, spade farms, and model smell-traps, rubricalities and sanitary reforms . . .'. He says he has been 'over head and ears in Young England, till I fled to you for a week's common sense'. Lancelot, who admits to having laughed at Young England for years, feels some compunction: 'Its little finger is thicker than my whole body, for it is trying to do something . . .'.

That evening Lancelot meets Vieuxbois at a dinner party. He finds him 'a quiet, truly high-bred young man, with a sweet open countenance, and an ample forehead, whose size would have vouched for great talents, had not the promise been contradicted by the weakness of the over-delicate mouth and chin'. Bracebridge recommends Lancelot to the young Lord with the words that he 'really ought to suit you for he raves about the Middle Ages, and chivalry, and has edited a book full of old ballads'. Vieuxbois turns out to be a determined paternalist. He does not see 'why people should wish to rise in life. They had no such self-willed fancy in the good old times.'

> [He] considered nothing more heterodox than the notion that the poor were to educate themselves. In his scheme, of course the clergy and the gentry were to educate the poor, who were to take down thankfully as much as it was thought proper to give them: and all beyond was 'self-will' and 'private judgement', the fathers of Dissent and Chartism, Trades'-union strikes, and French Revolutions, *et si qua alia.*

On another occasion Tregarva, the gamekeeper, describes Vieuxbois to Lancelot as

> as sweet a gentleman as ever God made ... He spends his whole life and time about the poor, I hear. But, sir, as sure as you live he's making his people slaves and humbugs ... Without meaning it, sir, all his boundless charities are keeping the people down ...

Lancelot cannot help thinking of the alms-giving scene in *Coningsby* where Lyle sets about restoring 'the independent order of the peasantry' by treating them as if they were 'middle-age serfs or vagabonds, and not citizens of modern England'.

In Kingsley's Epilogue, nevertheless, there is a tribute to Vieuxbois as the nearest to 'the ideal landlord' that the age is likely to see:

> Let him go on, like a gallant gentleman as he is, and prosper. And he will prosper, for he fears God, and God is with him. He has much to learn; and a little to unlearn. He has to learn ... to trust not in antique precedents, but in eternal laws: to learn that his tenants, just because they are children of God, are not to be kept children, but developed and educated into sons ...

Vieuxbois is, evidently, Manners. His 'sweetness', his 'overdelicate mouth', his medievalism, his paternalism, his Tractarianism, all testify to this. In real life Manners came to believe in universal education, though he had not done so originally; but it is true that he saw this as something to be handed down from above, rather than as something to be wrested from below. He did not want his tenants to remain 'children'; he wanted them to turn into 'sons'; but he also wanted them, as sons, to maintain respect for paternal authority.

Eleven years later, writing a Preface to the fourth edition (1859) of *Yeast*, Kingsley noted an improvement in conditions in the southern counties of England. Progress might be slow; but the labourers were better off than they had been:

> To a thoughtful man, no point of the social horizon is more full of light than the altered temper of the young gentlemen ... one finds everywhere, whether at College, in camp, or by the coverside, more and more, young men desirous to learn their duty as Englishmen, and if possible to do it ...

Kingsley attributed this 'improved tone' partly to the triumph of Whiggish principles, but also to the greater 'moral earnestness' fostered by the Anglican movement. Neo-Anglicanism had failed as an ecclesiastical system; it had 'proved itself, both by the national dislike of it, and by the defection of all its master-minds, to be radically un-English'. But

> it has sown in the hearts of young gentlemen and young ladies seed which will not perish; which, though it may develop into forms little expected by those who sowed it, will develop at least into a virtue more stately and reverent, more chivalrous and self-sacrificing, more genial and human, than can be learnt from that religion of the Stock Exchange, which reigned triumphant – for a year and a day – in the popular pulpits.

Kingsley does not mention Young England in this Preface, because it was no longer in being; but he had mentioned it in the novel and he must have regarded it as part of 'the Anglican movement' to which he was paying tribute. He put his finger on Young England's main achievement. But he had also, in *Yeast*, put his finger on what was most vulnerable about it – the charge that, for all its benevolence, its tendency was to keep the people down.

In Carlyle love of independence struggled with love of discipline and, still more, with love of leadership. In 1836 he adumbrated a sort of 'popular capitalism':

> Mine is that masculine species of charity which would lead me to inculcate in the minds of the labouring classes the love of independence, the privilege of self-respect, the disdain of being patronized or petted, the desire to accumulate, and the ambition to rise.

But he also thought that Independence should seek out his real superiors. His chief objection to Young England seems to have been its churchiness and medievalism (in spite of *Past and Present*) rather than its paternalism. Like Kingsley he thought that the movement had some potential for good. Thus he wrote to Richard Monckton Milnes, on 17 March 1844, apropos of his book of verse, *Palm Leaves*:

> One of the things I like in this book is the visible increase of earnestness. May it go on increasing! On the whole, if 'Young England' would altogether fling its shovel-hat into the lumber-room, much more cast its purple stockings to the nettles, and honestly recognizing what was dead ... address itself frankly to the magnificent but as yet chaotic Future ... telling men at every turn that it knew and saw for ever clearly the the body of the Past to be dead (and even to be damnable, if it pretended to be still alive and to go about in a galvanic state), what achievement might not 'Young England' manage for us! Whatsoever was noble and manful among us, in terrible want of a rallying-point at present, might rally then and march. But alas, alas!

Milnes himself described Young England in 1844 as

a good phenomenon in its way . . . The worst of them is that they are going about the country talking education and liberality, and getting immense honour for the very things for which the Radicals have been called all possible blackguards and atheists a few years ago.

His dislike of Smythe, or his dislike of Smythe's dislike of him, was not lessened when Smythe became Under-Secretary at the Foreign Office. This was a job that Milnes wanted himself; he wrote (too late) to Gladstone on 14 January 1846 asking him to intercede with Peel on his behalf; when he failed, he confessed himself 'thoroughly disappointed'. He had always admired Disraeli, seeing him as 'a son of the old jealous implacable Jehovah' with 'no Christian sentimentalities about him'; but, when Disraeli prospered, the admiration may have become a little soured. In any case, as Disraeli feared, he cannot have been 'over-satisfied' with the rather disparaging sketch of himself as Vavasour in *Tancred*.

Milnes wrote a critique of *Tancred* in the *Edinburgh Review* for July 1847. With an adroit left and right at Smythe and Disraeli he described Tancred as

a Coningsby of loftier aspirations and purer heart; a youth of the highest rank and station (why will Mr D'Israeli be so fond of dukes?) . . .

But the rest of the review was less personal and made some telling points. It conceded that *Tancred* was well written, that Disraeli was an effective orator and had written much successful fiction. At the same time it suggested that his habit of relying on portraitures of living people inevitably weakened the power of his novels as works of art. However good-natured and well executed the portraits might be, there was bound to be something superficial about them.

Then again, there was a contradiction between 'fraternity under a common father' and the assertion of 'the indefeasible superiority of one race over all mankind'. Disraeli had 'sacrificed to his national (Jewish) feelings his own good sense'.

But the worst of it was that the political philosophy behind the trilogy was wrong-headed. The object of the novels was 'the revolution and regeneration of modern society'; they proclaimed as delusive the ideals of progressive civilization and of advancing 'self-reliance and self-control'. Their philosophy was 'nothing less than the abandonment of all principles of individuality, responsibility and self-government; and a return to the narrowest principles of loyal dependence, hero worship and local patriotism'.

This presented the alternative philosophies in stark terms. It prejudged the choice between them by postulating that the principles of which Milnes disapproved must not only be 'narrow' but 'narrowest'. It attributed 'hero worship' to Young England, when it was a much more essential characteristic of Milnes's admired friend, Carlyle. Smythe might declare to Sir W. Fraser, in his romantic way, that he was 'all for a Radical party with Great Names'. But in fact, whereas Carlyle's whole system depended on heroes, the Young England system (so far as there was one) was likely to work better if decent men and women, without any extraordinary genius, performed the ordinary duties of their stations, both high and low.

These qualifications apart, Milnes summed up in his review what most people, then and since, have felt was wrong with Young England. This was the flank on which to mount an attack – even if it was not quite so defenceless as Milnes supposed.

5

Aftermath

Disraeli

The Duke of Rutland, John Manners's father, had been unnecessarily, though not unnaturally, suspicious of Disraeli and of his influence over his son. During the period when both were immersed in Young England, Manners's influence over Disraeli was probably at least as great as Disraeli's over him. It was only when Young England was no longer effective, and the Duke's suspicions of Disraeli had abated, that Manners's loyalty to Disraeli can have done any damage to his career, by consigning him to a background role. Ironically enough, it was as this second phase was opening that Disraeli saw Belvoir Castle for the first time. He attended a meeting of the Protectionist leaders there in 1846. Afterwards he told his sister that it was not at all like Beaumanoir, which he had pictured in *Coningsby* as Lord Henry's family seat, but Coningsby Castle 'to the very life'. Beaumanoir was 'one of those Palladian palaces, vast and ornate, such as the genius of Kent and Campbell delighted in at the beginning of the eighteenth century'. Coningsby Castle, on the other hand, where Lord Monmouth feasted the county in the conservative interest, was 'a castellated building, immense and magnificent, in a faulty and incongruous style of architecture . . .'. Neither of these fictional edifices can fully have satisfied Young England's romantic notions of what a ducal residence should be.

The real Belvoir compensates for any incongruity by the romantic beauty of its setting. Disraeli's admission to the Castle, however faulty its architecture, seems to symbolize his attainment of respectability as a Conservative leader. In another two years, at the age of 43, he was to succeed Lord George Bentinck as leader of the Protectionists in the House of Commons; from then on his career is part of British political history. He could no longer afford to have odd ideas, or to pose as any kind of rebel; he would find himself either in power or in direct search of it. Three times Chancellor of the Exchequer, though never for very long; Prime Minister, in succession to Lord Derby, in 1868; then again from 1874 to 1880; Earl of Beaconsfield in 1876; dead, and almost deified, in April 1881.

Caught up in the day-to-day management of a great party, Disraeli came to think of the 'Young England myth' as having 'evaporated'. It has often been supposed that he threw the movement over as soon as he found it no longer tactically useful; the detached way in which he recalled it in *Endymion* has been thought to typify his real attitude towards it. Sir William Gregory judged that Disraeli, though intimately connected with Young England, was 'far too intelligent to identify himself very much with their unpractical views'. If this were really so, it would be difficult to explain why in the General Preface to his Novels, written in 1870, he should have gone out of his way to vindicate his trilogy and to represent the views expounded in it as, in essence, those which he had always held himself. The truth is that the movement 'evaporated', not because he had willed it to do so, but as a result of causes that he would have prevented if he could. Nor did he ever renounce its guiding ideas.

No doubt Disraeli abandoned some of Smythe's more idiosyncratic fancies once he had the responsibilities of a party leader. He had at one time shared Smythe's Stuart, though not his Jacobite, sympathies; this part of the myth may indeed have evaporated. We no longer hear of the weaknesses of representative government, or of the probability (or even the possibility) that the House of Commons would 'fall more rapidly than it rose'. It is left to Waldershare in *Endymion* to describe the House of Commons, in an apparently whimsical paradox, as 'a mere vestry', living on capital accumulated during the pre-Reform era. For that matter, even in *Coningsby*, Disraeli had taken the precaution of making his hero reluctant to do away with Parliamentary government, on the ground that he deprecated political change of any kind.

There is only one respect in which the General Preface fails to endorse the guiding views of the trilogy: in the role it envisages for the Church. Here again, it is not a question of Disraeli having abandoned the Church, but of the Church having abandoned Disraeli. The secession of Newman and Faber destroyed his hopes that the Anglican Church, under Tractarian influence, could be used as a moral/political instrument to achieve national unity and class harmony. Thenceforward Disraeli supported the Established Church, as an ancient institution to be conserved with care and respect, but without any favouritism towards Puseyites and without much expectation of its making a dramatic contribution to the political welfare of the nation.

This apart, the basic views of Young England, whatever their origin, remained at the centre of Disraeli's political philosophy. His relations with Queen Victoria, and his bestowal on her of the title Empress of India, reflected the views on the monarchy he had shared with Smythe. The social legislation passed during his 1874–80 administration reflected the views on the welfare of the people he had shared with Manners and Cochrane. This legislation may not have been dramatic, but it was useful and wide-ranging (it included an Artisan Dwellings Act, a Friendly Societies Act, Labour Laws, Factory Acts, an Amendment of Education Act, an Agricultural Holdings Act, a Rivers Pollution Act and a Public Health Act). G. M. Young wrote in his *Victorian England* (1936):

> The reforms of the forties satisfied the aspirations of the poor and the consciences of the rich, until a new tide set in and carried us forward again with the Education Act of

1870, and the legislation of Disraeli's Government, with which Young England, now grown grey, redeemed the promise of its far-off fantastic youth.

Young England was not of course posthumously responsible for this social legislation; its main authors were, no doubt, civil servants. But Disraeli and Manners were influential members of the Government that pushed it through Parliament. Three decades earlier, in Young England's heyday, Manners and Cochrane had been actively concerned about labour conditions, housing and public health. In Kingsley's *Yeast* the young England peer, Lord Vieuxbois, was keenly interested in 'sanitary reforms'.

More broadly, devotion to the landed interest, and to the feudal principle that the tenure of property should be the fulfilment of duty, was as much a part of Disraeli's creed in the 1870s as in the 1840s. His political views had been formed in that decade, under the stimulus of Young England; thereafter he was too involved in practical affairs to adopt a fresh system; he could only prune the Young England system, where it seemed to have straggled out of control. Even the Imperialism of his Crystal Palace speech (1872), though a response to developments and preoccupations later than Young England, had its source in the Young England belief that statesmen should appeal to the imagination as well as to the reason of the masses.

Above all else, however, it was Young England that convinced Disraeli – or at least confirmed his conviction – that the Conservative Party could and should make allies of working men. This lifelong belief of Manners was a ruling, perhaps *the* ruling, principle of the whole Young England enterprise. Cochrane wrote, in *In the Days of the Dandies*; 'One of the principal tenets of Young England was perfect confidence in the people. There was an intense conviction that the Conservative strata was [sic], to be found in the lower classes . . .'. Whether or not Disraeli held this conviction with unwavering

intensity himself, he had enough confidence in it to pass the
Second Reform Act in 1867. When the suffrage was increasingly extended it became, and had to become, a good deal
more than a conviction. The Conservative Party could survive
only if it took care to make it true. But it was due more to
Disraeli than to any other statesman that this was seen as
being possible. It was his most valuable legacy to his party and
it was at least partly because of Young England that a daring
or a diffident hope developed into an article of faith.

Faber

Disraeli's life falls into two halves, before and after 1846. In
the first half he was still an adventurer, a brilliant young or
youngish man, with some social, literary and even political
success to his credit, but not widely trusted or respected and
with very uncertain prospects of becoming more than a
talked-about backbencher. In the second half he was a dedicated politician, still suspect to some moralists and most Liberals, but taken seriously even by them, and with a growing
reputation for wisdom and patriotism in the country at large.
He changed his dress and appearance to suit the change; in
his second incarnation he was no longer an extravagant
dandy, but one of those 'grave statesmen' whom a character
in *Endymion* thought an insular country of thick fogs and a
thick middle class required. The later Disraeli was absorbed
in, and disciplined by, his main life's work – though not so
totally absorbed and disciplined that he could not produce,
and publish, two very unusual novels.

Although Faber was a few years younger than Disraeli, his
life, too, fell into halves before and after 1846. In the first
half, while a devout Anglican, he was also a poet, with many
friends in the world and with literary, social and political
ambitions. Greatly admired by some, he was thought by
others to be too self-indulgent, too 'flashy', too wild and
theatrical in his pronouncements, too feminine in his tastes.

These qualities did not disappear when he became a Roman Catholic; but, just as Disraeli subdued his extravagances to the needs of a successful political career, so Faber subdued his to the needs of religion. As leader, first of an independent religious order, and then (from 1849) of the London Oratory, he displayed many of his old weaknesses, but within a framework, where his strengths – his energy, his will-power, his affectionate piety and his personal fascination – were more concentrated and more directed towards a single end. At times he seems to have lost his hold over his colleagues; but he always managed to reimpose it, because he was always 'the life and soul' of any group in which he was working. This is not the place to discuss his religion or what he achieved through or in it. He was engaged in a constant struggle with what he saw as his own wilfulness and sinfulness; to most religious people who knew him he seemed to have scored more victories than defeats. But he retained his gaiety and his humour and he never lost the ability, which he had shown so remarkably at Ambleside and Elton, to touch the sympathies of different classes.

If Disraeli changed his dress for the second half of his life, Faber changed his physique. In 1846 he was still a good-looking young man. Frances Trollope, meeting him at Florence in that year, was struck by his brilliance and eloquence, as well as by his best feature – the expressive mouth that a young lady in Oxford eight years earlier had found so irresistible. Mrs Trollope wrote: 'The charm and *power* of his countenance is in his mouth, which is not only peculiarly handsome, but has a variety of expression that is quite extraordinary.' The mouth never lost its expression: but the rest of Faber's physique was transformed in the course of the next few years. As his brother Frank wrote after his death:

Those who knew him in youth will remember him as eminently handsome, and of a slight and lithe figure. Such he still was in 1845; but when he paid me a visit

222

four years afterwards, all the *gracilis puer* had departed. The identity was gone; and though nothing could mar the beauty of his countenance, yet his augmenting bulk prevented any recollection of 'Faber of University'. This increased as life went on, and was, perhaps connected with the disease which proved fatal to him at the age of forty-nine.

Newman of course noticed this physical deterioration, too. He wrote to Frank Faber from Birmingham in October 1849: 'Your brother certainly has grown very large the last year or two, and is subject to very unequal health, and yet he gets through a great deal of work.'

By October 1852 Aubrey de Vere could write to Miss Fenwick that he had heard Faber preach at Limerick:

His own sufferings, which make him look fifteen years older than he is are so intense that when his headache is on him he can hardly speak or move . . . I passed almost a week with him in the house of my friend, W. Monsell . . . I can safely assure you that seldom in my life have I been so deeply impressed by any one as by Faber. I could hardly name another who . . . appears to live so entirely in and for God . . . There is a something almost tremendous in the earnestness, and at the same time simplicity, of his religious sense . . . In his manner there is at the same time an unguarded, and almost childlike, frankness and simplicity which make his whole being transparent to you. Not a trace do I find now of the faults chiefly attributed to him in early youth, such as affectation, insincerity or triviality . . . He still sometimes talks in a manner that some people would call *vain*; but this I think proceeds only from the simplicity, geniality, and love of sympathy that belong to him . . . Whatever he may once have been, he is now by nothing more marked than by simplicity, masculine strength, and spiritual power . . .

After his conversion Faber wrote devotional books and hymns, but no more poetry. For all practical purposes he had abandoned politics even in his Anglican days. He continued to do what he could to improve conditions for the poor, but never with any attempt or wish to subvert the existing order. The conversion of the country to the true faith was in any case bound to come before any political objective. In 1854 he was made a Doctor of Divinity by Pius IX. He wrote to Frank Faber in July of that year:

> I would have sent you some [of his devotional works] before, if I did not fear that each fresh exhibition of the distance to which we have drifted apart did not in some way widen a breach, which is almost the only heart-sorrow I have in life.

The breach between Faber and his family was never complete. Nor did he forget his old friends. In November 1857, Father Philip Gordon of the London Oratory wrote to the Duchess of Norfolk that the Father was 'much cut up by poor Lord Strangford's (George Smythe's) death'. At about the same time Faber wrote himself to the Duke: 'Strangford gone too – my letter reaching him the day *after* his death – and I *hindered* his being a Catholic in 1839.'

Faber died six years after Smythe, in 1863. Shortly beforehand, according to his brother, he was 'soothed and gratified' by a visit from his old Oxford friend, Roundell Palmer. Frank Faber was too much of an invalid to call on him himself; but his wife did so and found him shockingly ill and dropsical, though very affectionate. Manners, too, seems to have wanted to say goodbye. He wrote in his obituary of Faber:

> The last three years of his life were marked by acute sufferings, borne with singular courage and sweetness. Many of his old friends saw him during this period, and

much of the bitterness and misunderstanding which had accompanied his secession from the Church of England was removed.

Much, but not all. But the bitterness was not on Faber's side (there was no reason why it should be). He wrote to Manners from his deathbed:

My dearest John,
　　You know what a pleasure it would be to me to see you and bid you goodbye in person, but I feel also that it would be a great agitation and that I must obey Dr Bence Jones. Your friendship is one of the brightest pages of a happy life, for if my life has been imprudently full of hard work, the work itself has been a pleasure, and there has not been a single remorse to mar it . . . Of course, it is a regret to me that you are not of my faith, but of that I can say no more. Probably if it had not been for my sins and for the lukewarmness of my prayers, God among his many mercies would have given me that also . . .

For Manners Faber was 'far more successful than Newman, or any of his companions, in the work he undertook for his new communion'. At Cotton, soon after his conversion, he had showed the same power to attract farm labourers and their families to religion as he had shown at Elton. Preaching there in 1847 he said that no object had been so dear to him, when a Protestant clergyman, as 'the English poor so miserably neglected, ill used, or coldly treated as they are now . . . I feel even more strongly than ever the desire to devote all my health and strength to win my poor countrymen to the true light of the Gospel, to console them in all their tribulations, whether of body or of soul . . .'. At Faber's funeral there was a vast crowd, both inside and outside the church; according to a witness, those present ranged from the poorest Irish to 'the aristocracy in deepest mourning'. Manning spoke of him at a service next day as 'a great servant of God': 'He was a great priest; he was the means of bringing multitudes into the one fold, and he died as a priest should die, amid the prayers and tears of his flock. Though he lived in the world I never saw any one so detached from the world . . .'. The *Dublin Review* echoed this language: 'F. Faber died as a pastor ought to die, amidst the tears and prayers of a multitude of souls brought by him to the foot of the Cross . . .'. Newman, too, though still not fully reconciled to Faber personally, nor ever approving of his Italianate religious tendencies, wrote of his having 'departed amid the tears of hundreds'.

It is difficult to strike the right balance between hagiography and criticism. Faber was not a born saint; but he was one of those rare men who impress numbers of their contemporaries as having a quality of saintliness. Whatever this means, it must mean some power of goodness that is felt as such by people who encounter it. Those who do not share Faber's particular religious beliefs are likely to feel, as Manners felt, that he suppressed or distorted some of his most characteristic gifts in the service of the Roman Catholic Church. Yet some such suppression is the penalty that people who are both gifted and successful usually have to pay. Disraeli certainly had to do so. If Faber had lived as long as Disraeli, he would perhaps have seemed as eminent, in his calling, as Disraeli was in his. Not that there is any valid comparison to be made between two such different lives. One of the two men was concerned with worldly success, but only so far as it promoted religion. The other was concerned with religion, but only so far as it was compatible with political achievement.

Manners

Manners was the only one of the group to live into the present century. During his long life he held very consistently to the opinions and attitudes he had had as a young man. Loyal and affectionate by temperament, he clung more than any of his companions to the ideas of Young England, and to his memories of the movement. He was still thinking of it 'with a certain tenderness' at the end of 1880.

In 1847 Manners, though temporarily out of Parliament, had not lost all hope of reviving Young England. He wrote to Disraeli at the end of December: 'If we hold together we shall re-establish a "Young England" of greater weight and capacity than these Exeter Hall zealots conceive possible.' Two months later, in another letter, he reaffirmed his confidence in popular Toryism: 'The natural alliance between Toryism and the Church and People will conquer in the long run. I have faith in our cause.' Back in Parliament, he assured his father in December 1851:

I am nevertheless sanguine that I can see my way to a policy at once Tory, Protectionist and Popular. I lay it down as an axiom that the operatives can be, and ought to be, the firmest allies of a Tory and Protectionist Government; and that without their support in these times no Conservative Party can be really strong.

Even after the defeat of the Conservatives in 1880 Manners stuck to his guns. He wrote a commiserating letter to Disraeli just after Christmas, but refused to believe in any permanent alienation of 'the agricultural classes'. Properly led, they would 'fight for the existing order' and against 'democratic Revolution'. The real danger, he told Disraeli, was 'the growing reluctance of the highborn and wealthy to take the lead in and incur the trouble and expense of political life'.

Manners maintained his loyalty not only to his opinions but to his friends. He gave Disraeli constant support, particularly at the time of the Second Reform Bill. He wrote of Faber with kindness and esteem, in spite of the shock of his conversion; there is no sign of what must have been a heavy disappointment, except for a tendency to refer to his former friend as

227

'poor Faber'. He kept in touch with Cochrane and helped him by reminding Disraeli of his past service. His correspondence with Smythe continued warmly until the latter's death. In September 1850 he paid a visit, with Smythe, to the Ferrands in Yorkshire; later the two friends went to stay with the Cochranes at Lamington in Scotland. During their Yorkshire visit Mrs Ferrand took over a party to Haworth Parsonage. Charlotte Brontë wrote that this included 'two gentlemen; one tall and stately, black-haired and whiskered, who turned out to be Lord John Manners; the other not so distinguished, shy, and and a little queer, who was Mr Smythe, the son of Lord Strangford'. Predictably, it was Manners, and not Smythe, who thought of bringing a brace of grouse for Mr Brontë.

Manners's first marriage, absorbing as it was, did not disrupt his friendships. 'The days have glided away in one long dream of happiness,' he wrote in his diary. 'On Sunday we lunched with the Cochranes and G.S.S. dined with us afterwards. I try and hope to keep up all my old happy friendships and connections.' Smythe had died before Manners married for the second time. But his new wife seems to have stayed with him at Lamington for a couple of days in October 1880.

After his first marriage Manners gave up serious literary ambitions, though he occasionally published speeches or contributed to periodicals. But he remained politically active until 1892, with a total of over seventeen years as a Minister. He was three times First Commissioner of Works in Conservative Governments; twice Postmaster-General; once Chancellor of the Duchy of Lancaster. In all these capacities he sat in Derby's, Disraeli's and Salisbury's Cabinets. In 1866 Derby offered him first the Irish Secretaryship, with a seat in the Cabinet, and then the Lord-Lieutenancy of Ireland. Manners accepted, though with reluctance; but the plan was dropped. *The Times* brought up his Young England past against him:

> He is of the generous temper of the Princes of France, who would feed a hungry population with cakes, and we

are not satisfied that he would not have attempted to get rid of Fenianism by the erection of Maypoles, and cure pauperism by the multiplication of holy days.

In 1868 he declined to become Governor-General of Canada on 'private and family grounds'. In 1875 Disraeli offered him the Viceroyalty of India, but he again declined.

There was no lack of honours. At the end of his last administration Disraeli secured Manners a GCB and a pension of £1,200 a year. In 1888 he succeeded his elder brother as seventh Duke of Rutland. Three years later he was made a Knight of the Garter.

Manners died in 1906 at the end of a distinguished and useful career. He had been a good Departmental Minister; as Postmaster-General his concern for the welfare of his employees had made him extremely popular. In successive Tory administrations his advice on wider policy matters had been valued at Cabinet meetings. But he had never quite realized the expectations of him that had been aroused in some of his friends, particularly Disraeli, in his youth. Was this because he was not aggressive enough; because Disraeli was able to rely too absolutely on his loyalty and self-effacement? Disraeli can hardly be accused of ingratitude: this was never one of his failings, and he had recognized his debt in 1847, when he wrote:

What would I not give to find you again at my right hand, with the talent ever ready, the courage that never faltered, the indefatigable industry, and, above all, the honour and fidelity in which we could place implicit trust.

Disraeli had praised Manners's 'ability, acquirements and working powers' in emphatic terms, when he backed him as a candidate for Colchester in 1850. It was because of his gratitude that he invited him to take important posts abroad. But neither Disraeli nor Salisbury ever felt able to offer him a leading Ministerial appointment.

The Times, in its obituary of Manners, posed the same question, without really answering it. It recalled Manners's first meeting with Faber,

> whose character and talents had already won for him that saintly reputation which clung to him through life. Faber's influence over his new friend was all in the direction of strengthening the principles he had already imbibed with regard to the authority and prerogatives of the Church. The divine looked with great confidence to the future of the youthful politician, in whom he saw a greater capacity than circumstances ever adequately called forth.

Later in the obituary there are some hints of an explanation of this relative failure. Manners's 'ambition was hampered by his ideals as well as by his refinement'; though widely beloved, he was unwilling to adapt his convictions to changing circumstances.

Manners was never able to rid his reputation of a supposedly excessive attachment to monasteries, maypoles, holy days, old customs and old nobility. He could not free his image of these associations, because he did not want to. His attachment to such things had always been more reasonable than his critics had suggested – and he was not going to give them up at their behest. Perhaps his experience and his temperament combined to make him feel happier when pursuing causes that were lost or going to take a long time to win; success, as at the end of 1844, tended to make him uneasy. In any case he walked too much alone to carry great political weight.

Fraser's Magazine in March 1847 had observed that, with one or two exceptions, Manners's political and social aims were totally different from those of other public men; though not an absolutist in England – since this was not in our tradition – he perceived that 'in our dread of tyranny we have deprived ourselves of the advantage of legitimate authority'. Such acceptance of authority was less suspect to Disraeli than to many Victorians, with their firm belief in manly independence. Disraeli was prepared to say privately that, if the Prince Consort had out-lived 'some of our "old stagers", he would have given us, while retaining all constitutional guarantees, the blessings of absolute government'. But he knew better than to praise 'absolute government', or talk too much of 'legitimate authority', in public. Manners, on the other hand, could never be relied upon not to say exactly what he thought. His private and public postures were always the same.

For a short period in the 1840s Manners was able to pursue joint objectives with like-minded friends. He was never quite in this position again. Hence his nostalgia for Young England. But the nostalgia never became bitter; it was 'a certain tenderness', not a complaint.

Cochrane

Cochrane represented his old constituency, Bridport, in the Parliament of 1847–52. Then he was defeated in a contest for Southampton. In 1857 he was returned for his own county of Lanarkshire; from 1859 to 1868 he sat for Honiton; from 1870 to 1880 he represented the Isle of Wight. He was then raised to the peerage as Baron Lamington.

Cochrane never held office. He is said to have been offered the Governorship of Cape Colony in 1868; but Disraeli's Administration fell before the appointment was completed. Manners had written to Disraeli in September 1867 to say that he was 'growing nervous about Cochrane's position':

His seat at Honiton is cut from under him by the Reform Bill, and, knowing your good will towards him, I will ask you to consider what can be done for him . . . Forgive me for troubling you about this; but you know the interest I take in our old companion in arms.

Three months later Manners wrote again to say that Cochrane was grateful (Disraeli must have made some offer), but that he could not 'reconcile himself to the idea of relinquishing public life in England, while there is any hope of his continuing to take a part in it'. It is not clear whether this was an initial rejection of the Cape Colony Governorship, or whether some less attractive appointment had been offered.

Outside Parliament, where he kept up his reputation as a Greek expert, Cochrane was a well-known social and literary figure. In 1864–8 he was one of the editors of the satirical weekly, the *Owl*. He wrote a number of books, some of them with a French flavour. Among their titles: *Florence the Beautiful* (1854); *Justice to Scotland* (1854); *Francis I and other Historical Studies* (1869); *The Théâtre Français in the reign of Louis XV* (1870); *Historic Châteaux – Blois, Fontainebleau, Vincennes* (1876). His mellow reminiscences, *In the Days of the Dandies*, were running in *Blackwood's Magazine* at the time of his death in 1890. His only son succeeded him in his title and was appointed Governor of Queensland in 1895.

If Disraeli failed fully to reward Manners for his considerable services, he handsomely repaid Cochrane for lesser and shorter services by making him Lord Lamington at end of his last Government. Manners was able to report to his chief, after staying at Lamington in October, 1880:

> The gratitude and enjoyment the laird of the first ilk (Lamington) feels for and in his Peerage is great and ceaseless, and is in marked contrast to the indifference often shown by the wearers of new Coronets.

This was a sort of success; but it was no more than a compensation for a career that had on the whole been less of a success than a failure. Cochrane had had a varied and interesting life; but he must have hoped for some more solid achievement when he set forth from Cambridge, with confident enthusiasm, over forty years before. When he died, *The Times* compared his career with his novel *Ernest Vane*; in both there had been plenty of incident and plenty of chances for the hero: 'Yet the curtain falls on a half-told tale, and the novel is thus to some extent typical of the career of its author'. The second Lord Lamington wrote to the newspaper to add a couple of points, but otherwise seemed implicitly to accept this judgement: he meekly professed to have had 'much pleasure in reading your kind obituary-notice of my father'.

The Lamington peerage, like the Strangford peerage, is now extinct and Lamington House is no more than a pile of stones and rubble. But in Lamington Village a few sturdy cottages, in a plain Gothic style, commemorate the first Lord Lamington as a model landlord, who practised what he preached.

Smythe

After the 1847 elections Smythe was still sitting for Canterbury, while Manners was out in the wilderness. This was the beginning of a phase of 'brutal contentment', as he put it. But the letter he wrote to Manners from Paris in October, from the 'slough of my materialism', should not be taken too literally. Nothing that Smythe ever said should be taken too literally. In this case he was using his caressing tact to restore his friend's morale after electoral defeat. He wrote:

You have ... realized the prophecy of my boyish sonnet, are a perfect type among us of an older time, and the Christian Cavalier. In your love, your poetry, your politics, your popularity, your religion, you realize images and ideas, as obsolete as 'the mystic rose' or the Crusaders' faith, or the worship of a Masaccio or a

233

Raphael. You are a miracle of purity in an age of impurity . . .

This persistent purity contrasted with his own descent into the slough:

> I was a Poet-boy, such as Faber described, full of wild and audacious aspirations after the illimitable and the Unreal and of imaginative unhappiness because I could not master them. And now I am happy, contented, cynically happy, and brutally contented . . . with my intellect all gone, without ambition, without a desire except present ease, with a selfishness not unsocial – a mere incarnation of claret and cigars.

Smythe always had a weakness for claret and cigars, or their equivalents. But he did not pass the whole of his last decade in the supine state that this letter portrays. When Peel died, in July 1850, he began to think earnestly of mending his fences with Disraeli. That autumn he went with Manners to stay with the Ferrands and the Cochranes. During this tour he evidently discussed the possibility of a *rapprochement* between the Peelite Lord Aberdeen, his old Foreign Office chief, and the Protectionists; Manners reported to Disraeli on 10 September: 'G.S.'s idea of Aberdeen's politics is that he . . . would offer no opposition to a Protectionist government provided its foreign policy was Conservative.' Afterwards Smythe went on to Brussels, where he stayed with the Metternichs and was 'so flattered and made much of that I don't know whether I am standing on my head or feet'. He took care to let Manners know that both the Metternichs had spoken 'in the highest terms of Disraeli, whom they know and greatly admire, She, woman-like, eulogizing the genius of his face'. Early in 1852 he congratulated Manners on the birth of his son; then he wrote a few days later: 'I envy you all things, but nothing so much as acting with a man of genius, the friendship of whom is the gift of the Gods.' Later in the year he qualified the first part of this sentence, but not the second: 'I cannot envy you, for I love you too much; and I do not think that I am naturally envious . . .'.

Meanwhile Smythe had sent Disraeli himself a delightfully typical note of congratulations. This was in February 1852, when a Tory Government was briefly in office:

Those who hailed the dawn have the best right to salute the meridian. Believe therefore dear Dis. in the sincere congratulations with which I kiss Mrs. Disraeli's hand and am your affectionate opponent G. Sydney Smythe.

I can't help laughing at your having discovered Sir Roger de Coverly to stick him in the Colonies – it is so like one of your old strokes – in fiction –

Before the Parliamentary elections in July 1852 Smythe and Disraeli had a meeting, at which some sort of a deal seems to have been discussed. Smythe later wrote to him, on 2 July, to say that he meditated retirement and that there were several reasons why he could not help the Tories in at Canterbury by deliberately polling few votes himself. One was that if 'out of ancient sympathies, you were willing to give me a place abroad, neither you nor I would like to face the publick abuse inevitable upon what . . . would so flagrantly have the appearance of a bargain'. He proceeded, more ambiguously:

Let me recapitulate. You asked me at Malmesbury's whether I was going 'to bring in the Tories'. I said 'Yes'. You said 'You will have strong claims on us.' I answered, 'if I have, I will negotiate *only* with you.' . . . I said furthermore afterwards that I had faith in your star, and if I was returned off my own bat, and if I could come round to you again, I would do so . . . You were of old the Cid and Captain of my boyish fanaticism, and after that I was seduced to desert you (out of domestic reasons) I never could help feeling that you were still the Cid and Captain of my every sympathy.

It would be cruel in you – with your genius, your great qualities – your old affection for myself even if inverted now – to stab a corpse.

You will understand my metaphor and the fear it is meant to express.

You must also understand that whatever I can do for your two men here, I will do – short of the grave danger to myself – of polling so few votes – at considerable cost.

It is difficult to feel certain what this means, except that Smythe wished to find a way of renewing his alliance with Disraeli, without incurring public criticism. In the event he polled too few votes and never sat in Parliament again. His canvassing cannot have been helped by a duel he fought in May 1852 with Colonel Romilly, his colleague in the representation of Canterbury. Smythe had alleged in a speech at Canterbury that Romilly was in a cabal to injure him with the electors. According to Sir W. Fraser the duel, said to have been the last on British soil, took place 'in a secluded part of a solemn wood in Kent'. There was 'no sham about the encounter'; but it ended in fiasco, because, at the crucial moment, a cock pheasant, startled by the noise of the pistols, had an equally startling effect on the combatants.

Smythe's failure to get returned to Parliament put an end to his dreams of renewing his political association with Manners and Disraeli. It was, in any case, too late. He came to recognize this himself as he admitted in a letter to Manners:

When I came to you and your party, I foolishly fancied that it might be given one to redisintegrate and restore one's youth's dream. Ever together, I had imagined that Dizzy and you and I might have renewed the ancient faith with the ancient relations. But I had miscalculated all the vicissitudes of the long interval, in which, by

Ambition, we are separated. And I found you merging politics in far dearer ties, and Diz, with views, office-spurred, of the immediate and the practical, rather than with those of more difficult, but of graver inspiration, in their true influence upon a world which, let the positive say what it will, is governed by Idea.

This illustrates Smythe's insight, but also his unsuitability as a man of affairs. He saw, rightly, that Ideas do ultimately govern the world. But, for those who want to succeed as practical politicians, it is usually better not to adopt them too soon, or to have too many of them at any one time. Smythe's watch, as he boasted himself, was apt to be five minutes too fast; he might have been forgiven this, if he had not been in the habit of carrying different watches, one of which was always too fast for the average timekeeper, and the other too slow.

In the last years of his life Smythe largely disappeared from public view. According to his sister-in-law, his old chief, Aberdeen, offered him a place in his Peelite–Whig coalition in January 1853; but he declined – whether from ill-health, lack of ambition or reluctance to widen his breach with Disraeli. If this offer was seriously made it could suggest that Smythe's performance at the Foreign Office had not been as bad as Gregory supposed; but Aberdeen was perhaps more concerned with having his support as a speaker in the House of Commons. In 1855 Smythe's father died and he succeeded him as seventh Viscount Strangford. He was still active socially, though he never spoke in the House of Lords. In November 1855 Greville recorded him in his diary as expressing a high opinion of young Lord Stanley; Smythe

confirmed what Disraeli had told me of his notions and views even more, for he says that he [Stanley] is a real and sincere democrat, and that he would like if he could to prove his sincerity by divesting himself of his aristocratic character and even of the wealth he is Heir to.

At least on that particular evening Smythe's fast watch seems to have been ticking louder than his slow one. He always admired drastic action in others.

At the end of May Smythe had sent Croker, long retired, an agreeably written letter informing him of the death of his 'old college friend, and world-friend, and Tory-friend, Lord Strangford, my father':

> Since the death of Mr Canning you have ever been his intellectual chief; and from boyhood I remember that every solecism of my puerile English, or sciolism in more ambitious nonage, were met by the correction, 'What would Croker say?'

He ended warmly, 'with great admiration and respect'. It was a graceful way to make amends for Croker's rough handling in *Coningsby*.

Not long afterwards Smythe fell a victim to consumption, as his mother had before him. Gregory said that he was 'worn out by dissipation, brandy and water, and a delicate chest'. Early in 1857 he went to Egypt, in the hope of benefiting from the climate; but he returned to England, no better, in the autumn. On 9 November he married Margaret Lennox at Bradgate Park, near Leicester, the seat of the Earl of Stamford and Warrington. He died there a fortnight later. He was succeeded in his titles by his younger brother, a distinguished ethnologist. Since he, too, was childless, the peerages eventually became extinct.

As he grew weaker, Smythe thought of the friends of his not far distant youth. He asked his wife to read him one of Faber's poems and wrote to Manners:

> We have known a friendship together which has far passed that of ordinary comrades ... Wherein lies our

238

sympathy? ... I hardly open my lips but to make an
enemy. I am very lazy also, and so susceptible as to shut
up like a beaten hound. Yet I would fain think that our
sympathy lies in our love of truth.

To Disraeli he wrote of his 'morbid, keenly analytic, introspective, Jean-Jacques like temper', adding: 'I once heard that
you had said of me "that I was the only man who never bored
you".' On his deathbed he told him: 'I have no stamina, my
legs and arms are not larger than slate-pencils.' Then he got
his wife to write on his behalf, on 19 November. She said that
her husband had hoped, but was unable, to write himself;
there was a packet that he would like Disraeli to return:

> Lord Strangford bids me thank you for your kind
> letters, which have been amongst his greatest pleasures,
> and he says that the remembrance of your friendship,
> and of Mrs. Disraeli's goodness to him, often recurs to
> his mind ...

She described herself as helplessly watching his decease.
There was no improvement in his condition; he was not
currently in pain, but was increasingly weak.

The press reported that the Disraelis had left Torquay on
21 November for a visit to Hatfield House. It recorded
Strangford's death as it would that of a man who had once
been famous, but was no longer in the public eye. *The Times*
described him as having been, with Manners, 'the principal
disciples, if not the leaders' of the Young England party. 'His
style of speaking in the House was characterized by much
smartness and originality, which always commanded the
attention, if it did not influence the judgement, of that
assembly' – but he spoke rarely and came almost to be forgotten. The *Morning Chronicle* said nothing about Young England or about Smythe's work as a journalist. It recalled him as

a nobleman who formerly gave great promise of celebrity both in the literary and the political world in which his father . . . shone so conspicuously.

The peer whose decease we have now to chronicle was far better known to our readers, and we may add to fame also, as the author of 'Historic Fancies'.

Smythe's Cambridge friend, Lyttelton, who was to commit suicide in 1876 while under treatment for melancholia, summed him up as 'a splendid failure'. Lyttelton had been Under-Secretary for the Colonies, in Peel's last administration, at the same time as Smythe was Under-Secretary for Foreign Affairs. Smythe had voted against Lyttelton's election as High Steward for Cambridge University at the end of 1840; but he maintained some years later that Lyttelton was 'sorry, not angry' about this and that he was still among his friends. He would not have quarrelled with Lyttelton's judgement on his career. He had confessed several years earlier to his father: 'My life has been made up of two blunders. I am a failure, and – I know it!'

Endymion and Waldershare

Smythe cannot have been wrong in sensing Disraeli's 'old affection' for him. All the evidence suggests that, for three or four years from 1842, Disraeli was fascinated by Smythe's ideas, wit and personality – not so deeply infatuated as Faber, not so much in thrall, but nevertheless quite thoroughly bewitched. Smythe's desertion must therefore have been a bitter pill; affection could easily have turned to rancour, and perhaps almost did. Disraeli was not a man to forgive any sort of injury lightly. He told Sir W. Fraser that a man would enjoy Revenge 'when even Avarice has ceased to please'. Monckton Milnes had characterized him in March 1845, well before the fiercest of his attacks on Peel, as 'a regular "hip and thigh", "root and branch" sort of *Urmensch*'. Disraeli had not got over his dislike of Peel when he came to write *Endymion*; he does not actually name the Prime Minister of the early 1840s, but blames him for not trusting youth and compares his 'more solemn organization' with Roehampton's (Palmerston's).

If there were any doubt that Disraeli took Smythe's desertion hard, it must be dispelled by Smythe's reference, in his letter to Disraeli of 2 July 1852, to the 'humiliation – which you did all things – and you alone successfully – to make me feel'. Smythe's strenuous efforts to climb back into favour point the same way; so does Disraeli's dry comment in 1850 on *Sin and Sorrow*, alleged to have been the joint production of Smythe and Lady Sligo: 'I suppose he supplied the sin, and his sister the rest.'

In 1852 there was apparently a reconciliation, on which a seal was set the following year. Smythe was invited to stay at Hughenden. The visit was successful, though Smythe realized from the presence of Lord Henry Lennox that he could no longer be to Disraeli what he had been before. For his part Disraeli had by now decided that, although Smythe was remarkably clever, he was not a *practical* man. He anticipated the judgement of Mr Vigo in *Endymion*: 'He is a wonderful man – Mr Waldershare . . . but I fear not practical.' Reporting Smythe's visit to Mrs Brydges Williams, in a letter in September, 1853, Disraeli wrote of him: 'Both as to ability and acquirement, [he] is perhaps the most brilliant man of the day, tho' more adapted to social and literary pursuits than the stern business of politics'.

In 1857 Smythe bequeathed to Disraeli, on his deathbed, a cup of Derbyshire spar. Disraeli said to Sir W. Fraser 'with much feeling; "It is not a great thing; but for a man to remember one at all at such a time is most gratifying".' In the private memoranda Disraeli wrote in the 1860s Smythe's sayings are frequently quoted; in 1870 he paid a handsome tribute to Smythe's 'brilliant gifts' and 'fascinating manners' in the General Preface to his Novels.

Whatever bitterness there had been seemed to have gone.

But perhaps it had not been wholly removed. In May 1874 Disraeli met Lady Strangford, widow of Smythe's brother and a woman of formidable character and intelligence. He asked her whether the novel about which Smythe had written to him nearly thirty years before (*Angela Pisani*) had ever been finished. After a search she found the manuscript 'in an indescribable state of illegible confusion', about two-thirds finished, with one or two gaps and no real ending. She was impressed by its cleverness and beauty; tried it out on two men, one of them young, who were also impressed; briefly supplied the gaps and the ending; and had it printed. In December 1874 she sent Disraeli the proofs, lamenting that things were so quickly forgotten: 'If it was not for "Coningsby", the new generation would scarcely know the bright episode in political life of "Young England".' Would Disraeli do 'a little sketch of your dead friend . . . the one frame in which he would have desired to set his portrait for posterity?'

It was a difficult plea to resist; but Disraeli resisted it. Instead of replying himself, he seems to have sent a message to Lady Strangford through Manners. At any rate it was to Manners she next wrote, on 23 January. He forwarded this letter to Disraeli on 25 January with an apology for his only partially successful attempt to 'shield you from her importunity'. Finally she wrote again to Disraeli herself, a little stiffly, on 28 March 1875, with the completed copy, including her own sketch of her brother-in-law's life. She hoped for some reaction; there is no sign whether she got it.

Disraeli was by now Prime Minister. It is quite understandable that he should have felt too busy to write biographical sketches. He had discharged his debt to Smythe in his General Preface; in any case it would be difficult for him to write both sincerely and interestingly about a career that was not quite as edifying, in all its aspects, as most Victorians would have wished. Yet it is rather odd that he should not have offered to write a very short foreword commending the book. Perhaps he had simply no time to read the proofs. Or perhaps he did not want to commit himself to further praise of Smythe, when he meant to present him in a rather satirical light in *Endymion*.

Endymion came out in 1880. Disraeli had begun it in the early 1870s, continued it while he was Prime Minister and completed it after he left office. He is thought to have taken the name from Endymion Porter, a dedicated seventeenth-century royalist. This seems probable enough, since the hero of the book has an 'historic ancestor, Endymion Carey' who lived in 'the age of the cavaliers'. Endymion Porter is believed to have been an ancestor of Lady Beaconsfield. He was certainly an ancestor of Smythe's, his granddaughter having married the second Viscount Strangford. It is not surprising then to find that Waldershare, too, 'had some Stuart blood in his veins, and his ancestors had fallen at Edgehill and Marston Moor'. Fonblanque's *Lives of the Viscount Strangfords*, containing an account of Endymion Porter, as well as short lives of Smythe and his father, had been published in 1877.

Smythe and Endymion may have shared ancestors; but otherwise they have very little in common. Disraeli must have wished it to be quite clear that he was not resurrecting one of his Young England heroes in the book's central character. Endymion is credited with tact, industry and good judgement. He is also of course good-looking – though one suspects in a more regular way than Smythe. He is entirely governed by women and succeeds miraculously as a result; under their influence, although his father had been a Tory, he becomes a Whig; he has no ideas; he could never conceivably have boasted to Disraeli that he was the only man who had never bored him. In fact he is in almost all points the exact opposite of Smythe.

It is not only the hero in *Endymion* who has no ideas. The whole novel seems intended to confute Smythe's belief that the world 'is governed by Idea'. The characters who do have ideas dazzle their hearers with paradoxes, like Waldershare, or play uselessly with advanced opinions, like Mrs Neuchatel;

the characters who succeed do so because of their practical ability or their belief in their stars. Nothing could be further removed from the intellectual climate of the trilogy. The 'plastic' Endymion mounts to the top because he does not make mistakes and is pushed by powerful women. He is absolved from the need to have any ideas of his own about economic and social development, because he specializes in foreign affairs. (He had indeed read Adam Smith 'and not lightly', and visited Lancashire; but we are not told what, if any, conclusions he had formed as a result.) Lady Montfort seems to sum up much of the book in a well-known passage:

> Finance and commerce are everybody's subjects, and are most convenient to make speeches about for men who cannot speak French and who have had no education. Real politics are the possession and distribution of power. I want to see you give your mind to foreign affairs.

The way to get power is to be practical and the main place to deploy power is abroad. Disraeli allowed Lady Montfort some feminine, and some aristocratic, exaggeration; but, in his old age, he probably had a good deal of sympathy with this point of view.

So it is not suprising that Smythe, as Waldershare, should be confined to a secondary role and 'handled a little tartly' (Philip Guedalla's phrase). As usual, the portrait is not exact. Waldershare takes a degree at Paris as well as Cambridge; he has 'a moderate but easy fortune'; he enters Parliament in 1837, not 1841; he becomes Under-Secretary for Foreign Affairs in 1841, is delighted with his post, yet resigns in 1846 before the repeal of the Corn Laws. But his temperamental characteristics are clearly those of Smythe ('He was witty and fanciful, and though capricious and bad-tempered, could flatter and caress ... [he] was profligate, but sentimental; unprincipled, but romantic . . .'). They were both educated at

St John's, both Jacobites, both beautifully mannered and both inheritors of Irish peerages, besides both being Under-Secretaries of Foreign Affairs. A whole passage, in which Waldershare describes the Tory Party as 'a succession of heroic spirits' is lifted verbatim, except for a few words in the middle, from the speech Smythe made at Canterbury in 1847. Even if this was unconscious plagiarism, it puts beyond doubt whom Disraeli had in mind.

Waldershare's fancies, like Smythe's, 'alternated between Strafford and St Just, Archbishop Laud and the Goddess of Reason'. On taking Endymion in hand, he 'reverted for the moment to his visions on the bank of the Cam'; but he 'soon quitted the Great Rebellion for pastures new, and impressed upon his pupil that all that had occurred before the French Revolution was ancient history. The French Revolution had introduced the cosmopolitan principle into human affairs instead of the national . . .'. This was a schizophrenia that Smythe fully shared with Waldershare. In *Angela Pisani*, which has a strong French flavour (including a reference to Napoleon s 'divine and immortal lineaments'), there is nevertheless room for an 'old Tory', Sir Hilary Clifford, who belongs to the 'Bolingbroke and Wyndham school', and 'follows Mr Canning because he *feels* and supports the tradition . . .'. As we have seen, Smythe tried to reconcile national with cosmopolitan principles when he stood for Canterbury in 1847.

There is one rather puzzling sentence:

Mr Waldershare came down, exuberant with endless combinations of persons and parties. He foresaw in all these changes that most providential consummation, the end of the middle class.

This does not chime with Smythe's admiration of the Lancashire 'aristocracy of wealth', or his refusal to vote with the rest of Young England on Factory Hours. Manners did indeed believe that the middle classes had too much political power and that there was too much 'tyranny of the purse'; but this was a topic on which the views of the two friends, or at least their public language, differed. Yet, after all, Disraeli was writing fiction, not history. Although there were some very accurate strokes in his portrait of Smythe as Waldershare, it was not a photographic portrait. In particular he seems to have gone out of his way to emphasize that Waldershare's views were not to be taken seriously. It had been a different story at the time of the trilogy.

When all this has been said, Waldershare remains the second – and almost the real – hero of the book. In imagination Disraeli has given Smythe what he lacked for much of his life – success. Waldershare succeeds in educating Beaumaris, Imogene and Endymion; he is brilliant socially; he acquires considerable influence over Prince Florestan (Louis Napoleon); there is some real wisdom under his verbal 'coruscation'; he seems to do quite well as Under-Secretary of Foreign Affairs. At the end of the book he marries an heiress and, though not 'such a pattern husband as Endymion', he makes 'a much better one than the world ever supposed he would'. Disraeli had borrowed some of Smythe's ideas at a time when he needed them: he no longer thought them as important as he once had. In compensation he could allow Waldershare, however unpractical, a reasonable share of worldly success.

Evidently Manners did not get any impression that Disraeli had been unfair to the memory of his friend, or of the Young England movement in general. He did not mind Disraeli gently satirizing Smythe's love of paradox, his Stuart nostalgia, or his oscillation between Jacobitism and Gallomania. But he would not have been happy if there had been a direct assault on the basic principles of Young England. These had become almost as much a part of Disraeli's way of looking on politics as they were of Manners's; to the extent that they were not Disraeli's own, original principles, he had come to think of them as such; in *Endymion* they are neither challenged, nor endorsed – except in the sense implicit in the whole book that no principles really matter very much in comparison with power. This seems to have been one of Disraeli's latest masks, or poses. Manners rightly detected in it an almost youthful foppery. He wrote to Disraeli on 5 December 1880 that *Endymion* reminded him 'more of Vivian Grey than of any other book . . . consequently I was charmed with it'.

Another character in *Endymion*, Nigel Penruddock, exorcizes a part of the Young England dream. By the end of the book he has become a Roman Catholic Cardinal – both physically and spiritually modelled on Manning. But, in the earlier part, he is, or is destined to be, an Anglican clergyman, riding on the wave of 'the Oxford heresy' and convinced, like Faber and Gladstone in the early 1840s, that salvation could come only from the Church. He wants to see Endymion become a churchman:

> The Church must last for ever. It is built upon a rock. It was founded by God; all other governments have been founded by men. When they are destroyed, and the process of destruction seems rapid, there will be nothing left to govern mankind except the Church.

Disraeli missed the Eglinton Tournament in 1839, because he was on his honeymoon. In *Endymion* he re-creates it, without the rain, at Montfort Castle. Nigel Penruddock is found 'stalking about the glittering saloons', wrapped in 'a cassock that swept the ground'. 'I am thinking of what is beneath all this,' he tells Lord Montfort:

> A great revivication. Chivalry is the child of the Church; it is the distinctive feature of Christian Europe. Had it not been for the revival of Church principles, this glorious pageant would never have occurred. But it is a pageant only to the uninitiated. There is not a ceremony, a form, a

phrase, a costume, which is not symbolic of a great truth or a high purpose.

Disraeli was a little obsessed by Manning, whom he also introduced into *Lothair*. Manning was not a 'schoolman', like Newman, nor a 'monk', like Faber. If only he had arisen a quarter of a century earlier! He might have been 'equal to the occasion' and become, not a Roman Catholic Cardinal, but a new Laud! Then indeed, as Disraeli wrote in 1870, 'the position of ecclesiastical affairs in this country would have been very different, from that which they now occupy'.

6

A Harmless Dream?

I have tried in this book to portray the Young Englanders and their ideas as they saw themselves, or as their contemporaries saw them. I have not explored whether these ideas were better, or worse, suited to their era than those of other schools of thought: orthodox Conservatism, Benthamism, Liberalism, Democratic Radicalism. Young England held a certain view of what human society ought to be. Other views would place more emphasis on equality, on the one hand, or on competitive individualism, on the other. In any particular period a particular one of these views may seem to produce the best practical results. What results Young England would have obtained, if it had ever formed a government, is now impossible to say – except that, like all governing parties, it would have had to make some compromise out of its ideals.

Where there are no immediate results to judge (perhaps even where there are) the choice of political ideals will depend largely on temperamental bias. Whether what Young England preached was or was not right for its time – or for any time – it was capable of appealing to a certain type of temperament. For that type of temperament it will always have some appeal, however, unfashionable or unsuitable it may otherwise have become.

Any attempt to justify, or condemn, Young England's temperamental appeal would open up a discussion on political philosophy, or on the social history of the early nineteenth century, well beyond the scope of this book. If I have helped to explain the appeal that its ideas had for its founders, that is the most that I could expect to do in a historical sketch of this kind. But, of course, political ideas are not only to be judged by their temperamental or intellectual appeal. They are intended to have practical consequences of some kind, sooner or later, even when not launched by a government with immediate power to implement them. My sketch of the Young England movement would hardly be complete without an attempt to summarize what (if any) its practical consequences were.

To describe Young England (as Fonblanque did) as 'a pretty and a harmless dream' suggests that it never had any real influence on events. A number of historians have thought this, some more indulgently than others. Even Disraeli seems to have come to look at Young England rather in that light. In *Endymion* he makes Waldershare arrive at Paris 'full of magnificent dreams which he called plans'. Smythe himself had been ready to think of his plans as dreams; in 1851–2 he 'foolishly fancied that it might be given one to redisintegrate and restore one's youth's dream'; but then he would never give up the belief that, though dreams might not be real themselves, they could affect and even shape events in the real world.

If the Young Englanders really expected to be able to restore a society dedicated to medieval (or what they took to be medieval) values, they were of course deceiving themselves. It was unrealistic to think that the authority of the Crown could be substantially increased without exposing it to criticism and opposition. It was unrealistic to believe that a State Church, which was not universal and had been established by an act of political will, would be capable of reforming the political and economic conduct of the nation. It was unrealistic to expect that enough Victorian landowners and employers could be persuaded to put the physical and moral welfare of their tenants and workers above their own interests, efficiency and convenience – or that, if they did, the results would invariably be beneficial. It was unrealistic to hope that sentiments of feudal respect could be transplanted

from rural areas to the large and rootless working popula-
tions of the industrial towns.

After all, the Young Englanders were romantics before
they were realists. Yet they were by no means totally unrealistic. They were not so stupid as to believe that their objects
would be achieved miraculously; they knew that progress
towards them could be made only piecemeal and with patient
effort. Nor was it unreasonable for them to rely, as they did,
on the aristocracy and the Church. They were almost bound
to do so, since they believed (with Carlyle) that both plu-
tocracy and democracy were incompatible with good government. In any case they were aristocrats and Anglicans
themselves.

In the 1830s and 1840s rather more than half the population still lived in rural parishes, more often than not dominated by squires and parsons. The higher aristocracy still had
great power, and greater influence, both nationally and
locally. Even Cobbett, no friend to the 'Establishment', had
written a few years earlier: 'We should lose more than we
should gain by getting rid of our aristocracy.' Disraeli maintained in his biography of Lord George Bentinck (1852) that
England was 'the only important European community that is
still governed by traditionary influences'; if not actually governed by an aristocracy, it was at any rate governed 'by an
aristocratic principle'. The Church commanded great wealth
and controlled the established centres of education. In spite
of dissent, an effective parson could still prescribe public
morals and direct private consciences in many parts of the
country. Newman could still feel confident, in his *Apologia*,
that Liberalism was 'too cold a principle to prevail with the
multitude'.

Both before and after 1840 the aristocracy and the Church
were living bodies, which did not have to be resuscitated from
a vanished past. These instruments for 'regeneration' from
above were already at hand and needed only to be
regenerated themselves. But Young England did turn to the

past for help in defining the ends that these means were to realize. In an age of confident progress, such as the Victorian era was largely to become, this mood of restoratism would increasingly seem defeatist and reactionary. But, in the 1830s and 1840s, there was still much feeling of insecurity; a fear of revolutionary doom; a mood of anxious foreboding about the effects of industrialism, the advent of democracy and the decay of faith. To many Englishmen the French Revolution still served as a dreadful warning, showing how thin the veneer of eighteenth-century progress and enlightenment had been. The balanced pessimism of Coleridge and Southey still darkened men's minds. Science had not yet shaken the belief that Man was descended from Angels, rather than Apes, or persuaded the ordinary citizen that he was engaged in a process of evolutionary improvement.

Against this background it was not only the romantically minded who turned to the past for guidance and reassurance. The Young Englanders were in any case lovers of antiquity by temperament, keenly sensitive to its influence on the present; it came naturally to them to look for social models in a romanticized past, rather than in an idealized future. When he travelled in France Faber was distressed to find it a 'land of Conscription and Tricolor', miserably divided into departments 'in lieu of the old Provinces whose very names were precious sounds of history'. This seemed to him 'to *unfroissart* the country, and to hide, as it were, old France, the land of Catholicism and Chivalry ...'. Nevertheless, the most medieval of the group, Manners, explicitly admitted in *England's Trust* that there was no going back to the pre-industrial age. However convinced of the virtues of the Middle Ages, he could not ignore Sir Francis Palgrave's warning that complete restoration is never possible, because the circumstances can never be exactly similar. What he and his friends did set out to do was to steer society gradually on to a new tack, by counteracting some current attitudes and by reviving some old ones. No doubt they originally hoped to achieve much more in this way than they actually did. But it does not follow than they achieved little or nothing.

The wish of the Young Englanders to restore some medieval values might be compared with the wish of some modern Conservatives to restore Victorian values, or with the wish of the great Renaissance artists to restore the values of Greece and Rome. In each case the wish arose because some human capacities seemed frustrated by current attitudes. The Young Englanders were more concerned with emotional than with intellectual or technical capacities (though they were inclined to regard medieval cathedrals with reverential awe, as works of art that their own age could not rival). The renaissance in Victorian religion and art fell far short of the more comprehensive Renaissance of the fifteenth and sixteenth centuries. But it is undeniable that there was a renaissance of a kind – and that it created its own cultural atmosphere. That atmosphere can still be sensed in Victorian religious buildings or, for instance, in Pre-Raphaelite paintings. It is less easy to sense its political and social manifestations. Yet one such was the neo-feudalism that coloured, if it did not dominate, early Victorian and mid-Victorian society. Of course, neither Victorian Gothic, nor Victorian neo-feudalism, were genuinely medieval. Restorations can never reproduce the past exactly, not only because the agents, tools and materials are different, but also because replicas cannot be created in the same spirit as original works. A successful restoration, in any other than museum conditions, draws inspiration from the past, but must use it to create something that is effective in its own right.

Young England had less time to make an impact on Victorian politics than the Pre-Raphaelites had on Victorian art. But it contributed significantly to this cult of neo-feudalism. It was possible for it to make as much impact as it did only because, during its three years, its activities in Parliament, combined with Disraeli's trilogy, ensured it a continual supply of both favourable and unfavourable publicity. Being a movement of youth, it could not fail to make some appeal to the imaginations of the youth of the country; its burst of popularity after the Manchester and Bingley meetings is evidence of its doing so. Some of its ideas took at least temporary root – and some of these turned in time into elderly habits.

The sphere in which the movement was least effective was that of *reforming legislation*. With the exception of Smythe, Young England pressed for a Ten Hour Bill to limit the working hours of young persons and women in factories. The Ten Hour campaign was finally successful in 1847, after Young England had petered out. The Young Englanders' efforts, particularly those of Manners, who made a long speech on the subject in March 1844, had certainly contributed to this result; but of course they were not alone in working for it. The only other case in which they were able to influence current legislation was the New Poor Law. They could not get it repealed, but they did secure some modifications. At the end of the debate in July 1844 Graham acknowledged the effect of their representations, when he expressed

> a hope that the union of young England with old England would not be limited to any particular locality – that it would not be confined within these walls, but that when they met again in the next session of Parliament their union would prove to be strongly cemented whenever a party division including the fate of the Government might be attempted.

In both these cases Young England's influence, though by no means negligible, was marginal. It had more effect, at least in the long term, on *social habits*. Manners's hobby-horses – more holidays, more parks, more museums, more sports, more allotments, more public baths – were all eventual winners. We take all these things now so much for granted that it is easy to

254

forget how few opportunities there were for working-class recreation, particularly in the industrial towns, in the early nineteenth century. The Sunday game of cricket, even the Saturday game of football, the provision of a whole range of municipal facilities, all owe something to Young England's efforts. Of course the movement cannot claim any exclusive credit for them; Sadler, for instance, had pleaded in Parliament for allotments in 1831. But, at least as far as popular sport was concerned, Young England played an essential pioneering part. The ridicule it tended to provoke at the time is one proof of this. Even in the short term there were some practical results. Manners persuaded his father to give land for allotments; this was an example to other landowners. In his speech at Bingley at the end of 1844 Disraeli cited, as an instance of Young England's influence, the subscription of £21,000 at Manchester 'to form parks for the people'. In the long term, too, Manners's efforts to facilitate charitable bequests did lead to amendment of the law.

Young England also had considerable *aesthetic influence*. This is most obvious in the literary productions it produced or inspired. As we have seen, it spawned a whole crop of prose and verse. Most of this has been forgotten and, purely as literature, deserves to be forgotten. Disraeli's trilogy, and perhaps a few of the poems Faber wrote in 1838 and 1839, were the only Young England creations of lasting literary value. But the trilogy was a very important exception. Even without its political interest, it would still be enjoyed for its wit and for its observation of upper-class manners. Its political interest puts the three volumes in a category of their own. No English writer beforehand had used fiction (and/or history) in this way to propagate an exciting new political creed; nobody has done so since.

Less directly, Young England contributed to the Victorian Gothic Revival, if only through its adherence to the Oxford Movement. Churches up and down the country were restored, improved or spoilt (according to taste) under the inspiration of the Tractarians. Faber's restoration of churches at Sandford and Elton was typical; Newman recalls such activities, with a touch of gentle satire, in *Loss and Gain*. *Loss and Gain* also includes a dinner-table conversation about the relative merits of Gothic and Palladian religious architecture. Bateman, the host, says that 'if he had his will, there should be no architecture in the English churches but Gothic, and no music but Gregorian'. Reding, the hero, sees a difference of national taste, but not an intrinsic superiority of one style over the other. Campbell agrees: 'The basilica is beautiful in its place.' Yet even the Roman Catholic convert, Willis, says that 'the churches at Rome do not affect me like the Gothic; I reverence them, I feel awe in them, but I love, I feel a sensible pleasure at the sight of the Gothic arch'.

Faber, in *Sights and Thoughts*, quotes with approval a saying that 'the Homeric poems and Gothic architecture were the highest births of the human intellect'. He was particularly impressed by Amiens Cathedral: that 'miracle in stone' (as he wrote to Roundell Palmer) 'which haunts me as the *ne plus ultra* of religious architecture'. However, he began to waver towards Classical architecture in Greece and, after his conversion – unlike the more insular Newman – he became more and more Roman in his visual taste. Not that Faber was an architectural fanatic; it was religion, not art, that attracted him in Italy. In the days of his Wilfridian Order he was ready to collaborate with the architect Pugin who, although a Roman Catholic, was passionately convinced that religious architecture ought to be Gothic.

This conviction was shared by the Tractarians in general. As First Commissioner of Works Manners would have liked it to be agreed that the Gothic was the national style and, as such, should be adopted for civic, as well as religious, architecture. He was, however, reminded that the inspiration of two of our greatest architects – Inigo Jones and Christopher Wren – had been entirely Classical. The controversy came to a kind of head in the decision whether to rebuild the Foreign

Office in a Gothic or Palladian style. The Tories, vaguely influenced by the Oxford Movement, preferred the former; the Whigs/Liberals, who were victorious, preferred the latter. So both the Whig Foreign Office and the Roman Catholic Brompton Oratory were built to Classical designs. But a few minutes' walk in any city centre will show that Victorian Gothic was one of the least lost of Manners's causes.

It seems to me that the *political influence* of Young England, at least on the Conservative Party, has often been underrated. I have already argued that it had quite a lot to do with Peel's fall, even though it was not immediately responsible for it. This led to a division of the Party, for which Peel or his Protectionist opponents can be blamed. But it also led, eventually, to a revival of the Party on a sounder basis.

Young England was dead, as a Parliamentary force, by 1846. But two of its four 'esoterics', Disraeli and Manners, were members of every Conservative Cabinet until 1880. I have argued that Disraeli's basic political principles were confirmed or instilled during the time that he was working with Young England and that, thereafter, he was too caught up in practical politics to change them – perhaps no longer young enough to wish to do so. I believe that without Disraeli, who was at least the tactician behind the Second Reform Bill, the Conservative Party would have taken longer to come to terms with electoral expansion and to develop a programme of social reform. Even if there had never been a Young England, Disraeli would have seen the need for progress of this kind. But his confidence in the popular appeal of Toryism must have been strengthened by Young England's conviction that there could be an alliance of 'nobs and snobs', that Tory or Conservative sentiments were not confined to the upper classes. This conviction, which Cochrane in his old age declared had been central to the movement, proved to be much more firmly grounded in fact than hard-headed politicians in the earlier part of the nineteenth century can have expected.

Then again the growing importance of the monarch as a means of unifying the nation and occupying the imaginations of the people certainly owes something to Disraeli and, through him, to Young England. The Young Englanders wanted the Crown to retrieve some of its old power, whereas in practice its real power has continued to decrease. But they also wanted the Crown to appeal to the masses, as it has increasingly, and successfully, come to do.

Finally there is the romantic appeal that the movement has always had for a certain type of young Conservative supporter. The Primrose League in the 1880s kept some of its spirit alive, while Lord Randolph Churchill's Fourth Party was seen – not only by Manners – as picking up Young England's torch. Ralph Nevill, the youngest son of Lady Dorothy Walpole (George Smythe's summerhouse flame) wrote in his *Life and Letters* of his mother:

> She would invite to lunch on Sundays certain leading Conservatives and people not entirely out of sympathy with the Party's aims, especially the Fourth Party. It was in a sense the spirit of Young England all over again, in that those who met in her house were rebels and looked to a new England and a regeneration of the Party.

Some sixty years later (July 1943) Harold Macmillan, in his *War Diaries*, recorded his impressions of Hugh Fraser:

> I feel sure he will go into politics if he gets through and he ought to do well. It is curious how each generation in turn starts out with the sort of Young England idea. Disraeli left a great mark on England, and I am interested to find that the young men in the Tory Party now read his novels and study his life with the same enthusiasm as we did thirty years ago.

Young England's success in regenerating the nation, in

258

reviving a better feeling between classes, in 'raising the tone' of society, seems quite impossible to calculate, although this was always its principal objective. Clearly the movement was too short-lived to exercise any really profound or lasting *moral influence*; but, equally, it must have left *some* trace on the young people who were attracted to it during its three busy years. These were serious young men and women from the property-owning and professional classes, like the Oxonian squire who was full of Young England when he talked to Disraeli at a dinner party in September 1844. They did not form an extremely large class or an extremely powerful one; but it was large and powerful enough. Their behaviour, as they grew older, was one of the factors that combined to give the lower classes a degree of assurance that their interests would not be totally neglected. This feeling of trust, however limited, contributed to the mid-Victorian social equilibrium, which in some spheres and districts persisted well after the mid-Victorian era.

The anonymous 'Non-Elector', who wrote a pamphlet in 1872 (now in the Bodleian Library) on *Lord John Manners, the Young England Party and the Passing of the Factory Acts*, described Young England's motto as 'Restoration rather than Revolution' and its aim as the revival of Faith and Loyalty:

> Their proposals were vague, impracticable it may be, but the spirit which inspired them was undeniably a pure and noble one. As a party they did much to improve the moral atmosphere, and to dissipate the dogged bigotry and selfish materialism of Modern England.

If an observer thought this in 1872, not quite a generation after Young England's demise, he must have had some grounds for believing it in his personal experience. I have already quoted Kingsley's finding in 1859 that Whiggish/Liberal principles, on the one hand, and the Anglican

259

movement on the other, had brought about an 'altered temper of the young gentlemen'. Since undergraduate opinion in the 1830s seems to have been predominantly anti-Whig, the Anglican influence may have been the more important of the two. Certainly Tractarianism had enormous influence on Oxford undergraduates in the 1830s and early 1840s. Faber had himself gone up to Oxford with evangelical views and became a Puseyite after hearing Newman and Pusey preach.

Kingsley discerned a greater 'moral earnestness' up and down the country. No doubt, in the nation as a whole and over the century as a whole, Evangelicalism was a more potent force for moral earnestness than Tractarianism. But Kingsley was writing about the landlord class in the 1850s. Its 'improved tone' was, he thought, due 'in great part (that justice may be done on all sides) to the Anglican movement'.

This greater moral earnestness of the upper classes appears strikingly in a well-known novel published in 1853. Charlotte Yonge's *The Heir of Redclyffe*, although in no sense a political book, derives its religious and social assumptions from the Oxford and Young England movements. (It was Keble who encouraged Charlotte Yonge to write fiction.) She portrays a 'caring' upper (or lower-upper) class, cultivated and capable of innocent gaiety, but extremely serious-minded. Sir Guy Morville, the hero, is a born leader of men and adored by his people. He is so paternalist that he leaves his horse behind when he goes up to Oxford, for fear that the city 'would be a place of temptation for William' (his groom). Every contented village must have somebody – squire or clergyman – to 'look after it'. At Redclyffe itself the inhabitants have 'a very strong feudal feeling for "Sir Guy", who was king, state, supreme authority, in their eyes . . .'. Similarly the family at Holywell are spoken well of, not least because 'the young ladies looked after schools and poor people . . .'.

There are also minor indications of the cultural provenance of the novel. The hero finds solace in a quotation from one of Faber's poems ('Little things/On little wings/Bear little souls to heaven'). Like Faber, the young people approve of *I Promessi Sposi*; they share his distrust of Byron's immorality. Their Stuartomania knows no bounds. Guy asks Charles never to 'jest again about King Charles', while Amy weeps before the King's portrait and Philip finds his face 'earnest, melancholy, beautiful'. Guy chooses King Charles as his favourite historical character; Philip and Laura choose Strafford as theirs.

Whether they realized it or not, the numerous teenagers who read *The Heir of Redclyffe* throughout the nineteenth century must have imbibed some Young England attitudes, some sense of what the movement thought relations between classes should be. Superiors and inferiors should know their places, within a disciplined hierarchy. But there should be kindness and mutual respect between them – even decorous sociability. It was quite in accordance with Young England's doctrine that Prince Albert gave a banquet with music, dancing and games for nearly 500 estate workers and their families at Osborne in August 1846. He wrote to Peel:

> You will remember that we often talked about the use or possibility of giving public entertainments to the working class. I am therefore particularly glad, that this should have succeeded so well.

Peel replied that he himself was thinking about a holiday for his own labourers: 'To be able to look back on past and forward to future entertainments of this kind might cheer many a gloomy day.' At any earlier period an exchange of such sentiments between the Royal Family and a leading politician would surely have been improbable, if not unthinkable. The entertainments would either have been given as a matter of course, or they would not have been given at all.

The Young Englanders believed that everybody should have a place and an identity. Yet, in spite of Monckton Milnes's complaint against them, they did not want to prevent the able and independent-minded from rising. Even in the conservative rural areas Manners thought that a labourer should have some land of his own, and not merely work for a master. If there were no small farms, he said, how could there be any hope for the peasant to rise? But those who could not rise needed the protection of their landlords, or masters, and owed them duty in return. Lord Ashley, though evangelical and no Young Englander, put the theory succinctly, when he wrote in his diary for 29 June 1841, after visiting his family home in Dorset:

> What a picture contrasted with a factory district, a people known and cared for, a people born and trained on the estate, exhibiting towards its hereditary possessors both deference and sympathy, affectionate respect and a species of allegiance demanding protection and repaying it in duty.

This passage is a reminder that the Young Englanders were not the only paternalists of their time. Indeed, the more closely one looks at this period, the more difficult it becomes to find people in responsible positions who were not to some extent, in theory or in practice, paternalists. Perhaps no ruling class was ever reminded so frequently that it had duties as well as rights. Only the very thick-skinned and dogmatic – some of the more single-minded manufacturers, or some of the more Malthusian landlords – can have entirely escaped this moral pressure. The radicals among Young England's supporters felt that paternalism did not go far enough; but they liked it so far as it went. The weekly, *Young England*, took for granted the commonplace truths that 'wealth is not happiness – and property has its duties as well as its rights': although neglected in practice, nobody 'ever gravely doubted these axioms'. In an otherwise glowing review of *Coningsby* on 11 January 1845, it nevertheless struck a note that would have appealed to Monckton Milnes:

It is well to talk of a paternal government, and it were well if we had one. But the good would but be an accident; and the best security for the happiness of a people is alone to be found in institutions. What is wanted is some practicable scheme whereby the people of England in the nineteenth century might do without such helps and aids, which hurt their pride first, and next undermine their independence.

The hurting of pride, and the undermining of independence, have always been the faults of paternalism, practised insensitively, and always will be. Paternalism is after all a part of human life, not simply a phenomenon peculiar to the Early Victorian era. More individuals then than now found themselves exercising quasi-paternal control. But, however much the notion of paternalism may jar on egalitarianism, there will always be some room for it in practice, so long as there are any situations in which authority is exercised by an individual, or a group of individuals, over others. If these authorities do not see themselves in the role of fathers (or elder brothers) they will tend to take up roles still more likely to hurt pride and undermine independence.

The founders of the Young England movement went beyond a simple acceptance of paternalism as part of the human condition. They saw submission and deference as graceful things in themselves. They thought that people were the better for practising them; even rulers were expected to practise them towards God. This was part of a religious view of the world, which assumed that it was – or ought to be – under 'paternal government', that the happiness and duty of the individual consisted in discovering, and obeying, God's will.

The youthful Manners opened his poem, 'England's Trust', with a biblical text: 'In returning to rest shall ye be saved; in quietness, and in confidence, shall be your strength.' Everybody knows that some acceptance of things as they are, or have been, is an essential part of happiness, or at least of avoiding pain. Even the most restless progressive aims at a future state of blessedness, in which restlessness will no longer be so necessary. Yet the Young Englanders could not stop themselves seeing much that was currently wrong and that needed to be put right. They resolved the apparent contradiction between submission and reform by resorting to restoratism; by adopting the view that things had at one time been better and that human self-will, inspired by wickedness, had led the world astray. Once society was back on the right track, it could be kept there; the passive virtues would come into their own. The churchmen of the Oxford Movement had the same feeling of something having gone wrong, of the need to restore a pristine state of affairs.

If the Young England movement had continued and developed, this tension between its passive and active selves, which was already beginning to surface in 1845, must have developed, too. The active self would have needed to pre-dominate, if the movement was to succeed in a progressive age. But in that case the particular balance which Manners and his friends for a time achieved, and which still gives to Young England its particular flavour, would have had to yield to a more worldly, and less romantic, dynamism.

As it was, Young England turned, Janus-like, both towards the past and the future. Progressive in one sense, it was reactionary in another. Fearing the advent of total democracy, and convinced of the need for caring leadership it looked to the old world to redress the balance of the new.

Sources and Acknowledgements

Although I have not given detailed references, I have not made any statements of fact without (I hope) adequate authority. Sources of quotations are usually indicated in the text. Where this is not so, the following may help.

Letters from Smythe and his family to Disraeli are quoted from MS originals in the Hughenden Papers (there are only a few of them, since Disraeli passed on to Manners, during his lifetime, most of the letters he had received from Smythe); letters from Smythe to his father are quoted from extracts in Fonblanque's *Lives of the Lords Strangford*; letters from Smythe to Manners are quoted from extracts in Whibley's *Lord John Manners and His Friends*; Disraeli's letters and speeches are quoted from extracts in the *Life of Disraeli* by Monypenny and Buckle (or, in one or two cases, from Vols. 1 and 2 of his edited *Letters*); his memoranda are quoted from MS originals in the Hughenden papers; letters from Manners to Disraeli are quoted from MS originals in the Hughenden papers; other extracts from his letters and diaries are quoted from Whibley's biography of him; the few quotations from Cochrane's letters are taken from Whibley's biography of Manners; letters from Faber to Beresford Hope and Roundell Palmer are quoted from MS originals in the Brompton Oratory, together with one surviving letter from him to Smythe; letters from Faber to his brother, Frank, and other family letters, are quoted from MS originals in my own possession; Faber's letters to Manners, together with one or two other letters by him, are quoted from Addington's collection of his letters in *Faber. Poet and Priest*. I have also made some use of letters quoted in Bowden's and Chapman's biographies.

Published material, both by and about the Young Englanders, is listed in the bibliography that follows. Except for some of Cochrane's later books, I have studied all the publications of the group I could find in the London or Bodleian Libraries. I have looked through newspaper files, for the years when the movement was active, in the Colindale Newspaper Library. I have also drawn on Parliamentary Reports, particularly for the years 1841 to 1846. These Reports are of course the source of my quotations from the Parliamentary speeches of Smythe, Manners and Cochrane. For their speeches outside Parliament I have used press reports, a contemporary pamphlet reproducing the Manchester and Bingley speeches and a passage in Lady Strangford's memoir of her brother-in-law. The *Dictionary of National Biography* has been a constant standby.

I am grateful to the National Trust for access to the Hughenden Papers, now at the Bodleian Library, and for permission to reproduce portraits of Smythe and Manners at Hughenden Manor, Bucks. The Librarian of the Brompton Oratory most kindly allowed me to see Vols. 21 and 22 of Faber's miscellaneous correspondence. The Public Information Office of the House of Commons dealt quickly and courteously with an inquiry about Cochrane's Parliamentary career. I am also grateful to have had the opportunity of studying the records for the 1830s of the Oxford and Cambridge Union Societies. I regret that I was unable to obtain access to Manners's papers, or to Smythe's letters to Disraeli, at Belvoir Castle. Fortunately Manners's papers are quoted generously by his biographer, who did have access to them and who was also given access by Mrs Frank Russell 'to the papers of George Smythe which survive'. It was, too, from the originals at Belvoir Castle that the late Father Addington was able to reproduce the letters from Faber to Manners in his collection. Without all these published letters I could hardly have written this book.

266

I am very much indebted to Mr Charles Monteith, Lord
Blake and Professor Matthews, for their help and kindness.
Lord Blake encouraged me to write a history of the ideas of
the movement. I have tried to do that, though also to combine
it with some personal description of the chief characters and
their relationships. Professor Matthews took time from many
more pressing preoccupations to ensure that copies he had
had made of Belvoir Castle papers, some years ago, did not
contain important fresh evidence about the Young England
movement, that I ought to take into account.

Bibliography

Publications by the Young Englanders

BAILLIE-COCHRANE, Alexander (later Cochrane-Baillie and Lord Lamington), Poems, 1838; *The Morea* (poems) with *Some Remarks upon the Present State of Greece* (prose), 1840; *Lucille Belmont*, 1849 (revised edition); *Ernest Vane*, 1849; *A Young Artist's Life*, 1864; *Historic Pictures*, 1865; *In the Days of the Dandies*, 1906 (book form, but previously published in *Blackwood's Magazine*, 1890)

DISRAELI, Benjamin (later Earl of Beaconsfield), *The Revolutionary Epick*, 1834 (edition of 1864); *Vindication of the English Constitution* (A letter to Lord Lyndhurst), 1835; *Coningsby, or The New Generation*, 1844; *Sybil, or The Two Nations*, 1845; *Tancred, or The New Crusade*, 1847; *Lord George Bentinck*, A Political Biography, 1852; General Preface to his Collected Works, 1870; *Endymion*, 1880

FABER, the Revd Frederick William (later Father Faber), *The Cherwell Water-Lily and Other Poems*, 1840; *Sights and Thoughts in Foreign Churches and among Foreign Peoples*, 1842; *The Styrian Lake and Other Poems*, 1842; *Sir Lancelot, A Legend of the Middle Ages*, 1844 (second edition 1857); *The Rosary and Other Poems*, 1845; *Grounds for Remaining in the Anglican Communion – A Letter to a High-Church Friend*, 1846

MANNERS, Lord John (later Duke of Rutland); *England's Trust and Other Poems*, 1841; *What are the English Roman Catholics to do?* (under the pseudonym *Anglo-Catholicus*), 1841; *A*

Plea for National Holy-Days, 1843; *Notes on an Irish Tour*, 1849; '*F. W. Faber's Life and Letters*' (Review in *Blackwood's Magazine*), 1869 (December)

SMYTHE, The Hon. George (later Lord Strangford), *Historic Fancies*, 1844; Articles on Grey and Canning in the *Oxford and Cambridge Review*, 1845; *Angela Pisani*, with a brief memoir by his sister-in-law, 1875 (begun in Venice in 1845)

THE MANCHESTER SPEECHES, etc., *Young England* (Birmingham, Manchester and Bingley speeches), 1845; *The Importance of Literature to Men of Business*, A Series of Addresses delivered at Various Popular Institutions, 1852

Unpublished Contemporary Material

Disraeli's memoranda, and letters from the Strangfords and from Manners, in the Hughenden Papers (Bodleian Library, Oxford)

Vols. 21 and 22 of Father Faber's miscellaneous correspondence at the Brompton Oratory

A few letters from Newman, Faber, etc., in the author's possession

Records of the Oxford and Cambridge Union Societies

Published Contemporary Letters

CRABB ROBINSON, Henry (1775–1867), *Diary, Reminiscences and Correspondence* (ed. T. Saddler), 1872; *Henry Crabb Robinson, On Books and Their Writers*, (ed. E. J. Morley), 1938

CROKER, Rt Hon. John Wilson (1780–1857), *Correspondence and Diaries*, (ed. L. J. Jennings), 1884

DISRAELI, Benjamin, *Letters*, (eds. J. A. W. Gunn, John Matthews, Donald M. Schurman, M. G. Wiebe), Vols. 1 and 2, 1982

FABER, F. W., *Faber. Poet and Priest*, (Letters, 1833–1863, selected and edited by Raleigh Addington), 1974

MILNES, Richard Monckton (later Lord Houghton) (1809–1885), *Life, Letters and Friendships of Richard Monckton Milnes*, T. Wemyss Reid, 1890

NEWMAN, John Henry (later Cardinal) (1801–1890), *Letters and Correspondence of Newman in the English Church*, (ed. A. Mozley), 1891

WORDSWORTH, Mary, *Letters (1800–1855)*, (ed. Mary Burton), 1958

WORDSWORTH, William (1770–1850), *The Letters of William and Dorothy Wordsworth*, Vol. III (1841–1850), (ed. E. de Selincourt), 1939

Contemporary Publications

CARLYLE, Thomas, *French Revolution*, 1837; *Chartism*, 1839; *Past and Present*, 1843

COBBETT, William, *A History of the Protestant Reformation in England and Ireland*, 1829; *Rural Rides*, 1830

COLERIDGE, Samuel Taylor, *On the Constitution of the Church and State* (ed. H. N. Coleridge), 1839; review of Hallam in the *Quarterly Review*, 1828 (January)

DICKENS, Charles, *Bleak House*, 1852

DIGBY, Kenelm Henry, *The Broad Stone of Honour; or the True Sense and Practice of Chivalry*, 1822 (edition of 1876–7)

FABER, F. W., Obituaries in the *Saturday Review* (10 October) and the *Dublin Review* (no. III, Art. VI), 1863

GREVILLE, Charles (1794–1865), *Memoirs*

HALLAM, Henry, *View of the State of Europe during the Middle Ages*, 1818 (sixth edition, 1834)

d'ISRAELI, Isaac, *Commentaries on the Life and Reign of Charles the First*, 1830–2 (ed. by his son, 1851)

KINGSLEY, Charles, *Yeast*, 1848, (fourth edition, with Preface, 1859)

MADDYN, D. O., *Chiefs of Parties* (including Smythe on Disraeli), 1859

MANNERS, Lord John, *A Political and Literary Sketch, comprising some account of the Young England Party and the Passing of the Factory Acts*. By a Non-Elector, 1872

MILNES, Richard Monckton, Review of *Tancred* in the *Edinburgh Review*, 1847 (July)

NEWMAN, John Henry, *Loss and Gain*, 1848; *Apologia pro Vita Sua*, 1864; *Letter to the Rev. E. B. Pusey, D.D., on his recent Eirenicon* 1866

PALGRAVE, Sir Francis, *The Merchant and the Friar*, 1837 (revised edition 1844)

PEACOCK, Thomas Love, *Crotchet Castle*, 1831

SOUTHEY, Robert, *Sir Thomas More. Colloquies on the Progress and Prospects of Society*, 1829

THACKERAY, William Makepeace, Review of *Coningsby* in *The Pictorial Times* (25 May), 1844; *Punch's Prize Novelists*, 1847; *The Book of Snobs* (reprinted from *Punch* 1846–7), 1848

TROLLOPE, Anthony, *Barchester Towers*, 1857

YONGE, Charlotte, *The Heir of Redclyffe*, 1853;
Parliamentary Records, mainly 1841–6;
The Times, *The Morning Post*, *The Morning Chronicle*, *The Morning Herald*, mainly 1843–5; *The Oxford and Cambridge Review*, 1845–7; *Fraser's Magazine* (for sketches of Disraeli, Manners and Smythe as *Literary Legislators*), 1847 (January–May); *Young England, the Social Condition of the Empire, Nos. 1–14*, 1845 (January–April)

Later Publications

ARGYLL, George Douglas, 8th Duke of, Autobiography, edited by the Dowager Duchess, 1906

BATTISCOMBE, Georgina, *Shaftesbury*, 1974

BEATTY, Frederika, *William Wordsworth of Rydal Mount*, 1939

BLAKE, Robert, *Disraeli*, 1966

BOWDEN, John Edward, *The Life and Letters of Frederick William Faber, D.D.*, 1869

BRADFORD, Sarah, *Disraeli*, 1982

BUTLER, Marilyn, *Peacock Displayed*, 1979

CHAPMAN, Ronald, *Father Faber*, 1961

CROMPTON, Professor Louis, *Byron and Greek Love*, 1985

FABER, Rev. F. A., *A brief sketch of the Early Life of the late F. W. Faber, D.D. by his only Surviving Brother*, 1869

FABER, Geoffrey, *Oxford Apostles*, 1933

FONBLANQUE, E.B. de, *Lives of the Lords Strangford*, 1877

FRASER, Sir W., *Disraeli and his Day*, 1891

GASH, Norman, *The Life of Sir Robert Peel after 1830*, 1972

GIROUARD, Mark, *The Return to Camelot: Chivalry and the English Gentleman*, 1981

GRANT DUFF, Sir Mountstuart, *Frederick William Faber*, 1890

GREGORY, Sir William, Autobiography, edited by Lady Gregory, 1894

JERMAN, B. R., *The Young Disraeli*, 1960

LONGFORD, Elizabeth, *Victoria R. I.*, 1964

MACMILLAN, Harold, *War Diaries – The Mediterranean 1943–5*, 1984

MARTIN, R. B., *Enter Rumour. Four Early Victorian Scandals*, 1962

MONYPENNY, W. F. and BUCKLE, G. E., *Life of Benjamin Disraeli*, 1929 (revised edition)

NEVILL, Guy, *Exotic Groves. A Portrait of Lady Dorothy Nevill*, 1984

OGDEN, James, *Isaac d'Israeli*, 1969

PALMER, Roundell, Earl of Selborne, *Memorials, Part 1, Family and Personal*, 1889 (privately printed)

POPE-HENNESSY, James, *Monckton Milnes: The Years of Promise 1809–51*, 1949

ROBERTS, David, *Paternalism in Early Victorian England*, 1979

WARD, Wilfrid, *Aubrey de Vere: A memoir*, 1904

WHIBLEY, Charles, *Lord John Manners and His Friends*, 1925

WHISTLER, Rev. R. F., *History of Elton*, 1892

YOUNG, G. M., *Victorian England, Portrait of an Age*, 1936

Index